Praise for #1 *New York Times* bestselling author Lisa Jackson

Praise for *New York Times* bestselling author B.J. Daniels

Lisa Jackson is a #1 *New York Times* bestselling author of more than eighty-five books, including romantic suspense, thrillers and contemporary and historical romances. She is a recipient of the *RT Book Reviews* Reviewers' Choice Award and has also been honored with their Career Achievement Award for Romantic Suspense. Born in Oregon, she continues to make her home among family, friends and dogs in the Pacific Northwest. Visit her at lisajackson.com.

New York Times and *USA TODAY* bestselling author **B.J. Daniels** lives in Montana with her husband, Parker, and three springer spaniels. When not writing, she quilts, boats and plays tennis. Contact her at bjdaniels.com, or on Facebook, or Twitter, @bjdanielsauthor.

#1 *New York Times* Bestselling Author

LISA JACKSON

BEST-KEPT LIES

**HARLEQUIN
BESTSELLING
AUTHOR
COLLECTION**

**HARLEQUIN®
BESTSELLING
AUTHOR
COLLECTION**

Recycling programs
for this product may
not exist in your area.

ISBN-13: 978-1-335-40625-5

Best-Kept Lies
First published in 2004. This edition published in 2021.
Copyright © 2004 by Susan Lisa Jackson

A Father for Her Baby
First published in 1998. This edition published in 2021.
Copyright © 1998 by Barbara Heinlein

This edition published by arrangement with Harlequin Books S.A.

For questions and comments about the quality of this book, please contact us at CustomerService@Harlequin.com.

Harlequin Enterprises ULC
22 Adelaide St. West, 40th Floor
Toronto, Ontario M5H 4E3, Canada
www.Harlequin.com

Printed in Lithuania

MIX
Paper from
responsible sources
FSC® C021394

CONTENTS

Also by Lisa Jackson

Visit her Author Profile page at Harlequin.com,
or lisajackson.com, for more titles!

BEST-KEPT LIES

Lisa Jackson

This book is dedicated to Melissa, Joan, Karen, Tara and Isabel of Silhouette Books. Great editors. Wonderful women. You saw me through the bad times and the good. I can't thank you enough.

Prologue

"I'm dyin', Randi-girl, and there ain't no two ways about it."

Randi McCafferty stopped short. She'd been hurrying down the stairs, her new boots pinching and ringing on the old wooden steps of the house she'd grown up in—a rambling old ranch house set on a slight rise in the middle of No-Damn-Where, Montana. She'd been thinking of her own situation, hadn't realized her father was half lying in his recliner, staring at the blackened grate of the rock fireplace in the living room. John Randall McCafferty was still a big man, but time had taken its toll on his once commanding stature and had ravaged features that had been too handsome for his own good. "What're you talkin' about?" she asked. "You're going to live forever."

"No one does." He glanced up at her and his eyes held hers. "I just want you to know that I'm leavin' you half the place. The boys, they can fight over the rest of it. The Flying M is gonna be yours. Soon."

"Don't even talk that way," she said, walking into the dark room where the afternoon heat had collected. She glanced through a dusty window, past the porch to the vast acres of the ranch that stretched beneath a wide Montana sky. Cattle and horses grazed in the fields past the stable and barn, moving as restlessly as the wind that made the grass undulate.

"You may as well face it. Come over here. Come on, come on, y'know my bark is worse'n my bite."

"Of course I know it." She'd never seen the bad side of her father's temper, though her half brothers had brought it up time and time again.

"I just want to look at ya. My eyes ain't what they used to be." He chuckled, then coughed so violently his lungs rattled.

"Dad, I think I should call Matt. You should be in a hospital."

"Hell, no." As she crossed the room, he waved a bony hand as if he was swatting a fly. "No damn doctor is gonna do me any good now."

"But—"

"Hush, would ya? For once you listen to me." Incredibly clear eyes glared up at her. He placed a yellowed envelope in her palm. "This here is the deed. Thorne, Matt and Slade, they own the other half together and that should be interestin'," he said with a morbid chuckle. "They'll probably fight over it like cougars at a kill...but don't you worry none. You own the lion's share." He smiled at his own little joke. "You and your baby."

"My what?" She didn't move a muscle.

"My grandson. You're carryin' him, ain't ya?" he asked, his eyes narrowing.

A hot blush burned up the back of her neck. She hadn't told a soul about the baby. No one knew. Except, it seemed, her father.

"You know, I would have rather had you get married before you got pregnant, but that's over and done with and I won't be around long enough to see the boy. But you and he are taken care of. The ranch will see to that."

"I don't need anyone to take care of me."

Her father's smile disappeared. "Sure you do, Randi. Someone needs to look after you."

"I can take care of myself and…and a baby. I've got a condo in Seattle, a good job and—"

"And no man. Leastwise none worth his salt. You gonna name the guy who knocked you up?"

"This conversation is archaic—"

"Every kid deserves to know his pa," the old man said. "Even if the guy's a miserable son of a bitch who left a woman carrying his child."

"If you say so," she replied, her fingers curling over the edge of the envelope. She felt more than paper inside.

As if he guessed her question, he said, "There's a necklace in there, too. A locket. Belonged to your ma."

Randi's throat closed for a second. She remembered the locket, had played with it as a child, reaching for the shiny gold heart with its glittering diamonds as it had hung from her mother's neck. "I remember. You gave it to her on your wedding day."

"Yep." He nodded curtly and his eyes grew soft. "The ring is in there, too. If ya want it."

Her eyes were suddenly damp. "Thanks."

"You can thank me by namin' the son of a bitch who did this to you."

She inched her chin up a notch and frowned.

"You're not gonna tell me, are you?"

Randi looked her father steadily in the eye. McCafferty to McCafferty, she said, "Hell would have to freeze over first."

"Damn it, girl, you're a stubborn thing."

"Guess I inherited it."

"And it'll be your undoin', mark my words."

Randi felt a shadow steal through her heart, a cold premonition that settled deep inside, but she didn't budge. For her unborn child's protection, she sealed her lips.

No one would ever know who fathered her child.

Not even her son.

Chapter 1

"Hell's bells," Kurt Striker grumbled under his breath.

He didn't like the job that was set before him. Not one little bit. But he couldn't say no. And it wasn't just because of the substantial fee attached to the assignment, no, the money was good enough. Tempting. He could use an extra twenty-five grand right now. Who couldn't? A check for half the amount sat on the coffee table. Untouched.

Because of the night before. Because of his secret.

He stood in the living room, a fire crackling and warming the backs of his legs, the sprawling snow-covered acres of the Flying M Ranch visible through frosted windows.

"So, what do you say, Striker?" Thorne McCafferty demanded. The oldest of three brothers, he was a businessman by nature and always took charge. "Have we got a deal? Will you see that our sister is safe?"

The job was complicated. Striker was to become Randi McCafferty's personal bodyguard whether she liked it or not. Which she wouldn't. Kurt would lay odds on it. He'd spent enough time with the only daughter of the late John Randall McCafferty to know that when she made up her mind, it wasn't likely to be changed, not by him, nor by her three half brothers who all seemed to have developed a latent sense of responsibility for their headstrong sibling.

She was trouble. No two ways about it. The way she'd hightailed it out of here only a few hours earlier had clearly indicated her mind was set. She was returning to Seattle. With her child. To her home. To her job. To her old life, and the consequences be damned.

And she was running away.

From her three overbearing half brothers.

And from him.

Striker didn't like the situation one bit, but he couldn't very well confide in these three men, now, could he? As he glanced from one anxious McCafferty brother to the next, he didn't examine his own emotions too closely, didn't want to admit that the reason he was balking at the job was because he didn't want to get tangled up with a woman. Any woman. Especially not with the kid sister of these tough-as-nails, overprotective brothers.

It's a little too late for that now, wouldn't you say?

Randi was a sexy thing. All fire and attitude. A strong woman who would, he suspected, as any self-respecting child of John Randall McCafferty, bulldoze her way through life and do exactly what she wanted to do. She wouldn't like Striker nosing around, prying into her affairs, even if he was trying to insulate her from danger. In fact, she'd probably resent it. Especially now.

"Randi's gonna be ticked." Slade, the youngest McCafferty brother, echoed Striker's thoughts, even though he didn't know the half of it. In jeans and a faded flannel shirt, Slade walked to the window and stared outside at the wintry Montana landscape. Snow covered the fields where a few head of cattle and horses huddled against the cold.

"Of course she'll be ticked. Who wouldn't be?" Matt, brother number two, was seated on the worn leather sofa, the heel of one of his cowboy boots propped onto the coffee table only inches from a check for twelve thousand five hundred dollars. "I'd hate it."

"She doesn't have a choice," Thorne said. CEO of his own corporation, Thorne was used to giving orders and having his employees obey. He'd recently moved to Grand Hope, Montana, from Denver, but he was still in charge. "We agreed, didn't we?" he was saying as he motioned to his younger brothers. "For her protection and the baby's safety, she needs a bodyguard."

Matt nodded curtly. "Yeah, we agreed. That won't make it any easier for Randi to swallow. Even if Kelly's involved."

Kelly was Matt's wife, an ex-cop who was now a private investigator. She'd agreed to work with Striker, especially on this, her sister-in-law's case. Red-haired and quick-witted, Kelly would be an asset. But Striker wasn't convinced Kelly McCafferty would be the oil on troubled waters as far as Randi was concerned. No—having a relative involved would only make a sticky situation stickier.

He glanced to the window, toward the youngest McCafferty brother. The friend who had dragged him into this mess. But Slade didn't meet his eyes, just continued to stare out the frosty panes.

"Look, we've got to do something and we don't have time to waste. Someone's trying to kill her," Thorne pointed out.

Striker's jaw tightened. This was no joke. And deep down he knew that he'd take the job; wouldn't trust anyone else to do it. For as bullheaded and stubborn as Randi McCafferty was, there was something about her, a spark in her brown eyes that seemed to touch him just under the skin, a bit of fire that scorched slightly. It had gotten his attention and hadn't let go.

Last night had been proof enough.

Thorne was agitated, worry evident in the lines of his face, his fingers jangling the keys in his pocket. His stare held Striker's. "Will you take the job, or are we going to have to find someone else?"

The thought of another man getting close to Randi soured Kurt's gut, but before he could respond, Slade finally spoke.

"No one else. We need someone we can trust."

"Amen," Matt agreed, before Slade nodded toward the window where a Jeep was plowing down the lane.

Trust? Jesus!

His teeth clenched so hard they ached.

Slade nodded toward the window where an SUV was steadily approaching. "Looks like Nicole's home."

The tension in Thorne's features softened a bit. Within minutes the front door burst open, and a blast of cold Montana air raced into the room. Dr. Nicole McCafferty, still shaking snow from her coat, crossed the entry as the rumble of tiny feet erupted upstairs and Thorne's two step-daughters, four-year-old-twins, thundered down the stairs. Laughter and shouts added to the din.

"Mommy! Mommy!" Molly cried, while her shier sister, Mindy, beamed and threw herself into Nicole's waiting arms.

"Hey, how're my girls?" Nicole asked in greeting, scooping both twins into her arms and kissing them on the cheeks.

"You're coooooold!" Molly said.

Nicole laughed. "So I am."

Thorne, limping slightly from a recent accident, made his way into the entry hall and kissed his wife soundly, the girls wriggling between them.

Striker turned away. Felt he was intruding on an intimate scene. It was the same uncomfortable sensation that had been with him from the get-go when Slade had contacted him about helping out the family, and Kurt had first set foot on the Flying M. It had been in October when Randi McCafferty's car had been forced off the road at Glacier Park. She had gone into premature labor and both she and her new baby had nearly died. She'd been in a coma for a while and when she had awoken she'd struggled with amnesia.

Or so she claimed.

Striker thought the loss of memory, though supported by Randi's doctor, was too convenient. He'd also found evidence that another vehicle had run Randi's rig down a steep hillside, where she'd plowed into a tree. She'd survived, though as she'd recovered and regained her memory, she would say nothing about the accident, or guess who might have been trying to kill her. She'd incriminate no one. Either she didn't know or wouldn't tell. The same was true about the father of her kid. She'd told no one who had sired little Joshua. Kurt scowled at the thought. He didn't want to think of anyone being intimate with Randi, though that was just plain stupid. He had no claim to her; wasn't even certain he liked her.

Then you should have let it go last night...you saw her on the landing, watched her take care of her child, then waited until she'd put him to bed...

In his mind's eye, Kurt remembered her sitting on the ledge, humming softly, her white nightgown clinging to her body as she cradled her baby and fed him. He'd been upstairs, looking down over the railing, and moonlight had spilled over her shoulders, illuminating her like a madonna with child. The sight had been almost spiritual, but also sensual, and he'd slowly eased his way into the shadows and waited. Telling himself he just wanted to walk down the stairs unnoticed, one of the floorboards had creaked and Randi had looked up, seen him there on the upper landing, his hands over the railing.

"Come on, let's see what Juanita's got in the kitchen," Nicole was saying, bringing Kurt crashing back to the here and now. "Smells good."

"Cinn-da-mon!" the shier twin said while her sister rolled her eyes.

"Cinn-a-mon," Molly corrected.

"We'll find out, won't we?" Nicole shuffled the girls down the hallway toward the kitchen while Thorne returned to the living room.

The smile he'd reserved for his wife and family had faded and he was all business again. "So what's it gonna be, Striker? Are you in?"

"It's a helluva lot of money," Matt reminded him.

"Look, Striker, I'm counting on you." Slade gave up his position near the window. Lines of worry pinched the corners of his eyes. "Someone wants Randi dead. I told Thorne and Matt that if anyone could find out who it was, you could. So are you gonna prove me right or what?"

With only a little bit of guilt he slid the check into the battered leather of his wallet. There wasn't really any point in arguing. There hadn't been from the get-go. Striker could no more let Randi McCafferty take off with her kid and face her would-be killer alone than he could quit breathing.

He planned on nailing the son of a bitch.

Big-time.

"Great!" Randi hadn't gotten more than forty miles out of Grand Hope when her new Jeep started acting weird. The steering was off, and when she pulled to the side of the snow-covered road to survey the damage, she realized that her front left tire was low. And it hadn't been when she'd left. She'd passed a gas station less than a mile back, so she turned her vehicle around, only to discover that the station was closed. Permanently. The door was locked and rusted, a window cracked, the pumps dry.

So far her journey back to civilization wasn't going as planned—not that she'd had much of a plan to begin with. That was the problem. She'd intended to return to Seattle, of course, and soon, but last night...with Kurt...oh, hell. She'd gotten up this morning and decided she couldn't wait another minute.

All of her brothers were now married. She was, once again, the odd woman out, and she was the reason that they were all in danger. She had to do something about it.

But you're kidding yourself, aren't you? The real reason you left so quickly has nothing to do with your brothers or the danger, and everything to do with Kurt Striker.

She glanced in the rearview mirror, saw the pain in her eyes and let out her breath. She was no good at this, and had never wanted to play the martyr.

"Get on with it," she muttered. She'd just have to change the damn tire herself. Which should be no problem. She'd learned a lot about machinery growing up on the Flying M. A flat tire was a piece of cake. The good news was that she was off the road and relatively dry and protected from the wind under the overhang of the old garage.

With her baby asleep in his car seat, she pulled out the jack and spare, then got to work. Changing the tire wasn't hard, just tedious, and her gloves made working with the lug nuts a challenge. She found the problem with the tire: somewhere she'd picked up a long nail, which had created the slow leak.

It crossed her mind that maybe the flat wasn't an accident, that perhaps the same creep who had forced her off the road at Glacier Park, then attempted to kill her again in the hospital, and later burned the stable might be back to his old tricks. She straightened, still holding the tire iron.

Bitterly cold, the wind swept down the roadway, blowing the snow and lifting her hair from her face. She felt a frisson of fear slide down her spine as she squinted, her gaze sweeping the harsh, barren landscape.

But she saw no one.

Heard nothing.

Decided she was just becoming paranoid.

Which was a really bad thought.

Huddled against the rain, the intruder slid a key into the lock of the dead bolt, then with surprising ease broke into Randi McCafferty's Lake Washington home.

The area was upscale, and the condo worth a fortune. Of course. Because the princess would have no less.

Inside, the unit was a little cluttered. Not too bad, but certainly not neat as a pin. And it had suffered from neglect in the past few months. Dust had settled on the surface of a small desk pushed into the corner, cobwebs floated from a high ceiling, and dust bunnies had collected in the corners. Three-month-old magazines were strewn over a couple of end tables and the meager contents of the refrigerator had spoiled weeks ago. Framed prints and pictures splashed color onto warm-toned walls, and an eclectic blend of modern and antique furniture was scattered around the blackened stones of a fireplace where the ashes were cold.

Randi McCafferty hadn't been home for a long, long time.

But she was on her way.

Noiselessly, the intruder stalked through the darkened rooms, down a short hallway to a large master suite with its sunken tub, walk-in closet and king-size bed. There was another bath, as well, and a nursery, not quite set up but ready for the next little McCafferty. The bastard.

Back in the living room there was a desk and upon it a picture, taken years ago, of the three McCafferty brothers—tall, strapping, cocky, young men with smiles that could melt a woman's heart and tempers that had landed them in too many barroom brawls to count. In the snapshot they were astride horses. In front of the mounted men, in bare feet, cutoff jeans, a sleeveless shirt and ratty braids, was Randi. She was squinting hard, her head tilted, one hand over her eyes to shade them, that same arm obviously scraped. Twined in the fingers of her other hand she held the reins of all three horses, as if she'd known then that she would lead her brothers around for the rest of their lives.

The bitch.

Disturbed, the intruder looked away from the framed photograph, quickly pushed the play button on the telephone answering machine and felt an instant of satisfaction at having the upper hand on the princess. But the feeling was fleeting. As cold as the ashes in the grate.

As the single message played, resounding through the vaulted room, it became evident that there was only one thing that would make things right.

Randi McCafferty had to pay.

And she had to pay with her life.

Chapter 2

Less than two hours after his conversation with the Mc-Cafferty brothers, Striker was aboard a private plane headed due west. A friend who owned this prop job owed him a favor and Striker had called in his marker. He'd also taken the time to phone an associate who was already digging into Randi's past. Eric Brown was ex-military, and had spent some time with the FBI before recently going out on his own. While Striker was watching Randi, Brown would track down the truth like a bloodhound on the trail of a wounded buck. It was just a matter of time.

Staring out the window at the thick clouds, listening to the steady rumble of the engines, Striker thought about Randi McCafferty.

Beautiful. Smart. Sexy as hell.

Who would want her dead?

And why?

Because of the kid? Nah...that didn't wash. The book

she'd been writing? Or something else, some other secret she'd kept from her brothers.

She was an intriguing, sharp-tongued woman with fire in her brown eyes and a lightning-quick sense of humor that kept even her three half brothers at bay. True, Thorne, Matt and Slade could have held a grudge. All three of them had ended up sharing half the ranch while she, John McCafferty's only daughter, had inherited the other half. Though some of the townspeople of Grand Hope thought differently, Striker knew that the brothers were clean, their motives pure. Hadn't they hired him for the express purpose of saving their half sister's lovely hide? No, they were out as suspects. They weren't trying to murder her.

Chewing on a toothpick, he frowned into the clouds that were visible through the window. Most murders were committed because of greed, jealousy or revenge. Sometimes a victim was killed because they posed a threat, had something over on the killer. Once in a while someone was murdered to cover up other crimes.

So why would someone want to kill Randi? Because of her inheritance? Because of her son? A love affair gone sour? Had she swindled someone out of something? Did she know too much? Unconnected motives rattled through his brain. He scratched the side of his face.

There were two mysteries surrounding Randi. The first was the paternity of her child, a closely guarded secret. The second was about a book she'd been writing around the time of the accident.

None of her brothers, nor anyone close to her, professed to know who had sired the baby, probably not even the father. Randi had been tight-lipped on the subject. Striker wondered if she was protecting the father or just didn't want him to know. He thought it wouldn't be too hard to figure out who was little Joshua's daddy. Striker had already found out the kid's blood type from the hospital and he'd managed to get a few hairs from Joshua's head...just in case he needed a DNA match.

There were three men who had been close to Randi, close enough to be lovers, though he, as yet, had not substantiated which—if any—she had been intimate with. At that thought his gut clenched. He felt a jolt of jealousy. Ridiculous. He wouldn't allow himself to get emotionally involved with Randi McCafferty, not even after last night. She was his client, even though she didn't know it yet. And when she found out, he was certain the gates of hell would spring open and all sorts of demons would rise up. No, Randi McCafferty wouldn't take kindly to her brothers' safeguards for her.

He tapped his finger on the cold glass of the plane's window and wondered who had warmed Randi's bed and fathered her son.

Bile rose in his throat as he thought of the prime candidates.

Sam Donahue, the ex-rodeo rider, was at the top of the list. Kurt didn't trust the rugged cowboy who had collected more women than pairs of boots. Sam had always been a rogue, a man none of Randi's brothers could stomach, a jerk who had already left two ex-wives in his dusty wake.

Joe Paterno was a freelance photographer who sometimes worked for the *Seattle Clarion.* Joe was a playboy of the worst order, a love-'em-and-leave-'em type who'd been connected to women all over the planet, especially in the political hot spots he photographed. Joe would never be the kind to settle down with a wife and son.

Brodie Clanton, a shark of a Seattle lawyer who'd been born with a silver spoon firmly wedged between his teeth, was the grandson of Judge Nelson Clanton, one of Seattle's most prestigious lawmakers. Brodie Clanton looked upon life as if it owed him something, and spent most of his time defending rich clients.

Not exactly a sterling group to choose from.

What the hell had Randi been thinking? None of these guys was worth her looking at a second time. And yet she'd been linked to each of them. For a woman who wrote a column for singles, she had a lousy track record with men.

And what about you? Where do you fit in?

"Damn." Striker wouldn't think about that now. Wouldn't let last night cloud his judgment. Even if he found out who was the father of the baby, that was just a start. It only proved Randi had slept with the guy. It didn't mean that he was trying to kill her.

Anyone might be out to get Randi. A jealous coworker, someone she'd wronged, a nutcase who had a fixation on her, an old rival, any damn one. The motive for getting her out of the way could include greed or jealousy or fear…at this point no one knew. He shifted his toothpick from one side of his mouth to the other and listened as the engines changed speed and the little plane began its descent to a small airstrip south of Tacoma.

The fun was just about to begin.

Rain spat from the sky. Bounced on the hood of her new Jeep. Washed the hilly streets of Seattle from a leaden sky. Randi McCafferty punched the accelerator, took a corner too quickly and heard her tires protest over the sound of light jazz emanating from the speakers. It had been a hellish drive from Montana, the winter weather worse than she'd expected, her nerves on edge by the time she reached the city she'd made her home. A headache was building behind her eyes, reminding her that it hadn't been too many months since the accident that had nearly taken her life and robbed her of her memory for a while. She caught a glimpse of her reflection in the rearview mirror—at least her hair was growing back. Her head had been shaved for the surgery and now her red-brown hair was nearly two inches long. For a second she longed to be back in Grand Hope with her half brothers.

She flipped on her blinker and switched lanes by rote, then eased to a stop at the next red light. Much as she wanted to, she couldn't hide out forever. It was time to take action. Reclaim her life. Which was here in Seattle, not at the Flying M Ranch in Montana with her three bossy half brothers.

And yet her heart twisted and she felt a moment's panic. She'd let herself become complacent in the safety of the ranch, with three strong brothers ensuring she and her infant son were secure.

No more.

You did this, Randi. It's your fault your family is in danger. And now you've compounded the problem with Kurt Striker. What's wrong with you? Last night...remember last night? You caught him watching you on the ledge, knew that he'd been staring, had felt the heat between the two of you for weeks, and what did you do? Did you pull on your robe and duck into your bedroom and lock the door like a sane woman? Oh, no. You put your baby down in his crib and then you followed Striker, caught up with him and—

A horn blasted from behind her and she realized the light had turned green. Gritting her teeth, she drove like a madwoman. Pushed the wayward, erotic thoughts of Kurt Striker to the back of her mind for the time being. She had more important issues to deal with.

At least her son was safe. If only for the time being. She missed him horridly already and she'd just dropped him off at a spot where no one could find him. It was only until she did what she had to do. Hiding Joshua was best. For her. For him. For a while. A short while, she reminded herself. Already attempts had been made upon her life and upon the lives of those closest to her; she couldn't take a chance with her baby.

As she braked for a red light, she stared through the raindrops zigzagging down the windshield, but in her mind's eye she saw her infant son with his inquisitive blue eyes, shock of reddish-blond hair and rosy cheeks. She imagined his soft little giggles. So innocent. So trusting.

Her heart tore and she blinked back a sudden spate of hot tears that burned her eyelids and threatened to fall. She didn't have time for any sentimentality. Not now.

The light changed. She eased into the traffic heading toward Lake Washington, weaving her way through the red taillights, checking her rearview mirror, assuring herself she wasn't being followed.

You really are paranoid, her mind taunted as she found the turnoff to her condominium and the cold January wind buffeted the trees surrounding the short lane. But then she had a right to be. She pulled into her parking spot and cranked off the ignition of her SUV. The vehicle was new, a replacement for her crumpled Jeep that had been forced off the road in Glacier Park a couple of months back. The culprit who'd tried to kill her had gotten away with his crime.

But not for long, she told herself as she swung out of the vehicle and grabbed her bag from the backseat. She had work to do; serious work. She glanced over her shoulder one last time. No shadowy figure appeared to be following her, no footsteps echoed behind her as she dashed around the puddles collecting on the asphalt path leading to her front door.

Get a grip. She climbed the two steps, juggled her bag and purse on the porch, inserted her key and shoved hard on the door with her shoulder.

Inside, the rooms smelled musty and unused. A dead fern in the foyer was shedding dry fronds all over the hardwood floor. Dust covered the windowsill.

It sure didn't feel like home. Not anymore. But then nowhere did without her son. She kicked the door behind her and took two steps into the living room, then, seeing a shadow move on the couch, stopped dead in her tracks.

Adrenaline spurted through her bloodstream.

Goose bumps rose on the back of her arms.

Oh, God, she thought wildly, her mouth dry as a desert. The killer was waiting for her.

Chapter 3

"Well, well, well," he drawled slowly. "Look who's finally come home."

In an instant Randi recognized his voice.

Bastard.

His hand reached to the table lamp. As he snapped on the lights, she found herself staring into the intense, suspicious gaze of Kurt Striker, the private investigator her brothers had seen fit to hire.

She instantly bristled. Fear gave way to outrage. "What the hell are you doing here?"

"Waitin'."

"For?"

"You."

Damn, his drawl was irritating. So was the superior, know-it-all attitude that emanated from him as he lounged on her chenille couch, the fingers of one big hand wrapped possessively around a long-necked bottle of beer. He appeared as out of place in his jeans, cowboy boots and denim jacket as a cougar at a pedigreed-cat show.

"Why?" she demanded as she dropped her bag and purse on a parson's table in the entry. She didn't step into the living room; didn't want to get too close to this man. He bothered her. Big-time. Had from the first time she'd laid eyes on him when she'd still been recuperating from the accident.

Striker was a hardheaded, square-jawed type who looked like Hollywood's version of a rogue cop. His hair, blond streaked, was unruly and fell over his eyes, and he seemed to have avoided getting close to a razor for several days. Deep-set, intelligent eyes, poised over chiseled cheeks, were guarded by thick eyebrows and straight lashes. He wore faded jeans, a tattered Levi's jacket and an attitude that wouldn't quit.

Resting on the small of his back, sprawled on her couch, he raked his gaze up her body one slow inch at a time.

"I asked you a question."

"I'm trying to save your neck."

"You're trespassing."

"So call the cops."

"Enough with the attitude." She walked to the windows, snapped open the blinds. Through the wet glass she caught a glimpse of the lake, choppy, steel-colored water sporting whitecaps and fog too dense to see the opposite shore. Folding her arms over her chest, she turned and faced Striker again.

He smiled then. A dazzling, sexy grin offset by the mockery in his green eyes. It damn near took her breath away and for a splintered second she thought of the hours they'd spent together, the touch of his skin, the feel of his hands...oh, God. If he wasn't such a pain in the butt, he might be considered handsome. Interesting. Sexy. Long legs shoved into cowboy boots, shoulders wide enough to stretch the seams of his jacket, flat belly... Yeah, all the pieces fit into a hunky package. If a woman was looking for a man. Randi wasn't. She'd learned her lesson. Last night was just a slip. It wouldn't happen again.

Couldn't.

"You know," he said, "I was just thinkin' the same thing. Let's both shove the attitudes back where they came from and get to work."

"To work?" she asked, rankled. She needed him out of her condo and fast. He had a way of destroying her equilibrium, of setting her teeth on edge.

"That's right. Cut the bull and get down to business."

"I don't think we have any business."

His eyes held hers for a fraction of a second and she knew in that splintered instant that he was remembering last night as clearly as she. He cleared his throat. "Randi, I think we should discuss what happened—"

"Last night?" she asked. "Not now, okay? Maybe not ever. Let's just forget it."

"Can you?"

"I don't know, but I'm sure as hell going to try."

He silently called her a liar.

"Okay, if this is the way you want to play it."

"I told you we don't have any business."

"Sure we do. You can start by telling me who's the father of your baby."

Never, buddy. Not a chance. "I don't think that's relevant."

"Like hell, Randi." He was on his feet in an instant, across the hardwood floor and glaring down his crooked nose at her. "There have been two attempts on your life.

One was the accident, and I use the term loosely, up in Glacier Park, when your car was forced off the road. The other when someone tried to do you in at the hospital. You remember those two little incidents, don't you?"

She swallowed hard. Didn't answer.

"And let's not forget the fire in the stable at the ranch. Arson, Randi. Remember? It nearly killed your brothers." Her heart squeezed at the painful memory. To her surprise he grabbed her, strong hands curling around her upper arms and gripping tightly through her jacket. "Do you really want to take any more chances with your life? With your brothers'? With your kid's? Little J.R. nearly died from an infection in the hospital after the accident, didn't he? You went into labor early in the middle of no-goddamn-where, and by the time some Good Samaritan saw you and called for an ambulance, your baby almost didn't make it."

She fought the urge to break down. Wished to heaven that he'd quit touching her. He was too close, his angry breath whispering over her face, the raw, sexual energy of him seeping through her clothes.

"Now, I'm not moving," he vowed, "not one bloody inch, until you and I get a few things straight. I'm in for the long haul and I'll stay here all night if I have to. All week. All year."

Her stupid heart pounded, and though she tried to pull away he wouldn't allow it. The manacles surrounding her arms clamped even more tightly.

"Let's start with one important question, shall we?"

He didn't have to ask. She knew what was coming and braced herself.

"Tell me, Randi, right now. No more ducking the issue. Who the devil is J.R.'s father?"

Oh, God, he was too close. "Let go of me," she said, refusing to give in. "And get the hell out of my house."

"No way."

"I'll call the police."

"Be my guest," he encouraged, hitching his chin toward the phone she hadn't used in months. It sat collecting dust on the small desk she'd crammed into one corner of the living room. "Why don't you tell them everything that's happened to you and I'll explain what I'm doing here."

"You weren't invited."

"Your brothers are concerned."

"They can't control me."

He lifted a skeptical eyebrow. "No? They might disagree."

"Big deal," she said, tossing her head and pretending to be tough. The truth was that she loved all of her older half brothers, all three of them, but she couldn't have them poking around in her life. Nor did she want anything to do with Kurt Striker. He was just too damn male for his own good. Or her own. He'd proved that much last night. "Listen, Striker, this is my life. I can handle it. Now, if you'd be so kind as to take your hands off me," she said, sarcasm dripping from the pleasantry, "I have a lot to do."

He stared at her long and hard, those sharp green eyes seeming to penetrate her own. Then he lifted a shoulder and released her. "I can wait."

"Elsewhere."

His smile was pure devilment. "Is that a hint?" he drawled, and again her heart began to trip-hammer. Damn the man.

"A broad one. Take a hike."

"Only if you show me the city."

"What?"

"I'm new in town. Humor me."

"You mean so you can keep an eye on me."

Curse the sexy smile that crawled across his jaw. "That, too."

"Forget it. I've got a million things to do," she said, flipping up a hand to indicate the telephone, where no light blinked on her answering machine. "That's odd," she muttered then glanced back at Striker, whom she was beginning to believe was the embodiment of Lucifer. "Wait a minute. You listened to my messages?" she demanded, fury spiking up her spine.

"No, I actually didn't."

She made her way to the desk and pushed the play button on the recorder. "That's odd," she said as she recognized Sarah Peeples's voice.

"Hey, when are you coming back to work?" Sarah asked. "It's soooo boooring with all these A-type males." She giggled. "Well, maybe not that boring, but I miss ya. Give me a call and kiss Joshua for me." The phone clicked as Sarah hung up.

Randi bit her lower lip. Her mind was spinning as she jabbed a finger at the recorder. "You didn't listen to this?"

"No."

"Then who did?"

"Not you?" he asked and his eyes narrowed.

"No, not me." Her skin crawled. If Striker hadn't listened to her messages, then…who had? Her headache pounded. Maybe she was jumping at shadows. She was worried about her baby, exasperated with the man in her apartment and just plain tired from the long drive and the few hours' sleep she'd had in the past forty-eight hours. That was it; her nerves were just strung tight. Her brothers hiring this sexy, roughshod P.I. only made things worse. She rubbed her temple and tried to think clearly. "Look, Striker, you can't barge in here, help yourself to a beer, then sit back and make yourself at home…"

His expression reminded her that he'd done just that.

"So far," she went on, "I think you've committed half a dozen crimes. Breaking and entering, burglary, trespassing and who knows what else. The police would have a field day."

"So where's your son?" he asked, refusing to be sidetracked. "J.R. Where is he?"

She'd known that was coming. "I call him Joshua."

"Okay, where's Josh?"

"Somewhere safe."

"There is nowhere that's safe."

Her insides crumbled. "You're wrong."

"So you *are* afraid that someone is after you."

"I'm a mother. I'm not taking any chances with him."

"Only with yourself."

"Let's not get into this." She pressed a button and the answering machine rewound.

"Is he with your cousin Nora?"

Her muscles tensed. How had he learned about Nora, on her mother's side? Her brothers had never met Nora.

"Or maybe Aunt Bonita, your mother's stepsister?"

God, he'd done his homework. Her head thundered, her palms suddenly sweaty. "It's none of your business, Striker."

"How about your friend Sharon?" He folded his arms over his chest. "That's where I'm putting my money."

She froze. How could he have guessed that she would leave her precious child with Sharon Okano? She and Sharon hadn't seen each other in nearly nine months, and yet Striker had figured it out.

"You wouldn't take a chance on a relative, or you would have left him in Montana, and your coworkers are out because they might slip up, so it had to be someone you trusted, but not obvious enough that it would be easy to figure it out."

Her heart constricted.

He reached forward and touched her shoulder. She recoiled as if burned.

"If I can guess where you hid him, so can the guy who's after you."

"How did you find Sharon?" she asked. "I'm not buying the 'lucky guess' theory."

Kurt walked to the coffee table and picked up his beer. "It wasn't rocket science, Randi."

"But—"

"Even cell phones have records."

"You went through my mail to find my phone bill? Isn't that a federal offense, or don't you care about that?" she asked, then her eyes swept the desk and she realized that he couldn't have sorted through the junk mail and correspondence that was hers, as she'd had it held at the post office ages ago.

"It doesn't matter how I got the information," he said. "What's important is that you and your son aren't safe. Your brothers hired me to protect you, and like it or not, that's exactly what I'm going to do." He drained his beer in one long swallow. "Fight me all you want, Randi, but I intend to stick to you like glue. You can call your brothers and complain and they won't budge. You can run away, but I'll catch you so quick it'll make your head spin. You can call the cops and we'll get to the bottom of this here and now. That's just the way it is. So, you can make it easy for everyone and tell me what the hell's going on or you can be difficult and we'll go at it real slow." He set his bottle on one end of the coffee table and as he straightened, his eyes held hers with deadly intensity. "Either way."

"Get out."

"If that's the way you want it. But I'll be back."

So angry she was shaking, she repeated, "Get the hell out."

"You've got one hour to think about it," he advised her as he made his way to the door. "One hour. Then I'll be back. And if we have to, we'll do this the hard way. It's your choice, Randi, but the way I see it, you're damn near out of options."

He walked outside and the door shut behind him. Randi threw the bolt, swore under her breath and fought the urge to crumple into a heap. She forced starch into her spine. Nothing was ever accomplished by falling into a million pieces. It was hard to admit it, but Kurt Striker was right about one thing: she didn't have many choices. Well, that was tough. She wasn't going to be railroaded into making a wrong one.

Too much was at stake.

Chapter 4

Kurt slid behind the wheel of his rental, a bronze king-cab pickup. The windows were a little fogged, so he cracked one and turned on the defrost to stare through the rivulets of rain sliding down the windshield. He'd give her an hour to sort things out, the same hour he'd give himself to cool off. There was something about the woman that got under his skin and put him on edge.

From the first moment he'd seen her at the Flying M, he'd sensed it—that underlying tension between them, an unacknowledged current that simmered whenever they were in the same room. It was stupid, really. He wasn't one to fall victim to a woman's charms, especially not a spoiled brat of a woman who had grown up as the apple of her father's eye, a rich girl who'd had everything handed to her.

Oh, she was pretty enough. At least she was now that the bruises had disappeared and her hair was growing back. In fact, she was a knockout. Pure and simple. Despite her recent pregnancy, her body was slim, her breasts large enough to make a man notice, her hips round and tight. With her red-brown hair, pointed little chin, pouty lips and wide brown eyes, she didn't need much makeup. Her mind was quick, her tongue rapier sharp and she'd made it more than clear that she wanted him to leave her alone. Which would be best for everyone involved, he knew, but there was just something about her that kept drawing him in and firing his blood.

Forget it. She's your client.

Not technically. She hadn't hired him.

But her brothers had.

You have to keep this relationship professional.

Relationship? What relationship? Hell, she can't stand to be in the same room with me.

Oh, yeah, right. Like you haven't been through this before. And like last night never happened.

She'd put Joshua in his room and then after Kurt had sneaked down the stairway, she'd followed him and found him in the darkened living room, where only embers from a dying fire gave off any illumination.

He'd already poured himself a drink and was sipping it quietly while staring through the icy window to the blackened remains of the stable.

"You were watching me," she'd accused, and he'd nodded, not turning around. "Why?"

"I didn't mean to."

"Bull!"

So she wasn't going to let him off the hook. So be it. He took a sip of his drink before facing her.

"What the hell were you doing upstairs?"

"I thought I heard someone, so I checked."

"You did. It was me. This house is full of people, you

know." She was so angry, he could feel her heat, noticed that she hadn't bothered buttoning her nightgown, acted as if she was completely unaware that her breasts were visible.

"Do you want me to explain or not?"

"Yeah. Try." She crossed her arms under her breasts, involuntarily lifting them, causing the cleft between them to deepen. Kurt kept his gaze locked with hers.

"As I said, I heard something. Footsteps. I just walked upstairs and down the hall. By the time I started for the stairs you were there."

"And the rest, as they say, is history." She arched an eyebrow and her lips were pursed hard together. "Get a good look?"

"Good enough."

"Like what you saw?"

He couldn't help himself. One side of his mouth lifted. "It was all right."

"What?"

"I've seen better."

"Oh, for the love of St. Jude!" she sputtered, and even in the poor light, he noticed a flush stain her cheeks.

"What did you expect, Randi? You caught me looking, okay? I didn't plan it, but there you were and I was... caught. I guess I could have cleared my throat and walked down the stairs, but I was a little...surprised." His smile fell away and he took another long swallow. "We're both adults, let's forget it."

"Easy for you to say."

"Not that easy."

Her eyes narrowed up at him. "What's that supposed to mean?"

"You're pretty unforgettable."

"Yeah, right." She ran her fingers through her hair and

her nightgown shifted, allowing him even more of a view of her breasts and abdomen. As if finally feeling the breeze, she sucked in her breath and looked down to see her breasts. "Oh, wonderful." She fumbled with the buttons. "Here I am ranting and raving and putting on a show and…"

"It's all right," he said. "I lied before. I've never seen better."

She shook her head and laughed. "This is ridiculous."

"Can I buy you a drink?"

"Of my dad's liquor? I don't think so. I…I might do something I'll regret."

"You think?"

She let out a breath, glanced him up and down and nodded. "Yeah, I think."

He should have stopped himself right then while he still had a chance of taking control of the situation, but he didn't and tossed back his drink. "Maybe regrets are too highly overrated," he said, dropping his glass onto a chair and closing the distance between them. He noticed her pulse fluttering on the smooth skin of her throat, knew that she was as scared as he was.

But it had been a long time since he'd kissed a woman and he'd been thinking about how it would feel to kiss Randi McCafferty for weeks. Last night, he'd found out. He'd wrapped his arms around her and as a gasp slipped from between her lips, he'd slanted his mouth over hers and felt his blood heat. Her arms had instinctively climbed to his shoulders and her body had fitted tight against him.

Warning bells had clanged in his mind, but he'd ignored them as his tongue had slipped between her teeth and his erection had pressed hard against his fly. She was warm and tasted of lingering coffee. His fingers splayed across her back and as she moaned against him, he slowly started

inching her nightgown upward, bunching the soft flannel
in his fingers as her hemline climbed up her calves and
thighs. It seemed the most natural thing in the world to
use his weight to carry them both to the rug in front of the
dying fire...

Now, as he sat in his pickup with the rain beating against
his windshield, Striker scowled at the thought of what he'd
done. He'd known better than to kiss her, had sensed it
wouldn't stop there. He didn't need the complications of
a woman.

He hazarded a glance at the third finger of his left hand
where he could still see the deep impression a ring had
made as it had cut into his skin. The muscles in the back of
his neck tightened and a few dark thoughts skated through
his mind. Thoughts of another woman...another beautiful
woman and a little girl...

Angry with the turn of his thoughts, he forced his gaze
to Randi's condominium. This particular grouping of units
rested on a hillside overlooking Lake Washington. He'd
parked across the street where he had a clear view of her
front door, the only way in or out of the condo, unless she
decided to sneak out a window. Even then, he'd see her
Jeep leaving. Unless she was traveling on foot, he'd be
able to follow her.

He glanced at his watch. She had forty-seven minutes
to cool off and get herself together. And so did he. Leaning across the seat, he grabbed his battered briefcase and
reached inside, where he kept an accordion folder on the
McCafferty case. With one eye on the condominium, he
riffled through the pages of notes, pictures and columns
he'd clipped out of the *Seattle Clarion,* columns with a by-
line of Randi McCafferty and accompanied by a smiling
picture of the author.

"Solo," by Randi McCafferty.

Hers was an advice column for singles, from the confirmed bachelors to the newly divorced, the recently widowed or anyone else who wrote in, claimed not to be married and asked for her opinion. Striker reread a few of his favorites. In one, she advised a woman suffering from abuse to leave the relationship immediately and file charges. In another she told an overly protective single mother to give her teenage daughter "breathing space" while keeping in touch. In still another, she suggested a widower join a grief-support group and take up ballroom dancing, something he and his wife had always wanted to do. Her columns were often empathetic, but sometimes caustic. She told one woman who couldn't decide between two men and was lying to them both to "grow up," while she advised another young single to "quit whining" about his new girlfriend, who sometimes parked in "his" spot while staying over. Within each bit of advice, Randi often added a little humor. It was no wonder the column had been syndicated and picked up in other markets.

Yet there were rumors of trouble at the *Clarion*. Randi McCafferty and her editor, Bill Withers, were supposedly feuding. Striker hadn't figured out why. Yet. But he would. Randi had also written some articles for magazines under the name of R. J. McKay. Then there was her unfinished tell-all book on the rodeo circuit, one she wouldn't talk much about. A lot going on with Ms. McCafferty. Yep, he thought, leaning back and staring at the front door of her place, she was an interesting woman, and one definitely off-limits.

Well, hell, weren't they all? He scowled through the raindrops zigzagging down his windshield and his thoughts started to wend into that forbidden territory of his past, to a

time that now seemed eons ago, before he'd become jaded.
Before he'd lost his faith in women. In marriage. In life.
A time he didn't want to think about. Not now. Not ever.

"He's okay?" Randi said into her cell phone. Her hands
were sweaty, her mind pounding with fear, and it was all
she could do to try to calm her rising sense of panic. Despite her bravado and in-your-face attitude with Striker,
she was shaky. Nervous. His warnings putting her on edge,
and now, as she held the cell phone to her ear and peered
through the blinds to the parking lot where Kurt Striker's
pickup was parked, her heart was knocking.

"You dropped him off less than an hour ago," Sharon
assured her. "Joshua's just fine. I fed him, changed him
and put him down for a nap. Right now he's sleeping like
a...well, a baby."

Randi let out her breath, ran a shaking hand over her
lip. "Good."

"You've got to relax. I know you're a new mother and
all, but believe me, whatever you're caught up in, stress-
ing out isn't going to help anyone. Not you, not the baby.
So take a chill pill."

"I wish," Randi said, only slightly relieved.

"Do it... Take your own advice. You're always telling
people in your column to take a step back, a deep breath
and reevaluate the situation. You still belong to the gym,
don't you? Take yoga or tae kwon do or kickboxing."

"You think that would do it?"

"Wouldn't hurt."

"Just as long as I know Joshua's safe."

"And sound. Promise." Sharon sighed. "I know you don't
want to hear this, but you might consider going out. You
know, with a man."

"I don't think so."

"Just because you had a bad experience with one doesn't mean they're all jerks."

"I had a bad experience with more than one."

"Well…it wouldn't kill you to give romance a chance."

"I'm not so sure. When Cupid pulls back his bow and aims at me, I swear his arrows are poisoned."

"That's not what you tell the people who write you."

"With them, I can be objective." She was staring at Striker's truck, which hadn't moved. The man was behind the wheel. She saw movement, but she couldn't see his facial features, could only feel him staring at her house, sizing it up, just as he'd done with her. "Look, I'll be over tomorrow, but if you need to reach me for anything, call me on my cell."

"Will do. Now, quit worrying."

Fat chance, Randi thought as she hung up. Ever since she'd given birth she'd done nothing more than worry. She was worse than her half brothers and that was pretty bad. Thorne was the oldest and definitely type A. But he'd recently married Nicole and settled down with her and her twin girls. Randi smiled at the thought of Mindy and Molly, two dynamic four-year-olds who looked identical but were as different as night and day. Then there was Matt, ex-rodeo rider and serious. Had his own place in Idaho until he'd fallen in love with Kelly, who was now his wife. And then there was Slade. He was a rebel, hadn't grown up worrying about anything. But all of a sudden he'd made it his personal mission to "take care" of his younger, unmarried sister and her child.

A few months ago Randi would have scoffed at her brothers' concerns. But that had been before the accident. She remembered little of it, thank God, but now she had to figure out who was trying to harm her. She could accept Striker's help, she supposed, but was afraid that if she did, if she confided in anyone, she would only be jeopardizing her baby further and that was a chance she wasn't about to take. Regardless of her brothers' concerns.

Frowning, she remembered Matt and Kelly's wedding and the reception afterward. There had been dancing and laughter despite the cold Montana winter, despite the charred remains of the stable, a reminder of the danger she'd brought upon her family. Kelly had been radiant in her sparkling dress, Matt dashing in a black tuxedo, even Slade—who'd been injured in the fire—had forgone his crutches to dance with Jamie Parsons before whisking her away to elope on that snow-covered night. Randi had dressed her son in a tiny tuxedo and held him close, silently vowing to take the danger away from her brothers, to search out the truth herself.

Two days later when a breathless Slade and Jamie had returned as husband and wife, Randi had announced she was leaving.

"Are you out of your ever-lovin' mind?" Matt had demanded. He'd slapped his hat against his thigh and his breath had steamed from his lungs as all four of John Randall McCafferty's children had stood near the burned-out shell of the stable.

"This is beyond insanity." Thorne had glared down at her, as if he could use the same tactics that worked in a boardroom to convince her to stay. "You can't leave."

"Watch me," she'd baited, meeting his harsh gaze with one of her own.

Even Slade, the rebel and her staunchest ally, had turned against her. His crutches buried beyond their rubber tips in a drift of snow at the fence line, he'd said, "Don't do it, Randi. Keep J.R. here with us. Where we can help you."

"This is something I have to do," she'd insisted, and caught a glimpse of Striker, forever lurking in the shadows, always watching her. "I can't stay here. It's unsafe. How many accidents have happened here? Really, it's best if I leave." All of her brothers had argued with her, but Striker had remained silent, not arguing, just taking it all in.

Until last night. And then all hell had broken loose.

So she'd left and he'd followed her to Seattle. Now she realized she'd have one helluva time getting rid of him. It galled her that her brothers had hired him.

"What makes you think you'll be safer in Seattle than Grand Hope?" Thorne had asked as she'd packed her bags in the pine-walled room she'd grown up in. "You're still not healed completely from the accident. If you stayed here, we could all look after you. And little J.R, er, Joshua, would have Molly and Mindy to play with when he got a little bigger."

Randi's heart was torn. She'd eyed her bright-eyed nieces, Molly bold and impudent, Mindy hiding behind Thorne's pant leg, and known that she couldn't stay. She had things to do; a story to write. And she knew that if she stayed any longer, she'd only get more tangled up with Striker.

"I'll be all right," she'd insisted, zipping up her bag and gathering her baby into her arms. "I wouldn't do anything to put Joshua in danger." As she'd clambered down the stairs, she'd heard the twins asking where she was going and had spied their housekeeper, Juanita, making the sign of the cross over her ample bosom and whispering a prayer in Spanish. As if she would haul her own child into the maw of danger. But they didn't understand that in order for everyone to be safe, she had to get back to her old life and figure out why someone was trying to harm her.

And Joshua. Don't forget your precious son. Whoever it is means business and is desperate. She noted that Striker was still seated in his truck. Waiting. Damn the man. Quickly she closed the blinds, then took a final glance around the small nursery. Hardwood floors that were dusty, a cradle stuck in a corner, a bookcase that was still in its box as "some assembly" was required and she hadn't had time.

Because you were in the hospital.

Because you nearly died.

Because someone is determined to kill you.

Maybe, just maybe, your brothers have a point.

Maybe you should trust Kurt Striker.

Again she thought of the night before. Trust him? Trust herself?

What other choice did she have?

Much as she hated to admit it, he was right. If Kurt could figure out where she'd hidden Joshua, then the would-be killer, whoever he was, could, as well. Her insides knotted. Why would anyone want to harm her innocent baby? Why?

It's not about Joshua, Randi. It's about you. Someone wants you dead. As long as the baby isn't with you, he's safe.

She clung to that notion and set about getting her life in order again. She made herself a cup of instant coffee and dialed the office. Her editor was out, but she left a message on his voice mail, checked her own email, then quickly unpacked and changed into a clean sweater, slacks and boots. She wound a scarf around her neck and finger combed her short hair, looking into the hall mirror and cringing. She'd lost weight in the past five months; indeed she now weighed less than before she'd gotten pregnant, and she was having trouble getting used to the length of her hair. She'd always worn it long, but her head had been shaved before one of her lifesaving surgeries to alleviate the swelling in her brain and the resulting grow-out was difficult to adjust to though she'd had it shaped before leaving Montana. Instead, she went into the bathroom, found an old tube of gel and ran some of the goop through her hair. The result was kind of a finger-in-the-light-socket look, but was the best she could do. She was just rinsing her hands when her doorbell buzzed loudly several times, announcing a visitor. She didn't have to be told who was ringing the bell. One quick look at her watch showed her that it had been one hour and five minutes since she'd last faced Striker. Apparently the man was prompt.

And couldn't take a hint.

"Great," she muttered, wiping her hands on a towel and discarding it into an open hamper before hurrying to the front door. What she didn't need was anyone dogging her, bothering her and generally getting in the way. She was a private person by nature and opposed anyone nosing into her business, no matter what his reasons. Reining in her temper, she yanked open the door. Sure as shootin', Kurt Striker, all six feet two inches of pure male determination, was standing on her doorstep. His light brown hair had darkened from the raindrops clinging to it, and his green eyes were hard. Wearing an aging bomber jacket and even older jeans, he was sexy as hell and, from the looks of him, not any happier at being on her stoop than she was to find him there.

"What's with ringing the bell?" she asked, deciding not to mask her irritation. "I thought you had your own key, or a pick, or something. Compliments of my brothers."

"They're only looking out for you."

"They should mind their own business."

"And for your kid."

"I know." She'd already stepped away from the door and into the living room. Striker was on her heels. She heard the door slam behind him, the lock engage and the sound of his boots ringing on her hardwood floors.

"Look, Randi," he said as she stopped at the closet and found her raincoat. "If I can break in, then—"

"Yeah, yeah, I'm way ahead of you." She slid her arms through the sleeves and glanced up at him. "I'll change the locks, put on a dead bolt, okay?"

"Along with putting in an alarm system and buying a guard dog."

"Hey—I've got a baby. Remember?" She walked to the couch, found her purse and grabbed it. Now...the computer. Quickly she tucked her laptop into its case. "I don't think an attack dog would be a good idea."

"Not an attack dog—a guard dog. There's a big difference."

"If you say so. Now, if you'll excuse me, I've got to go to the office." She anticipated what he was about to say. "Look, it wouldn't be a good idea to follow me, you know? I'm already in enough hot water with my boss as it is." She didn't wait for him to answer, just walked back to the door. "So, if you'll excuse me—" She opened the door again in an unspoken invitation.

His lips twisted into a poor imitation of a smile. "You're not going to get rid of me that easily."

"Why? Because of the money?" she asked, surprised that the mention of it bothered her, cut into her soul. "That's what this is all about, isn't it? My brothers have paid you to watch over me, right? You're supposed to be...oh, hell...not my bodyguard. Tell me Thorne and Matt and Slade aren't so archaic, so controlling, so damn stupid as to think I need a personal bodyguard... Oh, God, that's it, isn't it?" She would have laughed if she hadn't been so furious. "This has got to end. I need privacy. I need space. I need—"

His hand snaked out, and fast as lightning, he grabbed her wrist, his fingers a quick, hard manacle. "What you need is to be less selfish," he finished for her. He was so close that she felt his hot, angry breath wafting across her face. "We've been through this before. Quit thinking about your damn independence and consider your kid's safety. Along with your own." He dropped her arm as suddenly as he'd picked it up. "Let's go. I won't get in the way."

The smile he cast over his shoulder was wicked enough to take her breath away. "Promise."

Chapter 5

"Don't even think about riding with me," she warned, flipping the hood of her jacket over her hair as she dashed toward her Jeep. The rain had softened to a thick drizzle, a kind of mist that made visibility next to nil. It was early evening, the sky dark with heavy clouds.

"It would make things a helluva lot easier."

Obviously, Striker wasn't taking a hint. Collar turned up, he kept with her as she reached the car.

"For whom?" She shot him a look and clicked on her keyless remote. The Jeep beeped and its interior lights flicked on.

"Both of us."

"I don't think so." She climbed into her car and immediately locked her doors. He didn't move. Just stood by the Jeep. As if she would change her mind. She switched on the ignition as she tossed off her hood. Then, leaving Striker standing in the rain, she backed out of her parking spot, threw the Jeep into Drive and cruised out of the lot. In the rearview mirror, she caught a glimpse of him running toward his truck, but not before she managed to merge into the traffic heading toward the heart of the city. She couldn't help but glance in her mirrors, checking to see if Striker had followed.

Not that she doubted it for a minute. But she didn't see his truck and reminded herself to pay attention to traffic and the red taillights glowing through the rain. She couldn't let her mind wander to the man, not even if she had acted like a fool last night.

She'd let him kiss her, let him slide her nightgown off her body, felt his lips, hot and hard, against the hollow of her throat and the slope of her shoulder. She shouldn't have done it, known it was a mistake, but her body had been a traitor and as his rough fingers had scaled her ribs and his beard-rough face had rubbed her skin, she'd let herself go, kissed him feverishly.

She'd been surprised at how much she'd wanted him, how passionately she'd kissed him, scraped off his clothes, run her own anxious fingers down his hard, sinewy shoulders to catch in his thick chest hair.

The fire had hissed quietly, red embers glowing, illuminating the room to a warm orange. Her breathing had been furious, her heart rocketing, desire curling deep inside her. She'd wanted him to touch her, shivered when his tongue brushed her nipples, bitten her bottom lip as his hot breath had caressed her abdomen and legs. She'd opened to him easily as his hands had explored and touched. Her mind had spun in utter abandon and she'd wanted him... Oh, God, she'd wanted him as she'd never wanted another man.

Which had been foolish...but as he'd kissed her intimately and slid the length of his body against her, she'd lost all control. All her hard-fought willpower...

She nearly missed her exit as she thought about him and the magic of the night, the lovemaking that had caused her to steal away early in the morning, before dawn. As if she'd been ashamed.

Now she wended her way off I-5 and down the steep streets leading to the waterfront. Through the tall, rain-drenched buildings was a view of the gray waters of Eliot Bay—restless and dark, mirroring her own uneasy feelings. She pulled the Jeep into the newspaper's parking lot, grabbed her laptop and briefcase and faced a life that she'd left months before.

The offices of the *Seattle Clarion* were housed on the fifth floor of what had originally been a hotel. The hundred-year-old building was faced in red brick and had been updated, renovated and cut into offices.

Inside, Randi punched the elevator button. She was alone, rainwater dripping from her jacket as the ancient car clamored upward. It stopped twice, picking up passengers before landing on the fifth floor, the doors opening to a short hallway and the etched-glass doors of the newspaper offices. Shawn-Tay, the receptionist, looked up and nearly came unglued when she recognized Randi.

"For the love of God, look at you!" she said, shooting to her feet and disconnecting her headset in one swift movement. Model tall, with bronze skin and dark eyes, she whipped around her desk and hugged Randi as if she'd never stop. "What the devil's got into you? Never callin' in. I was worried sick about you. Heard about the accident and..." She held Randi at arm's length. "Where's that baby of yours? How dare you come in here without him?" She cocked her head at an angle. "The hair works, but you've lost too much weight."

"I'll work on that."

"Now, about the baby?" Shawn-Tay's eyebrows elevated as the phone began to ring. "Oh, damn. I gotta get that, but you come back up here and tell me what the hell's been going on with you." She rounded the desk again and slid lithely into her chair. Holding the headset to one ear, she said, "*Seattle Clarion,* how may I direct your call?"

Randi slid past the reception desk and through the cubicles and desks of coworkers. Her niche was tucked into a corner, in the news section, behind a glass wall that separated the reporters from the salespeople. In the time she'd been gone, the walls had been painted, from a dirty off-white to different shades at every corner. Soft purple on one wall, sage on another, gold or orange on the next, all tied together by a bold carpet mingling all the colors. She passed by several reporters working on deadlines, though much of the staff had gone home for the day. A few night reporters were trickling in and the production crew still had hours to log in, but all in all, the office was quiet.

She slid into her space, surprised that it was just as she'd left it, that the small cubicle hadn't been appropriated by someone else, as it had been months since she'd been in Seattle or sat at her desk. She'd set up maternity leave with her boss late last summer and she'd created a cache of columns in anticipation of taking some time off to be with the baby and finishing the book she'd started. Between those new columns and culling some older ones, hardly vintage, but favorites, there had been enough material to keep "Solo" in the Living section twice a week, just like clockwork.

But it was time to tackle some new questions, and she spent the next two hours reading the mail that had stacked up in her in box and skimming the emails she hadn't collected in Montana. As she worked, she was vaguely aware of the soft piped-in music that sifted through the offices of the *Clarion,* and the chirp of cell phones in counterpoint to the ringing of landlines to the office. Conversation, muted and seemingly far away, barely teased her ears.

In the back of her mind she wondered if Kurt Striker had followed her. If, even now, he was making small talk with Shawn-Tay in the reception area. The thought brought a bit of a smile to her lips. Striker wasn't the type for small talk. No way. No how. For the most part tight-lipped, he was a sexy man whose past was murky, never discussed. She had the feeling that at one point in his life, he'd been attached to some kind of police department; she didn't know where or why he was no longer a law officer. But she'd find out. There were advantages to working for a newspaper and one of them was access to reams of information. If he wasn't forthcoming on his own, she'd do some digging. It wouldn't be the first time.

"Hey, Randi!" Sarah Peeples, movie reviewer for the *Clarion,* was hurrying toward Randi's desk. Sarah's column, "What's Reel," was published each Friday and was promoted as "hip and happening." A tall woman with oversize features, a wild mop of blond curls and a penchant for expensive boots and cheap jewelry, Sarah spent hours watching movies in theaters and on DVDs. She lived and breathed movies, celebrities and all things Hollywood. Today she was wearing a choker that looked as if it had been tailored for a rottweiler or a dominatrix, boots with pointed toes and silver studs, a gray scoop-necked sweater and a black skirt that opened in the front, slitted high enough to show off just a flash of thigh. "I was beginning to think I might never see you again."

"Can't keep a good woman down," Randi quipped.

"Amen. Where the hell have you been?"

"Montana with my brothers."

"The hair is new."

"Necessity rather than fashion."

"But it works for you. Short and sassy." Sarah was bobbing her head up and down as if agreeing with herself. "And you look great. How's the baby?"

"Perfect."

"And when will I get to meet him?"

"Soon," Randi hedged. The less she spoke about Joshua, the better. "How're things around here?"

Sarah rolled her eyes as she rested a hip on Randi's desk. "Same old, same old. I've been bustin' my butt...well, if you can call it that, rereviewing all the movies that are Oscar contenders."

"Sounds exhausting," Randi drawled.

"Okay, so it's not digging ditches, I know, but it's work."

"Has anything strange been going on around here?" Randi asked.

"What do you mean? Everyone who works here is slightly off, right?"

"I guess you're right."

Sarah picked up a glass paperweight and fiddled with it. "Now, when are you going to bring the baby into the office and show him off?" Sarah's grin was wide, her interest sincere. She'd been married three years and desperately wanted a baby. Her husband was holding out for the big promotion that would make a child affordable. Randi figured it might never come.

"When things have calmed down." She considered confiding in Sarah, but thought better of it. "He and I need to get settled in."

"Mmm. Then how about pictures?"

"I've got a ton of 'em back at the condo. Still packed. I'll bring them next time, I promise," she said, then leaned back in her chair. "So fill me in. What's going on around here?"

Sarah was only too glad to oblige. She offered up everything from office politics, to management changes, to out-and-out gossip. In return, she wanted to know every detail of Randi's life in Montana, starting with the accident. Finally, she said, "Paterno's back in town."

Randi felt the muscles in her back grow taut. "Is he?" Forty-five, twice divorced with a hound-dog face, thick hair beginning to gray and a razor-sharp sense of humor, the freelance photographer had asked Randi out a few years back and they'd dated for a while. It hadn't worked out for a lot of reasons. The main reason being that, at the time, neither one of them had wanted to commit. Nor had they been in love.

"He's been asking about you." Sarah set the paperweight onto the desk again. "You know, unless you're involved with someone, you might want to give him another chance."

Randi shook her head. "I don't think so."

"You hiding something from him?"

"What?" Randi asked, searching her friend's face. "Hiding something? Of course not... Oh, I get it." She shook her head and sighed. No one knew the identity of her son's father; not even the man himself. Before she could explain, Sarah's cell phone beeped.

"Oops. Duty calls," Sarah said, eyeing the face of the phone as a text message appeared. "New films just arrived. Well, old ones really. I'm doing a classic film noir piece next month and I ordered a bunch of old Peter Lorre, Bette Davis and Alfred Hitchcock tapes to review." She cast a smile over her shoulder as she hurried off. "Guess what

I'll be doing this weekend? Drop by if you don't have anything better to do...."

"Yeah, yeah, I know. I won't hold my breath."

Good thing, Randi thought, as she didn't seem to have a moment to breathe. She had way too much to do, she thought as she turned on her computer.

And first item on her agenda was finding a way to deal with Kurt Striker.

"...that's right. All three of 'em are back in Seattle," Eric Brown was saying, his voice crackling from his cell phone's connection to that of Striker's. "What're the chances of that? Clanton lives here but the other two don't. Paterno, he's at least got a place here, but Donahue doesn't."

Striker didn't like it.

"Paterno arrived three days ago and Donahue rolled into town yesterday."

Just hours before Randi had returned. "Coincidence?" Striker muttered, not believing it for a second as he stood on the sidewalk outside the offices of the *Clarion*.

There was a bitter laugh on the other end of the line. "If you believe that, I've got some real estate in the Mojave—"

"—that you want to sell me. Yeah, I know," Striker growled angrily. "Clanton lives here. Paterno does business in town. But Donahue..." His jaw tightened. "Can you follow him?"

"Not if you want me to stick around and watch the condo."

Damn it all. There wasn't enough manpower for this. Striker and Brown couldn't be in three places at once. "Just stay put for now. But let me know if anything looks odd to you, anything the least bit suspicious."

"Got it, but what about the other two guys? Paterno and Clanton?"

"Check 'em out, see what they're up to, but it's Donahue who concerns me most. We'll talk later." Striker hung up, then called Kelly McCafferty and left a message when she didn't answer. Angry at the world, he snapped his phone shut. All three of the men with whom Randi had been involved were here. In the city. Great... Just...great. His shoulders were bunched against the cold, his collar turned up and inside he felt a knot of jealousy tightening in his gut.

Jealousy, and even envy for that matter, were emotions Striker detested, the kind of useless feelings he'd avoided, even while he'd been married. Maybe that had been the problem. Maybe if he'd felt a little more raw passion, a little more jealousy or anger or empathy during those first few years of marriage, shown his wife that he'd cared about her, maybe then things would have turned out differently... Oh, hell, what was he thinking? He couldn't change the past. And *the accident,* that's how they'd referred to it, *the accident* had altered everything, created a deep, soul-wrenching, damning void that could never be filled.

And yet last night, when he'd been with Randi... Touched her. Kissed her. Felt her warmth surround him, he'd felt differently. *Don't make too much of it. So you made love to her. So what?* Maybe it had just been so long since he'd been with a woman that last night seemed more important than it was.

Whatever the reason, he couldn't stop thinking about it. Couldn't forget how right it had felt.

And it had been so wrong.

In an effort to dislodge images of Randi lying naked in front of the fire, staring up at him with those warm eyes, Striker bought coffee from a vendor and resumed his position not far from the door, protected by the awning of an antique bookstore located next door to the *Clarion*'s offices.

A familiar ache, one he rarely acknowledged, tore through him as he sipped his coffee. Leaning a shoulder against the rough bricks surrounding plate-glass windows etched in gold-leaf lettering, he watched the door of the *Clarion*'s building through a thin wisp of steam rising from his paper cup. Pedestrians scurried past in trench coats, parkas or sweatshirts, some wearing hats, a few with umbrellas, most bareheaded, their collars turned to the wind and rain that steadily dripped from the edge of the awning.

His cell phone rang and he swung it from his pocket. "Striker."

"Hi, it's Kelly."

For the first time in hours, he smiled as Matt's wife started rattling off information. The men at the Flying M were still upset about Randi's leaving. Kelly was working to find a maroon Ford, one that was scraped up and dented from pushing Randi's vehicle off the road in Glacier Park. Kelly was also double-checking all of the staff who had been on duty the night that Randi was nearly killed in the hospital. So far she'd come up with nothing.

Striker wasn't surprised.

He hung up knowing nothing more than when he'd taken the call. Whoever was trying to kill Randi was either very smart or damn lucky.

So far.

Cars, vans and trucks, their windows fogged, sped through the old, narrow streets of this part of the city. Striker glared at the doorway of the hotel, drank coffee and scowled as he considered the other men in Randi Mc-Cafferty's life, at least one of whom had bedded her and fathered her son.

Paterno. Clanton. Donahue. Bastards, every one of them.

But he was narrowing the field. He'd done some double-checking on the men who had been involved with Randi. It was unlikely that Joe Paterno had fathered the kid. The timing was all wrong. Kurt had looked into Paterno's travel schedule and records. Paterno had been in Afghanistan around the time the baby had been conceived. There had been rumors that he'd been back in town for a weekend, but Kurt had nearly ruled out the possibility by making a few phone calls to Paterno's chatty landlady. Unless Paterno hadn't shown his face at his apartment and holed up for a secret weekend alone with Randi, he hadn't fathered the kid. Since Randi had been out of town most of the month, it seemed Joe was in the clear.

Leaving Brodie Clanton, the snake of a lawyer, and Sam Donahue, a rough-around-the-edges cowboy; a man whose shady reputation was as black as his hat. Again jealousy cut through him. Clanton was so damn slick, a rich lawyer and a ladies' man. It galled Striker to think of Randi sleeping with a guy who could barely start a sentence without mentioning that his grandfather had been a judge.

A-number-one jerk if ever there had been one, Clanton had avoided walking down the aisle so far, the confirmed-bachelor type who was often seen squiring around pseudocelebrities when they blew into town. He was into the stock market, expensive cars and young women, the kind of things a man could trade in easily. Clanton had been in town around the time Joshua had been conceived, but, with a little digging into credit card receipts, Striker had determined that Randi, at that time, had been in and out of Seattle herself. She'd never traveled as far as Afghanistan or, presumably, into Paterno's arms, but she'd been chasing a story with the rodeo circuit, where Sam Donahue was known for breaking broncs and women's hearts.

If Striker had been a betting man, he would have fingered Donahue as the baby's daddy. Twice married, Donahue had cheated on both his wives, leaving number one for a younger woman who'd grown up in Grand Hope, Montana, Randi's hometown. And now he just coincidentally had shown up here. A day before Randi.

Striker's jaw tightened so hard it hurt.

DNA would be the only true answer, of course, unless he forced the truth from Randi's lips. Gorgeous lips. Even when she was angry. Her mouth would twist into a furious pout that Striker found incredibly sexy. Which was just plain nuts. He couldn't, *wouldn't* let his mind wander down that seductively dark path. No matter how attractive Randi McCafferty was, he was being paid to protect her, not seduce her. He couldn't let it happen again.

He felt a bit of hardening beneath his fly and swore under his breath. He shouldn't get an erection just thinking of the woman… Hell, this was no time. None whatsoever for ridiculous fantasies. He had a job to do. And he'd better do it quickly before there was another unexplained "accident," before someone else got hurt. Or before the would-be murderer got lucky and this time someone *was* killed.

Chapter 6

She pushed open the revolving glass doors and found him just where she'd expected him, on a rain-washed Seattle street, looking damnably rough-and-tumble and sexy as ever. Obviously waiting for her. Great. Just what she *didn't* need, an invitation to trouble in disreputable jeans and a beat-up jacket.

Yep. Kurt Striker in all his damn-convention attitude was waiting.

Her stupid pulse quickened at the sight of him, but she quickly tamped down any emotional reaction she felt for the man. Yes, he was way too attractive in his tight jeans, leather jacket and rough-hewn features. His face was red with the cold, his hair windblown and damp as he leaned a hip against the bricks of a small shop, his eyes trained on the main door of the building. He was holding a paper cup of coffee, which he tossed into a nearby trash can when he spotted her.

Why did she have a thing for dangerous, sensual types? What was wrong with her? Never once in her life had she been attracted to the boy next door, nor to the affable, respectable, dedicated man who worked nine to five, nor the warm, cuddly football-watching couch potato who would love her to the end of time and never once forget an anniversary. The very men she lauded in her column. The men she advised women to give second glances. The salt-of-the-earth, give-you-the-shirt-off-his-back kind of guy who washed his car and the dog on Saturdays, the guy who wore the same flannel shirt that he'd had since college—the regular Joe of the world. One of the good guys.

Maybe, she thought, crossing the street, that was why she could give out advice to the women and men who were forever falling for the wrong kind. Because she was one of them and, she realized, skirting a puddle as she jaywalked to the parking lot where Striker was posed, she knew the pitfalls of hot-wired attraction. She bore the burn marks and scars to prove it.

"Fancy meeting you here," she said, clicking her Jeep's keyless remote. "You just don't seem to get it, do you? I don't want you here."

"We've been through this."

"And I have a feeling we'll go through it a dozen more times before you get the message." She opened the car door, but he was quick, slamming it shut with the flat of his hand.

"Why don't you and I start over," he suggested, forcing a smile, his arm effectively cutting off her ability to climb into the Jeep. "I'll take you to dinner—there's a nice little Irish pub around the corner—and you can fill me in on your life before you got to Montana."

"There's nothing to tell."

"Like hell." His smile slid away. "It's time you leveled

with me. I'm sick to the back teeth of the clamped-lip rou-
tine. I need to find out who's been trying to hurt you and
your brothers. If you weren't so damn arrogant to think
this is just about you, that I'm only digging into all this
to bother you, then you'd realize that you're the key to all
the trouble that's been happening at the Flying M. It's not
just your problem, lady. If you remember, Thorne's plane
went down—"

"That was because of bad weather. It was an accident."

"And he was flying in that storm to get back to Montana
because of you and the baby, wasn't he? And what about the
fire in the stable? God, woman, Slade nearly lost his life.
The fire was ruled arson and it's a little too convenient for
me to believe that it was coincidence, okay?"

"Drop it, Striker," she warned, whirling on him.

"No way."

"Why do you think I left the ranch?" she demanded.

"I think you left because of me."

That stopped her short. Standing in the dripping rain
with his gaze centered directly on hers, she nearly lost it.
"Because of you?"

"And last night."

"Don't flatter yourself."

"The timing is right."

Dear Lord. Her stomach twisted. "Let's get something
straight, shall we? I left Montana so that the 'accidents' at
the Flying M would stop and my brothers and their fami-
lies would be safe. Whoever is behind this is after me."

"So you think you're what? Drawing the fire away from
your family?"

"Yes."

"What about you? Your kid?"

"I can take care of myself. And my baby."

"Well, you've done a pretty piss-poor job of it so far," he said, his skin ruddy with the cold, his eyes flashing angrily.

"And you think that confiding in you would help? I don't even know anything about you other than Slade seems to think you're okay."

"You know a helluva lot more than that," he said, and she swallowed against the urge to slap him.

"If you're talking about last night..."

"Then what? Go on."

"I can't. Not here. And...and besides, that's not the kind of knowing I was talking about. So don't try to bait me, okay?"

His jaw slid to one side and his eyes narrowed. "Fair enough and you're right. You don't know me, but maybe it's time. Let's go. I'll tell you anything you want to know." His grin was about as warm as the Yukon in winter. "I'll buy dinner."

Before she could argue, he grabbed the crook of her arm and propelled her around the corner, down two blocks and toward a staircase that led down a flight to a subterranean bar and restaurant. He helped her to a booth in the back before she finally yanked her arm away. "Where'd you learn your manners? At the Cro-Magnon School of Etiquette?"

"Graduated cum laude." One eyebrow cocked disarmingly.

She chuckled and bit back another hot retort. Goading him was getting her nowhere fast. But at least he had a sense of humor and could laugh at himself. Besides which, she was starved. Her stomach started making all sorts of vile noises at the smells emanating from the kitchen.

Kurt ordered an ale, and she, deciding a drink wouldn't hurt, did the same. "Okay, okay, so you've made your point," she said when he leaned back in the booth and stared at her. "You take your job seriously. You're not going away. Whatever my brothers are paying you is worth putting up with me and my bad attitude, right?"

He let it slide as the waitress, a reed-thin woman with curly red hair tied into a single plait, reappeared with two frosty glasses, twin dinner menus and a bowl of peanuts. She slid all onto the table, then ambled toward a table where a patron was wagging his finger frantically to get her attention.

The place was dim and decorated with leatherlike cushions, mahogany wood aged to near black, a scarred wooden floor and a ceiling of tooled-metal tiles. It smelled of beer and ale, with the hint of cigar smoke barely noticeable over the tang of food grilling behind the counter. Two men were playing darts in a corner and the click of billiard balls emanated from an archway leading to other rooms. Conversation was light, patrons at the long, battered bar tuned in to a muted Sonics basketball game.

"I'm going to check on the baby." She reached into her bag, retrieved her cell phone and punched out Sharon Okano's number.

Sharon picked up on the second ring and was quick to reassure her that Joshua was fine. He'd already eaten, been bathed and was in his footed jammies, currently fascinated by a mobile Sharon had erected over his playpen.

"I'll be by to see him as soon as I can," Randi said.

"He'll be fine."

"I know. I just can't wait to hold him a minute." Randi clicked off and tried to quell the dull ache that seemed forever with her when she was apart from her child. It was weird, really. Before Joshua's birth she had been free and easy, didn't have a clue what a dramatic change was in store for her. But from the moment she'd awoken from her coma and learned she'd borne a son, she could barely stand to be away from him, even for a few hours.

As for being with him and holding him, the next few weeks promised to be torture on that score. Until she was certain he was safe with her. She slid the phone into her purse and turned to Kurt, who was studying her intently over the rim of his mug. Great. Dealing with him wasn't going to be easy, either. Even if she didn't factor in that she'd made love to him like a wanton in the wee hours of this very morning.

They ordered. Two baskets of fish and chips complete with sides of coleslaw and a second beer, even though they weren't quite finished with the first, were dropped in front of them.

"Why are you keeping your kid's paternity a secret?" Kurt finally asked. "What does it matter?"

"I prefer he didn't know."

"Why not? Seems as if he has a right."

"Being a sperm donor isn't the same as being a father." Her stomach was screaming for food but the conversation was about to kill her appetite.

"Maybe he should be the judge of that."

"Maybe you should keep your nose in your own business." She took a long swallow from her drink and the guys at the bar gave up a shout as one of the players hit a three pointer.

"Your brothers made it my business."

"My brothers can't run my life. Much as they'd like to."

"I think you're afraid," he accused, and she felt the tightening of the muscles of her neck, the urge to defend herself.

"Of what?" she asked, but he didn't answer as the waitress appeared and slid their baskets onto the plank table, then offered up bottles of vinegar and ketchup. Only when they were alone again did Randi repeat herself. "You think I'm afraid of what?"

"Why don't *you* tell me. It's just odd, you know, for a woman not to tell the father of her child that he's a daddy. Goes against the grain. Usually the mother wants financial support. Emotional support. That kind of thing."

"I'm not usual," she said, and thought he whispered "Amen" under his breath, though she couldn't be certain as he covered up his comment with a long swallow of ale. She noticed the movement of his throat—dark with a bit of beard shadow as he swallowed—and something deep inside her, something dusky and wholly feminine, reacted. She drew her eyes away and told herself she was being a fool. It had been a long time since she'd been with a man, over a year now, but that didn't give her the right to ogle men like Kurt Striker nor imagine what it would feel like for him to touch her again, to kiss her, to press hot, insistent lips against the curve of her neck and push her sweater off her shoulder...

She caught herself and realized that he was watching her face, looking for her reaction. As if he could read her mind. To her horror she felt herself blush.

"Penny for your thoughts."

She shook her head, pretended interest in her meal by shaking vinegar over her fries. "Wouldn't sell 'em for a penny, or a nickel, or a thousand dollars."

"So tell me about the book," he suggested.

"The book?"

"The one you're writing. Another one of your secrets."

How could one man be so irritating? She ate in silence for a second and glowered across the table at him. "It's not a secret. I just didn't want to tell anyone about it until it was finished."

"You were on your way to the Flying M to finish it when you were forced off the road at Glacier National Park, right?" He dredged a piece of fish in tartar sauce.

She nodded.

"Think that's just a coincidence?"

"No one knew I was going to Montana to write a book. Even the people at work thought I was just taking my maternity leave—which I was. I was planning to combine the two."

"Juanita at the ranch knew about it." He'd polished off one crispy lump of halibut and was working on a second.

"Of course she did. I already explained, it really wasn't a secret."

"If you say so." He ate in silence for a minute, but she didn't feel any respite, knew he was forming his next question, and sure enough, it came, hard and fast. "Tell me, Randi," he said, "who do you think wants to kill you?"

"I've been through this dozens of times with the police."

"Humor me." He was nearly finished with his food and she'd barely started. But her appetite had crumpled into nothing. She picked at her coleslaw. "Who are your worst enemies? You know, anyone who has a cause—just or not—for wanting you dead."

She'd considered the question over and over. It had run through her mind in an endless loop from the moment her memory had started working again when she'd awoken from her coma. "I...I don't know. No one has any reason to hate me enough to kill me."

"Murderers aren't always reasonable people," he pointed out.

"I can't name anyone."

"How about the baby's father? Maybe he found out you were pregnant, is ticked that you didn't tell him and, not wanting to be named as the father, decided to get rid of you both."

"He wouldn't do that."

"No?"

She shook her head. She wasn't certain about many things, but she doubted Joshua's father would care that he'd fathered a child, certainly wouldn't go through the steps to get rid of either of them. She felt a weight on her heart but ignored it as Striker, leaning back in the booth, pushed his near-empty basket aside. "If I'm going to help you, then I need to know everything that's going on. So who is he, Randi? Who's Joshua's daddy?"

She didn't realize she'd been shredding her napkin in her lap, but looked down and noticed all the pieces of red paper. She supposed she couldn't take her secret with her to the grave, but letting the world know the truth made her feel more vulnerable, that she was somehow breaching a special trust she had with her son.

"My money's on Donahue," he said abruptly.

She froze.

He winked though his expression was hard. "I figure you'd go for the sexy-cowboy type."

"You don't know what my type is."

"Don't I?"

"Unfair, Striker, last night was…was…"

"What about it?"

"It was a mistake. We both know it. So, let's just forget it. As I said, you don't have any idea what 'my type' is."

One side of his mouth lifted in an irritating, sexy-as-hell smile. Green eyes held hers fast, and a wave, warm as a desert in August, climbed up her neck. "I'm workin' on it."

Her heart clenched. *Don't do this, Randi. Don't let him get to you. He's no better than…than…* Her throat tightened when she considered what a fool she'd been. For a man who'd seduced her. Used her. Cared less for her than he did for his dog. Silly, silly woman.

"Okay, Striker," she said, forcing the words through her lips, words she'd vowed only hours ago never to utter. "I'll tell you the truth," she said, hating the sense of relief it brought to be able to confide in someone. "But this is between you and me. Got it? I'll tell you and you alone. When the time comes I'll tell Joshua's father and my brothers. But only when I say."

"Fair enough," he drawled, leaning back in his chair and folding his arms over his chest, all interest in his remaining French fries forgotten.

Randi took in a deep breath and prayed she wasn't making one of the biggest mistakes of her life. She stared Striker straight in the eye and admitted to him something she rarely acknowledged herself. "You're right. Okay? Joshua's father, and I use the term so loosely it's no longer coiled, is Sam Donahue." Her tongue nearly tripped over Sam's name. She didn't like saying it out loud, didn't like admitting that she, like too many others before her, had been swept off her feet by the charming, roguish cowboy. It was embarrassing and, had it not been for her precious son, a mistake she would have rued until her dying day. Joshua, of course, changed all that.

Striker didn't say a word. Nor had his lips curled in silent denunciation. And he didn't so much as lift an eyebrow in mockery. No. He played it straight, just observing her, watching her every reaction.

"So now you know," she said, standing. "I hope it helps, but I don't think it means anything. Thanks for dinner." She walked out of the bar and up the steps to the wet streets. The rain had turned to drizzle again, misting around the street lamps, and the air was heavy, laced with the brine from Puget Sound. Randi felt like running. As fast and far as she could. To get away from the claustrophobic feeling, the fear that compressed her chest, the very fear she'd tried to flee when she'd left Montana.

But it was with her wherever she went, she thought, her boots slapping along the rain-slick sidewalk as she hurried to her car. The city was far from deserted, traffic rushed through the narrow old streets and pedestrians bustled along the sidewalks. She carried no umbrella, didn't bother with her hood, let the dampness collect on her cheeks and flatten her hair. Not that she cared. Damn it, why had she told Striker about Sam Donahue? Her relationship with Sam hadn't really been a love affair, more of a fling, though at one time she'd been foolish enough to think she might be falling in love with the bastard. The favor hadn't been returned and she'd realized her mistake. But not before the pregnancy test had turned out positive.

She hadn't bothered to tell Donahue because she knew he wouldn't care. He was a selfish man by nature, a rambler who followed the rodeo circuit and didn't have time for the two ex-wives and children he'd already sired. Randi wasn't about to try to saddle him with the responsibility of another baby. She figured Joshua was better off with one strong parent than two who fought, living with the ghost of a father whom he would grow up not really knowing.

She knew her son would ask questions and she intended to answer them all honestly. When the time came. But not now...not when her baby was pure innocence.

"Randi!" Striker was at her side, his bare head as wet as her own, his expression hard.

"What? More questions?" she asked, unable to hide the sarcasm in her voice. "Well, sorry, but I'm fresh out of shocking little details about my life."

"I didn't come all the way to Seattle to embarrass you," he said as they rounded a final corner to the parking lot.

"That's how it seems."

"No, it doesn't. You know better."

She'd reached her Jeep and with a punch of the button on her remote, unlocked it once more. "Why do I have the feeling that you're not finished? That you won't be satisfied until you've stripped away every little piece of privacy I have."

"I just want to help."

He seemed sincere, but she'd been fooled before. By the master, Sam Donahue. Kurt Striker, damn him, was of the same ilk. Another cowboy. Another rogue. Another sexy man with a shadowy past. Another man she'd started to fall for. The kind to avoid. "Help?"

"That's right." His eyes shifted to her lips and she nervously licked them, tasting rainwater as it drizzled down her face. Her heart thudded. She knew in that second that he was going to kiss her. He was fighting it; she saw the battle in his eyes, but in the end raw emotion won out and his lips crashed down on hers so intensely she drew in a swift breath and it was followed quickly by his tongue. Slick. Sleek. Searching. The tip touched her teeth, forcing them apart as he grabbed her. Leather creaked, the sky parted, rain poured and Randi's foolish, foolish heart opened.

She kissed the rogue back, slamming her mind against thoughts that she was making the worst mistake of her life, that she was crossing a bridge that was burning behind her, that her life, from that moment on, would be changed forever.

But there, in the middle of the bustling city, with raindrops falling on them both, she didn't care.

Chapter 7

Stop this! Stop it now! Don't you remember last night?

Blinking against the rain, fighting the urge to lean against him, Randi pulled away from Kurt. "This is definitely not a good idea," she said. "It wasn't last night and it isn't now."

His mouth twisted. "I'm not sure about that."

"I am." It was a lie. Right now she wasn't certain of anything. She reached behind her and fumbled with the door handle. "Let's just give it a rest, okay?"

He didn't argue, nor did he stop her as she slid into the Jeep and, with shaking fingers, found her keys and managed to start the ignition. Lunacy. That's what it was. Sheer, unadulterated, pain-in-the-backside lunacy! She couldn't start kissing the likes of Kurt Striker again.

Dear God, what had she been thinking?

You weren't thinking. That's the problem!

She flipped on the radio, heard the first notes of a sappy

love song and immediately punched the button to find talk radio, only to hear a popular program where a radio psychologist was giving out advice to someone who was mixed up with the wrong kind of man, the same kind of advice she handed out through her column in the *Clarion,* the very advice she should listen to herself.

First she'd made the mistake of getting involved with Sam Donahue and now she was falling for Kurt Striker... No! She pounded a fist on the steering wheel as she braked for a turnoff.

Cutting through traffic, she made a call on her cell phone to Sharon, was assured that Joshua was safe, then stopped at a local market for a few groceries.

Fifteen minutes later she pulled into the parking lot of her condo. Now away from the hustle and bustle of the city, the dark of the night seemed more threatening.

The parking lot was dark and the security lamps were glowing, throwing pools of light onto the wet ground and a few parked cars. The parking area was deserted, none of her neighbors were walking dogs or taking out trash. Warm light glowed from only a few windows, the rest of the units were dark.

So what? This is why you chose this place. It was quiet, only a few units overlooking the lake.

For the first time since moving here, Randi looked at her darkened apartment and felt a moment's hesitation, a hint of fear. She glanced over her shoulder, through the back windows of the Jeep, wondering if someone was watching her, someone lurking in a bank of fir trees and rhododendron that ringed the parking lot, giving it privacy. She had the uneasy sensation that hidden eyes were watching her through a veil of wet needles and leaves.

"Get a grip," she muttered, hoisting the bag and holding tight to her key ring. As if it was some kind of protection. What a laugh!

No one was hiding. No one was watching her. And yet she wished she hadn't been so quick to put some distance between herself and Striker. Maybe she did need a bodyguard, someone she could trust.

Someone you can't keep your hands off of?

Someone you've made love to?

Someone that even now, even though you know better, you'd love to take to bed? In her mind's eye she saw the image of Kurt Striker, all taut skin and muscle as he held her in front of the dying fire.

Oh, for the love of St. Peter! Hauling her laptop, the groceries, her briefcase and her rebellious libido with her, she made her way to the porch, managed to unlock the door and snap on the interior lights. She almost wished Kurt was inside waiting for her again. But that was crazy. Nuts! She couldn't trust herself around that man.

"You're an idiot," she muttered, seeing her reflection in the mirror mounted by the coatrack in the front hall. Her hair was damp and curly with the rain, her cheeks flushed, her eyes bright. "This is just what got you into trouble in the first place." She dropped her computer and bag near her desk, shook herself out of her coat and heard a pickup roaring into the lot. Her silly heart leaped, but a quick glance through the kitchen window confirmed that Striker had returned. He was already out of the truck and headed toward the condo.

She met him at the front door.

"You don't seem to take a hint, do you?" she teased.

"Careful, woman, I'm not in the mood to have my chain yanked," he warned. "Traffic was a bitch."

He was inside in a second and bolted the door behind him. "I don't like it when you try to lose me."

"And I don't like being manhandled." She started unpacking groceries, stuffing a carton of milk into the near-empty refrigerator.

"I kissed you."

"On the street, when I obviously didn't want you to."

One of his eyebrows lifted in disbelief. "You didn't want it?" He snorted. "I'd love to see what you were like when you did."

"That was last night," she reminded him, then mentally kicked herself. Lifting a hand, she stopped any argument he might have. "Let's not talk about last night."

He kicked out a bar stool and plopped himself at the counter that separated the kitchen from the living room. "Okay, but there is something we need to discuss."

She braced herself. "Which is?"

"Sam Donahue."

"Another off-limits subject." She pulled a loaf of bread from the wet sack.

"I don't think so. We've wasted enough time as it is and I'm getting sick of you not being straight with me."

"I should never have told you."

He shot her a condemning look. "I'd already guessed, remember?" He took a deep breath and ran stiff fingers through his hair. "You got any wood for that?" he asked, hitching his chin toward the fireplace.

"A little. In a closet on the back deck."

"Get me a beer, I'll make a fire and then, whether you like it or not, we're going to discuss your ex-lover."

"Gee," she mocked, "and who said single women don't have any fun? You know, Striker, you've got a helluva nerve to barge in here and start barking orders. Just because…because of what happened last night, you don't have the right to start bossing me around in my own home."

"You're right," he said without a trace of regret carved into his features. "Would you please get me a beer and I'll get the firewood."

"I might be out of beer. I didn't pick any up at the store."

"There's one left. In the door of the fridge. I checked earlier." The empty bottle on the coffee table stood as testament to that very fact.

"When you practiced breaking and entering," she muttered as he kicked back the stool and made his way to the deck. She opened the refrigerator again and saw the single long-neck in the door. The guy was observant. But still a bully who had barged unwelcome into her life. A sexy bully at that. Her worst nightmare.

She yanked out the last beer, twisted off the top and, as he carried in a couple of chunks of oak to the fire, took a long swallow. The least he could do was share, she decided, watching as he bent on the tiled hearth, his jacket and shirt riding up over his belt and jeans, offering her the view of a slice of his taut, muscular back. Her throat was suddenly dry as dust and she took another pull from the long-neck. What the hell was she going to do with him? She'd already bared her soul and her body, then, after insisting that she wasn't interested in him, kissed him on the street as if she never wanted to stop, and now... She slid a glance toward the cracked door of her bedroom and in her mind she saw them together, wrapped in the sheets, sweaty bodies tangled and heaving as he kissed her breasts. Her heart pounded as he pulled at her nipple, his hands sliding down to sculpt her waist as he mounted her, gently nudging her knees apart, readying himself above her, his erection stiff, his green gaze fiery. Then, eyes locked, he entered her in one long, hard thrust—

He cleared his throat and she was brought back to the living area of her condo, where he was still tending to the fire. Turning, she blushed as she realized he'd said something to her. For the life of her she couldn't remember a word. "Wh-what?"

"I asked if you had a match." His gaze was on her face, then traveled down the short corridor to the bedroom. Amusement caused an eyebrow to arch and she wanted to die. No doubt he could read her embarrassing thoughts.

"Oh, yeah..." While she'd been fantasizing, he'd crumpled old newspaper and stacked the firewood, even splintering off some pieces of kindling.

She took another swallow, handed him the bottle and hurried into the kitchen, where she rummaged through a drawer. *Don't go there. You're not going to tumble into bed with him. Not again. You're not even going to kiss him again. You're not going to do anything stupid with him. No more.* She found a pack of matches and tossed them over the counter to him, all the while trying to quell the hammering of her heart. Time to go on the offensive.

"Okay, Striker, so now I've told you my darkest secret. What's yours?"

"None of your business."

"Wait a minute. That's not fair."

"You're right, it's not." He struck a match and the smell of sulfur singed the air as he touched the tiny flame to the dry paper and the fire crackled to life. "But then not much is."

"You said I could ask you anything when we were in the pub."

"I changed my mind."

"Just like that?" she asked incredulously as she snapped her fingers.

"Uh-huh." He took a long pull from the bottle.

"No way. I think I deserve to know who the hell you are."

Rocking back on his heels as the fire caught, he looked up at her standing on the other side of the counter. "I'm an ex-cop turned P.I."

"I already figured that much. But what about your personal life?"

"It's private."

"You're single, right? There's no Mrs. Striker."

He hesitated enough to cause her heart to miss a beat. *Oh, God, not again,* she thought as she leaned against the counter for support. He'd kissed her. Touched her. Made love to her.

"Not anymore. I was married but it ended a few years back."

"Why?"

His jaw tightened. "Haven't you read the statistics?"

"I'm talking about the reason behind the statistics, at least in your case."

A shadow passed behind his eyes and he said, "It just didn't work out. I was a cop. Probably paid more attention to the job than my wife."

"And you didn't have any kids?"

Again the hesitation. Again the shadow. His lips tightened at the corners as he stood and dusted his hands. "I don't have any children," he said slowly, "and I never hear from my ex. That about covers it all, doesn't it?" There was just a spark of challenge in his eyes, daring her to argue with him. A dozen questions bubbled up in her throat, but she held them back. For now. There were other ways to get information about him. She was a reporter, for God's sake.

She had the means to find out just about anything that had happened to him. Newsworthy articles would be posted on the internet, personal stuff through other sources.

With Sam Donahue she'd been trusting and it had backfired in her face, but this time... Oh, God, why was she even thinking like this? There was no *this time!* There was no Kurt Striker in her life except as an irritating bodyguard her brothers had hired. That was it. He was here because he was hired to be here; she was a job to him. Nothing more.

"Look, I've got to get some work done," she said, motioning to her laptop. "I've been gone for months and if I don't answer some email and put together a new column or two, I'm going to be in big trouble. My boss and I are already not real tight. So, if you don't mind...well, even if you do, I'm going to start plowing through what's been piling up. I understand that you think you've got to be with me 24/7, but it's not necessary. No one's going to take a potshot at me here."

"Why would you think that?" Striker drained the rest of his beer.

"Because there are too many people around, there's a security guard for the condos always on the premises, and most importantly, Joshua is safe with Sharon."

The expression on his face told her he was of another mind. And wasn't she, really? Hadn't she, just minutes ago in the parking lot, sensed that someone had been watching her? She rounded the counter as he straightened and crossed the room.

"Look, I do know that I'm in some kind of danger," she said. "Obviously I know it or I wouldn't have taken the time to hide the baby. I came back here to try to figure this out, to take the heat off my brothers, to get on with my life and let them get on with theirs. And yeah, I'd be lying if I didn't say I was nervous, that I wasn't starting to jump at shadows, but I need to sort through some things, get a handle on what's happening."

"That's why I'm here. I'm thinking that maybe if we work together, we can make some sense of what's going on." He was close to her, near enough that she could smell the wet leather of his jacket, see the striations of color in his green eyes, feel the heat of his body.

She couldn't even make sense of the moment. "That might be impossible. I've been thinking about what happened from every angle and I come up with the same conclusion. I don't have any real enemies that I know of. At least not anyone who would want to hurt me and my family. It doesn't make any sense." To put some distance between her body and his, she walked to the couch and flung herself onto the cushions. *Who? What? Why?* The questions that had haunted her nights and caused her to lose sleep were still unanswered as they rolled around in her brain.

"So what does make sense?" he demanded. "Someone followed you from Seattle and on your way to Grand Hope, Montana, forced you off the road. Why?"

"I told you, I don't know. Believe me, I've been thinking about it."

"Think harder." He frowned and rammed stiff fingers through hair that was still damp. "If it doesn't have to do with the baby, then what about your job? Did you give someone bad advice and really tick someone off?"

She shook her head. "I thought about that, too. When I was back in Montana, I got online and searched through the columns for the two months prior to the accident and I couldn't find anything that would infuriate a person."

His head snapped up. "So you are worried?"

"Of course I'm worried. Who wouldn't be? But there

was nothing in any of the advice I gave that would cause someone to snap."

"You think. There are always nutcases." He set his empty bottle on the counter.

That much was true, she thought wearily. "But none who have emailed me, or called me or contacted me in any way. I double-checked every communication I received."

He nodded and she realized that he'd probably been privy to that information, as well.

"Well, there's got to be a reason. We're just missing it." He was thinking hard; she could tell by the way he rubbed his chin. "You write magazine articles under a pseudonym."

"Nothing controversial."

His eyes narrowed. "What about the book you were working on?"

She hesitated. The manuscript she was writing wasn't finished and she'd taken great pains to keep it secret while she investigated a payola scam on the rodeo circuit. It was while researching the book that she'd met Sam Donahue, a friend, he'd claimed, of her brothers'. As it turned out he hadn't been as much a friend as an acquaintance and somehow she'd ended up falling for him, knowing him to be a rogue, realizing that part of his charm was the hint of danger around him, and yet she'd tumbled into bed with him anyway. And ended up pregnant.

Which had been a blessing in disguise, of course. Without her ill-fated affair with Sam, she never would have had Joshua, and that little guy was the light of her life.

"What's in the book that's so all-fired important?"

Sighing, she walked to the couch and dropped into the soft cushions. "You know what's in it for the most part."

"A book on cowboys."

"Well, a little more than that." Leaning her head back,

she closed her eyes. "It's about all aspects of rodeos, the good, the bad, the ugly. Especially the ugly. Along with all the rah-rah for a great American West tradition, there's also the dark side to it all, the seamy underbelly. As I was getting information, I learned about the drugs, animal abuse, cheating, payola, you name it."

"And let me guess, most of the information came from good old Sam Donahue."

"Some of it," she admitted, opening an eye and catching Kurt scowling, as if the mere mention of Donahue's name made Striker see red. "I was going to name names in my book and, I suppose, I could have made a few people nervous. But the thing of it was, no one really knew what I was doing."

"Donahue?"

She shook her head and glanced to the window. "I told him it was a series of articles about small-town celebrations, that rodeos were only a little bit of the slice of Americana I was going to write about. Sam wasn't all that interested in what I was doing."

"Why not?"

"Oh, I don't know," she said, turning her attention to Kurt. The fire was burning softly, casting golden shadows on the cozy rooms. She snapped on a table lamp, hoping to break the feeling of intimacy the flames created. "Maybe it's because Sam's an egomaniac and pretty much consumed with his own life."

"Sounds charming," he mocked.

"I thought so. At first. But it did wear thin fast."

Striker lifted an eyebrow and she added, "I'd already realized that it wasn't going to work out when I suspected I was pregnant."

"What did he say about it?"

"Nothing. He never knew."

"You didn't tell him."

"That's right. Didn't we go over this before?"

Striker looked as if he wanted to say something but held his tongue. For that she was grateful. She didn't need any judgment calls.

"Besides," she added with more than a trace of bitterness, "I figure we're even now. He forgot to mention that he wasn't really divorced from his last wife when he started dating me." She wrinkled her nose and felt that same old embarrassment that had been with her from the moment she'd realized Sam had lied, that he'd been married all the time he'd chased after her, swearing that he was divorced.

Fool that she'd been, she'd fallen for him and believed every word that had tripped over his lying tongue.

Now a blush stole up her neck and she bit down on her back teeth. She'd always been proud of her innate intelligence, but when it came to men, she'd often been an idiot. She'd chosen poorly, trusted too easily, fallen harder than she should have. From Teddy Sherman, the ranch hand her father had hired when she was seventeen, to a poet and a musician in college, and finally Sam Donahue, the rough-and-tumble cowpoke who'd turned out to be a lying bastard if ever there was one. Well, no more, she told herself even as Kurt Striker, damn him, threatened to break down her defenses.

He walked to the fire, grabbed a poker and jabbed at the burning logs. Sparks drifted upward through the flue and one of the blackened chunks of oak split with a soft thud.

Randi watched him and felt that same sense of yearning, a tingle of desire, she'd experienced every time she was around him. She sensed something different in Kurt, a strength of character that had been lacking in the other men she'd found enchanting. They had been dreamers, or, in the case of Donahue, cheats, but she didn't think either was a part of Striker's personality. His boots seemed securely planted on the ground rather than drifting into the clouds, and he appeared intensely honest. His eyes were clear, his shoulders straight, his smile, when he offered it, not as sly as it was amused. He appealed to her at a whole new level. Man to woman, face-to-face, not looking down at her, nor elevating her onto a pedestal from which she would inevitably fall.

"So what do you think about your kid?" he asked suddenly as he straightened and dusted his hands.

"I'm nuts about him, of course."

"Do you really think he's safe with the Okano woman?"

"I wouldn't have left him there if I didn't."

"I'd feel better if he was with you. With me."

"No one followed me to Sharon's. Not many people know we're friends. She was in my dorm in college and just moved up here last fall. I...I really think he's safer there. I've already driven her nuts calling her. She thinks I'm paranoid and I'm not so sure she's wrong."

"Paranoid isn't all that bad. Not in this case." Striker reached into his jacket pocket, flipped open his cell and dialed. A few seconds later he was engrossed in a conversation, ordering someone to watch Sharon Okano's apartment as well as do some digging on Sam Donahue. "... that's right. I want to know for certain where he was on the dates that Randi was run off the road and someone attempted to kill her in the hospital... Yeah, I know he had an alibi, but double-check and don't forget to dig into some of the thugs he hangs out with. This could have been a paid job... I don't know but start with Marv Bates and Charlie... Damn, what's his name, Charlie—"

"Caldwell," Randi supplied, inwardly shuddering at the thought of the two cowboys Sam had introduced her to. Marv was whip thin with lips that barely moved when he talked and eyes that were forever narrowed. Charlie was a lug, a big, fleshy man who could surprise you with how fast he could move if properly motivated.

"That's right, Charlie Caldwell. Check prison records. See if any of Donahue's buddies have done time…. Okay… You can reach me on the cell, that would be best." He was walking to the desk. "I'll be in the condo, but let's not use the landline. I checked, it doesn't appear bugged, but I'm not sure."

Randi's blood chilled at the thought that someone could have tampered with her phone lines or crept into her home while she was away. But then Striker hadn't had any problem getting inside. He might not have been the first. Her skin crawled as she looked over her belongings with new eyes. Suede couch, faux leopard-print chair and ottoman, antique rocker, end tables she'd found in a secondhand store and her great-grandmother's old treadle sewing machine that stood near the window. The cacti were thriving, the Boston fern shedding and near death, the mirror over her fireplace, the one she'd inherited from her mother, still chipped in one corner. Nothing out of place. Nothing to give her pause.

And yet…something wasn't right. Something she couldn't put her finger on. Just like the eerie sensation that she was being watched when she parked her Jeep.

"Later." Striker snapped the phone shut and watched as Randi walked to her desk, double-checking that nothing had been disturbed. She'd already done a quick once-over when she'd come home earlier, but now, knowing that her phone could have been tapped, her home violated, her life invaded by an unknown assailant, she wanted to make certain that everything was as it should be.

Her phone rang and she nearly jumped through the roof. She snagged the receiver before it could jangle a second time.

"Hello?" she said, half expecting a deep-throated voice on the other end to issue a warning, or heavy breathing to be her only response.

"So you did get home!"

Randi nearly melted at the sound of Slade's voice. He was her youngest half brother, closest to her in age. Slade had been born with the same McCafferty wild streak that had cursed all of John Randall's children. Slade had just held on to his untamed ways longer than his older brothers.

"I thought you'd have the brains to call and tell us you'd arrived safely," he admonished, and she felt a twinge of guilt.

"I guess I hadn't gotten around to it," she said, smiling at the thought of her brothers, who had once resented her, now fretting over her.

"Is everything all right?"

"So far, although I have a bone to pick with you."

"Uh-oh."

"And Matt and Thorne."

"It figures."

"Who the hell do you think you are hiring a bodyguard for me behind my back?" she demanded and saw, in the mirror's reflection, Kurt Striker standing behind her. Their eyes met and there was something in his gaze that seemed to bore straight into hers, to touch her soul.

Slade was trying to explain. "You need someone to help you—"

"You mean I need a *man* to watch over me," she cut in,

irritated all over again. Frustrated, she turned her attention to the window, where just beyond the glass she could make out the angry waters of Lake Washington roiling in the darkness. "Well, for your information, brother dear, I can take care of myself."

"Yeah, right."

Slade's sarcasm cut deep.

Involuntarily, she squared her shoulders. "I'm serious."

"So are we."

Randi heard conversation in the background, not only the deep rumble of male voices, but others as well, the higher pitches of her sisters-in-law, no doubt, and rising above the rest of the conversation, the sharp staccato burst of Spanish that could only have come from Juanita, the housekeeper.

"You tell her to be careful. *Dios!* What was she thinking running off like that!"

More Spanish erupted and Slade said, "Did you hear that? Juanita thinks—"

"I heard what she said." Randi felt a pang of homesickness, which was just plain ludicrous. This was her home. Where she belonged. She had a life here in Seattle. At the newspaper. Here in this condo. And yet, as she stared out the window to the whitecaps whirling furiously on the black water, she wondered if she had made a mistake in returning to this bustling city that she'd fallen in love with years before. She liked the crowds. The noise. The arts. The history. The beauty of Puget Sound and the briny smell of the sea when she walked or jogged near the waterfront.

But her brothers weren't here.

Nor were Nicole, Kelly or Jamie, her new sisters-in-law. They'd become friends and she missed them as well as Nicole's daughters and the ranch and...

Suddenly stiffening her spine, she pushed back all her maudlin thoughts. She was doing the right thing. Reclaiming her life. Trying to figure out who was hell-bent on harming her and her family. "Tell everyone I'm fine. Okay? A big girl. And I don't appreciate you and Thorne and Matt hiring Striker."

"Well, that's just too damn bad now, isn't it?" he said, reigniting her anger.

Her headache was throbbing again, she was so tired she wanted to sink into her bed and never wake up and, more than anything, she wished she could reach through the phone lines and shake some sense into her brothers. "You know, Slade, you really can be a miserable son of a bitch."

"I try," he drawled in that damnable country-boy accent that was usually accompanied by a devilish twinkle in his eyes.

She imagined his lazy smile. "Nice, Slade. Do you want to talk to your new employee?" Without waiting for an answer, she slammed the phone into Kurt Striker's hand and stormed to her bedroom. This was insane, but she was tired of arguing about it, was bound and determined to get on with her life. She had a baby to take care of and a job to do.

But what if they're all right? What if someone really is after you? After Joshua? Didn't you think someone had already broken into this place?

Her gaze swept the bedroom. Nothing seemed disturbed...or did it? Had she left the curtains to the back deck parted? Had her closet door been slightly ajar...? She lifted her eyes, caught a glimpse of her reflection and saw a shadow of fear pass behind her own eyes. God, she hated this.

She heard footsteps approaching and then, in the glass,

saw Kurt walking down the short hallway and stop at the bedroom door.

Her throat was suddenly dry as cotton and inadvertently she licked her lips. His gaze flickered to the movement and the corners of his mouth tightened, and just the hint of desperation, of lust, darkened his eyes.

For a split second their gazes locked. Held. Randi's pulse jumped, as if it were suddenly a living, breathing thing. Her heartbeat thundered in her ears. Inside, she felt a twinge, the hint of a dangerous craving she'd experienced last night.

She knew that it would only take a glance, a movement, a whisper and he would come inside, close the door, take her into his arms and kiss her as if she'd never been kissed before. It would be hard, raw, desperate and they would oh, so easily tumble onto the bed and make love for hours.

His lips compressed.

He took a step inside.

She could barely breathe.

He reached forward, grabbed hold of the doorknob.

Her knees went weak.

Oh, God, she wanted him. Imagined touching him, lying with him, feeling the heat of his body. "Kurt, I…"

"Shh, darlin'," he said, his voice as rough as sandpaper. "It's been a long day. Why don't you get some rest." He offered her a wink that caused her heart to crack. "I'll be in the living room if you need me." He pulled the door shut tight and she listened to the sound of his footsteps retreating down the short hallway.

Slowly she let out the breath she'd been holding and sagged onto the bed. Disappointment mingled with relief. It would be a mistake of epic proportions to make love to him. She knew it. They both did. On unsteady legs she walked into the bathroom and opened the medicine cabinet. She reached for a bottle of ibuprofen and stopped short.

What if someone had been in her home?

What if someone had tampered with her over-the-counter medications? Her food?

"Now you really are getting paranoid," she muttered, as she poured the pills into the toilet and flushed them down.

Paranoid, maybe.

But alive for certain.

Making her way back to the bedroom, she slid under the covers and decided that she could work with Striker or against him.

With him would be a lot more interesting.

And together they might be able to get through the nightmare that had become her life.

Chapter 8

*H*e *was lying next to her, his body hard and honed, skin stretched taut over muscles that were smooth and fluid as he levered up on one elbow to stare down at her. Green eyes glittered with a dark seductive fire that thrilled her and silently spoke of pleasures to come. With the fingers of one callused hand he traced the contours of her body. She tingled, her breasts tightening under his scrutinizing gaze, her nipples becoming hard as buttons. He leaned forward and scraped a beard-roughened cheek over her flesh. Deep inside, she felt desire stretching as it came awake.*

This was so wrong. She shouldn't be in bed with Kurt Striker. What had she been thinking? How had this happened? She barely knew the man...and yet, the wanting was so intense, burning through her blood, chasing away her doubts, and as he bent to kiss her, she knew she couldn't resist, that with just the brush of his hard lips on hers she would be lost completely—

Bam!

Her eyes flew open at the sound. Where was she? It was dark. And cold. She was alone in the bed—her bed—and she felt as if she'd slept for hours, her bladder stretched to the limit, her stomach rumbling for food.

"Let's go, Sleeping Beauty," Kurt said from the vicinity of the doorway. She blinked and found him standing in the doorway, his shoulders nearly touching each side of the frame, his body backlit by the flickering light still cast from the living-room fire. In relief he seemed larger, more rugged. The kind of man to avoid.

So she'd been dreaming about making love to him again. Only dreaming. Thank God. Not that the ache deep within her had subsided. Yes, she was in her own bed, but she was alone and fully dressed, just the way he'd left her minutes— or had it been hours—before?

"Wha—What's the rush?" she mumbled, trying to shake off the remainder of that damnably erotic fantasy even though a part of her wanted to close her eyes and call it back. "So what happened to 'shh, darlin', you should get some rest'?" she asked sarcastically.

He took a step into the room. "You got it. Slept for nearly eighteen hours, now it's time to rock 'n' roll."

"What? Eighteen hours…no…" She glanced at the bedside clock and the digital display indicated it was after three. "I couldn't have…" But the bad taste in her mouth and the pressure on her bladder suggested he was right.

Groaning, she thought about her job and the fact that she was irreparably late. Bill Withers was probably chewing her up one side and down the other. "I'm gonna get fired yet," she muttered, then added, "Give me a sec."

Scrambling from beneath the warmth of her duvet, she stumbled over one of her shoes on her way to the bathroom.

Once inside, she shut the door, snapped on the light and cringed at her reflection. Within minutes she'd relieved herself, splashed water onto her face and brushed her teeth. Her face was a disaster, her short hair sticking up at all angles. The best she could do was wet it down and scrub away the smudges of mascara that darkened her eyes.

Thankfully her headache was gone and she was thinking more clearly as she opened the door to the bedroom and found Kurt leaning against the frame, a strange look on his face. She yawned. "What?" she asked and then she knew. With drop-dead certainty. Her heart nearly stopped. "It's the baby," she said, fear suddenly gelling her blood. "Joshua. What's wrong? Is he okay?"

"He's fine."

"How do you know?"

"I'm having Sharon Okano's place watched."

She was stunned and suddenly frantic and reached for the shoe she'd nearly tripped over. "You really think something might happen to him?"

"Let's just say I don't want to take any chances."

She crammed the shoe onto her foot, then bent down, peering under the bed for its mate. Her mind was clearing a bit as she found the missing shoe and slid it on. Striker was jumping at shadows, that was it. Joshua was fine. Fine. He had to be.

"Donahue's in town."

She rocked back on her heels. The news hit her like a ton of bricks, but she tried to stay calm. "How do you know?"

"He was spotted."

"By whom?"

"Someone working for me."

"Working for you. Did my brothers hire an entire platoon of security guards or something?"

"Eric Brown and I have known each other for years. He's been watching Sharon Okano's place."

"What? Wait! You've got someone spying on her?"

His face was rigid. "I'm not ready to take any chances."

"Don't you think someone lurking around will just draw attention to the place? You know, like waving some kind of red flag."

"He's a little more discreet than that."

She shook her head, clearing out the cobwebs, trying to keep her rising sense of panic at bay. "Wait a minute. This doesn't make any sense. Sam doesn't know about Joshua. He has no idea that I was pregnant...and probably wouldn't have cared one way or the other had he found out."

"You think."

"I'm pretty damn sure." She straightened.

"Then why would he be cruising by Sharon Okano's place?"

"Oh, God, I don't know." Her remaining calm quickly evaporated. She had to get to her baby, to see that he was all right. She made a beeline for the closet. "This is making less and less sense," she muttered and was already reaching for a jacket. Glancing at her shoes, she saw a pair of black cowboy boots, one of which had fallen over. Boots she hadn't worn since high school. Boots her father had given her and she'd never had the heart to give away. Ice slid through her veins as she walked closer and saw that the dust that had accumulated over the toes had been disturbed. Her throat went dry. "Dear God."

Kurt had followed her into the walk-in. He was pulling an overnight bag from an upper shelf. "Randi?" he asked, his voice filled with concern. "What?"

"Someone was in here." Fear mixed with fury. "I

mean…unless when you got here you came into my closet and decided to try on my cowboy boots."

"Your boots?" His gaze swept the interior of the closet to land upon the dusty black leather.

"I haven't touched them in months and look—"

He was already bending down and seeing for himself. "You're sure that you didn't—"

"No. I'm telling you someone was in here!" She tamped down the panic that threatened her, and fought the urge to kick at something. No one had the right to break into her home. No one.

"Who else has a key?"

"To this place?"

"Yes."

"Just me."

"Not Donahue?"

"No!"

"Sharon? Your brothers?"

She was shaking her head violently. Was the man dense? "I'm telling you I never gave anyone a key, not even to come in and water the plants."

"What about a neighbor, just in case you lost yours?"

"No! Jeez, Striker, don't you get it? It's just me. I even changed the locks when I bought the place so the previous owner doesn't have a set rattling around in some drawer somewhere."

"Where do you keep the spare?"

"One with me. One in the car. Another in my top desk drawer."

He was already headed down the hallway and into the living room with Randi right on his heels.

"Show me."

"Here." Reaching around him, she pulled open the center drawer, felt until her fingers scraped against cold metal, then pulled the key from behind a year-old calendar. "Right where I left it."

"And the one in your car."

"I don't know. It was with me when I had the accident. I assume it was in the wreckage."

"You didn't ask the police?"

"I was in a coma, remember? When I woke up I was a mess, broken bones, internal injuries, and I had amnesia."

"The police inventoried everything in the car when it was impounded, so they must've found the key, right?" he insisted.

"I... Jeez, I'm not sure, but I don't think it was on the report. I saw it. I even have a copy somewhere."

"Back at the Flying M?"

"No—I cleared everything out when I left. It's here somewhere." She located her briefcase and rifled through the pockets until she found a manila envelope. Inside was a copy of the police report about the accident and the inventory receipt for the impounded car. She skimmed the documents quickly.

Road maps, registration, insurance information, three sixty-seven in change, a pair of sunglasses and a bottle of glass cleaner, other miscellaneous items but no key ring. "They didn't find it."

"And you didn't ask."

She whirled on him, crumpling the paper in her fist. "I already told you, I was laid up. I didn't think about it."

"Hell." Kurt's lips compressed into a blade-thin line. His eyes narrowed angrily. "Come on." He pocketed the key, slammed the drawer shut and stormed down the hallway to the bedroom. In three swift strides he was inside the closet again. He unzipped the overnight bag and handed it to her. "Here. Pack a few things. Quickly. And don't touch the damn boots." He disappeared again and she heard him banging in the kitchen before he returned with a plastic bag and started carefully sliding it over the dusty cowboy boots. "I've already got your laptop and your briefcase in the truck."

Suddenly she understood. He wanted her to leave. Now. His jaw was set, his expression hard as granite. "Now, wait a minute. I'm not leaving town. Not yet." Things were moving too quickly, spinning out of control. "I just got home and I can't up and take off again. I've got responsibilities, a life here."

"We'll only be gone for a night or two. Until things cool off."

"We? As in you and me?"

"And the baby."

"And go where?"

"Someplace safe."

"This is my home."

"And someone's been in here. Someone with the key."

"I can change the locks, Striker. I've got a job and a home and—"

"And someone stalking you."

She opened her mouth to argue, then snapped it closed. She had to protect her baby. No matter what else. Yes, she needed to find out who was hell-bent on terrorizing her, but her first priority was to keep Joshua safe, and the truth of the matter was, Randi was already out of her mind with worry. Striker's concerns only served to fuel her anxiety. She was willing to bet he wasn't the kind of man to panic easily. And he was visibly upset. Great. She began throwing clothes into the overnight bag. "I can't take any chances with Joshua," she said.

"I know." His voice had a hint of kindness tucked into the deep timbre and she had to remind herself that he'd been hired to be concerned. Though she didn't believe that the money he'd been promised was his sole motivation in helping her, it certainly was a factor. If he kept both her and her son's skins intact, Striker's wallet would be considerably thicker. "Let's get a move on."

She was through arguing for the moment. No doubt Striker had been in more than his share of tight situations. If he really felt it was necessary to take her and her son and hide out for a while, so be it. She zipped the bag closed and ripped a suede jacket from its hanger. Was it her imagination or did it smell slightly of cigarette smoke?

Now she was getting paranoid. No one had been wearing her jacket. That was nuts.

Gritting her teeth, she fought the sensation that she'd been violated, that an intruder had pried into her private space. "I assume you've got some kind of plan."

"Yep." He straightened, the boots properly bagged.

"And that you're going to share it with me."

"Not yet."

"You can't tell me?"

"Not right now."

"Why not?"

"It's better if you don't know."

"Oh, right, keep the little woman in the dark. That's always a great idea," she said sarcastically. "This isn't the Dark Ages, Striker."

If possible, his lips compressed even further. His mouth was the thinnest of lines, his jaw set, his expression hard as nails. And then she got it. Why he was being so tight-lipped. "Wait a minute. What do you think? That this place is bugged?"

When he didn't answer, she shook her head. Disbelieving. "No way."

He threw her a look that cut her to the bone. "Let's get a move on."

She didn't argue, just dug through the drawers of her dresser and threw some essentials into her bag, then grabbed her purse.

Within minutes they were inside Kurt's truck and roaring out of the parking lot. Yesterday's rain had stopped, but the sky was still overcast, gray clouds moving slowly inland from the Pacific. Randi stared out the window, but her mind was racing. Could Sam have found out about Joshua? It was possible, of course, that he'd somehow learned she'd had a baby, but she doubted he would do the math to figure out if he was the kid's father. The truth of the matter was that he just didn't give a damn. Never had. She drummed her fingers against the window.

"I don't know why you think just because Donahue's in town that Joshua's not safe. If he drove by, it was probably just a fluke, a coincidence. Believe me, Sam Donahue wouldn't give two cents that he fathered another kid." She leaned against the passenger door as Kurt inched the pickup through the tangle of thick traffic.

"A truck belonging to Donahue has cruised by Sharon Okano's apartment complex twice this afternoon. Not just once. I wouldn't call that a coincidence. Would you?"

"No." Her throat went dry, her fingers curled into balls of tension.

"Already checked the plates with the DMV. That's what tipped Brown off—the license plates were from out of state. Montana."

Randi's entire world cracked. She fingered the chain at her throat. "But he's rarely there, in Montana," she heard herself saying as if from a long distance away. "And I didn't tell him about Joshua."

"Doesn't matter what you told him. He could have found out easy enough. He has ties to Grand Hope. Parents, an ex-wife or two. Gossip travels fast. It doesn't take a rocket scientist to count back nine months from the date your baby was born." Striker managed to nose the truck onto the freeway, where he accelerated for less than a mile, then slammed on the brakes as traffic stopped and far in the distance lights from a police car flashed bright.

"Great," Striker muttered, forcing the truck toward the next exit. He pulled his cell phone from the pocket of his jacket and poked in a number. A few seconds later, he said, "Look, we're caught in traffic. An accident northbound. It's gonna be a while. Stay where you are and call me if the rig goes by or if there's any sign of Donahue."

Randi listened and tried not to panic. So Sam Donahue was in the area. It wasn't as if he never came to Seattle. Hadn't she hooked up with him here, in a bar on the waterfront? She'd been doing research on her book and had realized through the wonders of the internet that he'd been in a rodeo competition in Oregon and was traveling north on his way to Alberta, Canada. She'd emailed him, met him for a drink and the rest was history.

"Good. Just keep an eye out. We'll be there ASAP." Striker snapped the phone shut and slid a glance in her direction. "Donahue hasn't been back."

"Maybe I should call him."

A muscle in Kurt's jaw leaped as he glared through the windshield. "And why the hell would you want to do that?"

"To find out what he's doing in town."

Striker's eyes narrowed. "You'd call up the guy who's trying to kill you."

"We don't know that he's trying to kill me." She shook her head and leaned the back of her crown against the seat rest. "It doesn't make sense. Even if he knew about Joshua, Sam wouldn't want anything to do with him."

"So why did you two break up—wait a minute, let's start with how you got together."

"I'd always wanted to write a book and my brothers had not only glamorized the whole rodeo circuit but they had also told me about the seedy side. There were illegal wagers, lots of betting. Some contestants would throw a competition, others drugged their horses, or their competitors' mounts. The animals—bulls, calves, horses—were sometimes mistreated. It's a violent sport, one that attracts macho men and competitive women moving from one town to the next. There are groupies and bar fights and prescription and recreational drug abuse. A lot of these cowboys live in pain and there's the constant danger of being thrown and trampled or gored or crushed. High passion. I thought it would make for interesting reading, so, while interviewing people, I came across Sam Donahue." Her tongue nearly tripped on his name. "He grew up in Grand Hope, knew my brothers, was even on the circuit with Matt. I started interviewing him, one thing led to another and…well, the rest, as they say, is history."

"How'd you find him?"

"I read about a local rodeo, down towards Centralia. He was entered, so I got his number, gave him a call and agreed to meet him for a drink. My brothers didn't much like him but I found him interesting and charming. We had a connection in that we both grew up in Montana, and I was coming off a bad relationship, so we hit it off. In retrospect, I'd probably say it was a mistake, except for the fact that I ended up with Joshua. My son is worth every second of heartache I suffered."

"What kind of heartache?" Striker asked, his jaw rock hard.

She glanced through the window, avoiding his eyes. "Oh, you know. The kind where you find out that the last ex-wife wasn't quite an ex. Sam had never quite gotten around to signing the divorce papers." She felt a fool for having believed the lying son of a bitch. She'd known better. She was a journalist, for crying out loud. She should have checked him out, seen the warning signs, because she'd always made a point of dating men who were completely single—not engaged, not separated, not seriously connected with any woman. But she'd failed with Sam Donahue, believing him when he'd lied and said he'd been separated two years, divorced for six months.

Striker was easing the truck past the accident, where the driver of a tow truck was winching a mangled Honda onto its bed and a couple of police officers were talking with two men near the twisted front end of a minivan of some kind. A paramedic truck was parked at an angle and two officers were talking with several boys in baseball hats who appeared unhurt but shaken. As soon as the truck was past the accident, traffic cleared and Striker pushed the speed limit again.

"So you didn't know he was married."

"Right," she replied, but couldn't stop the heat from washing up the back of her neck. She'd been a fool. "I knew that he was divorced from his first wife, Corrine. Patsy was his second wife. Might still be for all I know. Once I found out he was still married I was outta there." With one finger she drew on the condensation on the passenger-door window.

"You loved him." There it was. The statement she'd withdrawn from; the one she couldn't face.

Striker's fingers were coiled in a death grip around the steering wheel, as if somehow her answer mattered to him.

"I thought I loved him, but...even while we were seeing each other, I knew it wasn't right. There was something off." It was hard to explain that tumble of emotions. "The trouble was, by the time I'd figured it out, I was pregnant."

"So you decided to keep the baby and the secret."

"Yes," she admitted, strangely relieved to unburden herself as Striker took an off-ramp and cut through the neighborhood where Sharon Okano's apartment was located. She hesitated about telling him the rest of the story, but decided to trust him with the truth. "Along with the fact that Sam didn't tell me he was married, he also failed to mention that he and some of his friends had actually drugged a competitor's animals just before the competition. One bull reacted violently, injuring himself and his rider. The Brahman had to be put down, but not before throwing the rider and trampling him. The cowboy survived, but barely. Ended up with broken ribs, a shattered wrist, crushed pelvis and punctured spleen."

"So why wasn't Donahue arrested?"

"Not enough proof. No one saw him do it. He and his friends came up with an alibi." She glanced at Striker as he pulled into a parking space at Sharon's apartment building. "He never admitted drugging the bull, and I'm really not sure that it wasn't one of his buddies who actually did the injecting, but I'm sure that he was behind it. Just a gut feeling and the way he talked about the incident." She mentally chastised herself for being such a fool, and stared out the passenger window. "I'd already decided not to see him anymore and then, on top of all that, I discovered he was still married. Nice, huh?"

Striker cut the engine. "Not very."

"I know." The old pain cut deep, but she wasn't about to break down. Not in front of this man; not in front of anyone. Her jaw slid to one side. "Man, can I pick 'em."

Kurt touched her shoulder. "Just for the record, Randi. You deserve better than Donahue." She glanced his way and found him staring at her. His gaze scraped hers and beneath the hard facade, hidden in his eyes, a sliver of understanding, a tiny bit of empathy. "Come on. Let's go get your kid." He offered her the hint of a smile, then his grin faded quickly and the moment, that instant of connection, passed.

Her silly heart wrenched, and tears, so close to the surface, threatened.

She was out of the truck in a flash, taking the stairs to the upper-story unit two at a time. Suddenly frantic to see her baby, she pounded on the door. Sharon, a petite woman, answered. In her arms was Joshua. Blinking as if he'd just woken up from a nap, his fuzz of red-blond hair sticking straight up, he wiggled at the sight of her. Randi's heart split into a million pieces at the sight of her son. The tears she'd been fighting filled her eyes.

"Hey, big guy," she whispered, her voice hoarse.

"He missed you," Sharon said as she transferred the baby into Randi's hungry arms.

"Not half as bad as I missed him." Randi was snuggling her son, wrapped up in the wonder of holding him, smelling the baby shampoo in his hair and listening to the little coo that escaped those tiny lips, when she heard a quiet cough behind her. "Oh…this is Kurt Striker. Sharon Okano. Kurt is a friend of my brother Slade's." With an arch of her eyebrow, she added, "All of my brothers decided to hire him as, if you'll believe this, my personal bodyguard."

"Bodyguard?" Sharon's eyebrows lifted a bit. "How serious is this trouble you're in?"

"Serious enough, I guess. Kurt thinks it would be best if we kept the baby with us."

"Whatever you want." Sharon gently touched Joshua's cheek. "He's adorable, you know. I'm not sure that if you left him here much longer I could ever give him up."

"You need one of your own."

"But first, a man, I think," Sharon said. "They seem to be a necessary part of the equation." She glanced at Kurt, but Randi ignored the innuendo. She didn't need a man to help raise her son. She'd do just fine on her own.

They didn't stay long. While the women were packing Joshua's things, Kurt asked Sharon if she'd had any strange phone calls or visitors. When Sharon reported that nothing out of the ordinary had happened, Kurt called his partner and within fifteen minutes, Randi, Kurt and Joshua, tucked into his car seat, were on the road and heading east out of Seattle. The rain had started, a deep steady mist, and Striker had flipped on the wipers.

"You're still not going to tell me where we're going?" she asked.

"Inland."

"I know that much, but where exactly?" When he didn't immediately respond, she said, "I have a job to do. Remember? I can't be gone indefinitely." She glanced at her watch, scowled as it was after three, then dug in her purse, retrieved her cell phone and punched out the numbers for the *Clarion*. Within a minute she was connected to Bill Withers's voice mail and left a quick message, indicating she had a family emergency and vowing she would email a couple of new columns. As she hung up, she said, "I don't know how much of that Withers will buy, but it should give us a couple of days."

"Maybe that's all we'll need." He sped around a fuel truck, but his voice lacked conviction.

"Listen, Striker, we've got to nail this creep and soon," Randi said as the wipers slapped away the rain. "I need my life back."

The look he sent her sliced into her soul. "So do I."

The bitch wouldn't get away with it.

Three cars behind Striker's truck, gloved hands tight over the steering wheel, the would-be killer drove carefully, coming close to the pickup, then backing off, listening to a CD from the eighties as red taillights blurred. Jon Bon Jovi's voice wailed through the speakers and the stalker licked dry lips as the pickup cut across the floating bridge, over the steely waters of Lake Washington. Who knew where they were headed? To the suburbs of upscale Bellevue? Or somewhere around Lake Sammamish? Maybe farther into the forested hills. Even the Cascade Mountains.

Whatever.

It didn't matter.

Sweet vengeance brought a smile to the stalker's lips.

Randi McCafferty's destination was about to become her final resting place.

Chapter 9

"Get the baby ready," Kurt said as he took an exit off the freeway. Glancing in the rearview mirror to be certain he wasn't followed, he doubled back, heading west, only to get off at the previous stop and drive along a frontage heading toward Seattle again.

"What are we doing?" Randi asked.

"Changing vehicles." Carefully he timed the stoplights, making certain he was the last vehicle through the two intersections before turning down one street and pulling into a gas station.

"What? Why?"

"I'm not taking any chances that we're being followed."

"You saw someone?"

"No."

"But—"

"Just make it fast and jump into that brown SUV." He nodded toward the back of the station to a banged-up vehicle with tinted windows and zero chrome. The SUV was completely nondescript, the fenders and tires splattered with mud. "It belongs to a friend of mine," Striker said. "He's waiting. He'll drive the truck."

"This is nuts," Randi muttered, but she unstrapped the baby seat and pulled it, along with Joshua, from the truck.

"I don't think so."

Quickly, as Randi did as she was told, Striker topped off his tank.

Eric was waiting for them. He'd been talking on his cell phone and smoking a cigarette, but spying Striker, tossed the cigarette into a puddle and gave a quick wave. Ending his call, he helped Randi load up, then traded places with Kurt. The entire exchange had taken less than a minute. Seconds after that, Kurt was in the driver's seat of the Jeep, heading east again.

"I don't think I can stand all of this cloak-and-dagger stuff," Randi complained, and even in the darkness he saw the outline of her jaw, the slope of her cheek, the purse of those incredible lips. Good Lord, she was one helluva woman. Intriguingly beautiful, sexy as hell, smarter than she needed to be and endowed with a tongue sharp enough to cut through a strong man's ego.

"Sure you can."

"Whatever my brothers are paying you, it's not enough."

"That's probably true." He glanced at her once more, then turned his attention to the road. Night had fallen, but the rain had let up a bit. His tires sang on the wet pavement and the rumble of the SUV's engine was smooth and steady. The baby was quiet in the backseat, and for the first time in years Kurt felt a little sensation of being with family. Which was ridiculous. The woman was a client, the child just part of the package. He told himself to remember that.

No matter what else. He was her bodyguard. His job was to keep her alive and find out who was trying to kill her.

Nothing more.

What about the other night at the ranch? his damning mind taunted. *Remember how much you wanted her, how you went about seducing her? How can you forget the thrill of slipping her robe off her shoulders and unveiling those incredible breasts. What about the look of surprise and wonder in her eyes, or the soft, inviting curve of her lips as you kissed the hollow of her throat. Think about the raw need that drove you to untie the belt at her waist. The robe gave way, the nightgown followed and she was naked aside from a slim gold chain and locket at her throat. You didn't waste any time kicking off your jeans. You wanted her, Striker. More than you've ever wanted a woman in your life. You would have died to have her and you did, didn't you? Over and over again. Feeling her heat surround you, listening to the pounding of your heart and feeling your blood sing through your veins. You were so hot and hard, nothing could have stopped you. What about then, when you gave in to temptation?*

The back of his neck tightened as he remembered and his inner voice continued to taunt him.

If you can convince yourself that Randi McCafferty is just another client, then you're a bigger fool than you know.

It was late by the time the Jeep bounced along the rocky, mossy ruts that constituted the driveway to what could only be loosely called a cabin. Set deep in the forest and barricaded by a locked gate to which Kurt had miraculously had the key, the place was obviously deserted and had been for a long time. Randi shuddered inwardly as the Jeep's headlights illuminated the sorry little bungalow. Tattered shades were drawn over the windows, rust was evident in the few downspouts that were still connected to the gutters, and the moss-covered roof sagged pitifully.

"You sure you don't want to look for a Motel 6?" she asked. "Even a Motel 2 would be an improvement over this."

"Not yet." Kurt had already pulled on the emergency brake and cut the engine. "Think of it as rustic."

"Right. Rustic. And quaint." She shook her head.

"This used to be the gatekeeper's house when this area was actively being logged," he explained.

"And now?" She stepped out of the Jeep and her boots sank in the soggy loam of the forest floor.

"It's been a while since the cabin's been inhabited."

"A long while, I'd guess. Come on, baby, it's time to check out our new digs." She hauled Joshua in his carrier up creaky porch steps as Kurt, with the aid of a flashlight and another key, opened a door that creaked as it swung inward.

Kurt tried a light switch. Nothing. Just a loud click. "Juice isn't turned on, I guess."

"Fabulous."

He found a lantern and struck a match. Immediately the room was flooded with a soft golden glow that couldn't hide the dust, cobwebs and general malaise of the place. The floor was scarred fir, the ceiling pine was stained where rainwater had seeped inside and it smelled of must and years of neglect.

"Home sweet home," she cracked.

"For the time being." But Kurt was already stalking through the small rooms, running his flashlight along the floor and ceiling. "We won't have electricity, but we'll manage."

"So no hot water, light or heat."

"But a woodstove and lanterns. We'll be okay."

"What about a bathroom?"

He shook his head. "There's an old pump on the porch and, if you'll give me a minute—" he looked in a few cupboards and closets before coming up with a bucket "—voila! An old fashioned Porta Potti."

"Give me a break," she muttered.

"Come on, you're a McCafferty. Rustic living should be a piece of cake."

"Let me give you a clue, Striker. This is *waaaay* beyond rustic."

"I heard you were a tomboy growing up."

"Slade talks too much."

"Probably. But you used to camp all the time."

"In the summers. I was twelve or thirteen."

"It's like riding a bike. You never forget how."

"We'll see." But she didn't complain as they hauled in equipment that had been loaded into the Jeep. Sleeping bags, canned goods, a cooler for fresh food, cooking equipment, paper plates, propane stove, towels and toilet paper. "You thought this through."

"I just told Eric to pack the essentials."

"What about a phone?"

"Our cells should work."

Scrounging in her purse, she found her phone, yanked it out and turned it on. The backlit message wasn't encouraging. "Looking for service," she read aloud, and watched as the cell failed to find a signal. "Hopefully yours is stronger."

He flashed her a grin that seemed to sizzle in the dim light. "I already checked. It works."

"So what about a phone jack to link up my laptop?"

He lifted a shoulder. "Looks like you're out of luck unless you've got one of those wireless hookups."

"Not a prayer."

"Then you'll have to be out of touch for a while."

"Great," she muttered. "I don't suppose it matters that I could lose my job over this."

"Better than your life."

She was about to reply, when the baby began to cry. Quickly, Randi mixed formula with some of the bottled water she'd brought, then pulled off dust cloths from furniture that looked as if it was in style around the end of World War II. Joshua was really cranking it up by the time Randi plopped herself into a rocking chair and braced herself for the sound of scurrying feet as mice skittered out from the old cushions. Fortunately, as she settled into the chair, no protesting squeaks erupted, nor did any little scurrying rodent make a mad dash to the darker corners. With the baby's blanket wrapped around him, she fed her son and felt a few seconds' relaxation as his wails subsided and he ate hungrily from the bottle. There was a peace to holding her baby, a calm that kept her fears and worries at bay. He looked up at her as he ate, and in those precious, bonding moments, she never once doubted that her affair with Sam Donahuc was worth every second of her later regrets.

Kurt was busy checking the flue, starting a fire in an antique-looking woodstove. Once the fire was crackling, he rocked back on his heels and dusted his hands. She tried not to notice how his jacket stretched at the shoulders or the way his jeans fit snug around his hips and buttocks. Nor did she want to observe that his hair fell in an unruly lock over his forehead, or that his cheekbones were strong enough to hint at some long-forgotten Native American heritage.

He was too damn sexy for his own good.

As if sensing her watching him, he straightened slowly and she was given a bird's-eye view of his long back as he stretched, then walked to a black beat-up leather case and unzipped it. Out came a laptop computer complete with wireless connection device.

He glanced over his shoulder, his green eyes glinting in amusement.

"You could have said something," she charged.

"And miss seeing you get ticked off? No way. But this isn't the be-all and end-all. I have one extra battery. No more. Since there's no electricity here, the juice won't last forever."

"Wonderful," she said, lifting her baby to her shoulder and gently rubbing his back.

"It's better than nothing."

"Can I use it?"

"For a small fee," he said as the corners of his mouth twitched.

"You are *so* full of it."

"Wouldn't want to disappoint."

"You never do, Striker."

"Good. Let's keep it that way."

Joshua gave a loud burp. "There we go, big guy," she whispered as she spread his blanket on a pad and changed his diaper. The baby kicked and gurgled, his eyes bright in the firelight. "Oh, you're full of the devil, aren't you?" She played with him a few more minutes until he yawned and sighed. Randi held him and swayed a little as he nodded off. She couldn't imagine what life would have been like without this precious little boy. She kissed his soft crown, and as his breathing became regular and his head heavy, she placed him upon the makeshift crib of blankets and pillows, then glanced around the stark, near-empty cabin. "We really are in the middle of no-darned-where."

"That was the general idea."

She ran a finger through the dust on an old scarred table. "No electricity, no indoor plumbing, no television, radio or even any good books lying around."

"I guess we'll just have to make do and find some way to amuse ourselves." His expression was positively wicked, his eyes glittering with amusement. That he could find even the tiniest bit of humor in this vile situation was something, she thought, though she didn't like the way her throat caught when he stared at her, nor the way blood went rushing through her veins as he cocked an arrogant eyebrow.

"I think we'll do just fine," she said, hoping to sound frosty when, in fact, her voice was more than a tad breathless. Damn it all, she didn't like the idea of being trapped here with him in the middle of God-only-knew-where, didn't like feeling vulnerable not only to whoever was stalking her, but also to the warring emotions she felt whenever she was around Striker. *Don't even go there,* she told herself. *All you have to do is get through the next few days. By then, if he does his job the way he's supposed to, he'll catch the bad guy and you can reclaim your life. Then, you'll be safe. You and your baby can start over.*

Unless something goes wrong. Terribly, terribly wrong.

She glanced again at Striker.

Whether she liked it or not, she was stuck with him.

Things could be worse.

Less than two hours later, Striker's phone jangled.

He jumped and snapped it open. "Striker."

"It's Kelly. I've got information."

Finally! He leaned a hip against an old windowsill and watched as Randi, glasses perched on the end of her nose, looked up from his laptop. "News?"

He nodded. "Go on," he said into the phone and listened as Matt McCafferty's wife began to explain.

"I think I've located the vehicle that forced Randi off the road in Glacier Park. A maroon Ford truck, a few years old, had some dents banged out of it in a chop shop in Idaho. All under-the-table stuff. Got the lead from a disgruntled employee who swears the chop shop owner owes him back wages."

Striker's jaw hardened. "Let me guess. The truck was registered to Sam Donahue."

"Close. Actually was once owned by Marv Bates, or, precisely, a girlfriend of his."

"Have you located Bates?"

Randi visibly stiffened. She set aside the laptop and crossed the few feet separating them. "We're working on it. I've got the police involved. My old boss, Espinoza, is doing what he can." Roberto Espinoza was a senior detective who was working on Randi's case. Kelly Dillinger had once worked for him, but turned in her badge about the time she married Matt McCafferty. "But so far, we haven't been able to locate Mr. Bates."

"He had an alibi."

"Yeah," Kelly said. "Airtight. Good ol' boys Sam Donahue and Charlie Caldwell swore they were all over at Marv's house when Randi was forced off the road. Charlie's girlfriend at the time, Trina Spencer, verified the story, but now Charlie and Trina have split, so we're looking for her. Maybe she'll change her tune now that Charlie's no longer the love of her life and the truck she owned has been linked to the crime. We're talking to the employees of the chop shop. I figure it's just a matter of time before one of 'em cracks."

"Good. It's a start."

"Finally," Kelly agreed. "I'll keep working on it."

"Want to talk to Randi?"

"Absolutely." Striker handed the phone to Randi and listened to her end of the conversation as she asked about what Kelly had discovered, then turned the conversation to her family. A few minutes later, she hung up.

"This is the break you've been waiting for," she said, and he heard the hope in her voice.

God, he hated to burst her bubble. "It's a start, Randi. Time will tell if it pans out, but yeah, it's something."

He only hoped it was enough.

"Why don't you turn in." He unrolled a sleeping bag, placing it between the baby's makeshift crib and the fire.

"Where will you be?"

"Here." He shoved a chair close to the door.

She eyed the old wingback. "Aren't you going to sleep?"

"Maybe doze."

"You're still afraid," she charged.

"Not afraid. Just vigilant."

She shook her head, unaware that the fire's glow brought out the red streaks in her hair. Sighing, she started working off one boot with the toe of another. "I really can't believe this is my life." The first boot came off, followed quickly by the second. Plopping down on the sleeping bag, she sat cross-legged and stared at the fire. "I just wanted to write a book, you know. Show my dad, my boss, even my brothers that I was capable of doing something really newsworthy. My family thought I was nuts when I went into journalism in college—my dad in particular. He couldn't see any use in it. Not for his daughter, anyway. And then I landed the job with the paper in Seattle and it became a joke. Advice to single people. My brothers thought it was just a lot of fluff, even when the column took off and was syndicated."

She glanced at Striker. "You know my brothers. They're pretty much straight-shooter, feet-on-the-ground types. I don't think Matt or Slade or Thorne would ever be ones to write in for advice on their love lives."

Kurt laughed.

"Nor you, I suppose?"

He arched an eyebrow in her direction. "Not likely."

"And the articles I did for magazines under R. J. McKay, it was all woman stuff, too. So the book—" she looked up at the ceiling as if she could find an answer in the cobwebby beams and rafters "—it was an attempt to legitimatize my career. Unfortunately Dad died before it was finished and then all the trouble started." She rubbed her knees and cocked her head. Her locket slipped over the collar of her shirt and he noticed it winking in the firelight. His mouth turned dry at the sight of her slim throat and the curve of her neck where it met her shoulder. A tightening in his groin forced him to look away.

"Maybe the trouble's about to end."

"That would be heaven," she said. "You know, I always liked living on the edge, being a part of the action, whatever it was, never set my roots down too deep."

"A true McCafferty."

She chuckled. "I suppose. But now, with the baby and after everything that happened, I just want some peace of mind. I want my life in the city back."

"And the book?"

Her smile grew slowly. "Oh, I'm still going to write it," she vowed, and he noticed a determined edge to her voice, a steely resolve hidden in her grin. "Bedtime?"

The question sounded innocent, but it still created an image of their lovemaking. "Whenever you want."

"And you're just going to play security guard by the door."

"Yep." He nodded. "Get some sleep."

"Not until you tell me what it is that makes you tick," she said. "Come on, I told you all about my dreams of being a journalist and how my family practically laughed in my face. You know all about the men I've dated in recent history and I've also told you about my book and how I got involved with a man who was still married and might be trying to kill me. Whatever you're hiding can't be that bad."

"Why do you think I'm hiding something?"

"We all have secrets, Striker. What's yours?"

That I'm falling for you, he thought, then clamped his mind shut. No way. No how. His involvement with Randi McCafferty had to remain professional. No matter what. "I was married," he said, and felt that old raw pain cutting through him.

"What happened?"

He hesitated. This was a subject he rarely bridged, never brought up on his own. "She divorced me."

"Because of your work?"

"No." He glanced at her baby sleeping so soundly in his blankets, remembered the rush of seeing his own child for the first time, remembered the smell of her, the wonder of caring too much for one little beguiling person.

"Another woman?" she asked, and he saw the wariness in the set of her jaw.

"No. That would have been easier," he admitted. "Cleaner."

"Then, what happened? Don't give me any of that 'we grew away from each other' or 'we drifted apart.' I have readers who write me by the dozens and they all say the same thing."

"What happened between me and my ex-wife can't be cured by advice in your column," he said more bitterly than he'd planned.

"I didn't mean to imply that it could." She was a little angry. He could feel it.

"Good."

"So what happened, Striker?"

His jaw worked.

"Can't talk about it?" She rolled her eyes. "After I explained about Sam Donahue? That I was sleeping with him and he was still married. How do you think I feel, not seeing the signs, not reading the clues. Jeez, whatever it is can't be that humiliating!"

"We had a daughter," he said, his voice seeming to come from outside his body. "Her name was Heather." His throat tightened with the memories. "I used to take her with me on the boat and she loved it. My wife didn't like it, was afraid of the water. But I insisted it would be safe. And it was. Until…" His chest felt as if the weight of the sea was upon it. Randi didn't say a word but she'd blanched, her skin suddenly pale, as if she knew what was to come. Striker closed his eyes, but still he could see that day, the storm coming in on the horizon, remember the way the engine had stalled. "Until the last time. Heather and I went boating. The engine had cut out and I was busy fiddling with it when she fell overboard. Somehow her life jacket slipped off. It was a fluke, but still… I dived in after her but she'd struck her head. Took in too much water." He blinked hard. "It was too late. I couldn't save her." Pain racked through his soul.

Randi didn't move. Just stared at him.

"My wife blamed me," he said, leaning against the door. "The divorce was just a formality."

Chapter 10

Dear God, how she'd misjudged him! "I'm so sorry," she whispered, wondering how anyone survived losing a child.

"It's not your fault."

"And it wasn't yours. It was an accident," she said then saw recrimination darken his gaze.

"So I told myself. But if I hadn't insisted upon taking her…" He scowled. "Look, it happened. Over five years ago. No reason to bring it up now."

Randi's heart split. For all of his denials, the pain was fresh in him. "Do you have a picture?"

"What?"

"Of your daughter?"

When he hesitated, she crawled out of the sleeping bag. "I'd like to see."

"This isn't a good idea."

"Not the first," she said as she crossed the room. Reluctantly he reached into his back pocket, pulled out his wallet and flipped it open. Randi's throat closed as she took the battered leather and gazed at the plastic-encased photograph of a darling little girl. Blond pigtails framed a cherubic face that seemed primed for the camera's eye. Under apple cheeks, her tiny grin showed off perfect little baby teeth. "She's beautiful."

"Yes." He nodded, his lips thin and tight. "She was."

"I apologize if I said anything insensitive before. I didn't know."

"I don't talk about it much."

"Maybe you should."

"Don't think so." He took the wallet from her fingers and snapped it shut.

"If I'd known…"

"What? What would you have done differently?" he asked, a trace of bitterness to his words. "There's nothing you can say, nothing you can do, nothing that will change what happened."

She reached forward to stroke his cheek and he grabbed her wrist. "Don't," he warned. "I don't want your pity or your sympathy."

"Empathy," she said.

"No one who hasn't lost a child can empathize," he said, his fingers tightening, his eyes fierce. "It's just not possible."

"Maybe not, but that doesn't mean I can't feel some of your pain."

"Well, don't. It's mine. You can do nothing." A muscle worked in his jaw. "I shouldn't have told you."

"No…it's better."

"How?" he demanded, his nostrils flaring. "Tell me how you knowing about Heather helps anything."

"I understand you better."

"Jesus, Randi. That's woman patter. You don't need to figure out what makes me tick or even know about what I've been through. You weren't there, okay? So I'd rather you not try to 'feel my pain' or any of that self-aggrandizing pseudopsychological, television talk-show crap. You just need to do what I tell you to do so that we can make certain that you and your son are safe. End of story."

"Not quite," she whispered, and without thinking, placed a kiss on the corner of his mouth. The need to soothe him was overpowering, nearly as intense as her own need to be comforted. To be held. "If we're going to be sequestered from the rest of the world, I do need to understand you." She kissed him again.

"Don't do that." His voice was hoarse and she noticed that he shifted, as if his jeans were suddenly too tight.

"Why?" she asked, not budging an inch, so close she smelled the rain drying on his jacket. She felt reckless and wild and wanted to touch him and hold him close, this man who had seen so much of life, felt so much pain.

"You know why."

"Kurt, I just want to help."

"You can't." He turned to look her square in the eye, his nose only inches from hers. "Don't you know what you're dealing with here?"

"I'm not afraid." She kissed his cheek and he groaned.

"Don't do this, Randi," he ordered, but it sounded like a plea.

"You can trust me."

"This isn't about trust."

"No? Then why are we here? Alone together? If I didn't trust you, you can bet I wouldn't be locked away from the world like this. Believe me, Striker, this is all about trust. That's why you told me about Heather."

"Let's leave her out of this!" he growled.

"You have a right to be angry about what happened to your daughter."

"Good. 'Cuz I am and you're not helping!"

"No?" she said, her temper snapping. "Then I don't suppose I helped the other night, either?"

"Hell," he muttered, glancing away. His fingers were still surrounding her wrist, her pulse beating wildly beneath the warm pads.

"You remember that night, don't you?" she reminded him. "The one where you were watching me from the second story? *That* night, you didn't have any of these reservations."

"That night is the reason I'm having these reservations. It was a mistake."

"You didn't think so at the time."

"You're right, I didn't think period. But I'm trying to now."

"So it's okay for you to seduce me, but not the other way around."

He closed his eyes as if to gain strength. "I didn't bring you up here to sleep with you."

"No?" She kissed him again, behind his ear, and this time his reaction was immediate.

He turned swiftly, pinning her onto the floor and leaning over her. "Look, woman, you're pushing it with me. A man can only take so much."

"Same with a woman," she said. "You can't just—"

The rest of her sentence was cut off as his lips clamped over hers. Fierce. Hot. Hard. Desperate. He kissed her long and wildly and she responded, opening her mouth, feeling his tongue slide into her, arching as it probed. Her breath was trapped, her blood on fire, her bones melting as he slid his hands up and down her body. No longer did he deny what they both wanted. No longer did he say a word, just kissed and touched and tugged at her clothes.

She had no regrets. This was what she wanted. To touch him, physically and emotionally. Her own fingers struggled with the zipper of his coat and the shirt buttons below. She felt strong sinewy muscles covered by taut skin and chest hair that was stiff. Her fingertips grazed nipples that tightened at her touch.

"Oh, God," he rasped as he yanked off his shirt, then worked at the hem of her sweater. Strong, callused hands rubbed her skin as he scaled her ribs. She cried out as he touched beneath her bra, skimming the underside of her breasts. Her nipples tightened. Her breasts filled and she wanted him. With every breath in her body, she needed to feel him inside her, to have him rubbing and moving and balming the ache growing deep within. He peeled away her bra and scooped her into his strong arms, climbed to his feet and carried her to the sleeping bag, where they fell into a tangle of arms and legs. His mouth was ravenous as he kissed her face and breasts. Hard fingers splayed against the small of her back, pulling her tight against him, pressing her mound into the hardness of his fly, rubbing her sensually.

She moaned softly as he kissed her nipples, teasing them with his tongue and lips, biting softly before he nuzzled and sucked. Her mind spun in dizzying fragments of light and shadow. She saw his face buried into her breasts, felt his fingertips probing beneath the waistband of her pants, burned with a want so hot she was sweating in the cold room, aching for him, her fingers reaching for his fly. "Randi," he whispered across her wet breasts. "Oh, God, darlin'…" His hand slid down the slope of her rump, fingers stretching to find that sweet spot within her. She cried out and moved her hips as he yanked off her pants with his free hand and continued to explore with his other. Parting her. Delving deep. Causing her to gasp and throw her head back as she arched and he suckled at her breast. He scratched the surface of her need. Liquid warmth seared her.

"More," she whispered, lost.

He stripped her panties from her.

She fumbled with the buttons of his fly, but they came undone and, with amazing agility, he kicked out of his jeans to be naked with her. Skin on skin. Flesh on flesh. Blood heating, he pulled her atop him, and in one quick movement removed his hand and replaced it with his thick, hard erection.

"Oh!" she cried as he pushed her hips down and raised his buttocks in one swift motion. The world melted away as they began to move. Slowly at first. Friction and fire. Heat and want. All emotion and need. Randi closed her eyes and heard a slow, long moan. From her throat or his? She didn't know, didn't care. Nothing mattered but the man beneath her, the man she wanted, the man she feared she loved. This small moment in time could very well be their last, but she didn't care, just wanted to feel him within her.

Deep inside something snapped. She wanted more of him. More. So much more. Opening her eyes, she saw him staring at her, his own gaze bright with the same desire as her own. "That's it, baby," he whispered as she increased the tempo. He caught up quickly and took command, his hands tight on her as he began pumping furiously beneath her. Beads of sweat dotted his forehead, his skin tight, his hair damp with perspiration. Yet he didn't stop.

Hotter. Faster. The world spinning. "Oh, God, oh, God, oh…oh…" she cried as the world seemed to catch fire and explode around her. She convulsed, but still he held her upright, still he thrust into her, and though she'd felt complete surrender a minute before, she met each of his jabs with her own downward motion. Again. And again... Over and over until the heat rose in her in such a rush that she bucked. This time he came with her, his breath screaming out of his lungs, his body straining upward as he let go and finally emptied himself into her.

"Randi!" he cried hoarsely, his voice breaking, "Oh, love..."

She fell against him and felt his strong arms surround her and hold her close. One hand cradled her head, the other was wrapped around her waist. Tears sprang unbidden to her eyes as his words echoed through her head. Though they were spoken in the throes of passion, though she knew she would never hear them again, she clung to them. *Randi... Oh, love.*

They would be meaningless in the morning, but for now, for all of this night, they sustained her. She cuddled up against him, and knew a few moments' peace. For tonight, she would indulge herself. For tonight, she would sleep with this man she could so easily love. For tonight she'd forget that he was her bodyguard, paid to protect her, a man who no woman in her right mind would allow herself to fall for.

Lovers.

She and Kurt had become lovers.

The thought hit her hard, battering at her before she opened her eyes and knew that he wasn't in the sleeping bag with her. They'd made love over and over the night before and now... She opened one eye to the cabin as morning light streamed through the dusty windows. If anything, the dilapidated old cottage looked worse in the gloom of the day. The baby was rustling. It had probably been his soft cries that had cut through her thick slumber and roused her. So here she was, naked, cold, no sign of Kurt, in the middle of nowhere.

"Coming," she called to the baby as she found her clothes and slid into them. As she felt a slight soreness between her legs, a reminder of what had happened, what she'd instigated last night. What had she been thinking? Embarrassed at her actions, she crawled over to her baby and smiled down at his beatific face. "Hungry?" she asked, though she was already changing him. How quickly she'd become adept at holding him in place, talking to him, removing the old diaper, cleaning him and whipping a new diaper around him.

She found premixed formula in a bottle and, singing softly, fed her child. She heard the door open and looked over her shoulder to spy Kurt, carrying an armload of split kindling into the cabin. She felt heat wash up the back of her neck, but he didn't seem embarrassed. "Mornin'," he drawled, and the look he sent her reminded her of their lovemaking all over again. She'd been the aggressor. She'd practically begged him to make love to her. She'd definitely seduced him and now she felt the fool.

"I think I should say something about last night," she offered.

"What's to say?"

"That I'm not usually like that..."

"Too bad." One side of his mouth lifted. "I thought it was pretty damn nice."

"Really? But you...I mean you acted like it was a mistake. You *said* it was one."

"But it happened, right? I think we shouldn't second-guess ourselves."

"So it was no big deal?" she asked, and felt slightly deflated.

"It was a big deal, but let's not start the morning with recriminations, okay? I don't think that would solve anything. As I said, I'm not into overanalyzing emotions." He stacked the kindling in an old crate that was probably home to several nests of spiders. "I was hoping to make coffee before you woke up."

"Mmm. Sounds like heaven," she admitted.

"It'll be just a second." He dusted his hands and found a packet of coffee.

"I don't suppose you have a nonfat, vanilla latte with extra foam and chocolate sprinkles?" she asked, and he snorted a laugh.

"You lived in Seattle too long."

"Tell that to my boss," she muttered. "Actually, when I'm finished here…" She inclined her head toward her son. "I want to call him. If I'm allowed," she added.

"Just as long as you don't divulge our whereabouts."

"That would be tough considering that I don't know where we are." Randi finished feeding the baby and played with him as she changed his clothes. While Kurt heated water for the instant coffee, she balanced her son to her shoulder and put in another call to Bill Withers, only to leave another voice message when the editor didn't pick up his phone. "Withers must be ducking me," she muttered as she redialed and connected with Sarah.

"Where've you been?" Sarah demanded once she realized she was talking to Randi. "Bill gave me the third degree, and whenever your name is mentioned, he looks as if he's having a seizure."

"I can't really say, but I'll be back——" she glanced at Kurt, who was shaking his head "——soon. I don't really know when. In the meantime I'm going to email my stories. It shouldn't be that big of a deal, most of the questions I get come in over the internet."

"It's a control issue with Bill, but then it is with most men."

"Especially if the man happens to be your boss," Randi said. "Look, if he talks to you, tell him I'm trying to get hold of him. I've called twice and I'm going to email in a couple of hours."

"Well, hurry back, okay?"

"I'll be back as soon as I can," Randi assured her.

"Should I tell Joe?"

"What?"

"Paterno's back in town and he's been asking about you."

Randi and Joe had never been lovers; their relationship hadn't blossomed in a romantic way. She was surprised that he'd be looking for her. "Well, tell him I'll get back to him when I'm in town," she said, and saw Striker stiffen slightly. He couldn't help but overhear her conversation and she didn't like the fact that she had so little privacy. "Look, Sarah, I've got to run." She hung up, hoping to save as much battery as possible before Sarah could argue. Exchanging the phone for a cup of coffee, she said, "So I didn't lie, did I? This will end soon."

"I think so, but I did some checking this morning before you woke and so far no one's been able to locate Sam Donahue."

"You think he's hiding?"

"Maybe."

"Or...?" She didn't like the feeling she was getting. "Or you think he's followed us?"

"I don't know. Did he come looking for you at the office? I heard you tell your friend that you'd get back with him."

"That wasn't Sam." She hesitated, then decided to come clean. "It was Joe Paterno. We were...are...friends. That's all. That's all there ever was between us."

He looked as if he didn't believe her.

"Really." She lifted a shoulder. "Sorry to disappoint you. I get the feeling that you think I had this incredible love life, that I slept with every man I dated, but that just wasn't the case. I let everyone wonder about my baby's paternity to protect him. The fewer people who knew that Sam was the baby's father, the better it was for me and Joshua. At least that's what I thought, so I let people draw their own conclusions about my love life." She arched an eyebrow at him. "I might not have the best taste in men, but I am somewhat picky."

"I guess I should feel flattered."

"Damn straight," she said, sending a look guaranteed to kill, then took a long swallow of coffee before turning her attention to her baby. After all, he was the reason that everything was happening and Randi wouldn't have changed a thing. Not if it meant she never would have had her son. Joshua made it all worthwhile.

Even the accident, she thought as the baby giggled and cooed.

Late last fall she'd left Seattle intending to return to the ranch she'd inherited from her father. She'd just wanted some peace of mind and time alone in Montana, where she intended to write her book and do some serious soul-searching. Once on the ranch, she'd made some stupid mistakes including firing Larry Todd, the foreman, and even letting Juanita Ramirez, the housekeeper, go. Those decisions had been stupid, as Larry had known the livestock backward and forward and Juanita had not only helped raise Randi and her half brothers but had put up with their father until the grumpy old man had died. But Randi had been on a mission and had believed that before she could take care of a baby, she had to prove to herself that she could be completely self-reliant.

She'd thought that living on the Flying M, returning to her roots and running the ranch while writing her book might be the right kind of therapy she needed. After the baby came, she'd figured she could look after her child and raise him where she'd grown up, away from the hustle and bustle of the city. Plus, she still had her job at the *Clarion,* using email and a fax machine, until she could return to Seattle every other week or so if need be.

The prospect of becoming a mother—a single mother— had been daunting. How would she deal with her son's inevitable questions about his father? When she finished the book and the scam was exposed, many people in the rodeo world, including Sam Donahue, would be investigated and possibly indicted. How would she feel knowing that she'd sent her son's father to prison?

Nevertheless, because she'd been born a McCafferty, the kind of person who never shied away from the truth or tough decisions, she'd come to the conclusion that she had to let the truth be known and let the chips fall where they may.

But she hadn't gotten the chance. On her way back to Grand Hope, she'd had the accident that had nearly taken her life and sent her into premature labor. She'd been laid up in a coma, woken up to find out that she couldn't remember anything and that she had this wonderful infant son. As she'd recovered and her memory had returned in bits and snatches, she was horrified to realize that she'd been played for a fool, that Sam Donahue was Joshua's father and that he was a heartless criminal.

And now... *And now what?* She leaned closer to the baby and her locket swung free of her shirt. Joshua giggled and smiled, kicking and reaching for the glittering gold heart. "Silly boy," she said, leaning over to buss him in the tummy. He chortled and she did it again, making a game of it, closing out her doubts and worries as she played with her child.

Striker's cell phone rang, disturbing the quiet.

He flipped it open and answered, "Kurt Striker... Yeah, she's right here... I don't know if that's such a great idea.... Fine. Just a sec."

Randi turned her head and saw Striker glowering through the window, his cell phone pressed against his ear. He glanced her way and her heart nearly stopped. Something had happened. Something bad. "What?"

"Okay, put him on, but I don't have much battery left, so he'd better keep it short." He held the phone toward Randi. "That was Brown. He found Sam Donahue."

The floor seemed to wobble. "And?"

"It's for you, darlin'." Kurt's smile was cold as ice. "Seems as if good ol' Sam wants to talk to you."

Chapter 11

"What the hell's going on, Randi?" Sam Donahue shouted through the phone wires.

Randi braced herself for the onslaught. And it came.

"I've got some crazy son of a bitch telling me that I'm gonna be arrested because I tried to kill you or some damn thing and that's all a pile of crap. You *know* it's crap. Why would I want to hurt you? Because of the kid? Oh, give me a break! That story you're writing? Who would believe it? I've got an ironclad alibi, so call off your dogs!"

"My dogs?" she repeated as static crackled in her ear. The signal was fading and fast. Thankfully.

"Yeah, this guy. Brown."

"I can't hear you, Sam."

"…nuts! Crazy! He's talkin' about the police… Oh, God, they're here… Look, Randi, I don't know what this is all about, maybe some personal vendetta or something… This is all wrong," he said, swearing a blue streak that broke up as the battery in the phone began to give out. "…damn it… sue you and anyone…false arrest…no way… Leave me the hell alone! Wait…Randi…" His voice faded completely and the connection stopped just as the cell phone beeped a final warning about its battery running low.

Numbly, she handed the phone back to Striker.

"What did he want?"

"To protest his innocence," she said. "He told me to call off my dogs."

"They aren't yours."

"I didn't have time to explain. He didn't give me much of a chance and the connection was miserable." She shoved her hands into the pockets of her jeans. "Not that I wanted to straighten him out." She glanced at her baby, sleeping again, so angelic, so unaware.

"You okay?" Kurt asked, rubbing the back of her neck in that comforting spot between her shoulder blades.

"Yeah. It wasn't all that emotional for me. I was surprised." She managed a sad smile. "You know, I thought I'd feel something. Anger, maybe, or even wistfulness, *any* kind of emotion because he *is* the father of my child, but I just felt…empty. And maybe a little sad. Not for me, but for Joshua." She shrugged. "Hard to explain." She glanced around the cabin, her gaze landing on her baby, who despite the tense conversation had fallen asleep. "But the odd thing about the phone call was that I believed him."

"Donahue?" Striker snorted as he walked to the fire and warmed his hands.

"Yes. I mean, he was so vehement, so outraged that he was being arrested. It didn't seem like an act."

Striker barked out a laugh. "You thought he'd go quietly?"

"No, of course not, but—"

"You're still protecting him," Kurt said with a frown. "You know, just because he's the father of your child doesn't mean you owe him any allegiance or anything."

That stung. "Are you kidding? The last thing I feel for Sam Donahue is allegiance. He was married when he and I met. *Married.* Not just going with someone, or even engaged. When I asked him about it, he'd said he was divorced, that they'd been separated for some time and the divorce had been final for months. He flat-out lied. Silly me. I believed him," she admitted, but that old pain, the embarrassment of falling for Donahue's line and lies wasn't as deep. She'd fantasized about meeting or talking with him again, of either telling him to go to hell or advising him that he had a son who was the most precious thing on earth. And she'd hoped to feel some satisfaction in the conversation, but instead, all she'd felt was relief that she wasn't involved with him, that she was here, with Kurt Striker, that in fact, she'd moved on.

To what? A man who has been up front about his need to be independent; a sexy, single man who had no intention of settling down; a man who was so hurt after losing his child that he's formed a wall around his heart that no sane woman would try to scale. He's your bodyguard, Randi. Bought and paid for by your brothers. Don't be stupid enough to throw love into the mix. You'll only get hurt if you do.

Kurt added a chunk of wood to the fire. The mossy fir sizzled and popped. "And still you believe him. Defend him."

"That's not what I was doing. I was just...I mean, if he's guilty, okay. But...I still believe in innocent until proven guilty. That's the law, isn't it?"

"Right. That's the law. I'll just have to prove that he's the culprit."

"If you can."

A muscle jumped in Striker's jaw as he glanced over his shoulder. "Watch me." He swung the door of the woodstove shut so hard it banged, and Joshua, startled, let up a little cry.

Randi shot across the room and scooped up her baby. "It's all right," she whispered, holding him close and kissing a downy-soft cheek. But Joshua was already revving up—his cries, originally whimpers, grew louder, and his nose was beginning to run.

Striker looked at the baby and an expression of regret darkened his gaze. "I'll go see if I can recharge the cell's battery in the truck. I've got a second phone, but it doesn't hold a charge worth crap." With that he was out the door, letting in a gust of damp, cool air before the door slammed shut behind him.

"Battery, my eye," Randi confided to her tousle-haired son. "He just wants to put a little space between us." Which was fine. She needed time to think about the complications that had become her life and to hold her child. What was it about Striker that got to her? It seemed that they were always making either love or war. With Kurt, her passions ran white-hot and ice cold. There was nothing in between. And her emotions were always raw, her nerves strung taut whenever she was around him.

Because you're falling in love with him, you idiot. Don't you see? Even now you're sneaking peeks out the window, hoping to catch a glimpse of him. You've got it bad, Randi. Real bad. If you don't watch out, Kurt Striker is going to break your heart.

* * *

From a van near Eric Brown's apartment, the would-be killer hung up the phone and didn't bother smothering a smile. High tech was just so damn great. All one needed to know was how to tap into a cellular call, and that was pretty basic stuff these days. Easy as pie.

A fine mist had collected on the windshield and traffic, wheels humming against the wet pavement, spun by the parking lot of the convenience store where the van was parked. No one looked twice at the dark vehicle with its tinted windows. No one cared. Which made things so much easier.

Taking out a map, the stalker studied the roads and terrain of central Washington. So the bitch and her lover were in the mountains. With the kid. Hiding out like scared puppies. Which was fine and dandy. It wouldn't take long to flush her out and watch her run. The only question was, which way would Randi McCafferty flee?

To her condo on the lake?

Or back to Daddy's ranch and that herd of tough-as-nails brothers?

West?

Or east?

It didn't matter. What was the old saying? Patience was a virtue. Yeah, well, probably overrated, but there was another adage... Revenge is best served up cold.

Hmmph. Cold or hot, it didn't matter. Just as long as vengeance was served.

And it would be. No doubt about it.

The baby was fussy as if he, too, could feel the charged atmosphere between Randi and Kurt.

Randi changed Joshua's diaper and gave up on the column she'd been composing on Striker's computer. The article would have to wait. Until her son was calmer. Quieter.

Joshua had been out of sorts for two days now and Randi didn't blame him. Being here, trapped with Kurt Striker, was driving her crazy. It was little wonder her baby had picked up on the emotional pressure. But Randi was afraid there was more to the baby's cries than his just being out of sorts.

Joshua was usually a happy infant but now he cried almost constantly. Nothing would calm him until he fell asleep. His face seemed rosier than usual and his nose ran a bit. Randi checked his temperature and it was up a degree, so she was watching her child with an eagle eye and trying like crazy not to panic. She could deal with this. She was his mother. Okay, so she was a *new* mother, but some things are instinctive, right? She should know what to do. Women raised babies all the time, married women, single women, rich women, poor women. Surely there wasn't a secret that had somehow, through the ages, been cosmically and genetically denied to her and her alone. No way. She could deal with a little runny nose, a slight fever, the hint of a cough. She was Joshua's mother, for God's sake.

While trying to convince herself of her maternal infallibility, she wrapped Joshua in blankets, held him whenever she could, prayed that he'd snap out of it and generally worried that she was doing everything wrong.

"If he doesn't get better, I want to take him to a pediatrician," she told Kurt on the third day.

"You think something's wrong?" Striker had just finished stoking the fire and was obviously frustrated that he'd not heard back from the police or Eric Brown.

"I just want to make certain that he's okay."

"I don't think we can leave just yet." Striker walked over

to the baby. With amazing gentleness, he plucked Joshua out of Randi's arms and, squatting, cradled Randi's son as if he'd done it all his life. "How're ya doin', sport?" he asked, and the baby blinked, then blew bubbles with his tiny lips. With a smile so tender it touched Randi's heart, Striker glanced up at her. "Seems fine to me."

"But he's been fussy."

"Must take after his mother."

"His temperature is running a little hot."

He crooked an eyebrow and his gaze raked her from her feet to her chest, where he stopped, pointedly, then finally looked into her eyes.

"Say it and die," she warned.

"Wouldn't dare, lady. You've got me runnin' scared." He handed Joshua back to her.

"Very funny." She pretended to be angry, though she couldn't help but smile. "Okay, okay, so maybe I'm over-reacting."

"Give the kid a chance. He might have a little cold, but we'll keep an eye on it."

"Easy for you to say. You're not a parent..." She let her voice fade as she saw Striker flinch. "Oh, God, I'm sorry," she whispered, wishing she could take back the thought-less comment. But it was too late. The damage had been done. No doubt Kurt was reminded of the day he'd lost his own precious daughter.

"Just watch him," Striker advised, then walked outside.

Randi mentally kicked herself from one side of the cabin to the other. She thought about running after him, but de-cided against it. No...they all needed a little space. She thought of her condo in Seattle. If she were there...then what would she do? She'd be alone and have to leave Joshua with a babysitter.

Yeah, a professional. Someone who probably understands crying, fussy babies with runny noses a helluva lot better than you.

But the thought wasn't calming.

And there still was the issue of someone having been inside her place. Someone having a key. The more she considered it, the more convinced she was that someone had broken in—or just walked in—and made himself at home. A shiver ran across the nape of Randi's neck. The thought of someone being so bold, so arrogant, so damn intrusive bothered her. Of course, she could change the locks, but she couldn't change the fact that she and the baby were alone in a city of strangers. Yes, she had a few friends, but who could she really depend upon?

She glanced at the window and saw Kurt striding to his truck. Tall. Rangy. Tough as nails, but with a kinder, more human side, as well. Sunlight caught against his bare head, glinting the lighter brown strands gold and the dusting of beard shadowing his chin. He was a handsome, complicated man but one she felt she could trust, one she could easily love. She thought of their nights together, sometimes tempestuously hot, other times incredibly tender. Biting on her lower lip, she told herself he wasn't the man for her. Theirs was destined to be one of those star-crossed affairs that could never develop into a lasting relationship.

She twisted the locket in her fingers as she watched Kurt climb into the truck. She tried not to notice the way his jeans fit tight around his long, muscular legs, or the angle of his jaw—rock-hard and incredibly masculine. She refused to dwell on the fact that his jacket stretched over the shoulders she'd traced with her fingers as she'd made love to him. Oh, Lord, what was she doing?

* * *

It didn't feel right.

Something about the way the case was coming down felt disjointed, out of sync.

Two days had passed since Eric Brown had called and the police had taken Donahue into custody, and yet Striker had the niggling sensation that wouldn't let go of him that something was off. That he was missing something vital.

He stood on the porch of the cabin and stared into old-growth timber that reached to the sky. The air was fresh from a shower earlier. Residual raindrops slid earthward from the fronds of thick ferns and long needles. Earlier, as he'd sat in the broken-down porch swing, he'd spotted a doe and her fawns, two jackrabbits and a raccoon scuttling into the thickets of fir and spruce. The sun had been out earlier, but now was sinking fast and the gloom of night was closing in. Striker was restless, felt that same itch that warned him trouble was brewing. Big trouble.

He hankered for a cigarette though he'd given up the habit ten years earlier. Only in times of stress or after two beers did he ever experience the yen for a swift hit of nicotine. Since he hadn't had a drop of liquor in days, it had to be the stress of the situation. Maybe it was because both he and Randi were experiencing a bad case of cabin fever.

Even the baby was cranky. No doubt the little guy had picked up on the vibes within the cabin. During the days the tension between him and Randi had been so thick a machete would have had trouble hacking through it. And the nights had been worse. Excruciating. Sheer damn torture as he'd tried, and failed, to keep his hands off her. Though neither one of them admitted the wanting, it was there, between them, enticing and erotic, and each night they'd given in to the temptation, making love as intensely as if they both thought it would be the last time.

Which it should be, all things considered.

But the fire he felt for her, the blinding, searing passion, wasn't an emotion easily dismissed; especially not in the cold mountain nights when she was so close to him, as willing, as eager as he to touch and reconnect.

Just thinking of the passion between them caused a stiffening between his legs, a swelling that was so uncomfortable, he had to adjust himself.

Hell.

Just like a horny teenager.

He ran frustrated fingers through his hair.

Soon this would be over.

Yeah, and then what?

Are you just going to walk away?

He clenched his jaw so hard it ached, and kicked a fir cone with enough force to send it shooting deep into the woods. Not that anything was going to end soon. Unbelievable as it might seem, it looked as if Randi might be right about her ex-lover. Donahue's alibi for the day she'd been run off the road was airtight. Unbreakable. Donahue's two best friends swore that all three of them had been together in a Spokane tavern at the time. Though the border town was close enough to the Idaho panhandle and not that far from Montana, the time it would have taken Donahue to make the round-trip made it near-impossible for the cowboy or either of his cohorts to have actually done the deed.

Coupled with his friends' dubious testimony, a bartender at the tavern remembered the nefarious trio. Two other guys playing pool that day also acknowledged that the boisterous bunch had been downing beers like water that afternoon and into the evening.

Striker leaned against the weathered porch railing. There wasn't much chance that Sam Donahue had forced Randi off the road that day.

Unless he'd paid someone to try to kill her.

Kurt couldn't let it go.

Because you want it to be Donahue. Admit it. The fact that he's a mean son of a bitch and the father of Randi's baby bugs the hell out of you. You don't like to think of Randi making love to Donahue or anyone else for that matter. Just the thought of it makes you want to punch Donahue's lights out. Jeez, Striker, you'd better get out now. While you still can. The longer you're around her, the harder it's going to be to give her up.

Angry at the turn of his thoughts, he spat into the forest and rammed his hands deep into the back pockets of his jeans.

You have no right getting involved with her. She's your client and you don't want a woman fouling up your life. Especially not a woman with a kid. He thought of his own daughter and realized the pain he usually felt when he remembered her was fading. Oh, there were still plenty of memories, but they were no longer clouded in guilt. That seemed wrong. He could never forget the guilt he carried. And it stung like the bite of a whip when he realized that some of his pain had been eased by being near Randi's child. As if letting little Joshua into his heart allowed him to release the pain over Heather's loss.

"Kurt?"

The door creaked open and Randi appeared. Stupidly, his heart leaped at the sight of her.

Tousled red-brown locks, big eyes and a dusting of freckles assaulted him and he felt his gut tighten. She'd spent the morning on his computer working on a couple of new columns that she planned to email when they reached a cy-bercafé, and now, smiling enough to show off impossibly white teeth, she looked incredible. As sexy and earthy as the surrounding forest.

"How's the baby?" he asked, his voice a tad hoarser than usual.

"Sleeping. Finally." Arms huddled around her as if to ward off the cold, she walked outside and he noticed how her jeans fit so snugly over her rounded hips. The weight she'd gained while pregnant had disappeared quickly be-cause she'd been in the hospital, on IVs while in a coma; hence her inability to breast-feed, though she'd tried dili-gently once she'd awoken. So now she was slim and, if the little lines puckering her eyebrows could be believed, worried.

He felt the urge to wrap an arm over her shoulders, but didn't give in to the intimacy.

"Can we get out of here?" she asked.

"What? And leave all this luxury?" He forced a smile he didn't feel and noticed that her lips twitched despite the creases in her forehead.

"It'll be hard, I know. A sacrifice. But I think it's time."

"And go where?"

"Home."

"I'm not sure your condo is safe."

"I'm not talking about Seattle," she admitted, her brown eyes dark with thought. "I think I need to go home. Back to Montana. Until this is all sorted out. I'll call my editor and explain what's going on. He'll have to let me work from the ranch. Well, he won't have to, but I think he will."

"Wait a minute. I thought you were hell-bent to start over. To prove yourself. Take command of your life again."

"Oh, I am. Believe me." She nodded as if to convince

herself. "But I'm going to do it closer to my family." Staring at him, she inched her chin up in a gesture he'd come to recognize as pure unabashed McCafferty, a simple display of unbridled spirit, the kind of fortitude that made it impossible for her to walk away from a challenge. "Come on, Striker, let's get a move on."

He glanced around the cabin and decided she was right. It was time to return to Montana. This case had started there...and now it was time to end it. Whoever had first attacked Randi had done it when she'd attempted to go back to her roots at the Flying M. Somehow that had to be the key. Someone had felt threatened that she was returning. Someone didn't want her back at the ranch... Someone hated her enough to try to kill her and her unborn child....

His mind clicked.

New images appeared.

The baby. Once again, Striker thought Joshua was the center of this maelstrom. Didn't children bring out the deepest of emotions? Hadn't he felt them himself?

It was possible that whoever had started the attacks on Randi had done so with a single, deadly purpose in mind that Kurt hadn't quite understood. Perhaps Striker, Randi, the McCaffertys and even Sam Donahue had been manipulated. If so...there was only one person who would take Randi's fame and pregnancy as a personal slap in the face. And Kurt felt certain he knew who the culprit was.

"What do you know about Patsy Donahue?" he asked suddenly.

Randi started. "Sam's wife, or ex-wife, or whatever she is?"

"Yeah."

"Not a lot." Lifting a shoulder, Randi said, "Patsy was a year ahead of me in high school, the family didn't have much money and she got married right after she graduated, to her first boyfriend, Ned Lefever."

"You weren't friends with Patsy?"

"Hardly." Randi shook her head. "She never liked me much. Her dad had worked for mine, then her folks split up and I think she even had a crush on Slade, before Ned... well, it's complicated."

"Explain. We've got time."

"I won some riding competition once and edged her out and...oh, this is really so high school, but Ned asked me to the prom. He and Patsy were broken up at the time."

"Did you go?"

"To the prom, yes. But not with Ned. I already had a date. And I wasn't interested in Ned Lefever. I thought he was a blowhard and a braggart." Randi rested a hand against the battle-scarred railing as she rolled back the years. "It was weird, though. All night long, during the dance, I was on the receiving end of looks that could kill. From Patsy. As if I was to blame for Ned's—" She froze. "Oh, God, you think Patsy's behind the attacks, don't you?"

Kurt's eyes held hers. "I'd bet my life on it."

Chapter 12

"How could she let herself get tangled up with the likes of Donahue?" Matt grumbled to his brother as he uncinched Diablo Rojo's saddle. For his efforts, the Appaloosa swung his head around in hopes of taking a nip out of Matt's leg. Deftly Matt sidestepped the nip. "You never learn, do you?" he muttered to the fiery colt.

Rojo snorted, stamping a foot in the barn and tossing his devilish head. Matt, Slade and Larry Todd, the recently re-hired foreman, had been riding nearly all day, searching for strays, calves who might have been separated from the herd in the cold Montana winter. Spring was still a few months off and the weather had been fierce since Christmas, snow drifting to the eaves of some of the outbuildings.

Larry had already taken off, but Slade and Matt were cooling down their horses now that three bawling, near-frozen calves had been reunited with their mothers. The barn was warm and smelled of dust, dry straw and horseflesh. The same smells Matt had grown up with. Harold, their father's crippled old spaniel, was lying near the tack-room door, his tail thumping whenever Matt glanced in his direction.

Slade unhooked The General's bridle and the big geld-ing pushed against Slade's chest with his great head. He rubbed the horse's crooked white blaze and said, "I don't think Randi planned on getting involved with Donahue." The brothers had been discussing their sister's situation most of the day, hoping to find some answers to all of their questions.

"Hell, the man was married. I bet Patsy put up one helluva ruckus when she found out."

Slade nodded.

"She always was a hothead. She never liked Randi, ei-ther, not since Randi beat her out of some competition when they were in high school."

"What competition?" Slade scooped oats from a barrel with an old coffee can. The General, always eager for food, nickered softly. As Slade poured the grain into the manger, the old chestnut was already chomping.

"I can't remember. I wasn't around, but Dad mentioned it once. Something about horse racing, yeah, barrel rac-ing, when they were kids. Randi beat Patsy, and Patsy did something to her at school the next week."

Slade began rubbing The General down. "Wasn't that Patsy Ellis? Jesus, I think she had a thing for me once."

"You always think women are interested in you."

"Don't tell Jamie."

"Right." Matt was feeding Rojo. Thankfully the colt was finally more interested in food than in taking a nip out of Matt's hide. "That was her maiden name. Right after high school she married Ned Lefever. A few years later they were divorced and a while after that she took up with Donahue, married him. It must really have teed her off that he ended up cheating on her with an old rival."

"A woman scorned," Slade muttered as the barn door opened and Kelly, her eyes bright, her cheeks nearly as red as the strands of hair escaping from her stocking cap, burst inside. Harold gave off a gruff bark.

"Shh," Kelly reprimanded, though she bent over to pat the old dog's head. Snow had collected on her eyelashes and was melting on her skin. To Matt, as always, she looked sweet and sexy and was the most incredible woman to walk this earth. "I just got a call from Striker," she announced breathlessly as she straightened. "He and Randi are on their way back here, and guess what? They think Patsy Donahue is behind all this."

Matt and Slade exchanged glances.

"I've already checked with Espinoza, and the police are looking for her, just to ask her some questions. I put a call in to Charlie Caldwell's ex-girlfriend and guess who handed her over the keys to the maroon Ford van that edged Randi's Jeep off the road? Good old Patsy."

Slade's grin moved from one side of his face to the other. "Your husband and I had just come up with the same idea," he said.

"No way."

"Honest to God." Matt held up a gloved hand as if he was being sworn in at a trial.

"Great. Now you can both be honorary detectives and form your own posse or something."

Matt tossed aside the brush and walked out of Diablo Rojo's stall. "Don't I at least get a kiss for being so smart?" he teased.

"If you were so smart why didn't you come up with this

idea months ago and save us all a lot of grief. Forget the kiss, McCafferty." She winked at him and his heart galumphed. He'd never figured out why she got to him so, how when she walked into the room, everything else melted into the background. "Besides," she said coyly, "I expected smart when I married you."

"And good-looking and sexy?" he asked, and heard his brother guffaw from The General's stall.

"Minimum requirements," she teased. Matt dropped a kiss on her forehead and molded his glove over the slight curvature of her belly where his unborn child was growing. "Come on, you good-looking, sexy son of a gun," she began, pulling on the tabs of his jeans.

"On my way," Slade intercepted.

"I think she was talking to me." Matt shot his brother a look that could cut through steel.

"Both of you!" Kelly insisted, backing toward the door. "Let's go have a little heart-to-heart with Patsy Donahue."

"I think you'd better leave that to the police," Matt said.

"I was the police, remember?"

"Yeah, but now you're my wife, the mother of my not-yet-born child and Patsy could be dangerous."

"I'm not afraid."

"Spoken like a true McCafferty," Slade said as he slipped from The General's stall and tested the latch to make certain it was secure. "But maybe you should leave this to the Brothers McCafferty."

"We're like the Three Musketeers," Matt said.

"I won't say the obvious about a certain trio of stooges," she baited, and for her insolence, Matt whipped her off her feet and hugged her.

"Sometimes, woman, you try my patience."

She laughed and winked up at him with sassy insolence as he set her on her feet.

"Leave this to the men," Matt insisted as he held the barn door open and a blast of icy Montana wind swept inside.

"In your dreams, boys." Kelly adjusted the scarf around her neck as she trudged through the snow toward the ranch house. Not far from the barn stood the remains of the stables, blackened and charred, in stark contrast to the pristine mantle of white and a glaring reminder of the trouble that had beset the family ever since Randi's fateful drive east. "Look," Kelly said, sending her husband a determined glare. "I've been involved with this case since the beginning. Patsy Donahue is mine."

"Guess what?" Kurt asked as he clicked off the cell phone. They were driving east through Idaho, closing in on the western Montana border. Night was coming and fast, no moon or stars visible through the thick clouds blanketing the mountains. "That was Kelly. She and Espinoza and your brothers went over to Patsy Donahue's place."

"Let me guess." Randi adjusted the zipper of her jacket. "Patsy is missing."

"Hasn't been at her house for days, if the stacked-up mail is to be believed."

"Great." Randi was disheartened. Would this nightmare never end? It was unbelievable to think that one woman could wreak such havoc, be so dangerous or so desperate. Could Patsy hate her that much as to try to kill her? Kill her baby? Harm her brothers?

"I just don't get it," Randi said as she turned toward the backseat to check on Joshua. The baby, lulled by the hum of the truck's engine and the gentle motion of the spinning wheels, was sleeping soundly, nestled in his car seat. "Why take it out on the ranch…I mean, if she had a thing against me, why harm my brothers?"

"The way I figure it, Thorne's plane crash was an accident. Patsy wasn't involved in that. But the attacks on you were personal and the fire in the stable was to keep you frightened, maintain a level of terror."

"Well, it worked. Slade nearly lost his life and the livestock… Dear God, why put the animals in jeopardy?" She bit her lip and stared at the few flakes of snow slowly falling from a darkening sky. Sagebrush and scrub pine poked through the white, snow-covered landscape, but the road was clear, the headlights of Striker's truck illuminating the ribbon of frigid pavement stretching before them.

"She's angry. Not just at you but at your family. Probably because she doesn't have much of one. Besides, you own the lion's share of the ranch. She must've figured that hurting the ranch and hurting your brothers was hurting you." He flicked a look through the rearview mirror. "I just feel like a fool for not seeing it sooner."

"No one did," she admitted, though that thought was dismal. Maybe when they arrived at the ranch, Patsy would be in custody. Silently Randi crossed her fingers. "So what's going to happen to Sam?"

"He's being questioned. Just because he wasn't responsible for harming you doesn't mean he's not a criminal. If you testify about his animal abuse, illegal betting and his throwing of the rodeo competitions, we'll have a good start in bringing him to justice. There's no telling what the authorities will dig up now that they've been pointed in the right direction."

"Of course I'll testify."

"It won't be easy. He'll be sitting at the defense table, staring at you, hearing every word."

"I know how it works," she retorted, then softened her tone as they passed through a small timber town where only a few lights were winking from the houses scattered near the road and a sawmill stood idle, elevators and sheds ghostlike and hulking around a gravel parking lot and a pile of sawdust several stories high. "But the truth is the truth," Randi continued, "no matter who's listening. Believe me, I'm over Sam Donahue. I would have taken all of the evidence I'd gathered against him to the rodeo commission and the authorities if I hadn't been sidetracked and sent to the hospital." She leaned back against the seat as the miles sped beneath the truck's tires. "I had worried about it. Wondered how I would face Joshua's father. But that's over. Now I'm sure I can face him. The way I look at it, Sam Donahue was the sperm donor that created my son. It takes a lot more to be a real father."

The baby started coughing and Randi turned to him. Kurt glanced back, as well. Joshua's little face was bright red, his eyes glassy. "How much longer until we get to Grand Hope?"

"Probably eight or nine hours."

"I'm worried about the baby."

"I am, too," Kurt admitted as he glared at the road ahead.

Joshua, as if he knew they were talking about him, gave off a soft little whimper.

"Give me the cell phone," Randi said. She couldn't stand it another minute. Joshua wasn't getting any better; in fact, he was worsening, and her worries were going into overdrive. Kurt handed her the phone, and she, trying to calm her case of nerves, dialed the ranch house as she plugged in the adapter to the cigarette lighter.

"Hello. Flying M Ranch," Juanita said, her accent barely detectible.

Randi nearly melted with relief at the sound of the house-keeper's voice. "Juanita, this is Randi."

"Oh, Miss Randi! *¡Dios!,* where are you? And the *niño.* How is he?"

"That's why I'm calling. We're on our way back to the ranch, but Joshua's feverish and I'm worried. Is Nicole there?"

"Oh, no. She is with your brother and they are at their new house, talking with the builder."

"Do you have her pager number?"

"¡Sí!" Quickly, Juanita rattled off not only the telephone number for Nicole's pager, but Thorne's cell phone, as well. "Call them now, and you keep that baby warm." Juanita muttered something in Spanish that Randi interpreted as a prayer before hanging up. Immediately Randi dialed Thorne's cell and once he answered, she insisted on talking to his wife. Nicole had admitted Randi into the hospital after the accident, and with the aid of Dr. Arnold, a pediatrician on the staff of St. James, had taken care of Joshua during the first tenuous hours of his young life.

Now, she said, "Keep fluids in him, watch his temperature, keep him warm, and I'll put a call into Gus Arnold. He's still your pediatrician, right?"

"Yes."

"Then you're in good hands. Gus is the best. I'll make sure that either he or one of his partners meets us at the hospital. When do you think you'll get here?"

"Kurt's saying about eight or nine hours. I'll call when we're closer."

"I'll be there," Nicole assured her, and Randi was thankful for her sister-in-law's reassurances. "Now, how are you doing?"

"Fine," Randi said, though that was a bit of a stretch. "Eager to get home, though."

"I'll bet—oh! What...?" Her voice faded a bit as if she'd turned her head, and Randi heard only part of a conversation before Nicole said, "Look, your brother is dying to talk to you. Humor him, would you?"

"Sure."

"Randi?" Thorne's voice boomed over the phone and Randi felt the unlikely urge to break down and cry. "What the hell's going on?" Thorne demanded. "Kelly seems to think that Patsy Donahue is the one behind all this trouble."

"It looks that way."

"And now Patsy's gone missing? Why the hell hasn't Striker found her?"

"Because he's been babysitting me," Randi said, suddenly defensive. No one could fault Kurt; not even her brothers. From the corner of her eye Randi noticed Kurt wince, his hands gripping the steering wheel even harder. "He's got someone on it."

"Hell's bells, so does Bob Espinoza, but no one seems to be able to find her. It's time to call in the FBI and the CIA and the state police and the damn federal marshals!"

"She'll be found," Randi assured him, though she, herself, doubted her words. "It's just a matter of time."

"It can't happen soon enough to suit me." He paused, then, "Tell me about J.R. How is he?"

"*Joshua's* running a temperature and has a cold. I'm meeting Nicole at St. James Hospital."

"I'll be there, too."

"You? A big corporate executive? Don't you have better things to do?" she teased, and he laughed.

"Yeah, right now I'm discussing the kind of toilet to go into the new house. Believe me, it's a major decision.

Nicole's leaning toward the low-flow, water-conservation model, but I think we should go standard."

"I think I've heard enough," Randi said, giggling. Some of her tension ebbed a bit.

"You and me both. We haven't even started with colors yet. I'm leaning toward white."

"Big surprise, oh, conservative one."

He chuckled. "Well, it's too damn dark and cold to make many more decisions tonight. That's what happens when you're married to a doctor who works sixty or seventy hours a week and then gets detained at the hospital."

"Poor baby," Randi mocked.

"Uh-oh, they need me," he said, but his voice was fading, the connection breaking up. "I think…going to check into…sinks and…see you in a few hours…"

"Thorne? Are you there?"

Only crackle.

"I'm losing you!"

"Randi?" Thorne's voice was suddenly strong.

"Yeah?"

"I'm glad you're coming home."

"Me, too," she said, and her throat caught as she envisioned her oldest half brother with his black hair and intense gray eyes. She imagined the concern etched on his strong features. "Give my love to…" But the connection was lost, as they were deep in the mountains. Reluctantly, she clicked the cell phone off.

"He wants to know why I haven't tracked Patsy down yet," Striker surmised, his lips blade-thin.

"He wants to know why *no one's* tracked Patsy down. Your name came up, yes, but so did Detective Espinoza's, along with every government agency known to man. You have to understand one thing about Thorne. He gives an order and he expects immediate, and I mean im-me-di-ate, results. Which, of course, is impossible."

"I'm with him, though," Kurt said. "The sooner we nail Patsy Donahue, the better."

Randi wanted to agree with him, but there was a part of her that balked, for she knew that the minute Patsy was located and locked away, Kurt would be gone. Out of her life forever. Her heart twisted and she wondered how she'd ever let him go. It was silly really. She'd only known him for a month or so and only intensely for a week.

And yet she would miss him.

More than she'd ever thought possible.

This entire midnight run to Montana seemed doomed. Joshua's fever was worsening, there was talk of a blizzard ahead, and somewhere in the night, Patsy Donahue was planning another attack. Randi could feel it in her bones. She shivered.

"Cold?" Kurt adjusted the heater.

"I'm fine." But it was a lie. They both knew it. Every time a vehicle approached, Randi tensed, half expecting the driver to crank on the wheel and sideswipe Striker's truck. Silently she prayed that they'd reach Grand Hope without any incident, that her baby would recover quickly and that Kurt Striker would be a part of her life forever. It was a hard fact to face, one she'd denied for a long time, but no protests to herself or anyone else could overcome the God's honest truth: Randi McCafferty had fallen in love with Kurt Striker.

Patsy drummed gloved fingers on the wheel of her stolen rig, an older-model SUV that had been parked for hours at a bar on the interstate in Idaho. No one would be able to connect her to the theft. She'd ditched her van on an abandoned road near Dalles, Oregon, gotten on a bus and traveled east until the truck stop, where she'd located the rig and switched license plates with some she'd lifted while in Seattle. By the time anyone pieced together what she'd done, it would be too late. She was behind Striker's pickup, probably by an hour or so, but she figured she could make up the distance. It would take time, but eventually she'd be able to catch the bitch.

And then there would be hell to pay.

Her speedometer hovered near seventy, but she pushed on the accelerator and pumped up the volume on the radio. An old Rolling Stones tune reverberated through the speakers. Mick Jagger was screaming about getting no satisfaction. Usually Patsy identified with the song. But not tonight. Tonight she intended to get all the satisfaction she'd been lacking in recent years.

The SUV flew down the freeway. Patsy didn't let up for a second. She'd driven in dry snow all her life and felt no fear.

By daybreak her mission would be accomplished.

Randi McCafferty and anyone stupid enough to be with the bitch would be dead.

Chapter 13

The baby wouldn't stop crying.

Nothing Randi did stopped the wails coming from the backseat and Striker felt helpless. He drove as fast as he dared while Randi twisted in her seat, trying to feed Joshua or comfort him, but the baby was having none of it.

Striker gritted his teeth and hoped that the baby's fever hadn't climbed higher. He thought of the pain of losing a child and knew he had to do something, *anything* to prevent the little guy's life from slipping away.

He gunned the pickup ever faster, but the terrain had become rough, with sharp turns and steep grades as they drove deep into the foothills of the Montana mountains.

"He's still very warm," Randi said, touching her son's cheek.

"We'll be there in less than an hour," Striker assured her. "Hang in there."

"If he will," Randi whispered hoarsely, and it tore his heart to hear her desperation.

"I think it's better that he's crying rather than listless," Striker offered, knowing it was little consolation.

"I guess. Maybe we should get off and try to find a clinic."

"In the rinky-dink towns around here? At three in the morning? St. James is the nearest hospital. Just call Nicole and tell her we'll be there in forty-five minutes."

"All right." She reached for the phone just as Striker glanced in the rearview mirror. Headlights were bearing down on them and fast, even though he was doing near sixty on the straight parts of this curving, treacherous section of interstate. At the corners he'd had to slow to near thirty and he'd spotted the vehicle behind him gaining, taking the corners wide. "Hang on," he said.

"What?"

"I've got someone on my tail and closing fast. It would be best if I let them go around me." He saw a wide spot in the road, slowed down, and the other vehicle shot past, a blur of dark paint and shiny wheels.

"We'll probably catch up to him rolled over in the ditch ahead."

"Great," she whispered.

He took a turn a little fast and the wheels slid, so he slowed a bit. As he passed by an old logging road, he thought he saw a dark vehicle. Idling. No headlights or taillights visible, but exhaust fogging the cold night air. The same fool who'd passed them? The hairs on the back of his neck lifted.

It was too dark to be certain and he told himself that he was just being paranoid. No one in his right mind would be sitting in their rig in the dark. His gut clenched. Of course no one in his *right mind* would be there. But what about a woman no longer in control of her faculties, a woman hell-bent for revenge, a woman like Patsy Donahue?

No way, Striker. You're tired and jumping at shadows. That's all.

Pull yourself together.

He peered into the rearview mirror and saw nothing in the darkness. No headlights beyond the snow flurries…or did he? Was there a vehicle barreling after him, one with no headlights, one using his taillights to guide it? His mouth was suddenly desert dry. The image took shape then faded. His mind playing tricks on him. Nothing more. God, he hoped so.

"What?" Randi asked, sensing his apprehension. The baby was still crying, but more softly now. The road was steep and winding and he cut his speed in order to keep the truck on the asphalt.

"Look behind us. See anything?"

Again Randi twisted in her seat and peered through the window over the back of the king cab. She squinted hard. "No. Why?"

He scowled, saw his own reflection in the mirror. "I thought I saw something. A shadow."

"A shadow?"

"Of a car. I thought someone might be following us with his lights out."

"In this terrain? In the dark?" she asked, and then sucked in her breath and stared hard through the window. "I don't see anything."

"Good." He felt a second's relief. This would be the worst place to encounter danger. The road was barely two lanes with steep mountains on one side and a slim guardrail on the other. Beyond the barrier was a sheer cliff where only the tops of trees were visible in the glare of his headlights as he swept around the corners.

Randi didn't stop looking through the window, searching the darkness, and he could tell by the way she held on to the back of the seat, her white-knuckled grasp a death grip, that, she, too, was concerned. His hands began to sweat on the wheel, but he told himself they were all right, they would make it, they only had a few more miles. He thought of how, in the past few weeks, he'd fallen for Randi McCafferty hook, line and proverbial sinker. With a glance in her direction, his heart filled. He couldn't imagine life without her or without little Joshua. As much as he'd sworn after Heather's death never to get close to a woman or a child again, he'd broken his own pact with himself. And it was too late to change his mind. His stubborn heart just wouldn't let him. Maybe it was time to tell her. To be honest. Let her know how he felt.

Why?

Come on, Striker, are you so full of yourself to imagine she loves you? And what about the kid? Didn't you swear off fatherhood for good? What are you doing considering becoming a father again? Why would you set yourself up for that kind of heartache all over again? Remember Heather? Do you really think you have it in you to be a parent?

The arguments tore through his mind. Nonetheless, he had to tell her. "Randi?"

"What?" She was still staring out the back window.

"About the last few nights—"

"Please," she said, refusing to look his way. "You don't have to explain. Neither of us planned what happened."

"But you should know how I feel."

He noticed her tense. She swallowed hard. "Maybe I don't want to," she whispered before she gasped. "Oh, God, no!"

"What?"

"I think...I think there *is* someone back there. Every once in a while I see an image and then it fades into the background. You don't think..."

Kurt stared into the rearview mirror. "Hell." He saw it too. The outline of a dark vehicle without its lights on, driving blind, bearing down, swerving carelessly from one side of the road to the other and then melding with the night. He pressed hard on the accelerator. "Keep your eye on it and call the police."

She reached for the phone. Dialed 911.

Nothing.

"Damn."

She tried again and was rewarded by a beeping of the cell. "No signal," she said, staring through the window as the baby cried.

"Keep trying." Kurt took a corner too fast, the wheels spun and they swung wide, into the oncoming lane. "Damn it."

"It's getting closer!"

Kurt saw the vehicle now, looming behind them, dangerously close as they screeched around corners. "Hell."

"Do you think it's Patsy?"

"Unless there's some other nutcase running loose."

"Oh, God..." Randi sounded frantic. "What's she going to do?"

"I don't know." But he had only to think of the accident where Randi was forced off the road to come up with a horrific scenario.

Randi punched out the number of the police again. "The call's going through! Where are we? I'll have to give our location...oh, no...lost the signal again."

"Hit redial!" Kurt ordered. A sign at the edge of the road warned of a steep downgrade.

"Maybe you should just slow down," Randi said. "Force her to slow."

"What if she's got a gun. A rifle?"

"A gun?"

The vehicle switched on its lights suddenly and seemed to leap forward.

Kurt swung to the inside, toward the mountain.

The SUV bore down on them.

A sharp corner loomed. A sign said that maximum speed for the corner was thirty-five. The needle of his speedometer was pushing sixty. He shifted down. Pumped the brakes. Squealed around the corner, fishtailing.

The SUV didn't give up. "She's getting closer," Randi cried as she kept redialing. "Oh, God!"

Bam!

The nose of the trailing vehicle struck hard as Kurt hit a pothole. The truck shuddered, snaking to the guardrail, wheels bouncing over a washboard of asphalt and gravel. Kurt rode out the slide, easing into it, only changing direction at the last minute. His heart was pounding, his body sweating. He couldn't lose Randi and the baby!

"Hello! Hello! This is an emergency!" Randi cried, as if she'd gotten through to police dispatch. "Someone's trying to kill us. We're on the interstate in northern Montana." She yelled their approximate location and the highway number, then swore as the connection failed.

Thud!

Again they were battered from behind.

The front wheel hit a patch of ice and the truck began to spin, circling in what seemed like slow motion. Kurt struggled with the steering wheel, saw the guardrail and the black void beyond. Gritting his teeth, trying to keep the truck on the road, he felt the fender slam into the railing and heard the horrid groan of metal ripping. Over it all the baby cried and Randi screamed. "Come on, come on," Kurt said between clenched teeth, willing the pickup to stay on the road, his shoulders aching. He couldn't lose the woman he loved, nor her child. Not now. Not this way. Not again.

"Oh, my God, look out!" Randi cried, but it was too late.

The SUV hit the truck midspin, plowing into the passenger side with a sickening crash and the rending of steel. Kurt's fingers clenched over the wheel, but the truck didn't respond. The SUV's bumper locked to the truck and together the two vehicles spun down the road, faster and faster. Trees and darkness flashed by in a blur.

Randi screamed.

The baby wailed.

Kurt swore. "Hold on!" The two melded vehicles slammed into the side of the mountain and ricocheted across the road with enough force to send the entangled trucks through the guardrail and into the black void beyond.

Somewhere there was a bell ringing...steady...never getting any louder...just a simple bleating. It was so irritating. *Answer the phone, for God's sake...answer it!* Randi's head ached, her body felt as if she'd been beaten from head to toe, there was an awful taste in her mouth and... She opened an eye and blinked. Everything was so white and blinding.

"Can you hear me? Randi?" Someone shined a light into her eyes and she recoiled. The voice was a woman's. A voice she should recognize. Randi closed her eyes. Wanted to sleep again. She was in a bed with rails...a hospital bed... how did she get here? Vaguely she remembered the smell of burning rubber and fresh pine...there had been red and blue lights and her family…all standing around…and Kurt leaning over her, whispering he loved her, his face battered and bruised and bleeding… Or had it been a dream? Kurt… where the hell was Kurt? And the baby? Joshua. Oh, God! Her eyes flew open and she tried to speak.

"Jo…Joshua?"

"The baby's okay."

Everything was blurry for a minute before she focused and saw Nicole standing in the room. Another doctor was examining her, but her eyes locked with those of her sister-in-law. Memories of the horrible night and the car wreck assailed her.

"Joshua is at home. With Juanita. As soon as you're released you can be with him."

She let out her breath, relieved that her child had survived.

"You're lucky," the doctor said, and Nicole was nodding behind him. *Lucky? Lucky?* There didn't seem anything the least bit lucky about what happened.

"Kurt?" she managed to get out though her throat was raw, her words only a whisper.

"He's all right."

Thank God. Slowly turning her head, Randi looked around. The hospital room was stark. An IV dripped fluid into her wrist, a monitor showed her heartbeat and kept up the beeping she'd heard as she'd awoken. Flowers stood in vases on a windowsill.

"I…I want to see…my baby…and…and Striker."

"You've been in the hospital two days, Randi," Nicole said. "With a concussion and a broken wrist. J.R., er, Joshua, had a bad cold but didn't suffer anything from the accident. Luckily there was an ambulance only fifteen minutes away from the site of the accident. Police dispatch had gotten your message, so they were able to get to you fairly quickly."

"Where's Kurt?"

Nicole cleared his throat. "Gone."

Randi's heart sank. He'd already left. The ache within her grew.

"He had some eye damage and a dislocated shoulder."

"And he just left."

Little lines gathered between Nicole's eyebrows. "Yes. I know that he went to Seattle to see a specialist. An optic neurologist."

Randi forced the words over her tongue. "How bad is his vision?"

"I don't know."

"Is he blind?"

"I really don't know, Randi."

She felt as if her sister-in-law was holding back. "Kurt's not coming back, is he?"

Nicole took her hand and twined strong fingers between Randi's. "I'm not certain, but since you're going to ask, if I were a betting woman, I'd have to say 'No, I don't think so.' He and Thorne had words. Now, please, take your doctor's advice and rest. You have a baby waiting for you at the Flying M and three half brothers who are anxious for you to come home." Nicole squeezed Randi's fingers and Randi closed her eyes. So they'd survived.

"What about Patsy?" she asked.

"In custody. As luck would have it, she got away unscathed."

The doctor attending her cleared his throat. "You really do need to rest," he said.

"Like hell." She scrabbled for the button to raise her head. "I want to get out of here and see my baby and—"

Excruciating pain splintered through her brain. She sank back on her pillow. "Maybe you're right," she admitted. She had to get well. For Joshua.

And what about Kurt? Her heart ached at the thought that she might never see him again. Damn it, she couldn't just let him walk away.

Or could she?

Three days later she was released from the hospital and reunited with her family. Joshua was healthy again, and it felt good to hold him in her arms, to smell his baby-clean scent. Juanita was in her element, fussing and clucking over Randi and the baby, generally bossing her brothers around and running the house.

Larry Todd seemed to have forgiven Randi for letting him go, though he insisted on a signed contract for his work, and even Bill Withers, after hearing of the accident, had agreed to allow Randi to write her column from Montana. "Just don't let it get out," he said over the phone. "People around here might get the idea that I'm a softie."

"I wouldn't lose any sleep over it if I were you," Randi said before hanging up and deciding to tackle her oldest brother. She checked on the baby and found him sleeping in his crib, then, with her arm in a sling, made her way downstairs. The smells of chocolate and maple wafted from the kitchen, where Juanita was baking.

Though Slade and Matt were nowhere to be found, she located Thorne at his desk in the den. He sat at his computer, a neglected cup of coffee at his side. No doubt he was working on some corporate buyout, a lawsuit, the ever-changing plans for his house, or concocting some new way to make his next million. Randi didn't care what he was doing. He could damn well be interrupted.

"I heard you gave Striker a bad time." She was on pain medication but was steady enough on her feet to loom above the desk in her bathrobe and slippers.

Thorne looked up at her and smiled. "You heard right."

"Blamed him for what happened to me and Joshua."

"I might have come down on him a little hard," her brother admitted with uncharacteristic equanimity.

"You had no right, you know. He did his best."

"And it wasn't good enough. You were nearly killed. So was Joshua."

"We survived. Because of Kurt."

A smile twitched at the corners of his mouth. "I figured that out."

"You did?"

"Yep." He reached into his drawer and held out two pieces of a torn check. "Striker wouldn't accept any payment. He felt bad about what happened."

"And you made it worse."

"Nah." He leaned back in the desk chair until it squeaked and tented his hands as he looked up at her. "Well, okay, I did, but I changed my mind."

"What good does that do?"

"A lot," he said.

She narrowed her eyes. "You're up to something."

"Making amends."

"That sounds ominous."

"I don't think so." He glanced to the window and Randi heard it then, the rumble of an engine. "Looks like our brothers are back."

"They've been away?"

"Mmm. Come on." He climbed out of his desk chair and walked with her to the front door. She looked out the window and saw Matt and Slade climb out of a Jeep. But there was another man with them and in a pulse beat she recognized Kurt. Her heart nearly jumped from her chest and she threw open the door, nearly tripping on Harold as she raced across the porch.

"Wait!" Thorne cried, but she was already running along the path beaten in the snow, her slippers little protection, her robe billowing in the cold winter air.

"Kurt!" she yelled, and only then noticed the eyepatch. He turned and a smile split his square jaw. Without thinking, she flung herself into his arms. "God, I missed you," she whispered and felt tears stream from her eyes. His face was bruised, his good eye slightly swollen. "Why did you leave?"

"I thought it was best." His voice was husky. Raw. The arm around her strong and steady.

"Then you thought wrong." She kissed him hard and felt his mouth mold to hers, his body flex against her.

When he finally lifted his head, he was smiling. "That's what your brothers said." He glanced up at Thorne, who had followed Randi outside. He stiffened slightly.

"I'm glad you're back," Thorne said. "I made a mistake."

"What? You're actually apologizing?" Randi, still in Kurt's arms, looked over her shoulder. "This," she said to Kurt, "is a red-letter day. Thorne McCafferty never, and I mean, never, admits he's wrong."

"Amen," Matt said.

"Right on," Slade agreed.

Thorne's jaw clenched. "Will you stay?" he asked Striker.

"I'll see. Give me a second, will you." He looked at all the brothers, who suddenly found reasons to retreat to the house. "It's freezing out here and you're hurt…" He touched her wrist. "So I'll keep this simple. Randi McCafferty, will you marry me?"

"Wh-what?"

"I mean it. Ever since I met you…and that kid of yours, life hasn't been the same."

"I can't believe this," she said breathlessly.

"Do. Believe, Randi."

Her heart squeezed. Fresh tears streamed from her eyes.

"Marry me."

"Yes. Yes! Yes!" She threw her good arm around his neck and silently swore she'd never let go.

Epilogue

"I do," Randi said as she stood beneath an arbor of roses. Kurt was with her, the preacher was saying the final words and Kelly was holding Joshua as Randi's brothers stood next to Kurt and her sisters-in-law surrounded her. The backyard of the ranch was filled with guests and the summer sun cast golden rays across the acres of land.

It had been over a year since John Randall had passed on. The new stable was finished, if not painted, and Thorne and his family had moved into their house. Both Nicole and Kelly were nearly at term in the pregnancies.

"I give to you Mr. and Mrs. Kurt Striker…" The preacher's final words echoed across the acres and somewhere from Big Meadow a horse let out a loud nicker.

Randi gazed up at her bridegroom and her heart swelled. He had healed from the accident, only a small scar near one eye reminding her that his peripheral vision had been compromised.

Both Patsy and Sam Donahue had been tried and convicted and were serving time. Sam had agreed to give up all parental rights and Kurt was working with an attorney to legally adopt Joshua.

They lived here at the ranch house and Randi was able to keep working, though Kurt thought she should give up her column entitled "Solo" and start writing for young marrieds.

"Toast!" Matt cried as she and Kurt walked toward the table where a sweating ice sculpture of two running horses was melting and pink champagne bubbled from a fountain.

"To the newlyweds," Thorne said.

Randi smiled and fingered the locket at her throat. Once it had held a picture of her father and son. Now John Randall had been replaced by a small snapshot of her husband.

"To my wife," Kurt said, and touched the rim of his glass to hers.

"And my husband."

She swallowed a glass of champagne and greeted their guests. Never had she felt such joy. Never had she felt so complete. She held her son and danced on a makeshift floor as the band began to play and shadows began to crawl across the vast acres of the Flying M.

"I love you," Kurt whispered to her and she laughed.

"You'd better! Forever!"

"That's an awful long time."

"I know. Isn't it wonderful?" she teased.

"The best." He kissed her and held her for a long minute, then they walked through the guests and she saw her brothers with their wives... Finally all of the McCafferty children were married. As John Randall McCafferty had wanted. More grandchildren were on the way.

She could almost hear her father saying to her, "Good goin', Randi girl. About time you tied the knot."

As she danced with her new husband, she could feel her father's presence and she didn't doubt for a second that had he been here, the old man would've been proud.

Another generation of McCaffertys was on its way.

* * * * *

A FATHER FOR HER BABY

B.J. Daniels

This is for my brother, Charles Allen Johnson.
Here's wishing all your dreams come true.
A woman you can love. A life that makes you happy.
And above all the freedom to enjoy what you love most.
Good luck, little brother. I'm rooting for you.

Chapter 1

"Don't tell me you haven't found her," the angry voice bellowed on the other end of the phone line.

That was the *last* thing Sanders Killhorn wanted to tell his brother, Derrick.

"A woman that pregnant can't have just disappeared into thin air," Derrick snapped.

But Derrick's wife had done exactly that. Disappeared. Seven months of searching, and Sanders had found no trace of Kit. He crossed the room to the motel window, dragging the phone with him, and peered out. The sun hung on the Dallas skyline, fiery red. As red as Kit's hair.

"What about the guy who said he'd seen her in Texas City?" Derrick demanded.

"I talked to him." Behind Sanders, only the flickering television screen lit the nondescript motel room as another day dissolved into darkness and defeat. "He was only interested in the reward. He didn't know anything."

Derrick swore loudly. "I won't rest until I find my son."

His *son?* Sanders felt a chill. Derrick had no way of knowing if Kit had given birth to a boy. His brother's obsession with having a son scared him—just as it had Kit. Was that why she'd taken off?

"Someone has to have seen her," Derrick said. "Maybe she's cut her hair or dyed it."

Sanders couldn't imagine Kit doing either. But then, he couldn't imagine her taking off like she'd done, at nine months pregnant. Hadn't she known Derrick would never stop looking for her? Especially with her carrying his baby?

Sanders had tracked her from the Bozeman, Montana, bus station, where she'd abandoned Derrick's truck, as far as the Dallas, Texas, bus station. After that, she had vanished.

He'd checked every bus, train and airplane. And all the hospitals within a two-hundred-mile radius. No Kit Bannack Killhorn had given birth. At least not under her real name. Nor had anyone matching her description.

He'd also checked birth certificates for a two-month period. No Bannack. No Killhorn. Even the private investigator his brother had hired had come up empty-handed.

Sanders had grown weary of looking for his sister-in-law and wanted more than anything to return home to Montana. Especially with Christmas just days away.

"Something has to have happened to her," Derrick was saying. "Maybe she was in an accident and can't remember—"

The rest of his brother's words were lost as Sanders caught a familiar image out of the corner of his eye. He turned to stare at the television screen.

Kit's face stared back.

* * *

In a motel room across from Sanders's room, Luke stared at the same newscast, the same face on the TV screen, the same woman he'd also been chasing for seven months.

Just moments before, Luke had been electronically eavesdropping on Sanders's conversation with Derrick Killhorn and calling himself a fool. All this time, he'd been shadowing Sanders, hoping the man and his resources would lead him to Kit. But he was beginning to doubt even the great Killhorns could find the woman. And even if they did, Luke couldn't be sure she had the answers he so desperately needed.

He was ready to give up, admit he'd been wrong. He was sick of motel rooms, rental cars and eating out of foam containers. He was sick of tailing Sanders, and he damned sure hadn't done any good finding Kit on his own.

When her face flashed on the television screen, Luke gaped in disbelief, adrenaline singing through his veins. *I was right. Dammit, I was right.* He felt a jolt of satisfaction, followed quickly by fear and regret so strong that he could taste it. *Dear God, I was right.*

He kicked up the volume on the TV.

"…after an arsonist started a fire that destroyed the small private Galveston hospital last June."

Kit sat wrapped in a hospital blanket, the blazing building behind her. Her eyes caught the camera; her hand went up to shield her face from view. The image lasted only a few seconds, then was gone.

Luke cursed as he realized the newscast wasn't about Kit, but about a woman whose kidnapped baby had been returned to her.

What did any of that have to do with Kit?

A doctor came on the screen. Dr. Bernard explained that

three women had given birth on June third at the Galveston hospital just before the fire broke out. The mothers and their babies had been evacuated separately. It wasn't until later that authorities realized one of the babies had been kidnapped. The arson was still under investigation.

Luke felt his breath rush out of him. Kit. She had to be one of the mothers who'd given birth that night. That's why her face had been on the old file tape about the hospital fire back in June.

Luke shook his head in amazement. No wonder he and Sanders hadn't been able to find her. A hospital fire. That explained why no one at the area hospitals remembered Kit Killhorn.

Luke turned off the TV and stared at the empty screen, his heart pounding. He couldn't get the image of Kit out of his head. The stark terror in her eyes. The way she'd tried to hide from the camera. This lady was running scared. But what was she fleeing from? What had sent her hightailing it out of Montana? He couldn't wait to ask her.

Across town, Kit leaned over her son's crib and lovingly pulled the soft blanket up to Andy's dimpled chin. With warm fingers, she brushed his blond hair back from his angelic face and smiled down at him. She loved looking at him, and spent hours doing just that.

He'd had a big day today and she knew he must be exhausted. *She* was, after following him in all his explorations. It amazed her how quickly he learned, how quickly he changed. Over the last six and a half months she'd watched him grow, marveling at it all from his first smile and laugh to the first time he'd rolled over and crawled.

She'd named him Andrew, after her father. Unfortunately, she'd been unable to give him her father's last name,

Bannack. Nor had she used Killhorn. Either name would only have led Derrick to them. So she'd lied, providing fake names for the birth certificate to keep her baby safe.

Kit turned on the television in the room she shared with her son, hoping to catch the news and see if the predicted storm off the gulf had materialized.

But when the news came on, she found herself staring in confusion at the screen. Her face. What was she doing on TV? Old footage from the night of the fire! She remembered her terror that night when she'd seen the television news crew. Surely they hadn't ever shown this particular news clip before, or Derrick would have found her.

Her heart thudded. Why in God's name were they showing it *now?* Had the arsonist been found? Or was this about that poor woman whose baby had been kidnapped?

"After almost seven long months, Nina Fairchild and her son Dustin have been reunited," the newscaster said.

Kit felt a wave of relief. She'd silently feared that the kidnapper had taken the wrong baby the night of the fire—that Derrick had tracked her and Andy, and mistakenly stolen Nina's son.

Now the Fairchild baby was safe. Kit felt such gratitude that she hadn't caused the poor woman's pain. But at the same time, the newscast shattered any illusion that Kit could evade her past.

All these months, she'd hidden, terrified that Derrick would find her and Andy. As she'd watched her son grow and flourish, she'd convinced herself she'd done the right thing. Including lying to Dr. Bernard to get her job as a nanny. And lying to Tim Anderson so he'd pay her cash and there'd be no record of her employment.

But the moment she saw her face on TV, she knew she hadn't hidden well enough. She couldn't take the chance that Derrick hadn't seen the newscast somehow. Or at least hadn't heard about it.

She looked down at her son sleeping peacefully in his crib. Her heart thrummed with the sound of his rhythmic breathing. Tears welled in her eyes—tears of fear, anger and regret. She wiped at them, filled with another emotion, this one stronger than all the others put together: the need to protect her son. It felt almost primitive. She would give her life for Andy's.

She covered her son with a blanket and wondered if she would ever be able to find a place where they would be safe. As she began to pack, the answer chilled in her heart, filling her with terror.

As long as Derrick Killhorn was after her, no safe place existed.

Chapter 2

Luke wasn't surprised the next morning when he tailed Sanders to the office of Dr. Bernard, the obstetrician who'd probably delivered Kit's baby.

Only minutes later, Sanders came out smiling. And Luke had to give him credit. He'd gotten the information—and fast. Luke figured Sanders had greased a few palms: that would be the Killhorn way.

Luke waited, knowing the moment Sanders got into his rental car that he'd call his brother.

"I've got her," Sanders said excitedly into the cell phone. "She's working as a nanny in Galveston. I'm headed there now."

Luke would have loved to hear what Derrick was saying, because he was obviously giving Sanders instructions—long, detailed ones.

"Well, you know her better than I do," Sanders said, sounding dubious. "Okay. Sure, I can do that. Huntsville?

No, don't worry, I can convince her. All right, I'll meet you up at the airport, one way or the other."

Convince her to what? Luke wondered. Whatever it was, he didn't like the sound of it.

He followed Sanders at a safe distance into an old Galveston neighborhood with its neat rows of once-lavish houses. The sun hung high, the day was hot and humid, a sure sign of an approaching storm. But that was the least of Luke's worries. He had to get to Kit—before Derrick did.

Luke parked where he could watch Sanders approach the house and ring the doorbell. The house was large and sat on at least an acre of wooded land. *Secluded,* Luke thought. Ideal for his purposes.

And Sanders's?

He watched Sanders ring the bell again and wait. No one appeared at the door.

Luke swore under his breath. What if Kit had also seen the news program on television last night—and had taken off again? And just when he was so close.

Luke saw Sanders turn as if he'd heard something in the backyard. As Sanders started around the side of the building, Luke climbed out of the car with his equipment and headed into the trees beside the house.

The oaks had grown large and thick, making a perfect place to hide. Luke put on the headset and picked up the sound of a baby whimpering.

Through the branches, he could make out a woman with two infants in a double baby stroller on a patio in the shade of a large old oak. She was bent over, cooing softly to the fussing infant, when Sanders walked up behind her.

"Hi, Kit," Sanders said.

The woman jumped as if he'd touched her with a cattle prod. She spun around, fright evident in every line of her body. Even from this distance, Luke could see that she was ready to run. What in God's name had happened in Montana to make her this afraid?

Luke feared he already knew the answer.

"Where's Derrick?" Kit cried, fighting back a scream as her gaze leaped to look behind Sanders. "Where is he?" She reached for the stroller, her only thought to get the babies inside to safety.

"Kit, I'm here alone." Sanders had moved toward her, but stopped and held his hands out, palms up. She tightened her grip on the stroller, ready to run if she had to. "I'm here to help you."

"Help me? Derrick sent you to find me." She knew that Sanders acted as mediator, keeping peace and settling little problems for his older brother, and had since they were boys. Why else would he be here now?

"Kit, I've been worried sick about you," Sanders said. "I'm so glad I finally found you."

"How *did* you find me?" she said, glancing past him, afraid Derrick would appear at any moment.

"I saw you on TV last night."

Just as she'd feared. "I'd hoped Derrick had stopped looking for me."

Sanders smiled sadly, as if her innocence amazed him. "Kit, why did you run away in the first place?"

Didn't he know? She edged a little closer to the house.

"I'm not here to hurt you. You can tell me what's going on. I'm your friend."

She looked into his eyes and saw the same kindness she'd always seen there. Sanders had been her *only* friend in Big Sky. The only one Derrick allowed her.

"*Are* we friends?" she asked. "You're Derrick's brother. You work for him. I'm sure that's why you're here."

"That's not the only reason." He glanced into the stroller at the baby in blue. "I heard I have a nephew. He's adorable, Kit."

She nodded, her pride in her son hard to contain. At one time, she'd been excited at the prospect of Sanders being an uncle to her baby. She'd wanted Andy to have the family she'd never had.

"What's his name?" Sanders asked.

"Andrew. After my father." She saw disapproval in Sanders's eyes. Derrick had been determined the baby would be a boy—and would be named Derrick Killhorn Junior.

"Derrick's out of his mind with worry."

"I'm sure he is," she said. "But not for the reasons you might think."

"Kit, what's going on? The last time I saw you was at the clinic. You were thrilled because the doctor had said you'd be having the baby within the week. The next thing I know, you've taken off without a word."

Kit's young charge began to whimper again, and she knelt down in front of the stroller to check her, at the same time watching Sanders out of the corner of her eye. What did she think he'd do? Grab Andy and take off with him? That was more Derrick's style than Sanders's.

She straightened to find Sanders smiling at his nephew as if he'd never seen anything quite so amazing. Her heart ached with the need to trust him, to trust someone. She reminded herself of the time Derrick had wanted her to have a risky test late in her pregnancy to determine the sex of the baby. She had refused. Sanders had sided with her, saying it was too dangerous. Derrick had been furious but he'd backed down. From then on, she'd trusted Sanders to be on her side when it really mattered.

"I left the doctor's office that day to go to the construction site to see Derrick," she said. Killhorn Condominium Complex, the largest development in the history of Big Sky, Derrick had bragged. "Why didn't you let me drive you?" Sanders asked now.

Did he really not know what happened that day? Kit felt a chill and glanced toward the oak grove behind the house. Sunlight caught in the branches and dropped shadows into the dense undergrowth. She had the horrible feeling that someone was out there, watching, listening. Derrick.

She shifted her gaze back to Sanders. Seven months ago. That's when her life began to unravel. The day her husband's ex-wife, Belinda, showed up at her door.

Belinda had stared at Kit's swollen abdomen in shock. "I heard Derrick had a new wife but—"

"Derrick and I are expecting in June," Kit had said quickly.

Belinda laughed. "I can see that you're expecting, but that baby isn't Derrick's. I ought to know. I saw his test results. Derrick's sterile."

Sterile? Kit felt the earth crumble beneath her. She was one of the few people who knew Belinda could be telling the truth. Not even Sanders knew that the baby Kit carried wasn't Derrick's.

"That's ridiculous," Kit had said, fighting months of uneasiness about the odd circumstances surrounding her marriage. She clung to one statement her new husband had made. Derrick had promised her more babies, as many as she wanted. "What about the child you lost, the miscarriage?"

"What miscarriage?" Belinda gave Kit a pitying look. "I

left Derrick because he tried to get me to secretly adopt a son for him. The man's obsessed. He thinks not being able to father a son makes him less of a man." Belinda shook her head. "And now he's conned you into telling everyone this is his baby. He really got him an innocent this time."

Kit had been stunned. Did Derrick want a son badly enough that he'd lie to her?

When she'd questioned him about Belinda's claim that evening, he'd adamantly denied it, calling Belinda a liar. Kit had wanted to believe him. But the next day, when she'd seen Belinda at the doctor's office with a black eye and a cut lip, she'd known the cause before Belinda even confirmed her suspicions. Derrick had done it because of what Belinda had told her.

"Why did you go to the job site without me?" Sanders asked again.

"I wanted to talk to Derrick about Belinda," she said.

"Belinda? What lies is she spreading now? She'd do anything to hurt Derrick. I'm sure if you'd seen him on the job that day, he'd have straightened this whole thing out."

"I did see him."

Sanders frowned. "Derrick said he hadn't seen you since that morning at the house."

It came back in a flash of memory. Walking through the skeletal frame of the partially built block building, ducking beneath scaffolding, at first calling for Derrick, then moving forward silently as she followed the sound of raised voices. Deeper and deeper into the empty interior, she went, until she stood above the two men, looked down on them arguing below her.

And later, stumbling as she tried to flee, knocking over the stack of lumber. Her husband looking up at her. Had he really not seen her? "I saw him. I saw them both."

Sanders looked confused. "Them? It was after quitting time. Was one of the crew still there?"

She nodded. "A young man. I heard Derrick call him Jason."

Sanders closed his eyes and shook his head as if understanding had finally dawned. "Oh, Kit, you must have overheard the argument Derrick had with some college kid he'd fired."

"It was more than an argument."

"Come on, Derrick said the kid took a swing at him. But it couldn't have been much of a fight, because it was over by the time I got there, and I couldn't have been far behind you."

"How did Derrick seem when you arrived?"

Sanders shrugged. "He was upset. He'd left the keys in his pickup and when he saw it was gone, he thought Jason had stolen it."

"That was all he was upset about?"

"Well…" Sanders paused, then continued with a shrug, "You know how he feels about that truck. He was afraid the kid would wreck it. But then he realized you must have taken it."

"What made him think that if he didn't see me there?"

Sanders raised a brow. "The kid's motorcycle was gone. And so were you. I'd told him you'd left the clinic before I'd arrived. Who else would dare to take Derrick's new pickup?"

"You didn't see anything at the job?" she asked hopefully.

He frowned. "Like what?"

Tears filled her eyes. She shook her head slowly. Derrick had told Sanders just enough to cover for himself. "I know what I saw."

"What did you see, Kit?"

She blurted it out, desperate to say the words aloud, to finally tell someone. "I saw Derrick kill that man."

Chapter 3

"**W**hat?" Sanders stared at her. "Why would Derrick kill one of his employees?"

"I don't know why," she cried. "But I saw Derrick hit him with something." She started to describe the tool.

"A crowbar," Sanders interrupted, frowning.

"After Derrick hit him, the man fell to the ground." Her body began to tremble, her breath came hard and fast, her mind filled with the horror of the memory. "Then Derrick lifted him and dropped him in a tank filled with water." Tears coursed silently down her face. "The man struggled, but Derrick held him under. I saw the whole thing."

Sanders said nothing for a few minutes. "Kit, Derrick told me the same story but with just a little different ending. He said he tossed the kid into the tank to cool him off, letting him up as soon as he quit fighting. Then Derrick ordered him off the job site, and the kid left. And he told me about the fight *before* he knew you had taken off."

"He's lying. Don't you see—he made up that story after he saw me. I stumbled into some lumber. He looked up. He knows I saw what he did."

"Kit, I'm telling you, he didn't see you. And he certainly didn't—"

"Is everything all right, Kit?" asked a male voice from the house.

Kit turned to find her boss, Tim Anderson, in the doorway. "Fine, Tim," she said, unable to hide her relief that he'd come home early. "But would you mind taking the babies inside? I'll join you in just a minute."

"You didn't tell him, did you?" Sanders said after Tim had closed the door.

She shook her head. "I haven't told anyone. Just you." She glanced toward the grove of trees, unable to shake the feeling that they were being watched.

"I understand now why you ran, Kit." He sounded sympathetic, but also sad. "I just can't believe you'd think Derrick could kill someone. Let alone that he'd somehow gotten away with it."

"Everyone knows how powerful the Killhorns are in Big Sky—in the whole county."

"Do you really think my family has that much power?"

"Yes," she admitted, knowing that had been part of the reason she hadn't gone to the authorities once she reached Texas. "Your father's a judge, your uncle's the sheriff."

"You can't think they're in on it?"

It did sound ludicrous. It made her doubt herself. Hadn't Derrick always said she was foolish, young, incredibly naive? She replayed the memory of the last time she'd seen her husband. She studied each detail, looking for something, anything that proved Derrick's story, anything that proved her own vision somehow faulty. Sanders had explained it so well. Just a foolish misunderstanding by a pregnant woman. And yet...

"Who was the man, the one Derrick fought with? Jason what?"

"St. John," Sanders said. "Jason St. John."

"Has anyone seen him since?"

"Derrick has. He caught Jason sabotaging the job less than a week ago, but Jason got away."

Why didn't she believe that? Because she'd seen Derrick kill Jason seven months ago.

He must have seen the doubt in her expression. "Kit, I wouldn't be here trying to get you to come back if I thought Derrick was a killer. I think you know me better than that."

She felt in her heart that was true. She even started to concede, started to bend to his will the way she'd bent her whole life. But then she looked toward the house, thinking of her young son, and felt that jolt of motherness, that iron-strong will of protectiveness. "I believe you, Sanders. But I need you to find Jason St. John."

She knew he'd never locate him. Not alive, anyway.

"Find Jason St. John?" he repeated. "That's no small order. There's an APB out on him for sabotaging the job site, so I would imagine he's hiding."

Kit held her ground. "I need you to prove to me that Derrick isn't a murderer. Or help me to prove that he is."

Sanders looked at the toes of his shoes for a moment. "Kit, there's something I have to tell you. I called Derrick right after I saw you on television, then again this morning when I knew you and the baby were safe."

"You told him where I was?" she cried. Just the thought of her husband terrified her.

"Why wouldn't I tell him? I had no idea you thought he'd killed someone."

"Where is he, Sanders?"

"I'm meeting him up at the airport in less than two hours."

A shot of pure terror drove Kit back a step. "I've got to get out of here." Frantically, she turned and started for the house, but he stopped her.

"Where will you go?"

She shook her head, her eyes blurring with tears.

"You can't have saved much money," Sanders reasoned. "Do you know anyone in Texas you can stay with?"

She shook her head again. She had no one, no family. Derrick had cut her off from her friends, but she wouldn't have involved them in this, anyway, not with a murderer after her and Andy.

"What about the baby?" Sanders asked. "You won't be running alone now."

"I know," she said, hearing the panic in her own voice.

"Kit, be reasonable. How long can you and the baby last on the run? That isn't any kind of life for your son."

She knew he was right, but what choice did she have? She couldn't stay here. And she couldn't go to the authorities. Derrick Killhorn and his family were too powerful.

"You need some place to stay until Jason is found or I can prove your story. Somewhere you feel safe," Sanders said. "Maybe..." He seemed to hesitate.

Kit looked up at him hopefully.

"I know someone who has a place near Huntsville," he said after a moment. "She's a friend from college."

Kit wanted to grasp on to the idea as if it were a life raft in a stormy sea. But she hesitated. It seemed too easy. "Does Derrick know this friend?"

Sanders looked disappointed in her. "Kit, you have

to trust someone. If you can't trust me, then who do you have?"

The truth of his words hurt. She had no one but Sanders—and he knew it.

"All right," she said, praying she was doing the right thing.

He looked relieved. "I'll take you myself."

"No, you're supposed to meet Derrick at the airport. You're the only one who can convince him to leave me and Andy alone."

"All right. Then I'll hire a limo to take you to Huntsville."

"I don't need a limo."

"I want you and the baby to be comfortable," Sanders said, sounding a little hurt.

She nodded, ashamed for being so ungrateful.

"When can you be ready? I think the sooner you leave, the better, don't you?"

Just knowing Derrick would be flying in made her want to be out of Galveston as quickly as possible. "I don't have much. Besides… I've already started packing."

Sanders nodded as if not surprised. "I'll have the driver pick you up in an hour-and-a-half."

"Thanks."

He reached into his pocket and pulled out a cell phone. "Here, I want you to have this so I can make sure you're all right on the trip to Huntsville." He pressed the phone into her hand. "Keep it turned on in your purse."

She nodded, touched by his gesture.

"Don't worry," he said, giving her a reassuring smile. "I'm taking care of everything."

Chapter 4

When the limo pulled up in front of the house early, Kit was ready. She'd said goodbye to Tim and his daughter, as difficult as that was. Tim thought she was reconciling with her estranged husband. It was best to let him think that. She didn't want to involve him and his daughter anymore than she already had.

He'd insisted on carrying her bag out to the waiting car. Kit felt as if she were always saying goodbye to the people she cared about.

But now that Derrick had found her hiding place, she had no choice. She wouldn't be safe at the Andersons. Nor would the Andersons be safe from Derrick if she stayed.

She picked up the baby carrier, with her son sleeping peacefully inside, and, praying she'd made the right decision, headed for the waiting limo.

As she walked, she found herself glancing around, still feeling uneasy. She was relieved, however, to see no unfamiliar cars parked along the wide, tree-lined street. Knowing Derrick would be flying in terrified her more than she'd thought possible. What if he'd taken an earlier flight?

As she and Tim approached the long, sleek black car, the uniformed driver emerged from behind the wheel. Kit watched him move to the rear and open the trunk, unable to hide her surprise. She wasn't sure what she'd expected, but this man didn't fit her inexperienced image of a chauffeur. He looked too fit, his shoulders too broad, his arms too powerful, his body too compact and controlled. No, this man looked less like a chauffeur than a bodyguard— or a hired thug.

Her heart suddenly seemed a drum that she could not quiet. Did Sanders think she needed protection on the way to Huntsville? Was he worried that he wouldn't be able to talk Derrick into returning to Montana? All too easily panicked, she felt the way she had the day she left Montana. Here she was again. Running for her life. But this time with her baby son. What would she have done without Sanders here?

She hugged Andy to her as the driver took her single bag from Tim, placed it in the trunk and closed the lid.

"You're sure you're going to be all right?" Tim asked.

She nodded, dragging her gaze away from the limo driver to reassure Tim with a smile, to reassure *herself.* "We'll be fine."

The driver touched the brim of his cap as he moved past Kit to open the rear door. He looked strong and capable as both a driver and a bodyguard. He turned toward her, reaching for the baby carrier and diaper bag.

Reluctantly, she handed the carrier to him, watching closely as he leaned into the back of the car. He quickly strapped Andy into the rear seat, as if he'd done this sort of thing dozens of times before, and she began to relax a little.

As he stepped back, she noticed he wore a pair of worn brown cowboy boots. Only in Texas, she thought. Or Montana.

He stood back to hold the door for her, waiting, his eyes downcast, his demeanor subservient. And yet, Kit sensed a wariness in him that seemed to confirm her suspicion that Sanders had hired her a lot more than a limo driver.

"Good luck, Kit," Tim said. "If there's anything I can do…"

"Thank you. I really appreciate everything you've done for me and Andy."

She had wanted to say more, but afraid she'd cry, she quickly ducked into the back seat of the car beside her son. She was even more afraid she'd break down and tell Tim the truth. The last thing she would do was put any more lives in jeopardy.

The driver closed the door and hurried around to slide behind the wheel. Kit looked back through the dark tinted glass—one final goodbye to Tim and the sanctuary she'd found in Texas—as the limo pulled away from the curb. Beside her, Andy fell into the sleep of angels and babies.

"Please let me know if there is anything you need, Mrs. Killhorn," the driver said.

"Thank you," she said, surprised by how deep yet soft his voice was, and how completely free of a Southern accent.

Kit quickly dismissed the driver from her thoughts, confident that Sanders had seen to her safety in every possible way. As the car sped down the street, she didn't look back again.

"I'll give you and the baby some privacy. Just use the intercom."

The driver hit a power switch, and a tinted window went up between them, leaving her in the silent darkness of the back seat with only her sleeping son and her cell phone.

Kit watched the houses along the wide streets of old Galveston blur by: gleaming white works of art, ornate with spacious verandas and gentle roof lines, lounging in the shade of live oaks and palms under the Texas sun.

But the sky was filling with ominous dark storm clouds.

She closed her eyes, trying not to worry. About the past. Or the future. Sanders had seen to it that she and Andy were safe for the time being, she thought, glancing toward the privacy window that hid the limo driver. She snuggled against the deep leather of the seat. Warm and safe in this quiet cocoon, she drifted off.

Sanders got the page just as Derrick's plane touched ground at the airport. He hurried to the nearest phone and picked up, half expecting to hear Kit's voice, afraid she'd changed her mind or there'd been some sort of problem. He'd thought he'd covered everything. By now Kit should be safely in the limo and on her way with Derrick Jr. to Huntsville.

"Uh, this is Maury with Unlimited Chauffeur Service, and, you know that pickup you ordered? Well, I'm at the address, only she isn't here."

"What do you mean, she isn't there?" Sanders demanded.

"I was supposed to pick up a redhead and a baby, right? Well, I got here and the guy in the house says she left in another car with another driver about twenty minutes ago."

Sanders stared in stunned silence at the gate Derrick

would be coming out of at any moment. "Someone else picked her up?"

"A chauffeur in a limo," Maury said.

Sanders swore. "Unlimited sent two cars and drivers to the same address?"

"Afraid not," Maury said. "The other limo wasn't from Unlimited. The guy at the house saw an A-1 Rent-a-Ride sticker on the rear of the vehicle."

"A-1-Rent-a-Ride?"

"It's a place near the pickup address. So unless you called two limo companies, I don't know what to tell you."

Kit must have gotten cold feet, decided to take off and had called her own limo and driver. Only Kit would never do that even if she could afford it. She'd jump on a bus. Maybe even splurge and take a train or plane. But she'd never hire a limo and driver. Not Kit.

So what had happened? He'd been so sure he'd convinced her to go to Huntsville, or he would never have left her alone.

He spotted Derrick coming through the arrival gate and cursed his bad luck. Derrick stopped, caught sight of Sanders and no Kit or the baby, and scowled angrily, obviously unhappy that Sanders had had to go to Plan Two: Huntsville.

Wait until he heard that something had gone wrong with *both* plans and that Kit and baby were missing. Again.

Chapter 5

The sound of a phone ringing pulled Kit from a less-than-peaceful sleep. She sat up, disoriented, instantly afraid. Then she remembered where she was and realized the phone she heard was the cellular Sanders had given her. She reached into her purse.

"Hello?" Her son stirred beside her, stretching, his small fists reaching out, his sleep-wrinkled face so adorable and sweet. She leaned over and kissed his warm cheek.

"Kit." Sanders sounded far away. "Where are you?"

She glanced out at the passing landscape, at what appeared to be a tiny fishing village. She sat up a little straighter, surprised by what she was seeing. "I'm not sure." The sun had sunk beyond the front of the limo into scrub and sand. Off to her left, she caught a glimpse of a large body of water beneath a bank of dark clouds. The Gulf of Mexico? But Huntsville was to the north.

"Kit, I don't want to alarm you, but—"

She heard a thunk, then another voice.

"Is my son all right? What's going on? Where are you?"

Kit recoiled. "Derrick."

"Yes, your husband. I've been worried about you. You and the baby."

She swallowed, unable to force down the fear that threatened to choke her. And the revulsion. He was acting as if nothing had happened. "I told Sanders I didn't want to see you," she said.

"I know. Kit, you're confused. I don't want to argue about it. I want to see my son."

She closed her eyes. "No, Derrick." Her voice came out hoarse. "I saw you kill that man."

Silence. "You're wrong. You just made a mistake. But we can fix it. As soon as I see you."

"I want you to leave me alone," she demanded, glancing at the driver's outline through the privacy window. He had his back to her, his head facing forward, and seemed unaware of the drama being played out in the back seat. He must have the intercom turned off.

"Leave you alone?" Derrick repeated, sounding calm. Only someone who knew him the way Kit did could hear the rage behind his words. "For months you've denied me my son. You've made me look like a fool, marrying a woman who'd run off like you did." He took a breath. "And yet, I'm willing to forget and forgive, for my son's sake."

"He's not your son," she snapped, tired of the charade.

"Like hell." All pretense of calm was instantly gone from his voice. "Maybe you've forgotten, but my father's a judge. It shouldn't be too hard to convince him that my wife's unstable and an unfit mother—a woman who takes off nine months pregnant, then starts spreading some insane story about her husband being a murderer."

She could barely hear her own voice above the thunder of her heart. Hadn't this been her worst fear—that Derrick would somehow get Andy? "Running away from you wasn't insane and you know it."

He laughed; the sound had a bite to it. "It was insane for you not to take the limo Sanders hired for you. We could have worked this out."

She closed her eyes. What game was he playing now? "You know I took the car he sent."

"You stupid woman. You got into the wrong limo." He sounded confident that she'd just made the biggest mistake of her life. "Now who knows where you are or where you're going or what's going to happen to you. But I promise you this, Kit. I'll end up with my son."

Her gaze flew up. She stared at the back of the driver. He tugged at the collar of his white shirt with his index finger. Alarm knifed through her as she remembered the way his uniform looked on his powerful-looking athletic build, the jacket too snug in the shoulders, the pants too short. But it wasn't just the ill-fitting uniform, she thought, remembering the cowboy boots, the way he moved, the hidden power beneath his clothing and the wariness she'd sensed in him.

She noticed now that his dark blond hair needed trimming. It fell beneath the back of his cap to plaster damply against the tanned nape of his neck. And his hands—large, sun-browned, weathered and worn, like a pair of used leather gloves. Not the hands of a chauffeur.

She felt panic race through her veins. Hadn't she thought he looked like a bodyguard—or a thug? Only she'd believed Sanders had hired the man to *protect* her and Andy. Her heart pounded in her ears. "Who hired this limo?" she asked, her voice breaking.

Derrick made a pitying sound. "You were so busy trying to save yourself from me, you've gotten yourself into even worse trouble."

She turned her face to the side window and looked out at the miles of sand spit, feeling hot tears scald her eyelids. The line of clouds she'd noticed earlier now hung on the horizon above the darkening waters of the gulf. The driver had been following the coastline, not heading north, not going to Huntsville.

"Are you ready now to put all this foolishness behind us?" Derrick demanded as the telephone connection grew more faint. "Otherwise, what do I care what happens to you?"

He was just trying to scare her. He'd hired this limo and driver to confuse her, to bully and berate her—to frighten her into coming back to him, into forgetting she'd seen him murder a man.

She glanced over at her son. His eyes sparkled as he smiled up at her and waved his dimpled arms in the air. Anger, and her inborn need to protect her child at all costs, overpowered her fear and gave her a false confidence.

"You'd better hope nothing happens to me," she snapped. "I can prove that you murdered Jason St. John." The lie passed her lips before she could stop it. "I have evidence. And if anything happens to me or Andy—"

She didn't hear the privacy window slide down, didn't even realize the driver had seen her on the phone, not until he reached back and ripped it from her fingers. With a curse, he turned it off and tossed it onto the seat beside him as the window closed again.

She sat in stunned silence for a full minute, her anger spent, fear making her tremble.

"Who are you?" she demanded, pressing the intercom button. "What do you want with me and my baby?"

He pushed back his cap and met her gaze in the rearview mirror. A pair of startling steel gray eyes glared at her from a ruggedly handsome male face. His good looks surprised her. But the fury she saw in his expression left her stunned.

Her terror escalated. She was trapped in the back of a limo, racing along the two-lane at sixty-five miles an hour, with this man, who was no hired bodyguard, headed where? "Where are we?" she pleaded. "Where are you taking us?"

"We're almost there, Mrs. Killhorn."

She felt a fresh wave of panic. "That isn't what I asked you. Stop this car right now and let me out. Do you hear me?"

He didn't look back. Nor did he answer. She saw him reach for a car phone and begin speaking into it. She couldn't hear what he was saying.

She pushed the intercom again. But when she spoke into it, pleading with him to, please, not hurt her baby, she realized he'd turned it off.

"Damn you!" she cried, beating her fists against the window between them. "Damn you, stop this car! Let me and my baby out! Now!"

Andy began to scream, a high thin wail. Kit quit screaming, realizing she was only frightening the infant. She leaned over him, stroking his face, cooing softly as she soothed his cries. She had to try to quell her own panic. If she hoped to get them out of this, she had to keep her head.

Raindrops splattered the windshield as the storm moved inland. Through a break in the clouds, she could see the gulf, its surface a gunpowder gray. The driver had hung up the car phone.

Having calmed Andy, she gained a little control herself. She tried the intercom again. "Can you just tell me this—" she asked. "Did Sanders Killhorn hire you?"

She thought for a moment that he wouldn't answer, that he still couldn't hear her. But then he looked back in the mirror, his eyes almost silver in the darkness of the storm.

"No one hired me," he said.

Music suddenly filled the back of the limo. Soft but at the same time deafening to her. Christmas music.

Kit felt sick inside. Somehow, she knew, Derrick had outwitted his brother. Her mind refused to accept the possibility that Sanders had been in on this kidnapping all along.

Derrick had said she'd made a terrible mistake. And now he had her right where he wanted her.

Derrick slammed the pay phone receiver against the wall until the plastic flew in all directions. Slowly, he hung up what was left of the phone.

"Call her back," he commanded. "I have to talk to her."

"I don't think that's a good idea," Sanders said, noticing that people were watching. "Come on, let's get your luggage and get out of here before someone tells security about the phone you just destroyed."

Derrick handed his brother another receiver. "Call. If I can just talk to her, I know I can make her understand. She's just got it all wrong."

Sanders started to argue, decided it wouldn't do any good, and dialed.

He hung up when he got a recording saying that she was unavailable. She'd turned off the phone. "I still can't believe she rented a limo and driver."

Derrick swore. "She didn't, you moron."

Sanders stared at his brother. He had to admit he'd never seen Derrick this crazy over a woman. Not even Belinda could put him in this kind of a frenzy, and if there was one thing Belinda loved to do, it was set Derrick off. "She didn't rent the limo?"

"Someone's kidnapped her and the baby and she said that if anything happened to her—" He slammed a fist against the wall, once again drawing attention to them.

"Who would kidnap her?"

"How would I know that?" Derrick snapped.

Sanders reached for the pay phone. "We have to call the police—"

Derrick grabbed his wrist. "Are you crazy? We can't chance calling the cops. I won't risk my son's life. We have to wait until we hear from the kidnapper and see what his demands are. He'll call me back in Montana. I'm sure of it. I'll have to take the next flight home."

Sanders blinked. "You're going to just leave Kit and the baby in the hands of some kidnapper in Texas and go back to Montana?" He couldn't believe his brother. Couldn't believe Kit had been kidnapped. How had the kidnapper known where she was, let alone that she'd be taking a limo?

"I'm not just leaving them," Derrick snapped. "You're staying here. You track that limo and driver and call me as soon as you know something."

Sanders felt sick as he left the airport. Who would kidnap Kit and the baby? Only one man he could think of. The same man who'd known the address where Kit worked, who came up with the idea of a friend's secluded ranch in Huntsville, who anticipated Kit would insist on Sanders meeting him at the airport instead of driving her, and who'd suggested hiring a limo and driver to take her.

Derrick could easily have set up this whole kidnapping thing. To scare Kit into coming back to him.

The storm sucked the last of the light from the day, making the sky as gray as the gulf. Rain streaked the windows of the limo as it sped along the coast. Kit fought the urge to scream and pound again on the window. She knew it would only upset her son—and accomplish nothing.

She glanced at her watch, trying to calculate where they were. She had no idea. She didn't know Texas, never having ventured out of the house, let alone Galveston, for fear of running into Derrick. Through the rain, she glimpsed a highway sign: Brownsville, 170 miles. Dear God, they were headed south along the gulf toward Mexico.

Andy began to whimper. Kit unsnapped him from the carrier and changed his wet diaper, her hands trembling. She tried to stay calm, to think clearly, for the baby's sake.

"It's going to be all right," she said to him as she took a bottle from the warmer in the bag and put the nipple to his mouth. Andy took it greedily. She looked down at him, studying his precious face, promising him silently that she would get them out of this. Whatever she had to do.

Her head jerked up as she felt the car slowing. Her pulse was deafening in her ears as she fought to see beyond the rain. Why were they stopping? She quickly unsnapped Andy's car seat and buckled her son back into it as the driver turned onto a narrow shell road that ran through high dunes and scrub brush. Dense fog socked in the gulf. Fog and rain and night cloaked the car in darkness.

From what Kit could see, the area appeared seedy and deserted. The few shanties they passed stood on stilts like shore birds, but they too looked empty, boarded up as if anticipating a bad storm.

The driver pulled off on an even narrower side road and stopped between two tall dunes. He cut the engine.

Kit grabbed for the door, planning to leap out with her son and run. The door was locked.

Her gaze jumped to the driver as she heard the whir of the privacy window and saw him turning toward her.

Chapter 6

Kit hurriedly rummaged through her purse, looking for anything she could use as a weapon. She found nothing. Not even a metal nail file or a set of keys. For the first time in her life, she wished for a gun and the knowledge to use it.

The driver reached back and grabbed her arm, taking the purse from her with his free hand. She had the impression that he could have crushed her arm with the strength in his fingers alone, but he didn't. His grip was almost gentle, but firm. He left no doubt in her mind who would win if push came to shove.

"Take it easy, Mrs. Killhorn," he commanded as he dropped the purse on the seat beside him, but kept his hold on her arm.

"Don't call me that." She jerked free, as angry as she was afraid. "Derrick Killhorn hired you, didn't he?"

"I told you, no one hired me."

"Someone hired you to kill me and take my son," she cried in exasperation. "It had to be Derrick." Or Sanders.

The driver held up one of his large, weathered hands. "Hold on, I didn't bring you here to kill you or steal your son. If anything, I probably saved your life."

"What?" She glared at him. He didn't look like a crackpot.

He took off the chauffeur's cap, tossed it on the seat beside him and raked a hand through his full head of dark blond hair.

"I know you aren't a chauffeur," she said as she watched him shrug out of the uniform jacket and loosen his shirt collar. She remembered the anger she'd seen in his eyes—anger aimed at her. "Who are you?"

"I'm a carpenter." He met her gaze. "I make furniture."

What kind of answer was that? She felt her head spin. "Why would a carpenter want—"

"There was another limo and driver who were to pick up you and the baby. It was to come thirty minutes later than I did. That's the one Sanders hired."

Derrick had told her she'd taken the wrong limo. For once the man wasn't lying.

"If you'd gotten into the other limo, I doubt anyone would have ever seen you again," he said matter-of-factly.

She shuddered at the calm certainty in his voice. "How do you know that?" And for that matter, how did he know who she was, that a limo was going to pick her up, that Sanders had hired it?

He held up his hand and shook his head at her as if he found her lack of patience daunting. "I overheard Sanders making the arrangements. You were to go to Huntsville to an out-of-the-way ranch. Derrick would have been waiting there for you. All the arrangements were made before

Sanders even talked to you. It was Derrick's plan. Sanders just carried out his orders."

She felt sick inside but still didn't want to accept it. "And you just happened to overhear all this?"

He nodded. "I've been following Sanders for seven months." He sounded weary. "I've also been listening to him through the wonders of modern technology."

She frowned. "You *bugged* him? Isn't that illegal?"

He raised a brow as if to say that he'd done other things much more illegal than that. That scared her.

"Seven months?" The man was determined, she thought. "Why?"

He shrugged as if it should have been obvious. "I couldn't find you myself. I knew Sanders was looking for you. I thought with the Killhorn resources he had a better chance than I did."

She felt hesitant to ask the next obvious question. "Why did you want to find me so badly?"

"To talk to you."

She raised a brow. "You went to all that trouble just to talk to me?" He *was* a crackpot. Oh, God, could things get any worse? She held tightly to Andy and the baby carrier and glanced out at the fog and darkness. Rain fell in a thick gray sheet and drummed on the roof of the limo. How was she going to get away from this man?

"Originally that had been the plan."

Originally? The word snapped her attention back to him. Now he wanted more than to talk to her? "Are you a cop or something?"

"I'm Luke St. John. Jason's brother."

Chapter 7

Luke St. John? Sanders stared down at the name on the A-1 Rent-a-Ride rental form. St. John? Someone Derrick had hired? Now he wasn't so sure. It was too much of a coincidence not to be a relative of Jason's. Headed for Huntsville? He doubted that. But just seeing the name neatly printed on the paper, Sanders assumed that Luke St. John, whoever he was, knew about the plan to rent a limo and take Kit and the baby to Huntsville. How? But maybe more important, why had St. John used his real name on the rental agreement, as if he wanted Sanders to know that he knew?

No, Sanders thought, St. John wanted *Derrick* to know. Did Luke also believe that Derrick had killed Jason?

Sanders left, drove to the nearest pay phone and called the private detective Derrick had hired to find Kit when Sanders had failed. It gave Sanders no little satisfaction that the P.I. had been unable to find Kit.

Matthew Rustan, was a slimy, balding former high

school basketball star with a paunch, a lousy attitude and a hungry look in his eye that made Sanders nervous. The first time Sanders had seen the man's office, he could tell that all Rustan's good years were behind him—in more ways than one. The walls were lined with high school trophies, yellowed newspaper articles and old team photographs. Still, the man was handy—and willing to work.

"I need you to go over my rental car," Sanders said when Rustan answered. "I think there's a bug in it."

Thirty minutes later, the private eye slammed the rental car door and walked over to where Sanders stood waiting. "It's clean now."

"That's it?" Sanders asked pointing to the cell-phone size device the P.I. held in his hand.

He nodded. "This type works off a larger receiver, which can pick up pretty good as far away as five miles. Someone's probably heard every conversation you've had."

At least now he knew how Luke St. John had known so much. "One more thing. Can you run a check on a name for me?"

"Sure."

Sanders reached into his pocket. He'd copied the driver's license number off Luke St. John's A-1 Rent-a-Ride rental agreement. Beside it had been written the word *Montana,* one of the states where the license number was usually the social security number. "Try this."

Luke St. John. Kit gasped in surprise at the name and felt herself go cold as she stared at him.

He reached into his pocket, pulled out his wallet and flipped it open. As he handed it to her, he snapped on the overhead light. Kit looked down at the color photo on his Montana driver's license, then at the name. Lucas St. John.

He leaned over the seat to flip to a graduation photograph of a young man. Kit felt her throat constrict. Her heart pounded louder than the rain on the roof. She recognized the man in the photo instantly. This was the man she'd seen with Derrick at the construction site. The man she'd seen her husband murder. Jason St. John.

"Oh, God," she whispered. The young man in the photo had long, light brown hair and pale gray eyes. Intense, penetrating eyes, just like the ones gazing at her now.

"That answers at least one of my questions," Luke said, taking the wallet from her numb fingers. "It *was* my brother you saw your husband kill. I figured it had to be something like that. It was too much of a coincidence when you disappeared on the same day as Jason—and you nine months pregnant."

Kit's gaze jerked up at a sound outside the car. She let out a startled cry as a man's face appeared beyond the glass. He wore a bright yellow raincoat, the hood up, his features hidden in shadow.

"It's all right," Luke said, pocketing the wallet. "He's getting rid of the limo for me." He stepped out into the rain, leaving his door open.

Kit watched the man hand Luke two raincoats. She couldn't hear what they were saying as Luke shrugged into one of the coats then reached back in to toss her the second one. Luke went around the back of the limo with the man, opened the trunk and extracted her single bag. The man took the bag and disappeared into the darkness.

She pulled on the raincoat, chilled more by his words than by the weather or the raindrops that splattered her skin from the wet slick fabric. He was getting rid of the limo because Derrick would be looking for it—and them. Derrick would be tracking her down like a dog. She felt the weight of that thought and knew she could never be rid of the man.

Luke startled her, opening the door and climbing into the back of the limo. "There's a fishing cottage just over the hill," he said, reaching for the baby carrier. "We'll go there."

Kit glanced out into the night, unable to see a light or a building. She settled her gaze on Luke, wondering why he'd helped her, wondering what he wanted from her, suspecting she already knew the answer to that. She looked down at the baby in her arms. Andy had fallen back to sleep sucking his thumb; this kid could sleep through anything.

"Look," Luke said quietly, "I'm tired, cold and hungry and the best cook in Texas is waiting someplace warm and dry." He gave her a faint smile. It did something nice for his face, but it never reached his eyes. He didn't like her. She felt that from him. It was so strong that it was unnerving, especially since, on the surface, he seemed so affable.

"My aunt Lucille makes the best crab gumbo you've ever tasted," he said, his voice deeper, softer, cajoling.

Kit heard pride and tenderness in his tone at just the mention of his aunt's name. It warmed her a little to him. She reminded herself that he'd lost his brother. And she'd witnessed the murder and run instead of going to the police. That was the frightening bond they shared. That and the fact that now Derrick Killhorn would be looking for Luke St. John as well as for her and Andy. No wonder this man didn't like her.

She studied his face for a moment. At first she'd thought him ruggedly attractive, but now in the glare of the limo's overhead light, she realized that he could have been handsome if his features hadn't been so rigid, his gray eyes so cold.

"Well?" he asked, glancing out into the darkness with

a nervousness she found contagious. "We don't have a lot of time." He handed her the diaper bag and her purse from the front seat, then held out his hands again for Andy. "You don't know the terrain. It would be dangerous for you to carry the baby."

Still, it was all she could do to put Andy into the man's arms. But their lives were now in his hands, whether she liked it or not. Luke St. John had seen to that. She told herself that he had no reason to want to harm her or her son. In fact, he had every reason to want to see her stay alive. She hoped.

He covered the baby carrier with his uniform jacket, then he turned and ducked out of the car. Kit followed closely behind. She hadn't gone far when she heard the purr of the limo engine as it pulled away into the night.

They hurried through the downpour. The air smelled wet from the rain and salty from the sea. As they topped one of the dunes, she could see a shimmer of light in the distance. The light grew as they neared a fishing cottage on stilts, the exterior weathered as gray as the fog. It appeared out of the rain, a single golden light shining from the porch. It pulled them through the darkness, promising warmth and shelter from the storm. And, if Luke St. John were true to his word, crab gumbo.

Kit felt uneasy as they neared the house, questioning why she thought she could take Luke St. John at his word—including the fact that Derrick wasn't behind this abduction. For all she knew, the other limo would have taken her to Huntsville and safety.

"Lucas Allen St. John," the P.I. said, reading the report off his computer screen as a copy rolled out of the printer for Sanders. "Wow, who *is* this guy? Graduated at the top of his class from Montana Tech and went right to work as a structural engineer on some pretty impressive buildings around the world."

Sanders snatched up the sheets from the printer and scanned down what read like a résumé. It was *very* impressive.

"I wonder what happened," Rustan said thoughtfully. "Looks like he was good, really good. Then suddenly he drops out. Four years later he's building furniture out of his shed in Podunkland. Believe me, there's a story there. Something." Rustan rubbed his jaw. "Makes you wonder what happened. Want me to try to find out?"

Sanders shook his head. He couldn't care less about the man's past. He was more interested in the man's relatives. A brother named Jason. And Luke St. John's current address: Big Sky, Montana. How about that?

Sanders carefully folded the papers and put them in his pocket. "How much do I owe you?"

"Don't you want me to just put it on the bill I send to your brother?"

"No," Sanders said, pulling out two hundred dollars from the wad Derrick had given him. "This doesn't have anything to do with my brother."

Rustan shrugged and took the money. "You say you don't want me to keep looking for Kit Killhorn, right?"

"Right."

"But you want me to keep looking for Jason St. John, but you want me to bill you instead of your brother?"

Was the man stupid? "I believe that's simple enough."

"Oh yeah, it's simple all right. Just interesting."

"Maybe you should try to curb your interest in other people's affairs," Sanders suggested.

Rustan laughed in his face. "People's affairs *are* my

business. It's how I make a living, digging in other people's lives. I'll let you know if I find the answer to Luke St. John's past." He held up his hand before Sanders could protest. "It's on the house. A freebie. Sometimes I just like to satisfy my own curiosity."

Sanders left, his mind alive with worry. He didn't like the P.I. and suspected Rustan would call Derrick the moment he left the office and sell him the same information. But he didn't want any other outsiders involved in Killhorn business. Besides, he had more important things on his mind than Matthew Rustan. Why would this Lucas St. John kidnap Kit and the baby? Was he looking for his brother and thought Kit might know where Jason was? Or did he believe Jason had met with foul play?

Sanders felt his heart hammer harder. If Kit repeated that story about Derrick killing Jason... What would Lucas St. John do if he thought Derrick had killed his brother? Would he use Kit to try to get back at Derrick?

The possibilities terrified him. Then a new thought stopped him cold. What if this Luke St. John had kidnapped Kit to protect her from Derrick? Instantly, he rejected that theory as ridiculous. No one had to protect Kit from her own husband, nor the baby from his own father. Derrick might be a little out of control on occasion, but he'd married Kit, so he must have loved her. And more than anything in the world, Derrick wanted his son back.

Sanders glanced at his watch. By now Derrick was in Big Sky, waiting for his call.

Luke St. John led the way up the steep wooden stairs. Before he reached the door, it flew open and a matronly woman wearing an apron took the baby from Luke's arms and ushered them quickly inside.

Kit stepped into the warmth, surprised to find the place homey. A fire crackled in a woodstove in one corner, surrounded by an odd collection of comfortable-looking chairs. The opposite was lined with built-in bunk beds, with each covered with a worn handmade-looking quilt. Beside the bottom bunk was a white crib.

The kitchen took another corner of the room, where a delightfully spicy scent bubbled up from a huge pot on the stove. At the center of it all, a much-used high chair sat pushed up to a table set for three. Kit remembered seeing Luke on the car phone as they were leaving Galveston. They'd obviously been expected.

"I was getting worried about you," the woman said as she looked down at the baby. "Oh, what an adorable child."

Kit reached for Andy, surprised he wasn't howling his head off. He usually didn't like strangers, but he seemed to be intrigued by the woman's wide, open face and her deep Southern accent.

Before Kit could take Andy from the woman's arms, Luke reached for Kit's wet raincoat. She shrugged out of it, and he hung it on one of the hooks by the front door. "Aunt Lucille loves babies. Aunt Lou, meet Kit Kil—"

"Bannack," Kit said quickly, surprising herself at the vehemence she heard in her tone.

Luke's gaze flipped up to hers. "Kit Bannack," he corrected, studying her. "And her son, Andy."

"Well, come on in," Lucille said, eyeing her nephew curiously. "I hope you're hungry."

Luke said nothing, but Kit felt her stomach growl. When was the last time she'd eaten? She started to relax just a little. Derrick hadn't jumped out of any closets, and she was beginning to believe he wasn't going to. The only question that remained was what Luke St. John hoped to accomplish by scuttling her and Andy off to this place.

"The gumbo is ready," Lucille said, stealing another look at her nephew, worry on her face.

Andy began to whimper. "He probably needs to be changed," Kit said.

"Oh, please, let me," Lucille said. "If you don't mind."

Kit looked into the woman's face and found herself nodding. Andy had taken to her right away. But Kit didn't miss the look the woman gave her nephew—almost a warning look—before her gaze settled on Kit.

"Why, look at her, this woman is soaked to the skin," Lucille exclaimed. "Go warm up next to the fire," she told Kit. "Luke, get her a change of clothing," she ordered as she headed for the crib with Andy.

Luke obeyed, going to a built-in drawer and pulling out a pair of sweats. He held them up for Kit to inspect. They looked soft and comfortable, warm and way too large.

She went to take the clothes from him, knowing they would swallow her small frame. Which made them perfect. They would hide her figure, which was just fine with her. She'd always been thin. Since the baby, she felt too rounded, too full in places she'd never been full-figured before. She felt at odds with this new body, as if she hadn't yet grown into it—and might never do so.

Luke pointed her to the back of the house. She stepped through a doorway into what appeared to be a combination artist's studio and bedroom. Watercolors lined the walls, along with photos of weddings, baptisms and newborn babies. She stopped before a photograph, recognizing the man in the picture as the one now in the next room.

The photo had been taken on the beach—and not that long ago. And what made it so unusual was how different the smiling Luke St. John looked in the photo. The eyes weren't hard-as-steel gray, but soft, almost seductive. His rugged features weren't etched in unforgiving granite. He was handsome in a strong, very masculine way that had a strange effect on her. But it was the look on his face that drew her in, in a way she would never have expected. Luke looked happy. And that expression on Luke St. John was the most alluring of all.

Is this what he'd been like before his brother's death?

Then she saw the photograph next to it, and her heart thudded in her chest. It was of Jason at about age sixteen, squinting at the camera as he held up the huge fish he'd caught. He looked too serious for his age.

"She saw her husband kill Jason," Luke said the moment Kit had left the room.

Lucille covered her mouth with one hand, and her eyes swam with tears. "Dear God. You're sure?"

He nodded and reached over to take his aunt's hand. He squeezed it, then pulled back, as unable to give comfort right now as he was to receive it. "Jason's dead. Murdered." His jaw tightened. "And she saw the whole thing."

Lucille wagged her head, her gaze settling on him like an arm around his shoulders. "Oh, Luke, this must be killing you."

He looked away. "I have to see that this man gets what he deserves."

She brushed at her tears. "I know how angry you must be."

He doubted that. He'd never felt this kind of rage before. It thrummed through his body, vibrating inside him, causing a constant hum inside his head. He'd banked all but his frustration during the months he'd searched for Kit, waiting with infinite patience to find out exactly what had happened to his brother, not letting his suspicion that Derrick Killhorn was behind his brother's disappearance become any more than that: a strong suspicion.

Although he'd never met him, Luke knew who Derrick Killhorn was, had known people who'd worked with him in construction who'd found him pompous and often ruthless. Luke had seen Killhorn's photo in the *Lone Peak Lookout* a few times, where the man was always referred to as a prominent citizen and businessman from an old Montana family.

But Luke had only seen him once in person, outside a motel in West Yellowstone with a woman who was not his wife. Luke didn't like the man, nor did he like Jason working for him.

But when Luke heard Kit tell Sanders what she'd witnessed, he'd felt something explode inside his head, a time bomb that had been ticking for seven months.

Almost instantly, his rage had splintered, encompassing not only Derrick Killhorn but his wife, the woman who'd run and hid for months instead of going to the authorities. It had taken every ounce of willpower he possessed to remain in the trees when he'd heard her admit what she'd seen. He'd felt such wrath that he'd wanted to burst from his hiding place and—

And what? He balled his hands into tight fists. "I heard her tell her husband that she has evidence that can convict him."

"Dear heaven," Lucille said.

Luke nodded as he turned to look again at his aunt. "The woman had *evidence* and still she didn't come forward."

"She must be horribly afraid of her husband," Lucille said.

"Or still in love with him," Luke added, finding it almost

impossible to hold back the contempt he felt for Kit Kill-horn. Fear or love, it really didn't make a difference to him. Either way, he damned Kit Killhorn for what she'd done, adding her to his dark thoughts and, ultimately, to his plan.

"Luke, I know how upset you are, but do you realize what you've done? You've kidnapped this woman and her baby. What are you planning to do with them?"

"Whatever I have to." He could feel her gaze boring into him.

"I know you want justice for this terrible crime, but surely not at the cost of that woman and child." She sounded uncertain, as if she didn't know him anymore.

He didn't know *himself* anymore. "She's all that stands between Derrick Killhorn being punished or getting away with murder."

"Is that how you see her?" Lucille asked in shocked disbelief.

"That's all I can afford to see. She's an eyewitness," he said, fighting to keep his voice down, fighting to hold back his frustration. All these months of looking for her, and for what? He'd finally found her, heard her admit she'd seen Derrick kill Jason, and what good did it do unless he took her back to Montana and made her take her evidence to the authorities?

"Luke, she's a victim of this Derrick Killhorn just like Jason was. Can't you see that? A woman who runs and hides all this time isn't protecting her husband, she's scared to death of him."

He didn't pretend to understand the mind of a woman. And right now he saw nothing but his own rage, his own need for vengeance. "She married him, had his child. Surely she knew the kind of man she was marrying."

"Maybe not. And what about that child?" Lucille demanded. "My God, Luke, you've decided he's dispensable too because he's Killhorn blood?"

Luke turned at the sound of the studio door opening behind them. They abruptly stopped their conversation as Kit came back into the room. She halted, her gaze on them, no doubt aware they'd been talking about her. He watched her as she headed for the crib and her son. Derrick Killhorn's son. Luke clamped down his jaw, looking at her through unforgiving eyes.

"How are the clothes?" Lucille asked, her voice sounding strained to Luke's. "Oh, they're huge on you."

The sweatpants puddled at Kit's ankles, the sweatshirt billowed around her like a balloon. She looked almost comical, the clothing was so large on her slight form. Then he narrowed his eyes as he watched her pluck at the loose-fitting top, tugging it away from her breasts as if self-conscious about the curves that even the huge sweats couldn't hide. Her discomfort surprised him. And drew his attention.

He tried to remember what she'd been wearing before. Something bulky. Not that he'd really noticed. He'd been too anxious, too single-minded in his determination, too angry with her to care about anything but getting her into the car and getting away.

Now as he watched her move around the living room, studying his aunt's art work, he speculated about the body that was hidden under the clothing. The sexual nature of the thought amused him, but he reined in his thoughts. He was more interested in what *else* the woman was hiding from him.

Almost absently, she uncoiled her hair and shook out the waves of fiery red. They tumbled down to the middle of her back, thick and rich, with a texture that at one time would have made him want to run his hand over it, just as he would a fine piece of wood.

She turned, the movement accenting the swell of her breasts beneath the baggy sweats, the rounded curves of her hips. He was stunned by a sudden stab of longing that pierced his angry shell like an arrow.

But he recovered quickly and smiled to himself as he brushed the feeling away, finding it insignificant in light of his other emotions—disdain for Kit Killhorn being at the top of the list. She could call herself "Bannack" but to him she was Mrs. Derrick Killhorn. The name alone damned her.

He'd never before thought of himself as vengeful. But he'd never before dealt with the pain of losing a brother. That loss, coupled with the injustice of Derrick Killhorn going unpunished for the crime, burned within Luke stronger than any desire he'd ever felt—or thought he ever would. And this woman, he reminded himself, stood between him and the vengeance he demanded.

He concentrated on how Mrs. Kit Killhorn was going to help him. One way or the other. With the evidence she had and her eyewitness testimony, Derrick Killhorn would probably go to prison for most of his miserable life. But was that enough? No, Luke thought, as he looked at Kit. Not nearly enough.

Chapter 8

Kit could feel the tension in the air the moment she walked back into the room. There was no doubt that they'd been talking about her. Lucille looked upset and Luke… Well, he looked even more angry—if that were possible.

"Let's try some of this gumbo," Lucille said nervously.

Luke got up and moved to the fireplace to throw a log onto the dwindling blaze.

Kit pretended she hadn't noticed anything amiss as she pulled her hair up into a ponytail and went to the crib, where Andy sat surrounded by toys. He looked utterly content. She picked him up, hugging him to her tightly and dug into his bag for the baby food.

As she headed for the table, she noticed more water-color seascapes lining the walls. "Are these yours?" she asked Lucille.

"It's just a hobby," the woman said modestly.

"They're very good," Kit said, the cheerful bright paintings warming her all the more to Lucille.

"See, I told you you have talent," Luke said to his aunt as she placed a huge pot of steaming gumbo in the center of the table.

Kit noticed something odd in the way he moved toward the table, but before she could think of what it was, she heard Luke say, "Mrs. Killhorn is an artist herself. A painter. I've seen her work."

Kit felt as if he'd punched her. All the air rushed from her lungs; she thought she might faint. How could he know that? It wasn't as if it was common knowledge. And where could he have seen any of her work? She didn't like him calling her Mrs. Killhorn either, and he knew that—but it was her name, wasn't it? Did he think he needed to remind her what a fool she'd been to marry Derrick?

"I was at the house," he said sitting down at the table. "Killhorn's house. Twice, actually."

"When could you have—"

He looked up, pulling her down into the gray depths of his gaze until she thought she could see the dark bottom of his soul. "Seven months ago. One of my cousins is a locksmith."

Kit knew she shouldn't have been shocked by his confession. Nor by the open defiance in his eyes. The man had spent seven months tailing Sanders, bugging Sanders's car and his motel rooms, tracking her, then abducted her and Andy. Why was she so shocked that he'd broken into the house she used to live in with Derrick?

Because she was just beginning to understand how far Luke St. John would go to get what he wanted. And that was exactly what he wanted her to know.

She met his gaze with an angry one of her own. Her art

had always been private, painted in secret. First, because her aunt hadn't approved. Later, because Derrick didn't like her wasting her time painting.

But she *had* painted, filling the long hours alone in Derrick's huge house with the one thing she loved. When he'd seen her work before they were married, he'd shown no interest. His only concern was that she might want to hang some of them in the house, the house he'd spent a fortune paying an interior designer to decorate.

"I have a certain position in the community to uphold, you understand," he'd said. "I can't have amateur artwork on the walls."

He'd given her one room upstairs—what he called her sewing room; what she called her studio—and told her she could do with it whatever she wanted. So she'd put most of her paintings in storage. Only two, her favorites, were on the wall in her studio. Since Derrick never went in there, he hadn't noticed. Nor did he know that she'd begun to paint again.

But Luke had seen her paintings, had noticed they were hers and had probably seen her works in progress in the closet where she kept them. She felt as if he'd gone through her underwear drawer. Her paintings were extremely personal, and now, she realized, Luke St. John, a complete stranger, knew things about her, intimate things, things that made her feel vulnerable. She would have preferred him to go through her underwear drawer.

He raised a brow, challenging her to question his behavior. He'd broken into her house, tracked her, kidnapped her, and yet he still thought what she'd done—witnessing a murder and running instead of reporting it—was much worse than anything he'd done to reach her. He must think her a horrible coward. Or worse.

She dropped her gaze as she slipped Andy into the high chair and sat down at the table.

Out of the corner of her eye, she saw Lucille shoot Luke a warning look. He said nothing more as she ladled one of the bowls full of gumbo and handed it to Kit. "This will warm you up."

Kit took a bite, amazed at the incredible blend of tastes. "It's wonderful," she exclaimed.

Lucille smiled. "Food can make anything better."

"This problem takes more than gumbo," Luke said as he took the bowl Lucille offered him. "Even *your* gumbo."

Lucille ignored him as she served herself. Then she chatted about fishing, Texas, the weather, anything but what they were all doing here and why. Luke ate silently, his gaze on his gumbo, responding only when asked a direct question and then only in monosyllables.

Kit ate, listening to Lucille's wonderful Southern accent, feeling warmed by the woman's good nature as well as her spicy meal and cozy beach cottage. She fed Andy, who took spoonful after spoonful of baby food without even a whimper, but did pound the high chair tray occasionally and let out loud whoops, just in case anyone had forgotten he was there.

Several times during the meal, she felt Luke's gaze on her. It seemed fired by both hostility and curiosity. The anger she could feel coming off him like heat waves from the woodstove, but she understood the anger. And it bothered her much less than the open curiosity.

And she didn't understand the tension that arced between Luke and his aunt. It made Kit wonder what he'd done that had upset the woman. Kit suspected it was more than abducting her and Andy.

Kit found herself studying Luke out of the corner of her

eye while she ate. He was no hero who'd come riding up in a long black limo to save her and Andy. She knew that. Maybe he'd temporarily saved her from Derrick. But there was little doubt that his motivations were selfish ones. He'd kidnapped her for his own purpose. The question was: what purpose? To seek justice? Or did he just want revenge and not care who he had to hurt to get it? She worried it might be the latter.

She contemplated him for a moment. He *did* frighten her, she realized, but on a level that had nothing to do with his hostility over his brother's murder and the part she'd played by keeping it a secret.

No, what she feared in him was something more…primal. Something more… Luke looked up, his gaze connecting with hers, stunning her with its intensity, shocking her with its intimacy. In that instant she knew exactly what it was about Luke St. John that terrified her.

His lips turned up in a knowing smile and he nodded as if he'd read her thoughts and agreed wholeheartedly that she *should* fear him.

She looked away, shaken, and tried to focus on eating. But she could feel him, and realized she'd been keenly aware of him from the moment she'd looked into his gray eyes. Since then, she'd known where he was in the room without consciously looking for him. She *felt* his presence.

It suddenly hit her—the mannerism she'd noticed earlier when she'd watched him walk to the table. She knew, the same way she knew without looking right now that he was kneading his right thigh above his knee with the heel of his large hand. Luke St. John walked with a limp. It was so slight that it was almost unnoticeable, but she had noticed it. Because she noticed everything about the man.

That shocked her. And she told herself that it shouldn't.

Of course she'd be aware of him. He was her kidnapper. He held her and her son's welfare in his hands. Of course she would try to read this man, to gauge his behavior, the tone of his voice, the subtle meaning of his movements. It was some basic instinct that had been handed down for centuries to women, from a time when a woman's life depended on her ability to sense whether a man meant her harm.

Something just as basic told her this man wouldn't harm either her or Andy. Still, the ancient instinct that was making her so conscious of Luke St. John disturbed her. The same way she'd been disturbed when she'd looked at his smiling photograph. She glanced at him across the table now and realized that she was uncomfortable because she had the distinct impression that he was equally aware of her.

She took seconds on the gumbo at Lucille's prompting and concentrated on finding contentment in just being warm, dry and fed. It had never taken much to make her content because she'd never had much. So much of her life had been spent caring for other people, seeing to their comfort, their desires. She'd never given much thought to her own.

"So you're an artist," Lucille was saying.

Kit blinked and shot a resentful look at Luke. "No." She wouldn't consider herself an artist until her work was seen in a gallery showing. That would not only make her work complete, but make Kit's dream come true.

"I was a history major in college. Now I'm a…" She recalled the way Luke had said in the car that he was a carpenter, a furniture builder, as if that was *who* he was and the best he could explain himself.

She could see him gazing at her, waiting for her answer to the same question. Who *was* she? She hated to think how he would describe her. "I'm a mother."

Lucille smiled, as if that had been the perfect answer. Luke, of course, frowned.

"What made you major in history in college?" Lucille asked.

"My aunt," Kit said, happy to aid Lucille's attempts at dinner conversation, since Luke was having none of it, and the tension at the table was starting to get to Kit. Also she hoped talking to Lucille would make it easier to ignore Luke.

"My father's sister raised me after my parents were killed." Kit wished she couldn't feel Luke's gaze on her. "My aunt loved history and thought I'd make a good teacher." Kit would much rather have majored in art, but her aunt had scoffed at the idea.

"Teachers are respected," she'd contended. "Artists are nothing but hippies without jobs."

"I could teach art," Kit had suggested.

"To be truthful with you, you aren't that good," her aunt had said. "I know what's best for you."

And Kit had acquiesced to her aunt's wishes. It was Kit's nature to bend.

At the University of Montana, she'd met William, one of her professors. He'd talked her into taking art classes after he'd seen one of her paintings that she'd forgotten to hide. "You are good, really good," he'd encouraged. "Follow your heart, Kit. That is the best advice I can give you."

And she had, with both her art and William, right up until his death. Right up until she realized that she was pregnant with his baby. With William she was just beginning to realize her own potential. Then he was gone. And running scared, she'd put her life and that of her baby into Derrick's hands.

"You don't find history a little dry?" Lucille asked.

"Terribly," Kit said, being honest for the first time in a long time. "I was planning to enroll in some art classes, but then I—" She stopped. "I got married and—" She halted again, surprised she'd said so much, revealed so much about not only her life but her nature. What didn't surprise her was to see that both Lucille and Luke were staring at her, Lucille with sympathy and Luke with disgust.

She bristled at the contempt she saw in his face and felt indignation well up inside her at this man who had kidnapped her and Andy, and now stood in judgment. But she didn't kid herself. She knew the source of her resentment ran far deeper than Luke St. John. She'd let her life and Andy's get out of her control, and she'd done nothing to get power over it again.

"I've spent my life so far doing what other people wanted me to do," she said, shocked to hear herself finally admit it, shocked at the bitterness that clanged in her words and the tears that filled her eyes. "I've been bullied by the best."

Luke's gray gaze flickered up to hers. She fought not to recoil from the impotent fury she saw there.

When he finally spoke, his words hit her like stones. "Is that right?"

"Luke—" his aunt began, but he cut her off as he got to his feet.

"Under the circumstances, I'd say you narrowed down your options when you saw your husband kill my brother and did nothing about it." He shot a look at his aunt, as if daring her to say a word, then he slapped down his napkin and strode out of the cottage.

Kit let out the breath she'd been holding.

"Luke is a good person," Lucille said, her voice choked with emotion. "This thing with his brother is eating him up." She shook her head sadly. "Some people can accept injustice. They see it, but they don't let it destroy them if they can't or won't do anything about it." She sighed. "Luke isn't like that. He can't rest until Jason's murderer pays."

"What if there isn't a way to make Derrick pay?" Kit asked. "Do you think I would have run if I thought there was?"

"No one blames you, Kit."

"Luke does." She got up from the table and glanced toward the door he'd just exited. "Would you mind—"

"Don't worry, I'll watch Andy," Lucille said quickly. "Take a coat." She hesitated. "I'll be right here if you need me."

Kit smiled at the woman, comforted not only by her generosity but by her concern. "Thank you."

The rain had stopped. Thin clouds veiled the moon, making the gulf shimmer like polished pewter. The air still smelled of rain but the storm clouds were gone. Only a thin fog drifted past like ghosts lost at sea. Overhead, stars twinkled against the black velvet sky.

Kit joined Luke at the railing and looked out across the waves to the horizon, glad she'd taken Lucille's advice and worn her coat.

"What is it you want from me?" she demanded, looking over at him. "Retaliation for your brother's death. Or leverage? Or both?"

His large hands gripped the railing but his gaze stayed on the horizon. Not even the wash of the tide on the beach could drown out the silence between them.

"You were probably the last person to see my brother alive," he said finally, his voice rough as sand. "You're also the only person who can prove that Derrick Killhorn killed him."

He turned then, his eyes the same color as the gulf. She

wanted desperately to step back from the loathing she saw there, but she held her ground.

"I intend to make Derrick Killhorn pay for what he did to my brother. And—" his gaze locked with hers "—you're going to help me."

His words didn't surprise her. "What is it you think I can do to help you?"

"It's what you're going to do. You're coming back to Montana with me and you're going to tell the authorities that you saw Derrick Killhorn kill my brother and that you can prove it. You're going to give them the evidence you have."

"I can't—"

He didn't let her finish. "Don't tell me you can't because you have no choice," he said, his gaze as threatening as his words. "You haven't from the moment you got into my limo."

Sanders tried the cell phone again, not surprised to get the same message he'd had since being cut off from Kit earlier. "Unavailable."

Luke St. John had Kit and the baby. That much Sanders knew. What he didn't know drove him crazy. Were Kit and Andrew in any danger from Luke St. John? Where were they? Why had St. John kidnapped them?

He thought about calling the cell phone again and realized he was just wasting his time. There wasn't anything else he could do in Texas, there were no other leads to follow.

Convinced Derrick had been right about returning to Montana to wait out St. John's demands, Sanders called and booked a flight out for the next morning.

He started to hang up but realized he still hadn't called

his brother. Derrick would be furious. But that wasn't anything new.

As Sanders dialed the number, he tried not to think about what his brother would do when he learned that St. John had his wife and child.

"What?"

Sanders recoiled at the sound of his brother's drunken voice.

"I wondered when you'd get around to calling," Derrick said, his tone sharp as honed steel. Then he covered the phone and yelled at the top of his lungs. "Get out of here before I throw you out!"

"What's going on?" Sanders demanded.

"That damn Belinda," Derrick spat. "Her and her blood-sucking alimony check. I'd like to—" He took a drink and it seemed to steady him. "Was there a reason you haven't called?"

"I waited until I had as much information as I could get," Sanders lied. He'd put off calling because he'd known how upset Derrick was going to be, and he'd been worried that he would find him drunk. He'd been right on both counts.

"Have you heard anything from…the kidnapper?" Sanders asked.

He was answered with the rattle of ice cubes in a glass, and a drunken, "Who?"

Something in his brother's voice warned him. "Luke St. John. Jason was Luke's youngest brother. Luke's the one who rented the limo that picked up Kit. I was hoping you'd heard from him."

"No," Derrick said flatly.

But Sanders knew he had already heard, probably from P.I. Rustan. Derrick was taking the news much too calmly. He heard Derrick pour himself another drink. He could almost feel the depth of his brother's dark mood oozing through the phone lines.

"What do we do now?" he finally asked.

"What the hell *can* we do?" Derrick snapped back. "We wait. We wait for this Luke St. John to show himself. Then we deal with it."

What did that mean? *Deal with it.* Sanders wanted to ask, but decided now wasn't the time. Derrick was hard enough to talk to when he was sober; he was impossible when he was drunk.

"I've booked a flight back to Big Sky in the morning," Sanders told him. After what he'd heard tonight, it wouldn't be soon enough. "You sound like you might need help."

"Back here?" Derrick demanded as if just catching up with the conversation. "What for? There's nothing you can do here. I need you in Texas."

He'd expected Derrick to be relieved that he was headed home, not upset. "What do you need me to do here?"

Whatever reason Luke St. John had kidnapped Kit and the baby, it tied in with Jason's disappearance—and ultimately with Derrick. Sanders couldn't see how staying in Texas would accomplish anything. Like Derrick, he figured Luke would show himself in one way or another. If only Jason turned up before that. Otherwise… He didn't even want to think of the alternative.

"Just stay there," Derrick commanded. "I don't need any trouble out of you right now." He hung up.

Sanders called the airport to confirm his flight the next morning to Montana. It would be the second time he had openly defied his brother. He hoped he wasn't making a terrible mistake.

* * *

Luke saw Kit flinch at his words, then brace herself as if he were a windstorm she was determined to ride out.

Her eyes burned with anger. "Threatening me and my baby isn't going to bring your brother back."

Her words stung as effectively as if she'd slapped him, and he dropped his gaze from hers, feeling ashamed.

She let out an exasperated sigh. "I can't prove it. That's what I was trying to tell you."

He thought he'd misunderstood. "What?"

"I lied about having physical evidence."

Luke stared at her, disappointment and fury pumping through his veins. "Why?"

She shivered, pulling the coat around her, and stared out at the gulf as if it held the answers. "I was desperate. I thought Derrick might leave us alone if he thought I'd left evidence with someone. But I have nothing that can prove he killed your brother. Nothing but my word against his, and in Big Sky, that *is* nothing."

He grabbed her arms and pulled her around, then stared at her in disbelief. Hadn't she heard anything he'd said? "I don't think you get it," he said through gritted teeth. "This is something you *have* to do. If you don't go back, Derrick Killhorn will get away with murder."

Her voice came out a whisper. "You don't understand what's at stake. I can't go back. I have too much to lose."

Luke battled to keep his temper in check. "You think Derrick will ever stop looking for you now that he *knows* you saw him and *believes* you have physical evidence that can incriminate him?" Luke shook his head. "He will never give you a moment's peace."

"I'm not afraid for myself," Kit cried. "Don't you understand? It's my son." The fervor of her words, the fire in her eyes and the fierce strength he felt under his fingers reminded him of a mama grizzly bear protecting her young. "I can't let Derrick get *my* son."

Luke let go of her and stumbled back a step, frowning. Had he heard her correctly? Not her words so much as the emphasis she'd placed on them? "*Your* son?"

She bit her lip and leaned into the railing, into the darkness and the sound of the waves lapping at the beach.

His head spun in shock. "The baby isn't Derrick's?"

She huddled against the railing as if carrying the weight of the world on her slim shoulders. "No."

The baby wasn't Derrick's? He couldn't believe it. Because he didn't want to believe it. He wanted to think of this woman as Derrick Killhorn's wife. And that baby in the house as Derrick's son. It made what Luke intended to do easier that way. But hadn't he suspected there was more to it? Hadn't he even thought Kit might have taken off with his brother, Jason? "This baby…" he said, glancing toward the house. "It isn't… Jason's, is it?"

Her gaze leaped to his. "No. Why would you ask that? I didn't even know your brother."

Luke nodded. "It's just that when you and Jason both disappeared at the same time—"

She nodded. "You thought we ran off together."

"It crossed my mind." He wouldn't put anything past this woman. But he hadn't meant his words to sound so cold, so condemning.

"I might be a coward, but I'm not an adulteress."

He watched Kit chew at her lip for a moment. When she turned, he expected to see her eyes full of tears, but they seemed as hot and dry as a desert and just as bleak. "Andy's father died when I was two months pregnant. I met Derrick right after that. He convinced me it would be best if everyone thought it was his baby."

"And you went along with that?" She hadn't been kidding, he thought, when she said she'd been bullied into doing what everyone else wanted her to do.

"I didn't know how badly Derrick wanted a baby," she said patiently, but her blue eyes flared with irritation at his remark. "No, not a baby—a *son*. He wants *my* son. In some warped way, he believes that by marrying me, he bought and paid for Andy. Derrick hasn't just been searching for me to keep me from telling anyone about your brother's murder. He thinks he's above the law. And he knows that if he can get Andy back to Montana, it will only make it easier for him to take my son away from me."

"Not if the baby isn't Killhorn's and you can prove he's a murderer."

Kit shook her head. "You don't know the Killhorns."

"I think I do. That's why I won't let them get away with this."

"But what if Derrick *does* get away with it? What am I saying?" she cried, swinging her arms into the air. "He's *already* gotten away with it. With the help of his family, getting my son will be like child's play for him. And since I had to lie on the birth certificate, I can't even use that as proof."

"There are always tests that will show Derrick isn't the father," Luke said, amazed to find himself trying to give her some hope.

"Do you think Derrick will ever let it go that far?" she asked.

Luke saw her disgust for Derrick Killhorn and wondered what had ever made him think she might still love the man.

"Don't you see, it won't matter that Derrick's not Andy's

biological father. He has money and power on his side. I don't even have a job. And he's already told me he plans to prove I'm an unfit mother and take Andy away from me. I ran away nine months pregnant and hid out all this time. Saying I witnessed a murder without some kind of proof would only make me look all the more unstable. Or, like he said, something could happen to me, and he'd be able to take my son the easy way. No one would question Andy's paternity if I was dead."

Luke wanted to argue with her but her words rang with a certain amount of truth. He wasn't sure Derrick wouldn't beat this murder rap. He had so far, just as Kit pointed out. Why wouldn't he kill her if given the opportunity?

But what Derrick didn't know was that Luke planned to bring him down—one way or the other. And Mrs. Derrick Killhorn was going to help him.

Kit brushed a lock of hair from her forehead and shifted her gaze to the gulf. Her face, so etched with defeat, filled him with compassion for her and her son—the very last thing he wanted. He stared at her, feeling powerless without the hatred that had fueled his quest for the last seven months. He couldn't let this woman get to him. She would destroy his plans. Destroy him. Because ultimately, she could keep him from getting the vengeance his heart demanded.

Kit looked over at him. "I want to see Derrick pay for what he did just as much as you do," she said. "I will do everything I can to help you. Just don't ask me to jeopardize my son's life by taking him back to Montana where Derrick can get his hands on him."

He swore under his breath as he watched Kit pull her coat around her. The damp sea air seemed to penetrate his soul. Did he stand any chance at all against Derrick unless he could be just as ruthless?

"Let's go back into the house," Luke said. He put his arm around her shoulders and felt her flinch. Guilt over the realization that she feared him, and had good reason to, made his footsteps heavy as they crossed the porch. "I need you to tell me everything. About the murder. About Derrick."

"And then?" she asked, sounding worried.

"I don't know." All he knew for sure was that he couldn't let Derrick Killhorn get away with murder.

Chapter 9

When Kit entered the house, she found Lucille and Andy in the large old wooden rocker in front of the fire. Andy was in his pajamas, asleep, his chubby pink cheek nestled against Lucille's shoulder, one dimpled arm curled around her neck. Lucille was singing softly and rocking him, her hand patting his diapered bottom to the beat.

Kit stopped just inside the door, touched by the scene. Andy had taken to Lucille so quickly. Just as quickly as Kit herself.

Lucille quit rocking when she saw Kit. "Are you all right?" she asked in alarm.

Kit nodded, not sure that was true.

Lucille let out a sigh of relief and got up. She handed Andy to Kit, glancing from Kit's face to Luke's as if to read what had happened outside. When he didn't say anything, she squeezed his shoulder, walked past him, and went into her studio to close the door behind her.

Kit put Andy down in the crib and knelt to kiss the heat of his soft cheek. He stirred but didn't wake as she covered him. When she turned she caught Luke's gaze on her. He shifted his look to Andy, his large hand stroking his stubbled jaw, but she could see that his thoughts were as lost as he appeared. Lucille was right: this was killing him. She could see that, knew it in her heart in a way she couldn't explain. She'd just met Luke and yet she knew things about him, about who he was and what mattered to him, more than she ever had any other man.

This odd connection with him frightened her because she knew, ultimately, he was going to have to avenge his brother's death. She worried that would destroy the gentle, loving man she sensed in him. And she had no idea what part she and Andy would have to play in that plot.

As she sat down in front of the fire, he tossed another log onto the grate. Then he turned, sat down on a footstool by the woodstove and kneaded his thigh with the heel of his hand.

"Start from the beginning," he said, but it was less of a command than a plea. "Tell me everything, from the first time you ever laid eyes on Derrick Killhorn."

Kit took a breath and did as Luke asked, recounting every detail she could remember, starting that day at the clinic.

"My baby's father had died and I was a couple months pregnant and scared," she said. "On my way out of the clinic I collided with Derrick. He caught me and held me at a moment when I'd never felt more alone."

She avoided Luke's gaze, realizing how much she'd said about herself, about that point in her life. She'd been vulnerable and, looking back, she wondered if Derrick hadn't taken advantage of it.

"I was upset," she continued quickly before Luke could say anything. "Derrick insisted I sit while he went to get me some juice out of the vending machine. He was kind to me, and since I hadn't told anyone else what I was going through—"

"What about family or friends?" Luke asked, frowning.

She shook her head. "I don't have any family and I'd just recently transferred to the University of Montana. I hadn't really had time to make friends with my job, school and... William."

"William is the baby's father," Luke said.

She nodded. "He was one of my professors. No one knew about the two of us. Anyway, I poured out my predicament to Derrick and he told me about his loss, his unborn baby. He said his wife had never wanted a child and when she accidentally got pregnant they argued over keeping it, and one night, in her haste to leave, she fell and miscarried. Eventually, they divorced, but he'd never gotten over the loss. Of course later I learned that it had all been a lie."

"Did you ever ask Derrick what he was doing there at the college clinic?"

His question stunned her. Why hadn't she ever asked herself that before? Big Sky was a good four hours away. What *had* Derrick been doing there?

A thought struck her. "You don't think he'd heard somehow about my baby and—"

Luke shook his head. "I think he was there cruising, looking for someone just like you—a frightened, unmarried, pregnant young girl."

The whole idea was too horrible. That he'd purposely sought her out and the baby she carried from the very beginning.

"And there *you* were—young, unmarried, pregnant and frightened," Luke said.

Had it really been that easy for Derrick? Had that really been what he'd wanted? "I know I sound foolish. But I was touched by his loss and his concern for me and my baby. He offered me security, stability, a home and a family. Those were things I'd wanted my whole life."

"I'm sorry," Luke said. "I didn't mean to imply that you were foolish. Most everyone wants a home and family. But what about love?"

She avoided his gaze. "I thought love would come later." But it didn't.

"And in return for giving you those other things, you were to pretend the baby was his," Luke said.

"It seemed like such a small thing at the time," she said, feeling as naive as she must appear. "He said Big Sky was small and people would talk. It would be better for the baby if everyone thought it was his. And he said as far as he was concerned, the baby *was* his."

Kit glazed over her hurried marriage in front of a justice of the peace in Livingston, and skipped what her life had been like with Derrick in Big Sky.

From the first, he'd seemed overprotective, insisting she not drive, insisting she not leave the house without Sanders or himself with her.

She had thought he was just worried about her having a miscarriage and losing the baby the way his former wife had done. So Kit went along with his ridiculous rules, thankful to have a home and .

But she'd been disappointed when Derrick announced they wouldn't be making love until the baby was born. He said it was much too dangerous, and nothing she could say would convince him otherwise.

Then all Kit's fears about her husband came true.

Kit told Luke about the day Jason St. John was murdered, starting with her doctor's appointment and Belinda.

"Belinda?" Luke asked.

"Derrick's ex-wife. She'd been beaten. She said Derrick did it."

"He beat his ex-wife?" Luke asked, making it sound worse than murder.

Kit hadn't wanted to reveal Belinda's bombshell, but she realized there was no getting around it. "It seems Derrick is sterile. Belinda's the one who told me. Derrick swore it wasn't true, but the next day he'd given her a black eye."

She saw that Luke had tightened his fists. "Nice guy," he commented. "After you talked to Belinda, that's when you went to the condo job site?"

Kit nodded and, closing her eyes, recounted what she'd witnessed.

When she opened her eyes again, she saw Luke's face and realized she'd just made him live through his brother's murder with her. It broke her heart to see him in so much pain. "I'm sorry," she said, impulsively placing a hand on his.

He jerked back as if she'd slapped his hand, and gave her a look that warned her he would stand for no sympathy. "Did you see an old Harley motorcycle when you got to the site, or later when you took Derrick's truck?"

She withdrew her hand. Lucille was right; Luke took strength from his anger. Sympathy, pity, comfort—all would destroy the death grip he held on his emotions.

"Yes, it was parked in front of the job site trailer next to Derrick's new pickup."

"The pickup you took to the bus station, right?"

She nodded. "Derrick always leaves his keys in it."

"Then how did he get home?"

"Sanders came looking for me. I assume he gave Derrick a ride."

"Derrick must have been beside himself when he saw his new pickup gone, put two and two together, and realized you'd taken it—and what that implied."

"I would imagine he went nothing short of berserk since he never lets anyone drive that truck." The thought gave Kit no satisfaction, for from that moment on Derrick had been after her.

"Hopefully berserk enough that he was less worried about the crowbar than he was about getting rid of Jason's body and the bike—and finding you," Luke said. "You say he dropped the crowbar into the empty cells of the block wall. How high was the wall?"

"Maybe seven feet. He had to reach up to do it. I heard the crowbar fall down through the empty blocks."

Luke nodded. "I wonder how soon they were grouted."

"Grouted?"

"Filling the cells of the block walls with cement. It's part of the building code. Big Sky is in Zone Four, the highest risk for earthquakes. Buildings in that area have to be reinforced with steel and concrete."

"So you're saying Derrick has filled the wall with concrete?"

"I would imagine he did it the very next day, but we should be able to find out."

"Wouldn't any evidence on a tool be lost because of the concrete?"

Luke shrugged. "Who knows with today's forensics?" He hoped there would be enough evidence of foul play to get the sheriff's department to look into Jason's disappearance. "*If* the crowbar is still there," he added. "He could have hightailed it back to Montana yesterday and be in the process of disposing of it as we speak."

"I never should have told him I had evidence."

Luke shrugged. "It probably won't make any difference anyway. By now I'm sure Derrick has tracked down the limo I rented and knows that I'm the one who picked up you and Andy. It shouldn't take him long to figure out why. He'll be busy covering his tracks—if he can. I'm hoping he buried everything in so much concrete and steel that he can't get at it. At least not yet."

"Then you think Jason's...body and the bike are still at the job site?" Kit asked hopefully.

"From what you've told me, Derrick didn't have a lot of time before Sanders arrived."

She nodded. "Sanders said he went there right after he realized I'd left the doctor's office, so it couldn't have been that much later. Derrick wouldn't have had time to leave and come back."

"Unless Sanders is in on it. Then the two of them could have buried the body and bike anywhere with all the property and earth-moving equipment the Killhorns own."

She shook her head. "Sanders may be misguided when it comes to his brother, but he wouldn't help him cover up a murder."

"He was sending you to a secluded ranch in Huntsville, knowing Derrick would be there waiting for you," Luke reminded her.

"I'm sure he thought he was doing what was best for me, the baby and Derrick. He believes in his brother's innocence so he sees this as a simple misunderstanding that can be cleared up by Derrick explaining to me what happened."

"He can't be that naive," Luke said.

"Sanders and Derrick have an odd relationship. I think it's because Derrick's father—"

"Judge J. T. Killhorn."

"Yes, the judge thought the sun rose and set with Derrick. Sanders grew up thinking the same thing. Because of that, he's always been very protective of Derrick. But there is something inherently good in Sanders."

Luke didn't share Kit's faith in Sanders. "Then Sanders doesn't know Derrick isn't the baby's father?" he asked, watching Kit carefully as she responded.

She shook her head. "No one does. Except Derrick, you, me and Belinda."

Kit got up to check Andy, and Luke found himself wondering what kind of relationship Kit had had with her husband. Not that it made a damn bit of difference.

"Jason wasn't the hot-headed kid Derrick described to Sanders," Luke said when she returned to the fire. "He had some problems. I'd wanted him to finish college, he wanted to experience life. Because of that he didn't stay long at any one job. He liked to keep moving. But if he was anything, it was a pacifist. Jason would walk away from trouble rather than get involved. If Derrick had fired him, he would have just left peacefully. It wasn't like he needed the job. He could always get another. He definitely wouldn't have fought with his boss over something that meant so little to him."

"But I heard him arguing with Derrick," Kit said.

"I find that hard to believe. Our father died in Vietnam. Because of that, Jason didn't believe in wars or fighting. He was more of a modern-day hippie—probably what he wished our father had been. He never wanted anyone else to lose a father because of a war."

"I'm sorry about your dad," Kit said.

"Thanks. I have a few memories of him, but Jason never knew him at all. That always bothered him."

"I'm just starting to realize the effect that not having parents has had on me and my life," Kit said. "Is probably *still* having on me."

"It must have been hard growing up without even one parent."

"It was." She brushed a wisp of her hair back from her face and gazed into the fire. He could see her fighting old memories, old pains. He knew the look.

"You say you heard Jason and Derrick arguing—not just Derrick's voice?" Luke asked, drawing her back from what demons he could only imagine.

"I heard both voices raised in anger," she said. "But I never saw Jason even attempt to strike Derrick. It was strictly the other way around."

"If Jason was arguing with him, then it was about something my brother felt was too important to back away from." Luke ran the flat of his palm over his stubbled jaw. "Something was going on at the job, something that had Jason troubled enough to contact me. He'd called the day before he disappeared. I could tell he was upset. He said he'd stumbled onto a problem at the job. I think he would have told me then, but he was interrupted. Someone came into the room where he was calling from. He said he had to get off the line. He promised to call back. He never did."

"A problem?"

Luke shrugged. "I don't know, but I think, whatever it was, it's what got him killed. At one point, I thought the problem might be you because the two of you disappeared at the same time. I thought that you'd gotten involved with my brother and either talked him into taking off with you or got him killed. I've feared from the beginning it was the latter because of something I found at Jason's apartment."

"What was that?"

"I went to the room Jason rented, in a rundown seedy place at the edge of Big Sky owned by Derrick Killhorn. Jason's room had been cleaned out. Except for one thing. A photograph of our father in a small metal frame. It was on the floor next to the bed as if it had fallen there. Jason would never have left that behind." Unless he was in a tremendous hurry. Or was already dead when his room was cleaned out.

Luke got up to toss a couple more logs on the fire, afraid if he said another word that his emotions would betray him. He stared into the flames, listening to the dry wood pop and crackle.

Her touch, when it came, was hesitant. He felt her hand on his back. That was all. Just that one small palm. Branding his back with a warmth that radiated across his shoulders. He soaked up the feeling, his head down, his eyes closed, the firelight making flickering patterns across his eyelids. For that moment, he didn't care if she saw how vulnerable he was, how lost, how hurt or how much he needed to feel less alone, even for a moment.

Then he straightened and pulled away as he reached for another log and threw it into the blaze. When he turned, she had gone to the crib to check her son.

He thought about saying something, but when she came back to the fire, he realized he didn't know what to say. And the moment was lost.

"Do you think you could find that room again—the one where you saw Jason murdered?" he asked after a while.

"I don't know. I was so upset that day, I wasn't paying any attention to where I was going. I was just following the voices. It was the only time I was at the job. Derrick had this rule about no one but employees on the site. But I remember the spot where Derrick dropped the crowbar into the block cells. Once I find that room, I could tell you where on the wall the crowbar would be—if it's still there."

Like her, Luke had only been to the job site once, when he knew no one would be there. His first inclination had been to go straight to Derrick Killhorn and demand some answers. Fortunately, when he'd given it some thought, he decided working undercover would serve his purposes better. So he'd gone to the complex at night and looked around. He'd found nothing, but then he hadn't known what he was looking for. Now he knew.

He thought for a moment about finding the room and the evidence against Derrick Killhorn. As yet, he wasn't sure exactly what he planned to do with that evidence, since Kit had refused to go to the police. But he wanted that crowbar. He thought of it as gathering nails. Nails that would seal Derrick's casket. "It's on the ground floor, right?"

"At the back, deep in the building. The place was like a maze and with the complex finished by now, it will probably be impossible to find. I would imagine it's changed so much, and there are people living there by now, aren't there?"

Luke looked up at her. She didn't know. "The complex isn't finished. In fact, it will probably look pretty much like it did when you were last there."

"But that was seven months ago."

He nodded. "The job's been shut down. The word around town is that Derrick's in financial trouble." Luke looked to her for confirmation.

"I wouldn't know. I know nothing about Derrick's business. My name was never even on the checking account.

Derrick just had Sanders get me whatever I needed. But you've seen the house."

"Yes." It reeked of affluence but then it looked like that was exactly the image Derrick was shooting for. "Didn't you say Derrick was building this complex on his own?"

Kit nodded. "Last Christmas he was trying to get some investors but no one was interested. He was very upset. I remember he and Sanders arguing about it. Sanders is a partner in the construction company. He warned Derrick that financing such a huge project himself would be risky. Sanders was worried it would jeopardize the company."

"It sounds like the rumor might be true then," Luke said. He laughed and Kit looked over at him in surprise.

"I was just thinking how ironic it is. Imagine if you murdered someone and buried his body and his bike at your construction site. You're not worried because pretty soon it will be covered in concrete, carpet and residents. But then you run out of money and the building just sits there, partially completed, exposed. Any little construction problem could open up a can of worms—or in Derrick's case, uncover a body. Imagine how frustrating that must be for him. And then on top of that, he has you and me after him."

He could see the humor of the situation was a little too black for her.

"Do you think Derrick's financial problems might have had something to do with what he and Jason were arguing about that day?" she asked. "Maybe Derrick couldn't meet payroll."

"Money never meant that much to Jason. He might have quit and moved on, but he wouldn't have fought Derrick over a paycheck."

"But they *were* arguing," she pointed out.

Luke rubbed his jaw. "Then it had to be over something

else." He smiled, remembering his little brother. "Jason was the kind of guy who walked little old ladies across the street, shared his lunch with stray dogs, and always took his grocery cart back into the store. He believed this world could be better with a little kindness, a little caring."

Kit smiled. "He sounds like someone I would have liked."

Luke nodded, thinking that Jason would have liked Kit too. But that didn't help matters much. He tried to concentrate on what Derrick could have done to make Jason argue with him. Something. Something big. But instead he felt himself watching Kit, wondering about her.

She looked up at him. He could feel a hum between the two of them, like a power line.

"You think Derrick is back in Montana then?" she asked, almost sounding edgy. She must have felt it too.

He nodded, noticing how her hair shone in the firelight.

"Covering his tracks?" She had the bluest eyes he thought he'd ever seen. Clear blue. They reminded him of Montana summer skies.

"Probably," he said. "If he can."

"And Sanders?" she asked.

Her lips were full, slightly bowed: a classic kissable mouth. He reminded himself who this woman was. Mrs. Derrick Killhorn.

She licked her lips nervously and looked away, and he realized he'd been staring. For a moment, he had to struggle to remember her question. "Sanders? Doing whatever his brother tells him to do. Probably looking for us." He softened his tone. "Don't worry about it. He won't find us." At least not yet. "Get some sleep. We'll talk about it in the morning."

She nodded and closed her eyes.

Luke stood there for a moment, then he went over to his bunk. When he turned around, she was sound asleep in front of the fire. He tugged the quilt off her bunk and, putting her feet up on the ottoman, covered her to her chin.

He watched her sleep, wondering what had ever made her marry Derrick Killhorn.

He'd heard around Big Sky, after Kit had left town, that Derrick had robbed the cradle, taken himself a wife who was more child than woman, more cute than beautiful. Luke could see that that might have been true at one time. There was a freshness, an innocence about her, a girl-like quality in the sprinkling of freckles that ran across the bridge of her nose to add a flush to her cheeks.

He recalled the blue of her eyes and the sadness he'd seen there when she talked about her life with Derrick. Sadness. Worry. Fear. Her eyes seemed older than her face now. Older and wiser, he thought. After what she'd seen, he wasn't surprised—just sorry. But he still sensed an innocence, an innocence that intrigued him. And concerned him.

The light of the fire caught in her hair, inflaming it. In sleep she looked as defenseless as her baby son. His aunt was right. Kit Bannack was as much a victim as Jason had been. But Jason was dead, and Kit was still alive. All Luke had to do was keep her that way.

"Good night, Kit Bannack," Luke said quietly.

After he climbed into the top bunk, he lay for a long time watching the fire, watching Andy sleeping in the crib, trying to decide what to do next. Finally, he closed his eyes, content that Kit and Andy were safe. For the moment. He fell asleep thinking of them instead of his hatred of Derrick Killhorn.

Chapter 10

Sanders woke with a start. Immediately his conversation with Derrick began replaying in his head. His brother's reaction to the problem seemed…off. Sanders wasn't sure how he would respond to the same situation. Certainly, he'd do more than wait.

And why hadn't Derrick wanted him to return to Montana? That seemed strange at best. What could he possibly do in Texas? Nothing.

Feeling defeated, he stumbled into the bathroom and turned on the shower. When he came back out of the bathroom ten minutes later, he noticed the red light on the phone flashing.

He stopped in the middle of the room, at first confused, then alarmed. No one knew where he was. Derrick hadn't asked. Probably too drunk to care. Nor had Sanders offered the information. So who knew to call him here?

Sanders picked up the motel room phone, pushed the button for his voice mail and waited expectantly.

To his surprise, the message was from Matthew Rustan. He wondered how the P.I. had found him.

"Traced your credit card," Rustan said, as if Sanders had asked. "I've got something for you. Call me."

Kit woke in front of the fire to the smell of coffee, surprised to find it was morning and that she'd apparently slept the entire night curled in the chair. The last thing she remembered was Luke saying she should go to bed. She wondered who'd covered her with the quilt.

She glanced over at the crib, expecting to see Andy still asleep, and sat bolt upright when she saw the crib was empty. Then she heard his little laugh and turned to see Luke sitting at the table next to the high chair, feeding her son.

"Good morning," Luke said. Andy let out a squeal, and Luke smiled at him, the first real smile she'd seen from the man. The effect was amazing and unsettling.

Kit shrugged off the quilt and got up, feeling guilty for having slept so late. Normally she woke to Andy's cries. She wondered how she'd slept through them this morning, then realized she hadn't. Luke must have gotten Andy the moment the baby stirred. Luke had purposely let her sleep.

"Do you want me to help with that?" she asked as she headed for the table.

He glanced up, the lines of his face softer somehow, less darkness in the gray of his eyes. "Not unless you're worried I can't handle it."

"You seem to be doing just fine," she said, going into the kitchen to help herself to a cup of coffee. Luke did seem to know what he was doing. Andy let out a squawk and beat wildly on the high chair tray with his tiny palms.

"All right, buddy, I'm paying attention now," Luke said, getting the baby another bite. Kit noticed with surprise that he appeared to be enjoying himself as much as Andy was. She watched him put applesauce on the tip of the spoon, camouflaging the cereal behind it. Then he flew the spoon like a dive-bomber toward the baby's eagerly awaiting mouth, making Andy squeal again in delight.

Kit smiled. "How did you know he doesn't like cereal much?"

Luke shrugged and scooped up a spoonful to examine more closely. "Who would?" he said, making a face that made Andy laugh.

She took a chair across from Luke, remembering his expertise in buckling up the car seat yesterday, and his obvious experience in feeding babies. A thought struck her. "You must have children of your own."

He shook his head. "Just lots of nieces and nephews."

Kit watched him feed her son, amazed at the change in Luke. Had this been what he was like before his brother's death? Yes, she thought, remembering the photo of him. Watching him, she could almost convince herself that the other Luke St. John, the man filled with the desire for vengeance had never existed. But she glimpsed a sadness in Luke that seemed to pierce his very soul. And she knew the revengeful Luke would be back, and probably before very long, because, as his aunt had said, he wouldn't rest until he made Derrick pay. But at what cost to himself? she wondered. What cost to her and Andy?

Lucille came in, kissed the top of Andy's towhead and stopped behind Kit, her hand on Kit's shoulder.

"I've been doing some thinking," Lucille said.

"So have I." Luke looked up at her, the baby spoon in midair. "We can't stay here any longer."

Kit felt Lucille's fingers dig into her shoulder.

"Where are we going?" Lucille asked.

"Not *we*. I'm going back to Montana," he said, his tone taking on that hard edge again. "I'm going after Killhorn, just like I planned." His eyes moved to Kit's face. "Kit's going with me."

Sanders found Matthew Rustan in his office chair, looking like he'd had a rough night.

"Have you found Jason St. John?" Sanders inquired expectantly as he drew one of the straight-backed chairs up to the P.I.'s cluttered desk.

Rustan got up to make coffee. "No, and we're not going to find him until he gets a job. We need a paper trail. This kid has no credit cards, bank accounts, checking or savings, no electricity, water, sewage bills, no phone or address, and either is still unemployed or working off the books."

"Is there any way to prove he isn't dead?" Sanders asked and instantly regretted the question.

Rustan's head bobbed up. "Dead? You think he's dead?"

"No, I just asked if there was any way to prove he wasn't."

He hated the gleam that came into the P.I.'s eyes as he poured a cup of watery coffee and motioned to Sanders with the dirty cup. Sanders shook his head.

"Why don't you just tell me what's really going on," Rustan said as he sat back down. "First your brother has me looking for his wife, then you hire me to look for Jason St. John. Supposedly the wife gets found, but no sign of Jason. Then we've got you being bugged right before you start inquiring about Luke St. John." He took a sip of the coffee and made a face. "Come on, I know this isn't a simple missing person's case. We've got a few too many people missing and—" Rustan leaned toward him "—and too many with the same last name."

Before Sanders could tell him to mind his own business, the fax machine purred on and Rustan swiveled around in his chair to watch the paper roll out.

"I thought you said you had something for me," he reminded the P.I.

Rustan plucked up the paper the moment the machine freed it, scanned the page and swung back around, smiling. "Last night I cashed in a lot of old debts trying to get something on this Luke St. John. What happened four years ago? I got the answer." He held up the sheet of paper. "What's it worth to you? Or do you think your brother would be more interested?"

Sanders fought the urge to take the sheet of paper and cram it down the P.I.'s throat. He realized he was starting to act like his brother. A frightening thought.

"I'd fire you right now, but I don't think that would have much impact on you, would it?" Sanders said.

"No, I'd just dig a little deeper in the family's skeleton closet."

Sanders tossed a couple of twenties onto the P.I.'s desk. Rustan looked offended. Sanders threw down a hundred and started to pick up the twenties, but Rustan already had them in his greedy hand. The P.I. dropped the fax on a corner of the desk and sat back, waiting for Sanders's reaction.

Kit stared at Luke in amazement. How could he sit there and feed her child, laugh with him and tease him, and not even consider Andy's life? She felt sick. Was she wrong about the things she sensed in Luke St. John? "What about my baby?" she asked, her voice breaking.

He scraped the last of the applesauce from the baby food jar and fed it to Andy. But the mood had gone sour and even Andy seemed to sense it.

"You have to come with me," Luke said more softly to her. "I'm sorry, but I need you if I hope to prove Derrick killed my brother. You know which room Jason was killed in. The only way we can find it is to retrace your steps. If the crowbar is still there, I have to find it."

She heard the plea in his voice. He needed her to help him find the evidence. But it was more than that. What else did he want from her? "What about Andy?" she asked again.

Luke pushed back his chair and took the dirty spoon and baby food jars to the sink, limping. Sometimes his limp seemed more pronounced. When he was tired, she thought. When he was upset. He came back with a warm washrag.

She took it from him and began to clean the smears of applesauce and cereal from Andy's face. He wriggled and giggled, making her smile although her heart felt made of lead. When his face again glowed, shiny and bright, she leaned down to plant a kiss on his damp, chubby cheek and felt tears leap to her eyes.

"I won't take my son back to Montana," she declared and looked up, aware of the heat of Luke's gaze on her.

"You won't have to." He glanced toward his aunt. "I think I've come up with a way to protect your son."

"You know I'll do whatever you ask," Lucille said quickly.

He motioned for them both to sit down.

"I was thinking about that houseboat of Vernon's," Luke

said as he took a chair across from Kit. "Do you think he would take you and the baby on a little trip if I asked him?"

Lucille nodded. "Vernon would do anything for you and Jason." Her eyes welled with tears.

"Wait a minute," Kit interrupted. "What are you thinking about doing with my son?"

Luke reached across the table and secured her hands together on the table with one of his large ones. "You and Andy aren't safe anywhere right now. Am I wrong?" He continued before she could respond. "The only way to keep you safe is not to stay in one place too long. If Andy is with Lucille and Vernon on his houseboat, traveling around the inland waterways, Derrick won't be able to find them. And believe me when I tell you, Vernon would die before he'd let anything bad happen to that baby."

Lucille nodded in agreement and looked to Kit.

Kit could see Luke inspired that kind of loyalty in friends. She had sensed that in him and was glad to see that she had at least been right about that.

But that didn't mean she could leave her son behind. "I don't think you realize what you're asking me to do."

He squeezed her hands. "You're wrong. I understand the bond between a mother and her child. This may be the hardest thing you'll ever have to do. But it's also the only way you can guarantee your son's safety for the future. Are you willing to leave him for a few days to do that?"

She looked into Luke's gray eyes and knew the answer to her next question before she even asked it. "Do I have a choice?"

"No. But I'm trying to give you as much of a guarantee as I can that your son will be safe." He let go of her hands. "I can't give you the same guarantee about *yourself*. All I can tell you is that I will do everything in my power to keep you out of Derrick's hands. Both are better guarantees than what you would have gotten if you'd taken the limo Sanders sent for you, or just kept running. Let's get packed," he said, as if that ended the discussion. "I'll call Vernon."

Kit couldn't speak around the lump in her throat as she pulled her son from the high chair and hugged him to her. She felt Lucille's arms come around them both.

"Please try not to worry about Andy," the older woman said. "I'll take good care of him."

"I know," Kit cried. "It's just so hard."

"Of course it is, but how else are you going to end this terrible thing? Once it's over, you and Andy can be together and have nothing to fear."

Kit wondered. She'd lived in fear for so long, she couldn't imagine no longer being afraid.

She heard Luke hang up the phone. "Vernon will be by in ten minutes to pick up you and the baby," he told his aunt.

Lucille nodded. "I'll pack a few things, not much, because I know you won't be gone long." She stepped to her nephew and hugged him. "Be careful. Take care of Kit." Then she went to pack.

Kit took Andy to the crib to get him dressed for his trip, but tears blurred her eyes and her fingers trembled so hard that she gave up trying. Luke gently stepped in and changed Andy, dressing him in one of her favorite outfits: a little sailor suit.

She turned away to keep from sobbing and went to change out of her borrowed sweats into a pair of jeans and a light sweater of her own. When she came back, Luke handed her Andy and stepped away.

She held him, looking into his perfect little cherub face. He laughed and touched her cheek with his hand. She kissed his palm, holding it to her lips for a long moment. How could she not be with him? She couldn't even bear the thought. They'd never been apart.

"I will miss you so much, but I *will* be back," she told her son in a quiet whisper. "Be a good boy for Aunt Lucille and don't let anything happen to you, all right?"

A horn honked out front. Kit looked up to find Luke waiting to take the baby. Lucille stood by the front door, tears in her eyes, her overnight bag in her hand.

Kit hugged her son tightly, then kissed her own tears from his cheek, before she handed him to Luke. She followed them to the door and watched, choking back sobs, as Lucille and Andy climbed into a light blue van. She caught a glimpse of a nice-looking older man behind the wheel—and then her baby was gone.

Chapter 11

Shortly after Lucille and the baby left, another car pulled up out front and a man, probably the same one who had disposed of the limo, appeared at the door with an armload of packages. Luke didn't introduce him, and the man quickly left, leaving the tan, nondescript car behind.

"Here," Luke said without preamble.

Kit opened the boxes he handed her and stared at the winter clothing inside. "What do you want me to do with all of this?" she asked.

"Wear it," he said. "It's December in Montana and cold. Since you left in June, I would assume you don't have any warm clothing, right?"

She raised a brow. "How did you know my size?"

His gaze roved over her, almost intimately. "I have a good eye." He smiled. "Actually I guessed on some and cheated and looked in your suitcase on others, like shoe size. You'd better change and get ready," he said, opening the other boxes. "We have to leave soon."

At Luke's insistence, Kit put a dark brown rinse on her hair and pulled it back into a French roll. He'd had his friend pick up a pair of tortoiseshell glasses with clear lenses for her and a beautiful hunter-green sweater and tan wool slacks that accentuated not only her figure but her long legs.

She thought she'd feel self-conscious. But when she looked in the mirror, she didn't recognize the woman who peered back at her. Just a stranger in a beautiful outfit, a woman who looked confident and self-assured and—sexy. Not a woman who'd never owned clothing like this in her life and who'd never thought of herself as alluring.

She came out of Lucille's studio and stood nervously waiting for Luke's reaction.

He turned, his eyes widening at the sight of her, and let out a low whistle. "Wow. You look…sensational."

She blushed and brushed at the hem of the sweater with trembling fingers. "You're sure it isn't too—"

"It's not too anything," he said.

She smiled at him. He'd changed into slacks and a wool shirt.

"You look…" He looked very masculine, very virile, very strong. She was at a loss for words to describe what just the sight of him did to her. But she realized he'd look masculine in anything he wore—or nothing at all. The thought shocked her. She blushed again and ducked her head, but not before she'd seen a slow smile curl his lips.

"I take it I look all right?" he said and laughed softly. "Are you ready?"

Ready? She'd forgotten for a moment why they were doing this, what would happen when they reached Montana and, worse yet, what would happen when they went back to Big Sky. It was fun playing dress-up, pretending she was someone else, someone mysterious and sexy and self-confident.

On the ride to the airport, she felt like plain old Kit again. She missed Andy terribly and worried about what would happen when Derrick found out she was back in Montana. And she had no doubt that he would.

"Are you all right?" Luke asked as they took their seats together on the plane. He held her hand as if they were husband and wife, just another couple going to Montana for Christmas or a ski holiday.

She nodded, too close to tears to speak.

"Don't worry about Andy. He's in good hands."

"I know." She remembered her son's immediate reaction to Lucille. And her own sense of comfort. She'd felt safe and warm in the woman's hug, enveloped in the rich smells of her kitchen, cradled in the homeyness of the fishing cottage. It had made her realize how much she needed such a place—and not just temporarily. She needed it for her own peace of mind, but for Andy as well. And she wasn't going to get it until Derrick Killhorn was behind bars. That much she agreed with Luke about. The only way she and Andy could ever be free—or safe—was for her to help Luke get the evidence against Derrick.

But she also knew Derrick and what he was capable of. "I just want this to be over."

Luke said nothing. She glanced at him. He seemed deep in thought. Was he too wishing it was over? Or would it ever be over for him?

Luke played the role of attentive husband on the flight back to Bozeman. He almost looked relaxed, at ease with himself and her. And she enjoyed the reprieve, sitting with him as if they were husband and wife. The flight attendant had already assured them that they would be having a white Christmas.

Christmas. Kit couldn't believe it was just days away. She was thankful that Andy was so young. He wouldn't know if she wasn't there on Christmas morning. He would think it was no different from any other day. But Kit would know. They had only a few days. That didn't seem like enough time to trap a murderer. Especially one as ruthless as Derrick Killhorn.

It was early afternoon when they landed at Gallatin Field just outside of Bozeman. The moment they touched down, Kit saw what she'd originally believed to be a permanent frown crease Luke's brow again. His eyes took on that cold hard sheen of steel and she felt him draw away from her as if she were again Mrs. Derrick Killhorn, the wife of his enemy.

Luke was sorry when they landed. He'd enjoyed the flight, enjoyed Kit. Enjoyed talking to her. Enjoyed just looking at her. He'd known she would look beautiful in hunter green.

As she came out of the airport ladies' room, he watched her move through the small group by the baggage pickup. She looked good. Too good. The slacks hugged her buttocks nicely and the sweater accented the fullness of her breasts. She still wore the glasses, making her blue eyes seem very large and wide. Her hair hung down around her shoulders in waves of rich auburn brown. The woman was a walking distraction.

He frowned as he handed her the ski jacket, hat and mittens he'd had purchased for her along with the other clothing. "Let's get going," he said brusquely, resenting the way other men were looking at her and not really happy with the way she made *him* feel. All too well he remembered the jolt he'd felt when he'd brushed her arm on the plane. And she'd felt it too. He'd seen it in the way her eyes had widened. In the rapid beat of her pulse in the hollow of her throat. In the shocked, scared expression on her pretty face.

He had to remind himself that she was another man's wife. And that no matter what the circumstances, the other man was Derrick Killhorn. That thought worked as effectively on him as a dousing with a bucket of ice water.

He led her out to his pickup, an old black Chevy, parked in the lot where a friend of his had left it for him. He tried not to think about Kit as he drove down Jackrabbit Lane, following the Gallatin River past farmland and small subdivisions. Snowfields ran across the wide valley to lofty mountain peaks. This afternoon the Valley of the Flowers, as the Indians had named it, seemed filled with the lights strung for the holiday season.

Luke hadn't celebrated Christmas in years. Four, to be exact. He felt vulnerable, and told himself it was the season, not the woman beside him, making him feel that way.

Kit felt claustrophobic. Not that the pickup wasn't large and roomy enough. The problem was Luke. On the plane, there'd been other people around. But here in the darkness alone with him, it felt too intimate. He seemed to take up all the space, filling her senses with his presence. His scent. His body heat. His maleness. The soft rush of his breathing.

Even his movements seemed magnified, so filled with masculine confidence. This was a man who knew who he was. And, she feared, was aware of his effect on her.

It wasn't until they were headed south on the two-lane, that Kit realized she had no idea where they were going. She worried that someone would recognize her and tell Derrick if they went anywhere near Big Sky, and yet it looked as if that was exactly where they were headed. Just the thought of encountering Derrick sent her terror escalating.

"So where *are* we going?" she asked as if they'd just been discussing it. In fact, they hadn't discussed anything. Not where they were going or what they'd do when they got there. Their talk on the plane had been conversational and very general. She knew no more about Luke St. John than she had the previous day. And that was nothing.

Luke had been quiet from the time they left the airport. Kit couldn't blame him. Coming back here was even harder on him than it was on her. He'd come back knowing that Jason was definitely dead and probably buried somewhere in the Killhorn condo complex.

"South," he answered after a moment.

"Even I can see that."

He glanced over at her, appearing surprised by her tone.

"Don't you think you should at least let me in on what you're planning?" she asked.

He seemed to think that over and she got the impression he wasn't in the habit of sharing his thoughts—let alone his plans—with anyone. "To a friend's place at Big Sky."

Big Sky. Right into the lion's den. "Do you think that's a good idea?"

He shot her a look that told her he didn't appreciate her questioning his judgment. "Going to Twodot won't exactly help us get evidence on a murder that took place in Big Sky, don't you think?"

She ignored his sarcasm. "Where *you* live?" she asked, feeling as though she was prying, but at the same time keenly aware of how little she knew about this man.

"In the same area."

That was specific enough. She stared out the window, her heart aching for her son.

At the mouth of the Gallatin Canyon, snow began to fall, drifting down in a hypnotizing blur of white. Her arms felt so empty without him, as if a part of her were missing. She told herself they would be together again in a few days and that they would never have to fear Derrick Killhorn again. She silently prayed that would be true. But first, she reminded herself, she had to go back to Big Sky. And that meant facing Derrick.

Halfway down the Gallatin Canyon, Luke saw the flashing red and blue lights in his rearview mirror. He cursed under this breath and pulled over, reminding himself that Derrick's uncle was the sheriff.

But the cop car whizzed on past, siren blaring. Luke sat for a moment, letting his heart settle down again.

"Whoa," Kit said, looking pale in the dash lights. "I thought he was after us. I thought..."

"I know," Luke said. He knew exactly what she thought because he'd thought the same thing. He'd thought somehow they'd walked into a trap.

He studied Kit's face for a moment, remembering his promise to try to keep her safe. As much as he didn't like the idea, he knew he had to get a weapon. He knew he could kill Derrick with his bare hands, but only if he got close enough. A gun would help him protect Kit and possibly even increase their odds, because he didn't need anyone to tell him that Derrick would fight dirty.

He pulled back out onto the highway, watching his speed, feeling edgy, the hair on the nape of his neck prickly, his skin hot. Yeah, he needed a gun, but he also needed his wits about him. He'd been scared when he'd seen the cop car and the flashing lights behind him. But he hadn't been scared for himself. It was for Kit. She was his Achilles' heel. And he knew Derrick would try his best to use her against him.

Ahead he could see more flashing red and blue lights. As he drew nearer he saw that a semitrailer and truck had overturned on one of the sharp curves on the highway that wound along with the Gallatin River through towering granite bluffs and snow-crested pines.

The semi was blocking both lanes of the highway. A half-dozen cars and trucks were backed up. Luke joined the line to wait out the wrecker.

A phone rang. Luke turned to give Kit a puzzled look. It wasn't until the phone rang again that he realized the sound was coming from her purse.

"Sanders's cell phone." He vaguely remembered slipping it into her purse as they were leaving the limo the night before. He'd completely forgotten about it, he thought with a curse.

"Why hasn't it rung before?" Kit asked, fear in her eyes as she opened her purse and dug down to the bottom for the phone. She handed it to him as if it were a dirty diaper.

"It wasn't *on* before." He glanced at her. Had she turned it on? Maybe she'd tried to contact Sanders in the airport rest room. The fool woman still believed Sanders was on her side. Would she have called him? "Did you turn the phone back on?" He tried not to make it sound like an accusation.

"I didn't even know it was in my purse." Her eyes fired with irritation. So much for trying not to rile her.

"Maybe something jiggled against it in your purse," he suggested.

The phone rang again. One word glowed on the digital readout: Call. "It seems you have voice mail too."

He held out the phone for her to see. She pulled back as if the last thing she wanted to do was touch it again.

"Are you going to answer it?" she asked.

It had crossed Luke's mind. But he didn't really have anything to say to the Killhorns right now. And he didn't want Sanders trying to con Kit. Luke needed her, and he intended to hang on to her at all costs.

"No, I don't think answering it's a good idea."

"It's probably Sanders," she said, looking at the phone as if tempted. "I'm sure he must be worried about me."

Yeah, sure. Luke turned off the phone, studying her in the dash lights of his pickup for a moment. "You still trust him after everything that's happened," he said.

She turned away to look out the window toward the lights of Bozeman.

He had to admire her loyalty, misplaced as it was. Now all he had to do was keep her from doing something stupid because of that trust. If he wasn't careful, she could get them both killed.

Luke considered the cell phone in his hand for a moment, wondering if there was any way Killhorn could track the device. He didn't know anything about cell phones. He'd been living in isolation for too long. Not that it probably mattered. Derrick had to know Luke was coming for him. Luke just didn't see any reason to give him their itinerary. But first, he'd like to hear Kit's messages.

"Do you know how to listen to the voice mail on this?" he asked.

She nodded and gave him the code Sanders had provided her. Luke dialed it in and listened to several messages from

Sanders. They were pretty much as he'd expected: "Call me, Kit. I have to talk to you. I'm worried about you."

But the last message had a different ring to it, one that grabbed his attention.

"Kit, the man who's kidnapped you, Luke St. John. I just found out. Four years ago something horrible happened involving his former fiancée and his best friend. He's dangerous, Kit. Call me. It's urgent that I talk to you."

Luke didn't even realize he'd let out a low curse until Kit asked, "What is it? What's wrong?"

Luke shook his head as he rolled down his window. "Nothing. Just Sanders trying to get you back for his brother." Luke threw the phone high into the air out over the Gallatin River.

"He believes in Derrick's innocence," Kit said.

Maybe, Luke thought. *Or he just does whatever Derrick Killhorn says, right or wrong.* In either case, Luke couldn't let Kit talk to Sanders. Not now.

On the plane flying in from San Francisco, Sanders had tried the cell phone number again and had been surprised when the phone finally rang.

He jumped, startled. When had she turned it back on? He held his breath, willing Kit to answer. But the ringing stopped and the message read: *Unavailable.*

Again. Frustrated, he'd started to hang up, but changed his mind. Was there a way to trace Kit through the cell phone?

After a long conversation with the cell phone company, Sanders decided he was becoming quite adept at lying. Derrick would have been proud.

He'd discovered that his cell phone signal had been picked up from a Bozeman cell site tower. Bozeman. Not Texas. If the cell phone was back in Montana, then Sanders could only assume Kit was too. And the baby. And Luke St. John. The question was why?

Sanders had hung up with only one thought in mind. Getting home. And in a hurry.

He landed at Gallatin Field outside Bozeman, Montana, thirty minutes behind Kit and Luke. He'd left a message for Derrick with his flight number and time of arrival, but his brother was nowhere to be seen.

Sanders was in the process of renting a car when Derrick showed up, in a foul mood, reeking of whiskey.

"I thought I told you to stay in Texas," he snapped.

"I decided I'd better get back here and find out what's going on," Sanders said, returning the rental form to the clerk.

"When did you start thinking for yourself?" Derrick asked as Sanders picked up his suitcase and headed for the exit. He heard his brother behind him and put out his hand for Derrick's pickup keys.

Derrick hesitated for only a moment before he dropped the keys into Sanders's hand.

"Thinking for himself and driving too?" Derrick said, going around to the passenger side.

Sanders slid behind the wheel and started the pickup. "You'd better tell me just how much trouble you're in."

"Sand," Derrick said after a long moment. His voice sounded close to tears and Sanders felt himself pulled to his brother as if dragged by a rope. Derrick hadn't called him "Sand" since they were kids.

"I've got to get my son back, Sand. Tell me you're going to help me."

Sanders felt that last tug, their shared history, their shared blood. Brothers. "That's why I'm here, he told Derrick."

Chapter 12

Kit had been so lost in her thoughts, in her worries about Andy, that she hadn't even noticed the traffic had begun to move again. The afternoon light began to fade, the canyon to fill in with shadow. She wondered what Andy was doing right now and where he was and if he missed her. At least he was somewhere warm.

As Luke slowed the car, she looked up in surprise to see that the snow had stopped and they had reached Big Sky. The forty-mile trip from the airport had gone quickly. Too quickly.

Big Sky was one of those places you could pass and not really even know it. An unincorporated community made up of three villages, most of Big Sky could not be seen from the highway.

Canyon Village was the cluster of tourist convenience stores, gas stations, art galleries, fly-fishing shops and restaurants along the highway.

Luke turned into the Big Sky entrance and drove west a quarter of a mile to Meadow Village. Kit stared at Big Sky's one distinguishing feature: Lone Peak. It rose 11,166 feet above the meadow, snowcapped and elegant, against the navy blue of the sky and as dark as her memories, as ominous as her last time here.

"How are you doing?" Luke asked as he drove through Meadow Village with its assortment of condos, restaurants and ski shops.

"I'm all right," she lied, wondering where Derrick was right now. It terrified her to be this close. She felt Luke's gaze on her, but he said nothing as he drove along the edge of the golf course, now snow white and crisscrossed with cross-country ski tracks. Everything seemed to sparkle in Christmas lights and snow.

"I keep forgetting about Christmas," she said, staring at a huge tree glittering in one of the large houses in Meadow Village. She had such a longing for Andy that it brought tears to her eyes.

"Andy's all right, you know," Luke said.

She nodded, unable to speak.

"He and Lucille will be at a phone tonight. We'll call so you'll know he's fine."

She smiled at Luke. "Thank you."

Luke started up the snowpacked mountain road, winding through the pines and snow, higher and higher. They began to see the cars coming down the mountain, all with either skis or snowboards strapped on top, a sign that skiing had ended for the day.

"Where are we headed?" she asked again, afraid they were going straight to Derrick's job site, straight to Killhorn Condos and the murder scene.

"To a friend's cabin," Luke said, and kept driving. They

climbed until she could see the eighty miles of ski runs like pale white scars on the mountain, and finally the lights of Mountain Village nestled at the base of the peak.

Luke didn't turn into the resort but took a snowpacked unpaved road to the right. Dusk began to settle into the pines and lights winked on in the thick cluster of condos near the ski resort.

Kit felt herself tense as she realized how close they were to Derrick's condo development. She glanced at Luke. He drove past the road to the complex and didn't even look in that direction, but she knew he had to be thinking about it, just as she was.

A little farther up the road, Kit turned to glance back. She could see the silhouette against the sky. Killhorn Condos. The massive building sat on the edge of a cliff, odd-shaped because it was unfinished, looking out at the Big Sky resort, at Lone Peak, at her. She felt a chill and turned back to the road and to Luke.

They hadn't gone much farther when Luke pulled off in a plowed parking area and killed the engine. Just above them, in the pines, she could make out what appeared to be a two-car garage. "We have to take a snowmobile from here," he announced.

Kit pulled on her hat and mittens and followed him up the hill to the garage, remembering the other night when she'd followed him to Lucille's fishing cottage. She reminded herself how little she'd learned since then about the man she'd now been thrown in with.

They walked through the deep snow into the growing darkness, neither talking. Luke opened the garage door with a key and turned on a light. Kit saw a newer model snowmobile parked inside. Luke went to it and, a moment later, the machine leaped to life, motor thrumming. Luke motioned for her to climb on behind him as he pulled out of the garage. The garage lights went out and the door closed behind them.

They sped up a snowy path that led even higher into the woods and the mountains. The air smelled of snow and pines. The single headlight on the snowmobile flickered through the snow-laden boughs. To the west, the sun dipped deeper. Daylight faded. Shadows hunkered under the trees. She buried her face against the warmth of Luke's back and held on to his waist as they rode deeper into the woods.

At one point, he stopped and seemed to be studying the tracks in the snow. Then he gunned the snowmobile and they shot up into the pines. Not too much farther he stopped again, this time killing the engine and plunging them into the darkness of the winter evening.

Kit let go of Luke's waist and sat for a moment, unsure what to do next. One thing Luke St. John didn't do was communicate his intentions. It wasn't until he'd climbed off and handed her a flashlight that she realized they'd arrived wherever it was they'd been headed.

She swung off the snowmobile and trudged through the deep snow behind him, the beam of the flashlight pooling in his tracks as she followed.

At the top of the rise, she caught sight of a cabin overlooking the valley. Before taking the last few steps up to the wide rough wood porch, she stopped to look back and was amazed at the view. Mountains ran to the horizon. She felt as though she could see forever. No lights. Just landscape and lots of it. She marveled at the solitude. The seclusion. "What a view. It must be spectacular in broad daylight."

Luke grunted and reached under the porch. He pulled out a key, and Kit trailed after him. She turned to steal one last look at the twinkling valley below them before he swung open the cabin door, flicked a light and motioned her inside.

Kit stepped in, feeling as if she'd just stepped back in time. The cabin looked as though it could have existed a hundred years ago, from the worn pine floor to the stone fireplace, the log walls to the old cookstove in the kitchen.

"Make yourself at home," Luke said. "I need to find a few things."

"Oh, this is wonderful," Kit exclaimed. She saw Luke turn to look at her. Surprise lit his eyes.

"You have to be kidding," he said on his way to the bedroom. "This place is primitive at best."

Kit brushed away his words as she walked through the cabin, looking at the antiques, the old colorized black-and-white photos of Yellowstone Park, and the huge ornate cherry-wood bed that dominated the bedroom. "It's incredible. It's like a museum."

"Exactly," Luke said from in front of an ornate oak dresser, where he was searching for something. "Who'd want to live in a museum?"

Kit mugged a face at him. "If it looked like this, I would."

"Right. You forget, I've seen the house you used to live in. Villa Killhorn."

Kit recoiled from his words. "That wasn't my house. I never felt comfortable there."

He looked at her for a moment as if he was having trouble believing that. "Sorry, I thought that was the kind of house a woman dreamed of."

"Not this woman," she said. He didn't know her any better than she knew him, she realized. How could he not love this cabin? she wondered, disappointed by his attitude. She'd just assumed a man who worked with wood would have an appreciation for woodwork from another era.

She wandered around, looking at all the collectibles, and wondered if he planned to stay here tonight. She checked out the overstuffed sofa and couldn't decide if she'd rather sleep there in front of the rock fireplace or in the wonderful four-poster bed. She had a flash of Luke sitting up in that bed, the covers up to his waist, his chest bare. The image was so clear that she could see him patting a space beside him in the bed, motioning for her to join him.

Kit shook off the vision as Luke returned with a small duffel bag that he set on the floor. They weren't staying the night here, she thought, disappointed—and at the same time a little relieved. She hadn't been able to completely rid herself of the image of Luke in that beautiful bed.

She looked up at him and saw that he was watching her. She dropped her gaze and realized she'd stopped in the center of the room, her hand resting on the back of a large oak rocker that she hadn't noticed until this moment.

"It's an amazing rocker." The beautiful craftsmanship in the ornate wood-scrolled back and arms of the chair drew her attention the way a good painting drew her eye. "I've never seen anything like it."

"And you won't," Luke said almost grudgingly. "It's one of mine."

Her gaze shot up, but Luke had turned his back on her and was looking in another old cupboard for who knew what.

"This is yours?" She glanced around the room, seeing the man with different eyes. "This is *your* cabin. Not your friend's." No wonder she'd pictured him in that bed.

"That's why we can't stay long. Unless I miss my guess, the Killhorns know about this place by now. I don't want them catching us here."

She stared at him. "Why did you let me believe this cabin belonged to a friend?"

He shrugged and glanced around, seemingly at a loss for words. Then his gaze settled on her. The mood changed instantly. Something sparked in the depths of all that gray. His mouth quirked a little into a grin, and Kit looked down, shocked to realize what she'd been doing: stroking the wood of the rocker lovingly, intimately. She jerked her hand back and felt herself blush under the heat of his gaze.

"I thought you were in a hurry to get out of here," she demanded as she stalked past him and out the front door.

Luke stood for a moment after she'd gone outside, staring at the rocker, feeling shaken and thankful she'd left him alone. The rocker was one of his favorite pieces. He'd put so much of himself into it that the chair seemed an extension of his character. Because of that, he felt as if she'd brushed her fingers across his bare skin, as if he could still feel the imprint of her touch burning into his flesh. He closed his eyes, fighting to erase her from his memory, from his thoughts, from his emotions. His reaction to Kit amazed and terrified him on many levels.

He should never have brought her here. Why had he? And why had he pretended it was a friend's place? To get her reaction to his home, to his life, to his work? Her reaction to him?

He glanced around the cabin, cursing his own foolishness, remembering what his life had been like the last four years. He'd lost himself in the isolation, only going down to Big Sky or Bozeman when he couldn't get whatever it was he needed delivered—which was seldom. He hadn't needed or wanted anyone in that life.

But now he felt a stab of loneliness in this cabin, as if her brief presence here had changed everything, had changed him. It made him angry with himself. Angry with her.

He exchanged his ski jacket for his old wool hunting coat, then took his .357 magnum from the gun cabinet and stuck it and a box of shells into the pocket of his coat. He had to keep his mind on Derrick Killhorn. He was going up against a murderer. A man who had everything to lose—and therefore a dangerous man. Luke knew he was risking not only his life but Kit's—and ultimately her baby's. He couldn't fail.

And yet he couldn't hope to succeed at the rate he was going. He had to forget about this woman. Or she would be the death of him.

As he turned, he saw something glitter near the door. A thin silver string of light. He moved to it. Wire. He gave it a tug where it had been attached to his door. At the other end, a small battery pack appeared from behind a pair of his boots. He swore loudly. The door had been rigged so they would know when he came back. He'd walked right into the trap. What a fool.

"Luke," Kit called from the doorway. "Someone's coming."

He moved to her, dousing the lights, his hand finding her arm in the darkness as he guided her out to the porch. He could hear the sound of a snowmobile coming up the mountainside, see the flicker of the light through the pines.

"Do you think they're after *us?*" she asked. "You don't think it's Derrick...?"

He felt her shiver and drew her to him without thinking. Someone had been expecting them. Luke cursed that stupid cell phone, afraid it had alerted Derrick long before the wire job on the front door had.

"Not Derrick. I doubt he does his own dirty work." But

Derrick might make an exception this time, Luke thought. *Because I outmaneuvered him in Texas and I have something he wants dearly.*

"Dirty work?"

He couldn't see her face but he could feel her body tense against his. Her cheek nestled against his wool hunting coat and her fingers clutched the fabric. Her fear of Derrick filled him with an overwhelming need to protect her. But at the same time, he felt a desperate need to face Derrick Killhorn or whomever the man had sent to stop them. Luke wanted this fight, needed it, he thought, as he watched the snowmobile light bobbing up the mountainside. He also wanted Killhorn to know exactly who and what he was dealing with.

But not with Kit here. Luke would pick his battles in places where he knew he could protect Kit. He didn't want to risk it now, not here. Derrick had killed once. Luke didn't doubt that he'd kill as many times as it took to save his precious hide. Or hire someone who could.

"What are we going to do?" Her voice broke.

He looked down at her. She seemed so small, so defenseless in his arms. He knew she could be like a mama grizzly if provoked, especially when it came to her son. But her fear of Derrick was tangible.

"No reason to take any chances right now," he said, his need to protect her winning out. And yet he had taken a chance with her. He'd brought her here to his cabin. He couldn't believe he'd been so reckless. And for what purpose? To get his gun? No, to see what she thought of his cabin. It had been a test. And the fact that she'd passed gave him little satisfaction.

"Let's go. I know another way out of here."

He waited while Kit slid onto the seat of the snowmobile behind him and wrapped her arms around him, then he turned the key. The headlight came on, slicing through the darkness and the snow-filled pines.

"Hold on." He gunned the engine and took off down a path that led behind the cabin, away from the light of the other snowmobile.

He headed back into the mountains, picking up the trail that led to Beehive Basin. His plan was to circle around and come back down near the garage and his pickup. But that plan changed when he glanced back and saw the single snowmobile light behind them, grow closer. There was no doubt now that it was someone after them.

Luke felt Kit's arms tighten around him, felt her bury her face against his back. He wished he'd never gotten her into this. But she *was* in, and had been since the moment she witnessed the murder. Now he had to get her out. Before he got them both killed.

They hadn't gone far, when Kit felt Luke turn to look behind them. She saw the light of the other snowmobile behind them, coming fast, following them.

She held on tighter, peering around Luke to see where they were going, only to be blinded by the cold wind. She buried her face in his back again, feeling his warmth, his strength, and realized she'd put all her faith in Luke St. John from that first night on the gulf when she'd handed her son to him. She just hadn't realized that until this moment.

She looked over her shoulder. The light grew closer. Who was chasing them? Derrick? Or had he sent someone after them, just as Luke suspected he would? What could the person hope to accomplish by chasing them on a snowmobile?

And where was Sanders? Still in Texas? She hoped so. She refused to believe that he had any part in the murder cover-up. Nor did she believe he was the one after them right now.

Behind them, the approaching snowmobile light danced wildly as it bounced over the bumpy snow, the beam splashing across her back like a torch, marking her.

The pursuing snowmobile was closer now. She thought she could almost hear the roar of its engine. She clung more tightly to Luke as he wove in and out of the trees at a speed that made her dizzy. It was obvious he knew this route and she wondered if he'd ever had to run from anyone else this way before.

The trail widened a little. On either side of her she saw blackness darker than the night, as if the world had dropped away and left only this single ridge of snow and ice and rock. Beehive Basin. She'd heard about it. A long narrow ridgeline with cliffs and large steep bowls sweeping down on either side.

The light from the pursuing snowmobile washed over her back again, only this time she heard the vehicle coming up on her right. She could make out a figure in a snowmobile suit and helmet hunched behind the handlebars.

At first she thought he must be trying to pass them, as crazy as that seemed. The ridgeline was wide enough, but just barely. Then she realized that wasn't his intention at all.

"Luke!" she cried as she saw the rider swing his snowmobile into them. There was a *thud* as the other snowmobile hit theirs, then the loud crunch of metal. A piece of trim below Kit's feet flew into the air, cartwheeling in the lights of the machine behind them. They careened toward the edge of the cliff and the abyss.

Kit's heart leaped into her throat.

Luke regained control of the snowmobile and swerved to the right into the path of the other snowmobile, clipping one of its ski runners. The driver seemed to lose control and dropped back—but only momentarily.

"Are you all right?" Luke yelled.

She nodded against him, unable to speak. The other rider was trying to force them over the cliff!

She felt Luke digging into his coat with one hand and trying to steer and power the snowmobile with the other.

"He's coming again!" she cried. Her heart thundered in her chest as she saw the snowmobile racing up, this time on their left. The pursuing snowmobile was larger, faster and, because it carried only one rider, more maneuverable.

It came up beside them, its motor a roar in her ears. She felt Luke tense. She caught the glint of cold steel and saw that Luke held a pistol in his hand.

The report of the pistol was lost in the sound of the vehicles colliding. Luke's shot went wild and he dropped the pistol as their snowmobile shot off to the right.

The other snowmobile advanced so quickly again that Kit didn't even have a chance to warn Luke. It hit them from the rear, clipping them just enough to send them rocking toward the edge of the ridge.

"Luke—" That was all she got out as the other snowmobile bore down on them again.

"Hang on tight!" Luke yelled and took a hard left.

Before Kit knew what had happened, she and Luke were airborne, moving through the night into nothingness as she held tight to him and he anchored them both to the snowmobile. Time seemed suspended. They hung in the cold night air, a stillness around them.

Then they were free-falling, her arms wrapped around Luke, her face pressed into his back, the air whizzing by, until they hit bottom and Kit came down hard on the snowmobile seat.

Snow filled the air, a fine white powder that exploded around them. Kit felt herself being thrown forward, but Luke held them both to the snowmobile as he hit the throttle, driving her back onto the seat. She held her breath. Then the snow cleared and she could see that they'd landed in a wide steep basin. No trees to crash into, she thought with relief.

She looked off to her right and saw the other snowmobile's light. Their attacker had followed them off the ridge and was now just yards away in the same snowy bowl. They hadn't lost him!

But that wasn't what made her heart stop. It was the snow between the two snowmobiles. It was moving. They'd set off an avalanche, and now both snowmobiles were right in the middle of it.

The top couple of feet of new snow had broken loose and was now sliding down the mountain with them. The snow gained momentum, threatening to over take them and bury them alive.

"Are you still with me?" Luke called back to her as they raced downward, the avalanche with them.

"Yes, but—"

"I know," he yelled as he hurled the snowmobile and them down the mountain at a death-defying speed. Kit clung to him, watching the snow in the headlight accelerate in both speed and depth, so filled with fear that she felt frozen to Luke.

He stayed on the throttle as they barreled downward. Did he think he could outrun an avalanche? She held her breath, her heart in her throat.

The snowslide stayed with them…or they stayed with it. She couldn't be sure. At one point, she felt the snow building up behind her, and knew that if Luke let up on the throttle, that fast-moving wall of white would bury them.

Luke never let up. He careened down the slope with a fearless tenacity that awed her. The snow began to grow deeper around the snowmobile. Kit could feel them losing the race against the avalanche and realized, her heart breaking, that she might never see her son again.

Then she saw what Luke had done. They were no longer in the middle of the huge slab of tumbling snow. He'd been carefully driving them toward the left edge of the slide where the snow was less deep, less powerful. And he might have driven them out of the slide—if it hadn't been for the rock bluffs that rimmed the side of the bowl. The first bluff dropped away only yards ahead of them. Kit watched the avalanche just beginning to tumble in a waterfall of new light snow over the rock face.

"Hang on!" Luke called back as he swung the snowmobile to the left under the rock face of the cliff, and stopped so abruptly that she smashed into his back. But he turned around on the seat to face her and quickly pulled her into his lap, burying her face in his chest as snow thundered past them and the night sky turned a suffocating white.

It had all happened within a matter of seconds and yet it had seemed forever.

Luke had buried his face against the back of her neck.

As he raised his head, the cold rushed in, leaving only the warm memory of his face and breath against her skin. Kit lifted her face to find the night again clear, the avalanche now a powerless silent heap of crumpled snow wedged high among the pines below them.

"You're okay," he said quietly as he pulled off her knitted ski cap and shook out the snow, then brushed the snow from her shoulders and back.

Was he reassuring her? Or himself? She didn't feel okay. Her teeth chattered, she couldn't seem to stop shaking and tears burned her eyes. He wrapped her again in his strong arms, holding her until the shaking slowed a little, until the spilled tears threatened to freeze in icy rivulets on her cheeks.

She told herself that she shouldn't feel safe locked in his arms. Safety around Luke was an illusion, one she shouldn't trust.

"Don't worry," Luke whispered. "Derrick will pay dearly for this. I'll see to that." She could hear the lust for vengeance in his voice, the cold merciless conviction, and realized that while Derrick's attempts to kill them had made Kit more terrified of him, they had served to make Luke St. John a more dangerous adversary. Derrick had no idea what kind of man was coming after him.

Kit thought of the soft-spoken man who'd worked with his hands to make exquisite one-of-a-kind furniture. She couldn't imagine this man with her now, making that beautiful rocker. It filled her with a powerful sadness that brought tears again to her eyes.

"Maybe Derrick already has paid," she said quietly and looked over her shoulder. No snowmobile light shone from the field of avalanched snow. "Did you see what happened to the other snowmobile?"

"It was buried," he answered matter-of-factly. "I saw it go under almost right at the top."

Kit shuddered. She knew she should have little sympathy for the person who had tried to kill them, but she couldn't help thinking what a horrible way it had been to die, suffocating under the snow. "Do you think it was Derrick?"

"I don't know, but we're about to find out," he said.

The sound of voices and snowmobile lights came from

below them, from what Kit saw was a groomed snowmobile track, smooth and wide as a highway.

"Are you all right up there?" one of the voices called.

"Yes!" Luke hollered. "Let me do the talking," he said quietly to Kit. He put the snowmobile into gear and, circling around the snowslide, drove down to where the group of snowmobilers had gathered in the middle of the trail. Directly above them, the avalanche had curled up in the trees and died.

Several of the riders were already probing in the snow with limbs they'd broken off trees. Others with flashlights had climbed the crumpled snowfield to look for the downed rider.

"We saw the lights of the two snowmobiles coming off the top," one woman cried. "That other one got covered almost instantly. Were they with you?"

"There was another snowmobile?" Luke asked, sounding surprised. "I didn't see it." He looked back up the mountain. "I thought we were goners."

"Search-and-rescue is on the way," said one rider with a large snowmobile and a two-way radio.

One of the women pressed the plastic cup from her thermos into Kit's trembling hands. "Drink this. It's hot," she said.

Kit took it, cradling the cup in her mittened hands, but not even strong, black coffee would stop her shaking.

"Stay here," Luke told Kit, and left her sitting on the snowmobile with the woman, sipping the bitter coffee, feeling scared and cold and in shock.

Luke joined the search, becoming one of a half-dozen dark figures probing the remains of the avalanche. Kit could see him illuminated by the many flashlights on the snowfield.

One of the snowmobilers found the dead man before the-search-and-rescue team arrived. Kit heard the man say the body was with the snowmobile, buried under two feet of fresh snow.

Kit watched Luke walk over to where the men had dug out the snowmobiler. He stood among the small crowd of onlookers as one of the men tried to find some identification on the body.

"Here it is," the man said. He opened the dead man's wallet under the beam from his flashlight. He looked up. "Matthew Rustan."

Chapter 13

Kit watched Luke come out of the pines, out of the avalanched snow and the darkness.

"Who was it?" she asked, her heart in her throat.

"A private investigator named Matthew Rustan—"

She started to feel relief. There had to be a mistake. The man really wasn't after them.

" —from Galveston, Texas."

Galveston? She swallowed.

Luke put his arm around her shoulder and walked her back to the snowmobile. "Let's go home."

Where was home? she wanted to ask. She had no home. She didn't even know where her son was or if he was safe. All she knew was that a private investigator from Galveston had tried to kill them.

She began to shake again. She wrapped her arms around Luke's waist and leaned into his strength, closing her eyes to the night and the truth.

Luke drove slowly the rest of the way down the mountain, taking the groomed snowmobile trail back toward Big Sky and his pickup. He backed the truck up to a snowbank and loaded the snowmobile into the bed.

"I know a couple of places we can stay," he assured her. "We'll be safe."

She didn't ask where. She didn't care. He headed down the mountain, kicking up the pickup heater as if he thought mere heat could take away the core of cold inside her.

It seemed inconceivable that Derrick would think killing them would solve his problems. Had her threat of evidence scared him? Didn't he realize that if she'd had any physical evidence, she would have used it months ago? Or maybe he just knew her, knew how easily she could be swayed, manipulated, controlled, frightened—and thought if he didn't kill her, he could at least scare her off.

"You think Derrick knows that we're here?" she asked, watching the road twist off the mountainside in front of them. She could feel Luke's gaze on her.

"He knows, Kit. Or he will soon enough."

She nodded, and wondered if Derrick would think she and Luke had had something to do with Matthew Rustan's death. She decided it probably wouldn't matter one way or the other. The private investigator was dead. And Derrick Killhorn was still after her and Luke and Andy.

Kit looked out the window as they passed through Meadow Village, half expecting to see Derrick standing in the snow in front of one of the businesses, watching them pass, planning his next attack.

Instead of turning left toward Bozeman, Luke swung to the right on Highway 191, headed toward West Yellowstone, toward Derrick's house. The house sat back off the highway against the foothills. The lights were on and Derrick's pickup was parked outside. Being this close, knowing he was in the house, that he'd hired someone to try to kill her and Luke, chilled her to her soul. She had married a monster.

Luke pulled off at a small bar down the highway. "I need to make a phone call," he said motioning to the phone booth standing in the shadows. "I'll leave the truck running. I won't be long."

He pushed open the door to the booth and stepped inside, leaving the door open so he could hear, as well as see, Kit. He dialed Derrick Killhorn's number and waited. Derrick answered on the third ring.

"I have your wife. And your son."

Momentary silence. "I wondered when you'd call." Derrick's words slurred just a little. Was he drunk? Was he sitting in that big house all alone drinking himself into a stupor? All the better. "Are you familiar with the penalty for kidnapping, St. John?"

"Are you familiar with the penalty for murder, Killhorn?"

Luke heard the tinkle of ice in crystal, the sound of Derrick downing whatever liquid had been poured into the glass. "I don't know what you're talking about."

"Sure you do. You killed my brother and now you're going to pay. By the way, have you heard that the private investigator you hired failed? But I won't fail when I come after you, Killhorn."

"Making threats, are you?" Derrick's laugh had a nasty drunken ring to it. "Do you know who I *am*?"

"Oh, yeah, I even know *what* you are. That's why it's going to make taking you down all the more enjoyable."

"How do you hope to do that? You have no proof, in fact you have nothing."

"I have your wife."

"Like I said, you have nothing."

Luke turned to look back at Derrick's house. "You're despicable."

"Without evidence—"

"Evidence?" It was Luke's turn to laugh. "Do you really think I give a damn about evidence? I don't want to see you go to prison. That's too good for you."

"What *do* you want?" Derrick fell quiet for a moment. "Maybe there's a way we could work this out."

The bastard thought he could buy Luke off? Luke spit out his next words. "I want vengeance. I want you and I'm coming for you. Maybe it will be in that fancy house of yours tonight while you sleep. Or maybe when you get into your pickup in the morning. But believe me, I will get you and you won't know what hit you."

Luke slammed down the phone and turned to see Kit standing behind him. From her expression, he figured she'd heard just about everything he'd said.

"You were just trying to scare him, right?" she said, her voice thin.

Luke stepped out of the booth and pulled her back toward the pickup. "I scared him."

He opened the passenger door for Kit, then went back around and slid behind the wheel again. He put the pickup into Reverse and backed out onto the highway. He could feel her looking at him.

"I have to try and keep him away from the job site tonight so we can look for the crowbar," he said.

She nodded, but she still looked worried and scared and upset with him. It surprised him how much that bothered him. But he could think of nothing more to say to her. Even if he had thought of something, it would have been a lie.

* * *

Kit felt numb. She sat against the pickup door, watching the highway roll by. She didn't want to feel. She definitely didn't want to think. Too much had happened. Too many things worried her. Like Derrick. And Luke, she thought, looking over at him.

She'd seen in his photograph what he'd been like before his brother's death. She'd seen that man feeding her son that very morning, the man who made the beautiful furniture with his hands. It was that man who haunted her. She'd come to care about that Luke St. John.

But his hatred of Derrick frightened her. She didn't want that rage to kill the old Luke, to kill the good man she sensed in him.

He turned a couple of miles farther up the highway onto a narrow snowpacked road that led back into the woods to a row of old log cabins hidden in the pines.

He glanced over his shoulder. Kit looked back, but there were no headlights. Nothing but darkness behind them.

He drove past the cabins to the farthest one. It was the only cabin with an attached single-car garage, also made of logs.

The garage door gaped open, a small light glowing inside. Luke pulled in and cut the engine, but didn't move to get out. A single bulb hung at the back of the garage, making the space a little less cold, a little less scary.

"I'm sorry about that," Luke said as he reached over to brush a lock of her hair from her cheek. He sounded as if he were apologizing for messing up her hair, not for anything that had happened earlier.

She thought about the Luke on the mountain, the one who'd outrun the avalanche and saved them. "I owe you my life. Again."

He shook his head and looked away. "It doesn't count when I keep risking it. We can stay here for a day or so. Then I have other friends and other places we can go if we need to."

She said nothing, hoping it would all be over by tomorrow and she would be headed back to Texas and her son. She didn't even try to think past that. If they could find the crowbar tonight—

Luke opened his pickup door and got out. The garage suddenly seemed too closed in without him beside her. She opened her door and slid out, feeling trapped in the tight space as she edged past the truck door, closed it, and stood for a moment. She felt a little wobbly, as if she'd just run all the way from Lone Peak.

"Kit?"

She heard his voice outside the garage and moved toward it as if sleepwalking. Nothing seemed real, not the winter night nor the sky masked with clouds nor the smell of new snow and pines.

"Kit?"

She felt the snowy ground move beneath her, twisting as if to throw her off. Luke's arms enveloped her and she didn't go down, but her head swam.

"Here, let me help you," he said.

"I'm fine," she said, reminding herself that she hadn't eaten much of anything all day. Her near-faint was the result of that rather than weakness, rather than fear.

"You're not fine." He swept her up in his arms and carried her toward the cabin door.

She started to argue, decided it wasn't worth the effort, and, looping her arms around his neck, laid her head on his shoulder. He felt so solid, so strong. Just the opposite of how she felt right now.

She felt tears sting her eyes and fought not to cry, but the huge gulping sobs came anyway, refusing to be held back.

Luke hugged her to him, tighter, closer.

"It's all right," he whispered. "Let it out. It's all right."

She closed her eyes and burrowed into him, soaking in his warmth, his strength, breathing in the male scent of him as if it were pure oxygen. In Luke's arms, she felt safe, secure, sexy. She opened her eyes at the first sense of alarm. Sexy? The crying stopped and Kit became intensely aware of Luke's body, vividly aware of his maleness. This was dangerous uncharted territory. She'd gone from feeling safe and secure to sexy and…scared. Luke affected her in so many ways, some she didn't even understand, ways that she suspected other women knew about. She didn't.

Luke swung open the front door of the cabin and carried her inside. He turned on a light, illuminating knotty pine walls that glowed golden against the faded yellow of a shag rug and bright citrus-and-green daisies in a white chenille spread on the double bed in the middle of the room. He approached the bed and set her down carefully, as if she would break.

"I'm fine, really." And she was. She didn't feel like passing out anymore. But she did feel light-headed, as if she'd just stuck her finger into an electrical outlet.

Kit was off the bed and standing on the other side in an instant, wiping hastily at her tears. Luke had never seen anyone so skittish. Her cheeks flushed and she fidgeted uncomfortably as if afraid to go near the bed again. He fought a smile. He found it so incredibly appealing, her lack of sophistication. It made him wonder about her level of sexual experience. It wasn't as though she was a virgin;

she had a child. But still, he found something captivating about her ingenuousness.

"You can have the bed," he said, trying not to enjoy her obvious discomfort. Did the thought of sleeping with him give her that much distress? Well, she need not worry. "I'll take the floor," he assured her.

"No, I can sleep on the floor—"

He raised his hands. "Please, all of these cabins have only one bed and I don't want you out of my sight, especially after what happened tonight. So, you sleep on the bed, I sleep on the floor."

She nodded as if everything he said was too reasonable to contest, and yet she looked as if she thought he'd jump her the instant she went near the bed again. He wondered idly if she was afraid of him—or herself.

"Let me take your coat." He held out his hands and waited while she unzipped the ski jacket with trembling fingers. He could almost hear the fine-tuned hum of her apprehension coming off her in waves. She'd seemed less nervous on the mountain with a killer after them and an avalanche trying to bury them. Well, at least she'd forgotten about Derrick for the moment.

He took her coat and hung it in the closet. Then he watched her pluck nervously at her clothing. The thin sweater had molded to her body the way none of her previous clothing came even close to doing. He could see what appeared to be a black lace bra beneath the sweater. Black lace? He felt a tug in his groin strong enough to knock him to his knees.

Black lace and skimpy, too. He told himself he shouldn't have been surprised. He'd seen that sensual side of her in her paintings. Sensed it in her. But she kept it so well-hidden that he *was* surprised.

He hung up his coat in the closet. When he turned back to her, he felt something break loose inside him. Kit looked so damned guileless standing there, so vulnerable, so open. He'd never met a woman like her.

He knew when he closed his eyes tonight that he would feel the avalanche beneath him, hear the sound of tearing metal as the other snowmobile slammed into them, feel Kit's arms wrapped around him, her face pressed into his back.

But right now it wasn't the rush of the avalanche or the sound of tearing metal that possessed him. It was the woman. And not just her body, although he wished that was all it was.

He liked her.

He liked the way she loved her son, for one. She would do anything to protect Andy—even come back to Montana and risk her own life. Luke didn't kid himself. He couldn't have hog-tied her into coming back here if she hadn't believed that Andy would be safe in Texas with Lucille. And that the only way to keep Andy safe was to face Derrick on his turf.

But it wasn't the fact that she was a good mother that was making Luke's pulse race at this moment. It had more to do with the girl-woman standing in front of him. He couldn't say why or how, but he knew Derrick had never released the latent passion he sensed in her. And no matter how hard Luke tried, he couldn't seem to dampen the desire he felt when he looked at her. It came with a speed and force that floored him. It had been a hell of a long time since he'd felt anything for a woman, any woman. And it had never been like this.

He reminded himself that Kit was still Derrick's wife. Married. Off-limits. Forbidden. Normally just knowing a woman belonged to another man would have cooled his desire like snow on fire. But not this woman.

"Are you hungry?" he asked, hoping his aunt Lucille's theory that food solved most problems covered this one. "I thought we'd order a pizza."

She nodded, looking as uncomfortable as he felt.

"Let me guess," he said, narrowing his gaze at her, desperately trying to lighten the mood, to still the charged air between them. He'd seen fear in her eyes earlier but this fear was different. He wanted to tell her she had nothing to fear from him. Absolutely nothing.

"You look like a veggie pizza kind of woman," he said.

She smiled and maybe didn't look quite so leery of him. "Not on your life. What are you? A pepperoni-and-mushroom man?"

He returned her smile. "No way. Italian sausage, green peppers, onions and anchovies."

He raised an eyebrow in anticipation of her reaction to anchovies.

"I happen to like anchovies on my pizza," she said with pretended indignation.

He clutched his heart and laughed. "My kind of woman. And tonight, I feel like living dangerously." He saw her tense. "I was talking about pizza," he reminded her quickly. "But while we're on the subject, we probably won't be getting that much sleep tonight. I want to go to the condo complex."

She actually seemed to relax a little, and he wanted to laugh. She would feel more comfortable creeping around the complex looking for dead bodies with a murderer after her than she would in a room with him. What *was* this woman so afraid of?

He called in the pizza order, a large loaded including anchovies. It pleased him that she liked anchovies.

"I'm sure word is out about the snowmobiler who was killed in an avalanche tonight," Luke told her after he'd hung up the phone. "I would imagine Derrick's already taken care of the crowbar, but we have to try to find it just in case it's still there."

She nodded and looked around the cabin as if she'd like to sit down. But she obviously wasn't about to sit on the bed and that was the only piece of furniture in the room.

He noticed her eyeing him warily again. "I should go out and close the garage door," he said.

"I think I'll wash up," she said.

"Great." He edged toward the door.

Luke went outside, closed the garage door and stood staring up at the heavens.

In truth, he just needed to get some fresh air and the freezing December breeze felt like a cold shower. The cabin had seemed too small with both of them in there. He studied the starry sky and tried to refocus his thoughts, his emotions. He needed desperately to hang on to his anger, he told himself. It was his strength, his key to survival.

When he was around Kit, she seemed to take the edge off that anger, seemed to replace his need for vengeance with other needs that wouldn't help him do the job he'd come home to Montana to do. She weakened his resolve, and when he thought too much about her, he made mistakes. He'd done something incredibly stupid earlier, taking her to his cabin. He didn't want to make another mistake that could cost her her life. He'd come close enough already.

He walked out past the stand of timber and looked down the dark road toward Derrick's house. The lights were on but he couldn't be sure Derrick was home now. He thought about Matthew Rustan, the private investigator on the other snowmobile. Luke had never doubted Derrick would try to kill them. Kit, it seemed, had. He felt all his animosity for the man. The anger was there, just beneath the surface, ready to bubble up and boil over, ready to take control. He felt a little better, or at least a little safer, knowing it was still there and that he could still call on it when he needed it.

He stood outside until he saw the lights of the pizza delivery van coming up the road toward the cabins. It was just a little after eight o'clock but full dark. After they ate, they'd go up to the building site at Killhorn Condos. He felt his heart quicken at the thought and the air suddenly felt colder.

Luke wished he'd grabbed his coat. But he knew it wouldn't take him long to warm up again. Not once he'd gone back into the cabin, back into that small room with Kit.

Kit could smell snow in the air again by the time they left Luke's truck in a pull-off near Mountain Village and hiked under the cold cover of darkness and the pines up the mountain toward the complex.

Only the jagged outline of evergreens and the sharp edge of the mountains against the skyline broke the great expanse of white.

Kit could see her breath in the freezing night air, hear her pulse pounding in her ears, see Luke in front of her leading the way toward Derrick's construction site.

She smiled to herself, remembering earlier in the cabin. They'd eaten pizza, sitting on the bed across from each other. Luke had tried so hard to make her feel comfortable, making jokes, laughing, teasing her. But she hadn't felt comfortable. She doubted that she *could* feel comfortable in any small quarters with the man. Then he'd called someone, and a few minutes later a man arrived with a pistol for him.

"How are you doing?" he whispered now, stopping partway up the mountain. He'd been moving fast, an urgency in him that matched the intensity of his expression. If she'd forgotten what was at stake here, one look at Luke certainly reminded her. If Derrick caught them, he would try to kill them again. She didn't doubt that anymore. She knew Luke never had.

"All right." All right? She couldn't remember the last time she'd been all right. She buried her mittened hands deep in her pockets, snuggled down into the collar of her coat and looked up the mountain.

The condo complex loomed, a sinister shell, dark and foreboding against the bleak white of the snowfall.

Luke gave her a moment to catch her breath, but only that. "Stay close." He touched his fingers to his lips and started up again. Tucked in his jacket, he carried a small tool bag. The borrowed pistol was in the bag.

Kit followed, the memory of the last time she'd been to the job site forming a weight around her shoulders. Snowflakes began to fall, spiraling down in large, lacy disks. As they drew nearer the condo, wind whipped the falling snow, making it steal around the structure like ghosts.

She was startled to see how little had changed since the last time she'd been here. Except now the building's block skeleton had been encased in dense plastic, making it resemble a cocoon. From deep inside came a steady roar like a blast furnace. Closer, the plastic drummed in the wind, an unearthly sound.

Luke skulked down the side of the structure to the corner and peered around it, then motioned for Kit to follow. "The coast is clear," he said, pointing toward the small trailer Derrick used for an office. No vehicles were parked near it, nor were there any near the building.

She stared into the plastic wall, trying to see what waited for them inside the opaque protective cover, unable to make out anything. Too easily she could remember the man on the snowmobile.

Luke peeled back the plastic and motioned for her to enter. She stepped into the warm darkness and stopped, instantly convinced they weren't alone. Derrick. It was as if she could feel his warm breath caress her cheek, as if he wanted her to know he was now standing only inches from her, waiting to surprise her. Luke collided with her back.

"What is it?" he whispered, his hands clutching her shoulders.

Unable to speak, she reached back to grab his forearm.

Luke wrapped his free arm around her and pulled her behind him. She buried her face in his back, in the rough wet wool of his coat, and steadied herself against him. Her heart drummed like the plastic in the wind, her pulse roaring louder than the heater deep within the building.

"Kit?" Luke whispered, snapping on the flashlight he'd brought.

She lifted her head and peeked around his broad back. The beam made a thin golden slice into the black, ending in a pool on the rough plywood flooring, illuminating the empty cavity of building where they stood. And nothing more.

No Derrick. And she realized that the warmth now brushing against her cheek was from waves of air moving through the vacant building from the heater. Kit let out the breath she'd been holding, feeling foolish, feeling weak with relief and fear. She felt Luke's gaze and looked up at him, giving him a feeble shrug and an even feebler smile. "I thought I felt—"

He nodded, his look sympathetic. He reached into the bag and pulled out the pistol, glanced at her, then stuffed it in the waistband of his jeans.

"I'm fine," she said, straightening her shoulders, telling herself to stop being such a coward.

Luke seemed to study her for a full minute, then nodded. "Come on."

She led the way through the dark hollows of the building, getting turned around in the maze of rooms. She was beginning to doubt that she could ever find the room Jason was killed in, when she saw something that jogged her memory like a pinprick.

A set of temporary stairs led up to a sort of second-story gallery. She licked her dry lips and swallowed, her throat parched by the dry air circulating around her, her ears humming with the roar of the heater, her heart pounding.

It was from that gallery that she'd witnessed the murder. Only then, it had been just a plywood walkway.

She felt Luke watching her, waiting. She raised an arm and pointed to the stairs. "Up there."

He nodded and headed for the steps, trailing the beam of the flashlight up the wooden stairs in front of her. Kit clambered up to the gallery, her gaze on her footing rather than on the view until her hands latched onto the makeshift two-by-four railing and she finally looked out.

It took her a moment to orient herself. Before, the structure had been open, the block walls only up about seven feet high, no floor, just dirt, a large pile off to one side, and, at its center, the water tank Derrick had thrown Jason into. All that was gone now, replaced by a large enclosed room with a high ceiling, concrete floor and towering block walls with rectangular openings where windows would one day go.

"Is it coming back?" Luke asked.

She almost smiled at that. The images had never left her, as hard as she'd tried to force them away. They hovered in her brain waiting for a weak moment. She'd had a lot of weak moments.

In a hushed whisper she explained what it had looked like that afternoon, ending with where she'd seen Derrick throw the crowbar. Then she followed Luke back down the stairs, through a narrow doorway and across the great expanse of concrete floor to the block wall.

Luke bent down, shining the light on the wall, starting at eye level and slowly descending as he studied each cinder block. They all looked the same to Kit. The flashlight stopped about two feet off the floor and she heard Luke curse.

"What is it?" she asked, crouching down beside him.

"These blocks, they've been replaced."

On closer inspection, she could make out the difference in coloration. Four blocks in a square looked newer, cleaner.

Luke pulled a sledgehammer from his tool bag and struck one of the newer blocks. The surface shattered and he peered inside the block cell with the flashlight.

"It's empty," Luke said. "No crowbar. Not even any grout or steel. He must have replaced these recently."

Luke had been right: Derrick had rushed back to Montana to destroy any and all evidence. And it was Kit's fault for telling him that she had proof. "I'm sorry."

Luke shook his head and pushed himself back up. "It was a long shot, anyway, and he could have replaced them months ago for all we know."

The crowbar had been in there, Kit thought. If only she'd gone to the police. If only—

"Don't," Luke said, shifting the flashlight so the wider, softer beam shone on their faces. He reached out, his gloved hand cupped her jaw and lifted her face until he could look into her eyes. "We're going to get him. Nothing he can do can save him at this point."

If Luke thought his words reassured her, he was wrong. She feared that he planned to take the law into his own hands if they couldn't prove Derrick's guilt. He didn't realize how much that scared her.

He stared into her eyes for a moment, then drew back as if he could tell from her expression that she disapproved. He skimmed the flashlight beam across the concrete floor. "I wonder when this was poured."

"Why?"

"If it was poured soon after Jason's murder, then I'd say there's a good chance this is where his body is buried. Derrick would have wanted to get the evidence covered as quickly as possible and—" he shone the flashlight on the rough surface of the concrete "—it looks like it might have been poured in a hurry."

Kit felt her eyes widen as she looked down at the concrete floor. My God, Jason could be under there. Quite possibly *was* buried beneath their feet. She felt a shudder and a wave of sympathy for Luke that threatened to drown her. Her hand found his arm. Tears filled her eyes.

He glanced over at her and shook his head. "Come on, let's see what we can find in Derrick's office." He gently pulled his arm free. "There should be records of when the concrete was poured."

They moved in silence to the construction job office, the twenty-four-foot trailer parked at the side of the building.

As they stepped through a break in the plastic and out of the heated building, large wet snowflakes floated down on them. Kit trudged behind Luke through the falling snow. She waited while he tried the door. Locked.

He was reaching into his tool bag when the sound of a motor cut through the wind. A pair of headlights flashed across the landscape on the narrow snowpacked road that led to the complex.

Luke grabbed Kit and quickly pulled her behind a fork-lift parked beside the trailer. "I want to see who this is," he whispered.

They waited as the vehicle made its way to them. A dark-colored Suburban finally lurched to a stop in front of the trailer. The driver cut the engine, and the lights and darkness took back the night.

Kit heard the car door open. Then close. She watched in trepidation as a figure appeared out of the storm, headed right for them. The newcomer wore a large full-length dark coat with the hood up, and snowboots.

Luke motioned for Kit not to move as the figure sneaked along the side of the trailer to the door just feet from where the two of them were crouched.

Kit held her breath, afraid to blink an eye as she watched the person try the door of the trailer with the same result. Locked.

A muttered curse drifted with the wind and snow. Then the figure reached into a deep pocket and extracted a set of keys that jingled softly. After a moment, the trailer door opened. The person glanced around, then hurriedly stepped inside.

The beam of a flashlight darted around in the trailer. Kit could hear the banging of what sounded like metal drawers, and more curses, the voice now definitely that of a woman.

Luke shot Kit a questioning look.

"It's Derrick's ex, Belinda," she whispered.

He nodded. "Come on. Let's see what she's looking for." Luke opened the door to the trailer and they quickly stepped in.

Belinda jumped a good foot, clutched a hand over her heart and swore profusely. "You just scared the hell out of me."

Luke doubted that. In the golden beam of his flashlight, she still looked full of the devil.

She flipped back her hood. Her brassy dyed hair was cut in a severe wedge above her ears, making her mascara-lined eyes appear too large for her face. Two-carat diamonds glittered from her earlobes like trophies. But it was her large, full mouth that dominated her perfectly made-up face. She'd painted her mouth fire-engine red, and now sucked at the corner of her lower lip nervously.

She could have been pretty, Luke thought, except for the raw greed in her eyes.

"You have a lot of guts being here," Belinda said to Kit, obviously forgetting that she too was trespassing and in dangerous territory. She snapped off her flashlight and put it back into her purse. "Derrick is looking for you and, let me tell you, he's way beyond furious." She made a face as if Kit should be scared. The woman had no idea just how scared Kit was—or how afraid Belinda herself should be.

Belinda glanced at Luke and raised an eyebrow to Kit. "You hire yourself a bodyguard?"

"In a manner of speaking," Luke answered before Kit could. He wondered what men like Derrick saw in women like Belinda. The woman he'd seen Derrick with in West Yellowstone could have been this woman's twin, they were so much the same type.

All gussied up, his grandmother St. John would have said. "Only birds looking to mate put on such plumage," she would say with a laugh. "Not that there is anything wrong with mating, mind you. But the kind of woman you want won't need all those trappings to attract her mate."

Luke glanced over at Kit, her face flushed from the cold, her eyes bright, her hair simple and back to its natural brilliance and color. The one time he'd seen her in makeup, that day in the limo, the sparseness of it had accentuated her beauty, not created it.

No, a real woman didn't need artifice, he thought, looking at Kit. But Derrick Killhorn needed artifice. So why had he married Kit? Was he only after the baby? Could the man really be that blind that he hadn't even noticed what he had? Hadn't appreciated his own wife?

"Want to tell us what you're looking for?" Luke asked, dragging himself back to the moment. He motioned with his flashlight beam to the fingernail file in Belinda's hand and the recently defiled file cabinet.

She looked contrite for a moment but it passed quickly. "Derrick's up to something."

"Want to elaborate?"

She shot him a look as if to say, "Why should I?"

"We know something's going on," Kit said. "That's why I came back."

Her words must have been music to Belinda's ears. "So you've come back to stick it to him. Good for you. Just remember, kid, he's a mean one." She glanced at Luke. "You were smart to get someone…big and strong and tough-looking, but Derrick plays dirty."

They didn't need to be reminded of that, Luke thought. "Do you know what you're looking for?" he ventured as he shone the light into the file cabinet, looking for the condo complex invoices.

She appeared offended, but only for an instant. Her moods changed more quickly than Montana weather. "Of course, I know what I'm looking for. What are *you* looking for?"

Luke kept searching the files. "An invoice for concrete. I need to know when concrete was poured in one of the rooms."

"Well, you aren't going to find it in there," Belinda said. "Earlier today I stopped by here to pick up my check. Derrick didn't seem to be around but there was a folder on his desk. I just kind of glanced at it. It had a bunch of figures scrawled on the outside and bills inside, all boring stuff to do with the complex as far as I could tell." She brushed her bangs back and took a breath. "I didn't think anything about it until Derrick came in, caught me and threw a conniption fit. Whatever was in that folder, he definitely didn't want me looking at it. He locked it in this cabinet. So I thought, why not check it out, you know?"

Luke knew. "Did you find it?"

She shook her head at the file drawer now hanging open. "It's not in there. He must have hidden it."

Luke shone the flashlight around the small trailer. "Where would he hide it?"

Belinda seemed to think for a moment. Luke noticed that the obviously expensive outfit she wore was canary yellow and everything she had on matched, including her nail polish. This was a woman with a lot of free time on her hands and obviously more money than she needed. It made him wonder how she'd managed to get alimony out of Derrick. The word blackmail sprang to mind.

"If that folder is as important as I suspect it is, he put

it someplace real safe," she said. She glanced at Kit. "You don't happen to know the combination to the wall safe at the house, do you?"

Kit looked surprised. "I didn't even know there *was* a wall safe."

Belinda mugged a face at Luke. "She really was out of her league, you know?"

"I know," he said, glancing over at Kit, then settling his gaze on Belinda again. "You don't have the combination?"

She guffawed. "That was the second thing he changed right after the locks on the doors at the house." She jingled the keys in her pocket. "He forgot about my keys to his trailer, though."

Luke thought he heard a noise outside and flicked off his flashlight. "I think maybe we should all get out of here before someone else shows up." He went to the window, pulled back the curtain and glanced out. Nothing but snow and darkness.

"How are we going to get the combination to the wall safe?" Belinda asked, not easily sidetracked. "I can tell you where it is."

Luke flicked his flashlight back on so he could see Kit. He didn't like the idea of having her out of his sight. "Where?"

"Derrick has the mind of a gopher," Belinda said. "He can't remember anything so he carries any numbers he needs in his wallet—including the combination to the safe. Of course, as cheap as he is, he never lets the wallet out of his sight."

"Then we'll have to get his wallet," Luke said.

"Whatever you two have planned, I want in on it," Belinda said quickly.

He studied her a moment, wondering about her motives.

She certainly seemed eager to get more ammunition against Derrick. "I don't think you realize how dangerous it is."

Belinda let out an oath. "You think breaking into here isn't dangerous? You think just being married to him wasn't dangerous?"

"You've already done enough just telling us about the file folder," Kit assured her. "I don't want to see you get hurt again because you were trying to help me."

Belinda patted Kit's shoulder. "Look, I owe the SOB and I want in on this. It's *my* behind, all right?"

"Then you have to know," Luke said. "Derrick killed a man, and Kit and I have come back to town to prove it."

"Whoa." Belinda sat down hard in Derrick's office chair. She blinked. "Murder?"

Kit nodded. "I saw him kill Luke's brother, Jason, when Jason was working for Derrick seven months ago."

Belinda glanced over at Luke as if she was just starting to get it. She put a diamond-encrusted hand to her forehead. "I knew he had a mean streak—but murder?"

"Now you know the kind of man we're dealing with," Kit said.

Belinda chewed at her lip. "Derrick knows that you saw him?"

Kit nodded.

She let out a gusty sigh. "No wonder he's been out of his mind. I thought it was just you leaving him. Derrick has an ego the size of Alaska. He doesn't take rejection well. Who knew it was something much worse?" She laughed. "Oh, you have to let me help. I'm probably one of the few people in town who really understands the terrible odds you're up against if you think you can bring a Killhorn to justice in this county. And I'm the only person who wants to see it happen as much as the two of you. Maybe more."

Before either one of them could respond, the sound of a vehicle bucking snowdrifts filled the trailer.

Chapter 14

Luke switched off the flashlight and reached for Kit. "Let's get out of here."

As they filed out of the trailer, Luke spotted Belinda's Suburban parked nearby. In the distance, a set of headlights wound its way toward the job site, busting through drifts blown into Belinda's earlier tracks.

"Give me your keys," Luke ordered Belinda. "Kit, you get in the front with me. Belinda, get in the back seat and stay down."

He took the keys Belinda handed him. Since whoever was coming up the road would no doubt recognize Belinda's Suburban, Luke knew he had to get her, as well as himself and Kit, out of here.

Hurriedly he ushered Kit into the front seat. She huddled on the floorboards, looking up at him, and he read both concern and trust in her eyes. He heard Belinda climb into the back and slam the rear door.

Luke slid in behind the wheel, cranked over the engine and put the car in four-wheel drive. Then he swung around and headed back up the road at a speed that he hoped would brook no arguments from the approaching vehicle.

"Stay down," he ordered the women. "And hang on."

As he neared the other vehicle, Luke caught a glimpse of its size, shape and color against the snowfall and recognized the make. "Who do you know that owns a newer pale green Dodge pickup?"

"Derrick," came the answer in chorus.

Luke smiled. He'd been looking forward to this for a long time now. He revved the engine and kept the Suburban busting through the snowdrifts, driving it forward on the one-way road headed right for the approaching pickup.

When they were down to only a short, narrow stretch of straightaway between them, Luke increased his speed and flashed on his brights.

He saw the pickup slow. It was that moment of hesitation that he'd hoped for. He drove the Suburban forward, sending snow and ice cascading over the top of the car, the motor roaring in his ears as he got ready. One of them would have to go off the road into the deep, soft, snowy ditch. Luke had no intention of it being him, but he was ready just in case Derrick Killhorn had played chicken before. But Luke was betting on Derrick's attachment to his truck to decide the fate of things.

They were within a few yards of each other, Luke refusing to back off on his speed, when Derrick, at the last minute, jerked his wheel. The pickup careened off the road, burying its hood in the deep snow-filled ditch.

Luke roared on past. But he knew Derrick had seen that it wasn't Belinda driving the rig. When Luke looked back, the pickup was high-centered on its axle in the drift, the driver's door was open, light spilling out, and Derrick Kill-horn was standing in the middle of the road, his posture beyond furious. Luke smiled.

Kit sat huddled on the passenger side of Luke's old Chevy pickup. He'd left the engine running, the heater blasting cold air. Not that it mattered. She had her window down so she could hear what he was saying to Belinda, who'd parked next to them. The air outside the pickup seemed warmer than what was coming out of the heater.

"Tell Derrick I took your Suburban." Luke stood beside Belinda's car, her window down, talking. "I don't want Derrick to think you're the one who ran him off the road."

She snorted. "It wouldn't be the first time. Don't worry about me. You just figure out a way to get that safe combination. I know there's something in that folder that Derrick doesn't want us to see." She sobered. "Hopefully it will be what you need to get him for your brother's murder. I've always said Derrick should be behind bars."

Kit watched Luke rub his thigh with his leather-gloved palm. He looked so capable, so self-assured. She felt safe with him. And at the same time... She studied his profile, her gaze lingering on his lips. She trembled again, this time not from the cold.

"If you call Derrick and tell him to meet you somewhere, will he do it?" Luke was asking Belinda.

"Depends on what I'm offering," she said with a coy smile.

"The Mountain Village mall will be busy tomorrow night with all the skiers and shoppers," Luke said. "There's one shop that always has a crowd outside. Tell him to meet you there. I'll get his wallet."

"Just name the time," Belinda said.

"What about me?" Kit asked.

"Oh, I haven't forgotten you," Luke assured her, flashing her a look that said he'd tried, though.

Back at the cabin, Luke dialed the number for Kit and handed her the phone. She waited, her heart a thunder in her ears. Just the sound of Lucille's soft Southern drawl made her choke back tears.

"How is everything?" Kit asked, trying to keep the panic out of her voice.

"Fine, honey, we're both just fine. We've been having a grand old time. Andy's been an angel and he seems to love boating."

Kit held the phone, crying softly, unable to speak. Luke took the receiver from her and spoke for a moment with his aunt. Then he handed it back to Kit.

"Just give him a hug for me," she said, her voice cracking with emotion. "I miss him so much."

"Of course you do, honey. But don't worry. You two will be back together soon. Luke will see to that."

Kit glanced up at Luke. There was a softness to his expression, a look of compassion and concern. At that moment, she'd never seen a more handsome man.

"Yes," she said into the phone, her gaze locked with Luke's. "I know Luke will see that Andy and I are together soon."

Luke didn't sleep well that night and he knew it had nothing to do with the accommodations. He'd slept on harder floors in less hospitable places.

He didn't kid himself about the problem. It was Kit. He'd lain awake long into the night thinking about her, cursing himself for involving her and the baby in his plot to avenge his brother's death. If he'd never picked her up in the limo, he'd be getting a good night's sleep right now, he'd told himself—all the time knowing that wasn't true.

What choice had he had? Let her go to Huntsville and Derrick? He hated to think what would have happened to her and Andy if she'd gotten into the other limo.

No, he was stuck with her and it was normal that he felt responsible for her and the baby. He'd just make the best of it. They'd work together to stop Derrick Killhorn. Luke wouldn't get any more involved in this woman's life than he had already.

But as he lay there on the floor listening to the rhythmic sound of her breathing, he felt a connection to this woman that scared him more than all the Derrick Killhorns in the world.

Kit woke to sunshine streaming through a crack in the drapes. She could hear the shower running and Luke humming. Obviously, he'd gotten more sleep last night than she had. She got up to peek outside. The morning sun caught in the new snow, making it sparkle like the blinding brilliance of zillions of diamonds.

"I thought we'd go into Bozeman today," Luke announced behind her, making her jump. She hadn't heard him turn off the shower. She spun around to find him toweling his blond hair dry. He wore only a pair of blue jeans and a white T-shirt.

She hadn't let herself think about the body hidden beneath Luke's winter clothing. But now that was all she *could* think about. All she could see. The T-shirt hugged his attributes, accenting the broadness of his shoulders, the rounded contour of his pecs, the chiseled waist. Even his muscular, smooth forearms with the light dusting of blond hair stirred something in her, awakening desires she hadn't even known existed. She looked away, embarrassed at her own thoughts.

"We have time to kill," Luke was saying. "We can't get the combination to the safe until after dark. I don't think staying here all day will do either of us any good. I know I'm lousy at just sitting around."

She nodded quickly in agreement. How could he make her feel sexy with just a look, even a look often laced with self-deprecating humor?

"Is something wrong?"

"No." She tried to avoid looking at anything but his face. "Nothing."

He nodded. "I need to buy a metal detector, the kind you use to find large objects."

"To find Jason's motorcycle."

He raised a brow. "We know Derrick poured concrete after Jason was killed. Now all we have to do is find the motorcycle." He studied her for a moment. "You're sure nothing's wrong."

She gulped and looked away. "What is the plan for to-night?" she asked, quickly going to the bed to make it.

He didn't answer right away. "Am I making you un-comfortable?"

She intended to lie but when she looked up, her gaze met his and she recognized the gleam in those gray eyes of his. "All right, maybe I'm not used to sharing a room with a strange man."

"Strange?" He grinned. "You think I'm strange?"

"No," she said, flustered. "I meant—" She stopped, eyeing him. "You know what I mean. I know you find it silly—"

"No, not silly," he said, the grin fading. "I find it…you… refreshing." He picked up his flannel shirt and pulled it on, turning away from her to tuck it into his jeans. "Is this better?"

Much. "I should get ready," she said, hurrying past him. She could have sworn that she heard a soft chuckle as she passed.

The plan was simple. Maybe too simple, Luke thought. But it was one he'd seen work. One he'd used himself in his misspent youth. Luke couldn't believe he was about to use skills he'd picked up as a wild kid on the streets of Butte, Montana. Petty larceny, here I come again, he thought, as he and Kit worked their way toward Mountain Village.

They'd spent the day in Bozeman. He'd found himself studying her every opportunity he got. Her reaction to him that morning had surprised him and pleased him. That she was attracted to him and that the feeling frightened her was something new for him. What she didn't know was that he felt the same way about her. Only, she frightened him, he'd bet, a whole lot more than he did her.

He'd felt torn all day. He'd been anxious for night to fall so they could get the combination to Derrick's home safe, and hopefully not only find the concrete invoice but anything else Derrick might be hiding in that file folder. But at the same time, Luke hadn't wanted his time with Kit to pass too quickly. For a few hours, he'd forgotten everything but her. They'd walked the busy streets, looking into the holiday-decorated store windows, doing a lot more than killing time.

He'd suggested getting a present for Andy. They'd spent the better part of the morning searching stores for the ideal gift. Against Kit's protests, he'd ended up buying a shopping bag full of gifts for the baby.

"It's his first Christmas," Luke had argued, and when he

saw her tears, had stopped in the middle of the sidewalk to pull her to him and promise she'd be with Andy on Christmas morning to open the packages.

It was a promise he shouldn't have made but wanted more than anything to keep. He'd found himself caught up in the excitement of Christmas for the first time in years, maybe the first time ever, and knew it had more to do with Kit than the decorations hanging from the street corners, the bell ringers or the music that played from store doorways. The season seemed to make Kit glow with a warmth that he wanted to share. She would see things in store windows that would make her eyes light up like a child's. He found that he could make her laugh—and he didn't want to stop.

He'd taken her to lunch at a cute, out-of-the-way Chinese food place and challenged her to try chopsticks. He laughed through most of lunch and marveled at how easy it was to please this woman. At the same time it embarrassed him that it took so little and delighted him. He found himself wanting nothing more in life than to please her. Dangerous thinking.

Eventually, they'd gone to the metal detector shop and purchased one specifically designed to find large steel objects—such as a motorcycle under two feet of concrete or more. The mood had changed the moment he put it in the back of his pickup and headed south, toward Big Sky. Kit's eyes had taken on a faraway look; she was no doubt worried about tonight, about the future.

Luke drove back in silence, lost in his own thoughts. When he thought of Jason, which was often, it now seemed to be with less anger and hatred and more intense pain and sadness. Jason was gone. And it broke his heart.

He sometimes felt as if he were betraying his brother's

memory by not hanging on more tightly to that hatred. He worried that this change in him would dim his desire for vengeance. He still had to bring Derrick Killhorn to justice, one way or the other. But there were moments now when he knew that no matter what he did to his brother's killer, it wouldn't bring Jason back. And that he wouldn't get the satisfaction he'd once thought he would. But, he told himself, when the day came to settle the score with Derrick, he would do what had to be done.

Just like he would do what had to be done now, he thought as he and Kit made their way, through the throng of people, toward the lodge. The ski hill had closed for the day and the hallways in the lodge were packed. Beside him, Kit walked with an armful of brightly wrapped empty boxes. He carried a shopping bag filled with empty wrapped packages.

Christmas music played. "Jingle Bells."

"White Christmas."

"Hark the Herald Angels." Luke looked over at Kit, wisps of her brilliant red hair escaping from under her ski hat, her coat buttoned up to her chin against the cold, her eyes as shiny and bright as the winter evening. She was about to come face-to-face with Derrick Killhorn and she looked more terrified than he'd ever seen her.

Luke realized he'd lost that Christmas spirit he'd felt with Kit earlier in Bozeman. He'd come to the Village not to shop, but to shoplift. If he succeeded, it would bring him one step closer to his ultimate goal of bringing down Derrick Killhorn. If he failed—

He couldn't even consider that possibility.

Inside the lodge, Luke began searching the faces of the crowd for one face in particular: Derrick Killhorn's.

Belinda had been so sure that he would come. Luke

glanced at his watch. Two minutes to seven. Belinda said he wouldn't be late.

With a jolt Luke realized she was right. Derrick was elbowing his way through the crowd. He wore a ski jacket with a fur-trimmed collar, jeans, expensive boots and an air of superiority. Luke supposed some women might find him attractive. He had little-boy looks and a charm that seemed to ooze from his pores like oil. Luke reminded himself that Kit had once been one of those women. She'd found Derrick charming and handsome enough to marry him. Luke felt a painful stab of jealousy that did nothing to improve his mood.

He glanced over at Kit and nodded slightly, then he stepped away from her, skirting around the shoppers and skiers and snowboarders. Luke was banking on Derrick's surprise at seeing Kit—that and his own ability to keep Derrick from ever getting near Kit once that happened.

Luke never took his eyes from the man as he closed in. He wanted to see the expression on Derrick's face when he recognized Kit coming toward him. It was a moment Luke had no intention of missing for several very good reasons. Kit's safety was at the top of that list.

Derrick was frowning as he scanned the crowd, no doubt looking for Belinda and wondering why they had to meet here, of all places. His gaze brushed over Kit, then flicked back to her. His eyes widened and several emotions seemed to flicker across his face in an instant. Surprise. Shock. Fear. It was the fear that Luke took guilty pleasure in.

Derrick stumbled, all the superiority of his step instantly gone, leaving him fighting to keep his feet under him.

Luke smiled and moved in for the kill.

Derrick was only a few feet from Kit when she bumped

one of the skiers, sending her armload of packages spilling to the floor between her and Derrick.

The crowd parted. Shoppers and skiers stopped to help pick up the packages, moving between Derrick and his wife. Kit stumbled back. "Watch that one," she cried pointing to a large box at Derrick's feet. "It's breakable."

Derrick quickly bent down to pick it up. The package and several too-helpful skiers who'd stopped to lend assistance were all that stood between him and Kit. At that exact moment, Luke jostled Derrick ever so slightly. Derrick didn't even notice.

Derrick straightened with the package in his hands and glanced around in surprise. The crowd flowed again around him. Kit was gone and Luke was walking away, enjoying the look of consternation on Derrick's face. Derrick stood for a moment, shook the empty package and glared angrily about him. Then he walked to a trash can and smashed the brightly wrapped box into the can.

Luke rounded the corner. He could see Kit waiting expectantly at the far end of the hallway. He hurried to her.

"Did you get it?" she cried.

He held up Derrick's wallet, the expensive leather still warm.

She smiled then, relief washing over her beautiful face.

"Come on," he said, returning her smile. He took her hand. They ran down the hall and out into the night. It felt good to run. Luke knew Derrick wasn't after them. There was no way he'd be able to find them in that crowd, but Luke didn't want to stop running any more than he wanted to let go of Kit's hand.

Luke ran with Kit down the wide trail that led from Mountain Village to the lagoon, the scent of pines and snow and winter filling his nostrils, his lungs. They ran until he could feel Kit slowing and he eased up, stopping beside her, still holding her hand. She leaned against him, he against her.

Luke pulled back to see her face. The laughter seemed to bubble up from deep inside her. She looked at him and the first nervous giggle spilled out. He grinned at her and they both began to laugh, the hearty laughter of children who'd just pulled off the perfect harmless prank. Somewhere in the distance, sleigh bells jingled and Christmas music played. The snow fell around them and the air smelled of evergreen.

Their eyes met and locked and, abruptly, they stopped laughing. Snow filled the silence, falling in large floating flakes that caught on Kit's eyelashes, on her nose, on her lips. Luke followed the lazy drift of a snowflake to her lips. Without thinking, he leaned down to touch the tip of his tongue to the side of her mouth to capture the delicate ice crystal before it could melt. Their breaths mingled, snow white in the freezing night air. Luke didn't feel the cold or the snow. He felt nothing but Kit, as she released his hand to press her palms against his chest, her gaze still locked with his, her lips parted slightly. Somewhere close by "Silent Night" played on a car radio.

He lowered his lips to hers, barely brushing her mouth. He heard her sharp intake of breath, felt her sway against him. His arms encircled her and pulled her closer. His mouth dropped to hers, the pressure gentle, the kiss tentative. She tasted sweet, her lips cool, her breath warm, her mouth now an open invitation. He deepened the kiss, greedily seeking the pleasures of her mouth while his hands roamed over her back, her shoulders and finally cupped her bottom to pull her into him, into his kiss.

She groaned softly and melted into him, opening to

him in a way that ignited his passion and stole his heart. He couldn't ever remember wanting a woman the way he wanted her. He slipped his hand up under her coat, under her sweater until he felt the warmth of her bare flesh.

She gasped as his hand slipped under her bra and cupped her full breast in his palm. Her eyes flew open and she drew back, a look of surprise and caution on her face.

He could feel her trembling as he let go of her warm breast. His heart banged around in his chest. They stood looking at each other for a long moment, the snow falling between them, a wall of cold white. He yearned to kiss her again, to hold her, to press his body to hers. He wanted to feel her warmth beneath him, to make love to her.

"I'm sorry." He stopped. "No, I'm not sorry. I wanted to kiss you."

She shook her head, dropping her gaze. He saw tears bead in her eyes and fought the urge to reach for her. "I sometimes forget why we're here," she said. "What it is we're doing." Her eyes lifted to meet his. "I forget that I'm married."

Married. To Derrick Killhorn. He took a deep breath. "So do I." He *wanted* to forget. "I have to be honest with you. I don't just want to kiss you, Kit. I want to make love to you."

She gazed into his eyes. "Because I'm his wife? Is this just another way to get back at him?"

She thought that he wanted her as a way to get revenge against Derrick Killhorn? "I want to make love with you in spite of that fact, not because of it." He took her shoulders in his hands and pulled her close again. "This has nothing to do with the Killhorns, nothing to do with Jason. This is about you and me."

"I know nothing about you," she said, her voice filled with emotion.

"You know everything about me that matters," he said.

He felt her tremble, saw the raw desire in her gaze, and would have kissed her again right there if it hadn't been for the sound of a vehicle coming quickly up the road, headed their way.

"Come on," he whispered and took her hand again. This time they didn't stop running until they reached his pickup.

Chapter 15

Luke wanted more than anything to kiss Kit again, but he knew that wouldn't be a good idea. They had to hit Killhorn's house *now*. It couldn't wait. Soon Derrick was bound to realize his wallet was missing. Would he realize why and try to hurry home?

If Luke hoped to get into the safe, it had to be done immediately. While all of that was true, it didn't make things any easier, he thought. His desire for Kit seemed a fire inside him and the kiss had only fanned the flames.

"Here, make sure the combination is in there," he said handing Derrick's wallet to Kit when they reached the pickup. He turned on the cab lights as he backed up and headed for Derrick's house.

She opened the wallet as if she thought it might be full of vipers. "I think this is it," she said after a few moments. She held up a slip of paper with a series of numbers on it.

"Let's hope so," Luke said. He drove the eight miles

down the mountain to the highway. Ahead he could see Killhorn's large-ranch-style home. Just the sight of it made him grit his teeth.

"Are we going to break in?" Kit asked, sounding worried.

"Not this time." He reached into his coat pocket and extracted a key. "Last time I was here I borrowed the back door key, duplicated and returned it."

She nodded. "Derrick always kept an extra set of keys by the back door. Belinda's right about him. He's pretty predictable in some ways. But not in others."

Luke glanced over at her, wondering what her life with Derrick had been like. Hell, he thought. Then he wondered if that was true or just what he wanted to believe.

He parked under a stand of pines up the road from the house, and they walked back following the contours of the land to keep out of sight of the highway. A yard light burned golden in the snowfall. Derrick's truck was nowhere to be seen. Nor were there any lights on in the house. But Luke knew Derrick wouldn't have had time to get back to the house ahead of them even if Belinda hadn't been able to take care of her part of the plan—disabling Derrick's precious pickup.

Luke used the key to open the back door. "Let's make this quick." He hurried up the stairs, headed—as per Belinda's directions—for the master bedroom and the wall safe.

When he opened the door to the massive bedroom, he tried to ignore the king-size bed with the velvet cover, tried not to think about Kit lying in that bed with Derrick.

It took only a moment to push aside the painting and dial the numbers on the safe. No alarms went off as he swung open the door and quickly riffled through the meager contents. He found a file folder with numbers scrawled on the outside. He glanced in it. Invoices. *Bingo.*

Tucking the folder under his arm, he spent a few more minutes looking for anything else that might pertain to the condo complex and Jason's murder. A couple of insurance policies, some papers on the house, a passport, a marriage license, titles on vehicles and construction equipment. Nothing else about the complex.

Luke had started to close the safe door when one of the items drew his attention again. He pulled out the marriage license form and frowned down at it. He remembered filling one of these out four years ago but that was as far as he'd gotten. He tossed it back into the safe, and with the folder under his arm, closed the door and turned, expecting to find Kit behind him.

"Kit?" he called quietly.

No answer. He rushed out of the room, anxious to find Kit and get out of this house, hoping the plan hadn't gone awry. That Derrick hadn't returned.

To his relief he spotted her coming out of a room down the hall. She carried the two paintings he'd seen on the wall. He smiled and went to help her.

Luke led the way down the wide curved stairway and Kit followed, glancing around the house that had been her home for a few, long miserable months.

Everything about this house gave her the creeps and reminded her how unhappy she'd been here. She'd tried to hide that fact from Derrick, who'd become angry when she'd attempted to talk to him about it.

"No woman could be unhappy in a house like this," he'd protested. "What's wrong with you? Are you crazy? Look around you. This is a palace, and you're the queen."

He didn't understand that she would gladly have traded the house and everything in it for a tiny shack and a husband who spent more time with her, a husband who she felt loved and cherished her and accepted her for the person she was, rather than for his image of what Mrs. Derrick Killhorn should be.

"I'd just like to be with you more," she'd said. "Feel like you're with me. That we're truly husband and wife."

"Grow up," he'd snapped angrily. "You expect everything to be perfect instantly. It's going to take some time. After the baby comes, after my son is born, then we'll go on a honeymoon or something." He walked away from her. "I have the condos to finish. It's not like I'm asking you to do anything. Just stay here and let me get my work done."

"And if it's a daughter?" she'd cried.

He'd turned and narrowed his gaze at her. "If you'd have had that damn test, we wouldn't have to keep arguing about the baby's sex, now would we?" He'd glared at her as if he hated her. "You're Mrs. Derrick Killhorn. Try to act like it. A lot of women would love to be in your shoes, sweetheart."

"Are you all right?" Luke asked from the bottom of the stairs.

Kit blinked and looked down at him, surprised to see that she'd stopped partway down the steps, her mind replaying that old scene with Derrick as if she had lived it yesterday. "Fine," she said and hurried down to Luke.

He studied her for a moment, concern in his expression.

"I have a lot of bad memories here," she explained, her voice sounding close to tears. She realized that they weren't tears of remorse, but of relief. She'd never have to come back to this house. Her son would never have to live here. She lifted her chin and gave Luke a smile. "I'm fine."

Luke smiled back. "Yeah, I can see that."

Headlights flashed across the living room window. A vehicle pulled up in front of the house. Car doors slammed, and Kit could hear voices approaching the front door, the sound of snow being stomped off two pairs of boots.

Kit had worried that, while her luck and Luke's had been holding, it would eventually run out. She feared that was the case as she heard the boom of Derrick's angry voice, followed by another equally angry voice, one she'd heard only a few times before but recognized instantly—Judge J. T. Killhorn's. Derrick's father.

A key clicked in the front door lock. Luke grabbed Kit and pulled her into the closest hiding place he could see: a wide hall closet by the living room. There was just enough room between the back wall and the doors for him and Kit and the paintings, but nothing else. He felt the file folder slip from under his arm and hit the floor. Papers fluttered at his feet as he heard the front door open off to the right and the sound of raised voices.

"I want to know what the hell's going on," Judge Killhorn bellowed. "And don't give me that nonsense about nothing."

A light came on. A thick sliver cut a swath between the double closet doors, illuminating the interior enough that Luke could see Kit's pale face and get a pretty good view of the living room.

He heard what sounded like Derrick opening the coat closet by the front door and banging the metal hangers around as if looking for one in particular. Luke just hoped that whatever Derrick was looking for wasn't in *this* closet.

"I told you—"

The judge cut his son off. "You *told* me a lot of things."

Luke saw the judge move into the olympic-size living

room. He seemed to be looking for a place to sit but none of the fancy furniture appeared to appeal to him. "I had a talk with John Stockwell at the bank this afternoon."

"I'm having a little cash flow problem. It's nothing to concern yourself with," Derrick snapped as he joined his father in the living room. Luke saw Derrick glance up the stairs. "Maybe I should find a banker who can keep his mouth shut."

"Don't you blame John for this. I strong-armed him into telling me. You've gone and run that construction company into the ground, haven't you? I told your brother not to get involved in any business dealings with you because you'd end up screwing him."

"Your faith in me, Father, has always amazed me," Derrick said. "I have to check something. I'll be right back." He left his father before the man could respond, and ran up the stairs.

When Derrick came back down, he looked as though he'd seen a ghost. He went straight to the liquor cabinet and poured himself a drink.

"I'll take one of those," J.T. announced behind him. "Make it a double. You want to tell me what the hell's going on?"

"Nothing."

"Nothing?" the judge roared.

"I told you, I'm a little short of cash right now. Nothing serious." Derrick made another drink and handed it to his father, then went to stand behind one of the high-back chairs as if for protection.

"Someone slashed your tires at Mountain Village to-night, your wallet was stolen, someone's been sabotaging your job, and you call that *nothing?*"

"Just a little random violence," Derrick said, and took a long swallow of the liquor.

The old man finally sat down, but didn't look comfortable. "I didn't give you a ride home to talk to you about money or your damn tires."

"And I thought you gave me a ride out of the kindness of your heart," Derrick quipped.

J.T. frowned at his son. "You know, I'd heard things about you, things I didn't want to believe, and I ignored them. But I couldn't keep ignoring what's going on. For some time now I've been keeping an eye on you and I don't like what I see."

Derrick let out a nasty laugh. "Not that it's any of your business—"

"You don't understand," his father cut in. "I'm *making* it my business. I want to talk to you about your wife."

Luke felt Kit tense beside him.

Derrick's face closed in anger. "I can handle my wife."

"Is that right?" The judge rattled his ice and stared down into the amber liquid. "I ran into Bob Haskins, my friend who's a J.P. over in Park County. He likes Scotch, and over a bottle of the expensive stuff he got to talking about you and your so-called marriage. He just assumed it had been a practical joke and thought I knew. You want to let me in on the joke?"

"It's complicated."

"Dishonest, may describe it better, if not morally corrupt," the judge said. "What exactly was the purpose of making that woman think you married her?"

Luke shot a look at Kit. Her eyes were wide, her look one of shocked disbelief. Kit and Derrick weren't married?

"I'm waiting for an answer and I'm not leaving until I get

one. You involved a friend of mine in one of your scams. That is unforgivable."

"I *was* going to marry her," Derrick whined. "I was just waiting until I was sure she was going to give me a son."

"What?" The judge slammed his glass down on the coffee table. Derrick grimaced.

Beside Luke, Kit looked as if she might faint. Luke carefully balanced the paintings on the toes of his boots. She looked too upset to comfort even if they hadn't been in a narrow closet. He knew she had to be furious—not only with Derrick but with herself. No one liked being duped. Especially by someone as loathsome as Derrick Killhorn. Cautiously, he took her hand in his and squeezed it gently, hoping she'd take the gesture as one of comfort and concern.

She squeezed back with a force that told him that along with shock, she was feeling some anger. He felt the same way about Derrick Killhorn. Luke could not believe the man, could not believe the depth of his depravity.

"You're telling me you knocked up that woman, then pretended to marry her, then waited to see what the sex of the baby was?" the judge was saying loudly.

"I *would* have married her if I'd known it was going to be a boy." He shrugged. "She wouldn't take the damn test so I could find out for sure."

The judge let out an oath. "What the hell is wrong with you?"

"Nothing," Derrick cried. "I just want a son. What's wrong with that? You got *two* of them."

The judge narrowed his eyes. His expression said that having a son wasn't all it was cracked up to be, especially right now. "There's more to this and don't you dare lie to me."

Derrick shook his head and looked away. "You always want to think the worst of me."

"You always want to take shortcuts—as if the rules were made for everyone but you." J.T. sighed and motioned for his son to sit down. "It's my fault. You knew you were my favorite. Sanders knew it as well. Look how he caters to you."

With obvious reluctance, Derrick came around the chair and sat across from his father.

"So what happened?" the judge asked. "This woman find out about the phoney marriage? Is that why she left you?"

"No, she's just flighty as all hell, that's all. I gave her everything but it wasn't enough. She knew how badly I wanted a son and now she's busting my chops, the stupid cow."

"Someone ought to bust *your* chops," the judge said in disgust. He shook his head at his son. "Is that any way to talk about the mother of your child?"

"She left me."

"I shouldn't wonder." J.T. got up and went to the bar to refill his glass. "I saw your ex the other day," he said, his back to Derrick.

"Belinda? That moronic—"

The judge swung around. "Belinda gave you every chance, and you blew it. I know that for a fact." He walked back to the couch with his drink and sat down, leaning forward, his elbows on his thighs. "She told me something that deeply disturbs me. She says you can't father children of your own and that's why you've been acting so irrationally. You think you need this baby to prove your manhood."

Derrick's face turned purple and he looked as if he might explode. "She's a damn liar."

The judge glared at his son. "This isn't your baby, is it?"

"Look, I don't have to—"

Derrick didn't get another word out of his mouth before his father was on his feet, holding Derrick's collar. He jerked his son to his feet and stuck his face in his.

"You listen to me, Derrick. I'm sick of your lies and your excuses. Sanders tells me you've had him searching for that poor woman for seven months. No wonder you're having financial problems at that condo complex. You leave that woman alone. She's not your wife, that's not your son. You get your brother back here and take care of business. Sanders idolizes you. Don't you hurt him or I swear—"

J.T. let go of his son, then turned, picked up his drink and drained it. Carefully, he set the empty glass on the coffee table. "I'm not bailing you out anymore, Derrick. Not financially. Not legally. Not any way."

Derrick didn't say a word as his father walked out. But the instant the front door closed, he threw his glass against the wall, shattering a huge ornate mirror and sending his own image splintering into knife-sharp shards.

He stood for a moment, then grabbed up the phone and beat out a number. He waited, then slammed down the phone, grabbed his coat and stormed out of the house.

The rage Luke saw in the man's face as he left was nothing compared to Luke's own. He couldn't believe what Derrick had done to Kit. Luke made a silent promise to Kit and his brother Jason. This man would pay for everything he'd done. He'd pay, if it was the last thing Luke St. John ever did.

Kit's world tilted precariously. She held on to Luke's hand, an anchor in a storm that she'd thought couldn't get any worse. The marriage had been a fake. Derrick had only wanted her son.

Suddenly there was no air in the closet. Derrick had barely slammed the front door behind him, when Luke threw open the closet doors, caught the paintings before they tumbled off his toes, and hurriedly, but carefully, put them out of harm's way. Then he swept Kit up in his arms and carried her to the couch.

"What if Derrick comes—"

"If he comes back, I'll take care of him," Luke assured her in a tone that did, indeed, reassure her. "Just breathe."

She gulped air as if fighting for her last breath. She could still hear the roar of Derrick's snowmobile dying off in the distance. Luke pressed a glass of sherry into her hand.

"Drink," he insisted. "It can't hurt."

She saw that he had poured himself a glass of whiskey. She emptied the glass as he did his own.

He let out a long sigh and looked at her, concern in his expression. "You want another one?"

She shook her head. "Derrick and I were never married."

"Sounds that way."

Kit couldn't believe it. "I fell for his lies. He seemed so caring, so sincere at first."

"You saw only what he wanted you to see." A muscle in his jaw jumped and in his eyes she saw mirrored her own anger. "The man was a damn fool," Luke said as he knelt in front of her. "He didn't even know what he had."

She smiled at Luke. The lava-hot veneer of her anger fell away and she felt such intense relief that it made her want to laugh. *Not married.* This explained so much about her so-called relationship with Derrick. Why he hadn't slept with her. Why he had seemed to have no interest in her other than the baby she carried. Why he'd demanded that the baby had to be a boy—and that she have the test to prove it.

She shook her head again and did laugh. She wasn't Mrs.

Derrick Killhorn. She wasn't married to a murderer. She didn't have to worry about Derrick trying to take Andy legally. She met Luke's puzzled gaze. She wasn't married at all. The intensity of his look stilled her laughter, stilled everything but her heart. It slammed around in her chest.

"Maybe you'd better have some more sherry," Luke said, and started to rise.

She touched his arm, and he stopped, his gaze coming back to hers. "Thank you."

"For dragging you back here, for making you have to hear all this? Yeah, you owe me a lot of thanks."

She remembered the way he'd taken her hand in the closet. The gentle squeeze of his fingers. And the care he'd shown her paintings, which now rested safely by the door. Derrick had tried so hard to seem gentle, loving and caring; and Luke tried so hard to hide what was second nature for him.

She reached out to cup his jaw in her hand. It felt wonderfully rough and warm and strong. "Just knowing Derrick has no legal hold over me or my son was well worth the trip. But I'm not quitting now. After everything Derrick has done, I won't let him get away with your brother's murder."

"Are you sure? I wouldn't blame you if you wanted to bail out and go be with your son."

She shook her head. "I've never wanted to see anything through to the end more in my life."

He covered her hand with his own, sliding it from his jaw to his lips. He kissed her open palm.

"I owe it to myself," Kit whispered. "To my son. To you."

The touch of his lips at the heart of her palm started an avalanche of feelings cascading through her.

"You owe me nothing," he said, releasing her hand as he got to his feet and dragged her up and into his arms. He held her tightly, his large, powerful arms gentle, protective. Her world felt solid again. "You owe me nothing, Kit Bannack. Absolutely nothing."

She gazed up at him, hearing the emotion in his voice, the way he said her name. She wasn't Mrs. Derrick Killhorn anymore. And Luke St. John seemed as relieved as she felt.

She circled her arms around his neck, her gaze locked with his, as he bent to kiss her.

Car lights flickered across the living room window.

Luke swore softly. "I guess it's time to get moving," he said, drawing back to look into her eyes. He held her a few more moments, as if he didn't want to let go, then released her.

She watched him hurry to the open closet and scoop up the folder and papers he'd dropped. She closed the closet doors quickly behind him as he handed her the folder and went to get her paintings. At the sound of the doorbell, they slipped out the back door and disappeared into the night.

Sanders stood outside Derrick's house, listening. The night was quiet and cold. Where was Derrick?

Sanders had run into his father down the road. J.T. had pulled alongside him and rolled down his window. Sanders had seen right away that his father was upset. What had Derrick done now? "What's wrong?"

J.T. had only wagged his head. He looked angry. Sanders figured his father had fought with Derrick, which surprised him.

"I can talk to him," Sanders offered.

J.T. laughed without humor. "Don't waste your time. Or your life."

"Derrick's under a lot of strain."

J.T. looked over at Sanders as if he was seeing him for

the first time. Sanders felt the heat of his father's gaze, felt surprised at the emotion he saw there. He'd seen this same expression on his father's face before, but it had always been for Derrick—never for J.T.'s younger son. The face held sadness, regret, worry. But what shocked and scared Sanders was the unspoken apology he saw on his father's forlorn face.

"Sanders—" J.T. stared at his son for a long moment. Finally he shook his head, shifted his car into gear and drove away, whatever he'd planned to say never making it into words.

Sanders rang Derrick's doorbell a second and third time, knowing it was useless. Derrick was gone. He must have left by snowmobile. Sanders had seen his truck up on the mountain with all four tires slashed. He turned from the door and headed for his car, wondering what was going on.

But it was his father Sanders thought about as he left. He'd seen something in his father's face tonight that had Sanders terrified something horrible was about to happen. Or maybe already had.

Chapter 16

Everything had changed. And nothing had changed. But Luke found himself feeling better than he'd felt in a long time. Kit didn't belong to Derrick. She never had. It made him smile to himself. She'd never been Mrs. Derrick Killhorn.

He knew it was foolish. It meant nothing. But it meant everything. He wanted to kiss her again. That's all he could think about as they left Derrick's house and trudged through the snow and cold. Over his shoulder, he watched the house disappear behind him in the storm, then disappear from view entirely as if it had never existed any more than the marriage.

He'd heard whoever had come to visit Derrick finally leave and the night had grown still again, leaving him and Kit alone.

She walked next to him through the snow. The clouds broke above Lone Peak and the moon hung, a thin sliver of silver, the stars around it like bright sparks in the black velvet sky. The air had a bite to it that braced him.

He glanced over at her. Her breath came out frosty white. Earlier, she'd gone so pale. It had frightened him. Now her color had returned and she looked more beautiful than ever, stronger than ever, a woman to reckon with. He liked that.

At his pickup, he stowed Kit's paintings safely behind the seat, then climbed in beside her and started the truck.

"I thought we should change our hideout. I have a friend who owns a motel south of Big Sky. He's expecting us." It was a little nicer, a little more private, a lot more intimate.

Kit didn't answer. She seemed lost in her own thoughts. He wondered if she was as relieved as he was that she'd never been married to Derrick Killhorn.

"Derrick will never quit looking for us now," she said, her face troubled. "He's being pushed in too many directions. He couldn't tell his father that he had to find me because I witnessed him murder Jason. Or that now the victim's brother was after him." She met Luke's gaze. "Derrick must be going crazy."

"Can't think of anyone who deserves it more. Can you?"

She shook her head. "But it only makes him more dangerous." Her voice sounded small. "I'm afraid what he'll do to you, Luke."

"Kit—"

"There may be a way to end all of this," she said, meeting his gaze. "I'm going to call Judge Killhorn. You heard what he said. Maybe he'll help us."

Luke wished he shared her faith in J. T. Killhorn. "I wouldn't get your hopes up. Even though he came down hard on Derrick, I think when push comes to shove, he'll protect his son."

"I have to try," Kit said without hesitation, and he

thought about the young woman who used to be easily swayed. Not this Kit. Not this woman that he was beginning to admire more and more.

He checked them into the Pinecone Motel, a small out-of-the-way place, and pulled up to the last unit in the row, the one closest to the Gallatin River.

"I'll get your paintings and our bags out. Why don't you go call," he said, handing her the key to number nine.

When he came into the room a few minutes later she was sitting on the bed, her head in her hands. He almost hoped that she hadn't been able to get through to the judge, but he could tell by her expression, when she looked up, that she had. "Well?"

"He listened, then he said I'd best not make accusations against his son unless I had proof to back them up." Kit made a discouraged face. "I told him I had come back to Montana to get proof, but Derrick had destroyed it before I got here. I told him about the snowmobile accident and the man who'd tried to kill us—Matthew Rustan. Luke, he sounded like he believed me. He sounded scared."

"But he refused to do anything," Luke guessed.

She nodded.

"You gave it your best shot." He had expected this. Kit, however, seemed disheartened. She still believed in justice, that life should be fair, that good conquered evil without all-out war. Luke had stopped believing in that years ago. Four to be exact. Jason hadn't believed in war, and look where it had gotten him.

Luke put down her paintings, then stood back to admire them. They were full of life with a boldness and a passion he recognized—in both the paintings and the artist. He felt drawn to them, the same way he felt drawn to Kit.

He looked up to see her watching him.

"You like my paintings." She seemed pleased.

"Very much. I see you in them."

She smiled nervously. "What? You see all the tragedies of my young life?"

He shook his head. "I see desire in them, a need and a fear of that need, of that unsatisfied longing. I recognize those feelings."

He found that he couldn't take his eyes from her. A slight blush stained her cheeks, making her look as new and fresh as a Montana morning. Her lips had a natural rosiness to them and her eyes shone bright as sunlight on snow.

She bit her lower lip as he moved to the bed. She tilted her head back, her gaze locking with his, and he saw everything he'd seen in her paintings. It was now in her eyes.

"There is something so sensual, so provocative, so alluring about you, Kit Bannack. I don't think you know what you do to a man."

She started to look away, but he touched her cheek with his fingers and held her gaze. Then he let his hand slide down, along the slim column of her neck, to the hollow at her throat, down to the rise above her breasts.

He heard her intake of breath when he stopped. He freed the top button of her shirt, skimming his fingers across the silken warmth of her skin to the next button. His gaze held hers, never wavering. Her eyes widened as he freed the next button and the next, brushing the fabric back to let his fingers trail along the smooth white tops of her breasts.

Desire shone naked in her eyes and he felt her tremble as he let his hand skim over the outside of her thin lace bra and felt her nipple leap to his touch, rock hard.

She groaned as he brushed his fingertips over the other breast. The nipple pressed against the sheer lace as if aching for his touch, for his lips, for the feel of his wet tongue, just as he ached to feel every inch of her.

He freed the rest of the buttons and pushed the fabric aside. Only then did he break eye contact to look down at her. He felt himself catch fire at just the sight of her. The full white breasts peeked above the black lace of the bra. Nipples strained at the lace. He trailed his fingers from the brilliance of her fiery hair, down her shoulder, over her one breast to her slim waist, stopping at the buttons of her jeans. Then he looked up at her again.

Her gaze seemed to beg him to prove his desire for her.

He opened his own shirt and, taking her hand, pressed her palm against his thundering heart. "That's what you do to a man," he whispered. "That's only part of what you do to me."

She shook her head, her look still disbelieving.

He took her hand and pressed it against his maleness, now hard and full of yearning.

She closed her eyes, a soft groan escaping her lips.

"You are so incredibly sexy, Kit," he whispered, raising her hand to brush his lips across her fingertips, then across her palm.

"Derrick never wanted me," she said so quietly that at first he thought he hadn't heard correctly. "He never made love to me."

He thought she was talking semantics.

"He didn't want me. He said it was because he was afraid of hurting the baby, but the truth is—" she opened her eyes and met Luke's gaze "—I never saw desire in his eyes. In fact, I've never seen desire like this in any man's eyes before you."

"Oh, Kit," he said, understanding at last the longing he'd sensed in her paintings, in her. She'd felt rejected, unloved, undesirable. He knew that feeling only too well. He knew what that kind of hurt could do.

He pulled her into his arms, rocking her gently, his hand stroking her hair, his heart picking up her beat.

After a few moments, he pulled back to look at her. "You are so beautiful, my sweet Kit." His gaze caressed her face. "*I* want you. I want you more than I've ever wanted anyone, anything."

Her gaze fired with such open desire that he thought he would die in his need to fulfill it. He ached to free the woman he saw trapped in her eyes, to show her that she was no longer that young college girl...that this body of hers was no longer that of a girl-woman...that her desires, her fantasies, her longings were all those of the woman she'd become.

"I want to make love to you. With you." He wanted at that moment more than anything else in the world to show her the joys of her own body, to make her understand at last what a desirable, beautiful woman she'd become. And what pleasure that gave a man.

She touched his cheek with her hand. "Oh yes, please. Please make love to me."

Kit shivered at the look in Luke's eyes and started to draw her shirt back over her breasts, shy and embarrassed by her aching hard nipples pressing against the thin lace of her bra.

He stopped her, slipping the shirt from her shoulders.

His gaze felt as hot on her skin as his fingertips had been. And it made her feel naked. And on fire. He'd been right about the yearning in her. That yearning for him had become agony.

He reached behind her to unsnap the lacy bra and toss it

aside. His gaze fell on her breasts and she closed her eyes, anticipating his touch, dying for it.

He cupped each breast in his large hands and thumbed her aching nipples to hard points. Her eyes flew open at the feel of his tongue, rough, hot and wet. He trailed across her skin with his mouth, branding her tender flesh. She groaned and buried her fingers in his hair, pulling him into her as he suckled at her breasts until she felt a burst of pure pleasure scorch her skin, melt her center.

"Oh, Kit," Luke whispered as he lifted her head to look into her face.

She trembled as she wrapped her arms around his neck and held him close for a few moments while her heart slowed down and the sharp elation eased a little. But the desire didn't dim. Instead it flared brighter at the feel of his chest against hers.

She pulled back just enough to slip his shirt off his wonderfully broad shoulders, letting her fingers and her gaze caress his rich, warm skin.

He smiled down at her as she leaned up to kiss his lips, then trailed kisses down to his nipples. She flicked each with her tongue and thrilled at his immediate reaction.

He pulled her to her feet. His eyes had taken on a sheen, deepening with desire. He began to unbutton her jeans. She reached for the buttons on his, holding his gaze, trembling at just the thought of the two of them naked.

He pulled off her jeans, stopping for a moment to eye her lacy panties. He smiled up at her as if her lingerie told him everything he needed to know about her, then stripped off her panties.

She wanted to tell him how inexperienced she was, how unsure, but oh, so willing. He pulled her to him before she could say a word. His kiss, so filled with passion, penetrated her very soul. Then he dropped his jeans and swept her up and onto the bed again.

Their bodies melded soft and hard, one forming to the other in a blaze of heat. Skin on skin, they exchanged caresses. Kit thrilled to the feel of him, to his touch, to his body's reaction to hers. She had never known such pure joy. She opened her heart and her body to Luke, rejoicing in the pleasure it gave her, rejoicing in the pleasure she seemed to give him. She had never dreamed making love could be like this.

And just when she thought she could experience no more, that no other pleasure beyond this could exist, he proved to her how little she knew about lovemaking. He caught her up in his rhythm, a primal dance, his own unique beat drumming inside her, thrumming through her veins, a steady throb that thundered in her pulse. Heart pounding to that bilateral beat, he took her to a place she had only dreamed of, a place where there was nothing but rapture. She cried out, her release coming fast and furious, sending her spiraling out of control.

"What in the hell happened to you?" Sanders cried at the sight of his brother's bruised and bloodied face the next morning. He'd already heard at the gas station earlier that Derrick had been in another bar fight. This time in West Yellowstone.

"You wouldn't believe me if I told you," Derrick said, closing the door behind Sanders and heading into the living room to the bar to pour himself a drink. "You want one?"

"It's a little early for me," Sanders said and dropped into one of Derrick's living room chairs. The house felt empty without Kit. Empty and cavernous. "Why do you say I won't believe you?"

Derrick finished making himself a Bloody Mary, then stood for a moment, eyeing him. "Because I haven't been totally honest with you." He sat down across from Sanders and took a sip of his drink.

I knew it, Sanders thought and braced himself.

"I'm sure you've wondered why Luke St. John kidnapped Kit and my son," Derrick said.

Oh, yeah. Sanders had thought about nothing else—and Derrick's strange reaction to it.

"Surely you must wonder why, after being abducted, Kit fell in with this…man and has now come back to Montana to try to prove I'm a murderer."

Sanders wished now that he'd taken that drink.

"She knew him," Derrick said and swore. "Kit knew Luke St. John before I married her, before she came to live in Big Sky. They were seeing each other here."

"What?" How could that be? Kit never left the house without Sanders driving her. Sanders had been her only friend. There wasn't any way she could have been seeing another man, especially as pregnant as she was.

Derrick slammed his drink down. "I knew you wouldn't believe me. They were involved, dammit." He turned away and Sanders felt his heart drop.

"The baby—?"

Derrick swung back around. "He's mine! But don't you see? She and St. John are trying to frame me. Jason disappearing is all part of the plot."

"Why wouldn't she just divorce you?"

"Because she knows I will never let her have my son."

That made a strange kind of sense to Sanders. But Kit having an affair with Luke St. John? Did she know what he'd done four years ago?

"Luke St. John is the one who slashed my tires, the one who beat me up last night."

Sanders stared at his brother as Derrick told him how he'd gone to West Yellowstone, looking for Kit. When he hadn't found her, he'd gone to the nearest bar for one drink. Luke had jumped him in the shadows when he came back out.

"I think he would have killed me if a car hadn't come by," Derrick finished.

Sanders's heart ached at the anguish in his brother's face. Kit had betrayed him, stolen his son. And now he'd been beaten up by her boyfriend...

"I'm so sorry." Sanders knew he was apologizing for doubting his big brother, as much as anything.

"It's all right," Derrick said remorsefully. "I should have told you sooner. I just couldn't bear to have anyone find out. Not even you."

It explained Derrick's protectiveness with Kit, Sanders thought. Kit and Luke St. John. He still had trouble believing it. But unless Derrick had killed Jason St. John, it was the only thing that made any sense.

"I can't let this man get my son, Sand," Derrick said, his voice cracking with emotion.

"No." Sanders felt as betrayed by Kit as his brother did. "He won't. We won't let him."

Derrick smiled. "I knew I could count on you, little brother."

When Kit opened her eyes the next morning, she found Luke studying her. He smiled shyly as if she'd caught him at something he hadn't meant for her to see. She returned his smile, only a little worried about what she'd witnessed in his gaze. He rolled to one side and pulled her into him, spooning her against him, his lips next to her ear, his arms wrapping her in a warm cocoon. "How are you this morning?" he whispered.

She laughed softly. "I've never been better."

He chuckled. "Me neither."

Her skin felt hot and tender and damp. It was as if no man had ever touched her before. But one had now. He'd touched her in a way that she knew had changed her forever. She snuggled against Luke, feeling strong and confident that together they could do anything. Even beat Derrick at his own evil game. At that moment, she really believed love could conquer all—even Luke's need for vengeance. She didn't even question that the feelings between them were love.

"Tell me about Andy's father," Luke said softly behind her, wanting to know everything about this woman. "That is, if you don't mind talking about William."

Kit sighed and snuggled deeper in his arms. "He taught one of my literature classes and I had the worst crush on him. He didn't want to get involved with me. I thought it was the difference in our ages—he was a lot older. I didn't know about his heart. I found out that I was pregnant with his baby a few weeks after his death. He never knew. I like to think he would have been happy about it."

Luke pulled her closer. He couldn't believe all the loss this young woman had had in her short life. Her parents, then the first man she'd ever loved. He could see how easily she'd become Derrick's prey. "You've had quite a time, haven't you?"

"I guess this was the way it was meant to be," Kit said. "I think it's made me stronger. I can see things so much clearer. My relationship with William was never...passionate. I think I was looking for security. He seemed so worldly, so safe. That's what I wanted then."

"And now?" Luke asked.

"Now I know about passion and desire and I would never settle for anything less."

He liked her answer.

"What about you?" She turned in his arms to face him. "Was there someone in your past?"

He shook his head and sat up. He should have anticipated this. "No one." It wasn't a lie, he told himself. "No one who mattered." He leaned over the side of the bed to pick up the file folder they'd stolen from Derrick's safe. He opened it. And closed the discussion permanently, he hoped.

Kit sat up beside him. She said nothing as he thumbed through the contents, but he knew he'd hurt her by not talking about his past. He hated hurting her. He chastised himself for having made love to her. It had been a foolish thing to do. He would end up hurting her even more. And yet all he could think about was making love to her again.

He tried to concentrate on the invoices, studying each closely. Belinda had been right; they all dealt with the condo complex. He found what he'd been looking for at the bottom of the pile—an invoice for concrete dated the day after Jason disappeared. He felt cold with dread.

Surely this wasn't what Derrick had been trying to hide. It proved nothing. Just that a large amount of concrete had been poured the next day, making Luke suspect that the concrete had been used to bury his brother and the bike.

But there was nothing really incriminating in the bunch of invoices, and certainly nothing worth hiding in a safe. Was he missing something?

"I can't imagine what Derrick didn't want Belinda to

see in here," he said after a while. "I can't find anything out of the ordinary."

"Maybe Belinda would know if she saw the papers," Kit suggested.

"Could be, but she said when she was looking at them, she didn't see anything odd about them."

"Then there is nothing in there that helps?" Kit asked, sounding disappointed.

"Derrick did pour a large amount of concrete the day after Jason disappeared," Luke said.

"Oh, Luke."

He put the invoices back and set the folder on the floor beside the bed. The room seemed suspended in silence. Slowly he turned to look at Kit. Her cheeks were still flushed from lovemaking, her hair a wild mane around her shoulders, her lips dark from his kisses. Just the thought of her naked body under the blankets made him want to unwrap her like an early Christmas present.

"Kit—"

He had no idea what he was going to say. Maybe nothing. Maybe he was going to tell her what had happened four years ago. One moment he was looking at her, the next he was kissing her and throwing back the covers so he could wrap his arms around her, hold her a little longer, make love to her one more time. Everything else could wait, he told himself.

Much later, Luke opened his eyes to find Kit smiling at him, surprised he'd fallen asleep again. Through the window, it looked like late afternoon. He couldn't remember a time he'd spent the day napping, even though he hadn't had a lot of restful nights in the last four years.

"Hello," she whispered and leaned over to kiss him.

He felt her hand trail over his ribs and down to his hip,

his leg. He reached to stop her but she'd already traced her fingertips along the scar that ran the length of his right thigh. He saw her frown as he pulled her hand to his lips and kissed it.

"Do you want to tell me about it?" she asked.

He shook his head. "It happened a long time ago. I don't even think about it."

He could see that she wasn't buying that, just like he was sure she hadn't bought that there had never been anyone who'd mattered in his life.

"I know it still bothers you," she said. "I've seen you rubbing it. Sometimes, when you're tired, you limp just a little though you seem to try very hard not to."

He didn't like the fact that she'd noticed so much about him. "You're very observant," he said. Too observant. He didn't realize he'd revealed so much of himself to this woman. Yes, woman, he thought looking into her eyes. He felt a stab of desire and knew in his heart that he'd always feel it with her. "My injury isn't anything to concern yourself with. I try not to think about it."

He freed himself from her, physically, if not emotionally, and threw back the covers. He swung his legs over the side of the bed, looking for his jeans. He told himself he had to take care of Derrick and that was what stood between him and Kit, but he knew it was fear—fear of the past repeating itself. He knew he was running scared.

"I'm sorry for bringing it up. I didn't mean to pry," she said quickly, reaching for him as if to draw him back into the bed. "What did I say that was wrong?"

"Nothing." He could hear the hurt in her tone and cursed himself. "I think I *will* call Belinda."

Just moments before, he'd been beside her, warm, sated and content. Too content. He'd felt as if he could stay in that bed with Kit forever and never have any reason to get up again because everything he needed or wanted would be there with her. That scared him. That made him feel guilty. What the hell was he doing? He was here with her to avenge his brother's death, wasn't he?

"You get the combination?" Belinda asked when she answered his call.

"Got it and the folder in the wall safe at the house."

She let out a laugh. "All right! And there's something there that will nail Derrick's sorry behind?"

Luke hated to tell her. "Nothing I can find. It all looks pretty straightforward to me. We think one of the invoices might indicate where he buried Jason's body and his motorcycle, but that's a long shot at best."

Belinda swore. "That can't be the right folder then. I saw his face. He was almost messing his pants, he was so afraid I'd seen something. I know a little something about construction after the years I spent with Derrick, but only because I listened and butted in. Whatever was in that folder was something he was afraid I would understand, and he thinks I'm as dumb as a door. It would have to be something pretty obvious, don't you think?"

Luke agreed. "But believe me, there's nothing here."

"All right," she said, sounding less defeated than challenged. "Then there's *another* folder somewhere. Maybe I underestimated him. I'll get back to you." She hung up before Luke could warn her to be careful.

Luke could feel Kit's gaze on him. "I shouldn't have made love to you," he said, pulling on his shirt, his back still to her. He had no right to this woman. Not now. Maybe not ever.

"How can you say that?" she cried.

He swung around to face her. "I don't know what's going to happen. You've already lost so many people in your life. I don't want to be another one."

"Then don't be," she said, getting up to go to him, wrapping the blanket around her nakedness.

He held her at arm's length. "I made a promise to my brother that I have to keep, Kit. Don't ask me to break it, please."

"I'm not asking you to break any promises or make any to me. Just don't pretend that something didn't happen here tonight. Was I the only one who felt something?"

He saw the sudden worry in her face. He shook his head. "God, no, Kit." He'd felt more than he'd wanted to, much more, and just the thought that he might never get to make love to her again nearly tore his heart from his chest.

He had to finish things with Derrick, one way or the other, and soon. Even if he lived through this, he wasn't sure after he finished with Derrick that Kit would want him. Eventually she would learn about his past too, about him and, as hard as it was to accept, she might not ever want him again.

"Luke, I don't know what happened to you, why you're so sensitive about your injury or what it is you don't want me to know about your past. But nothing that happened or is going to happen will change how I feel about you. I love you, Luke St. John."

He felt his heart implode. "Don't, Kit, please. You don't know me."

"You once told me that I knew everything about you I needed to know." She looked up at him, her face filled with eagerness, with love. "After making love with you, I know that's true. I know you, Luke. I know you in my heart. Nothing is going to change that or the man I know you to be."

He smiled at the sincerity in her voice. "Kit, don't put so much stock in me. Desiring a man is one thing. Loving him is something entirely different." He knew that only too well. And as much as he wanted to believe her words, he'd heard them before, from another woman, another time. The outcome was a jagged scar in his memory as ugly and painful as the one on his thigh.

"I *do* know you, that's why I love you."

He reached out to run his hand down Kit's hair, loving the feel of it. Her gaze burned into his when he looked into her blue eyes. "If that's true, Kit, then you know that I have to finish what Derrick Killhorn started, or I won't be able to live with myself. Do you understand that about me, the kind of man I am?"

"Yes," she said, stepping back to take his full measure. "But I'm afraid, Luke. I think you want more than to see Derrick in prison. I think your idea of justice means killing him—or being killed."

He turned away, unable to look at her and lie. "I don't know what it will take, Kit. Please don't love me. Don't ask me to love you right now."

She said nothing. Her silence rang louder than anything she could have said.

He glanced toward the window. It would be dark soon. "I have to try to find Jason's bike."

"I'm going with you," she said behind him. "You'll need a lookout. You won't be able to hear someone coming with the metal detector headphones on."

"No," he said harder than he meant to. All he wanted was for her to be safe. He didn't want her near Killhorn or the condo complex. He cursed himself for forcing her to come back with him.

He turned to look at her, her hair flamed by the light, her

cheeks still glowing from the exertion of making love. She pulled the blanket around her naked body and looked up at him, her eyes so filled with compassion that he thought his heart would break.

"We're in this together," she said, her voice pleading with him. "I came back with you because you needed me, so we could end this once and for all."

He shook his head. "No. This is between me and Derrick now." He didn't like going off without her, but he had no choice. She would be safer here than any other place he could leave her.

"You plan to kill him, don't you?" she said, shaking her head. "What is the point of looking for the bike if you don't plan to use that evidence? And why did you need me here?" she demanded. "You want an eye for an eye. You want blood. It seems the only thing that will satisfy the vengeance in you. So why did you force me to come here with you?"

He stared at her, the truth in her words flaying him. "I thought you could keep me from killing Derrick, but I realize now that you can't. No one can."

"That's why you don't want me telling you I love you," she said. "You would much rather hate than love."

"It's not that simple and you know it," he shot back at her.

"No. But Derrick could be punished for what he did without you throwing away the rest of *your* life," she cried. "It doesn't have to be all or nothing."

He looked away, not sure she was right. He owed his brother. That debt was eating him alive.

"The choice will ultimately be yours," she said, sounding defeated.

He turned away from her. "I have to go try to find my brother's body."

"Then what?"

He could hear the tremor in her voice. "Settle the score."

Luke turned from her, and she felt as if he'd been ripped from her arms. The ache for him was heart deep, soul deep. She knew it would never go away and that no other man would be able to satisfy it.

He dressed quickly and left, not looking back as he closed the door behind him. Kit sat down on the bed. It still held his heat, his scent. She buried her face in his pillow—still showing the depression his head had made—and cried.

Chapter 17

The night was clear and cold. The river ran ice-green through the soft, smooth white of the snowdrifts. Luke drove the snowmobile up the mountain to within a few hundred yards of the condo complex. Overhead, the sky had turned cold blue, the stars like tiny snowflakes. He breathed in the night air, trying to rid himself of Kit's scent. It seemed to be branded on his skin. Or maybe it was only etched in his memory. He wondered if he would ever be able to breathe again without her fragrance being there, tantalizing him, just as the woman herself had done...continued to do.

The pines groaned in the light breeze. Snow crystals showered down from the heavy boughs. Ahead, he could see the complex. It sat hunkered in the darkness, waiting. He drove the snowmobile a little closer and stopped.

His thoughts kept drifting back to Kit and the way she'd looked when he left. And how she'd looked earlier: her hair fanned out across the bed, her body bathed in candlelight, her eyes shiny and bright with desire as he leaned over her.

He shook off the memory and concentrated on what he had to do as he carried the metal detector toward the building.

He'd expected the complex to be heavily guarded. What he hadn't expected was to find it wide open and not a soul around. Not even the heater ran inside the massive structure. No cars were parked by the trailer and the road looked blown in with snow, as if no one had been there for some time.

Where was Derrick? Was he so unconcerned because there was nothing to find in the building? Luke didn't believe that, yet he couldn't explain the absence of guards or the lack of fear on Derrick's part. It made no sense.

Derrick had failed with the snowmobile attack, his files had been broken into, he'd been run off the road, his wallet had been stolen and his wall safe had been breached.

Derrick knew exactly what Luke was looking for. He'd gotten rid of the crowbar, but Jason's body and the bike would have been impossible to jackhammer up out of the cement. It would be covered not only with concrete but by a mesh of steel—that is, if Jason was buried where Luke suspected he was—in the room he died in.

Luke was positive Derrick had hidden what he could. What he couldn't, he should be guarding with his life. So why wasn't he? Because guards would be witnesses and Derrick had no intention of ever letting Luke take the evidence to the police.

Luke stopped at the edge of the complex. His instincts told him that he was walking into a trap. His instincts? He almost laughed. His instincts had told him to take Kit to his friend's motel. Obviously, he could no longer trust his instincts.

Luke hefted the metal detector over his shoulder, hoping he wasn't about to make the biggest mistake of his life. His last mistake.

And for what? Kit was right. Why did he need to find the motorcycle? Did he really plan to use the evidence to try to get Derrick convicted of murder? Or was finding the bike simply a way to put off what he had to do? He knew Derrick had killed his brother. Why did he need more evidence?

He told himself that he had to have the motorcycle. He had to know where his brother was buried before he finished with Derrick.

Luke entered the building through the hole in the plastic, wondering if Derrick was in there, waiting for him. It didn't matter, he told himself. They would have to face each other sooner or later. He turned on his flashlight in the cavernous structure, his footsteps echoing on the concrete, sounding cold and totally alone. He knew he was about to find the motorcycle—and his brother.

Nothing could stop him now. Nothing. And nobody. But as he stepped deeper into the complex, he couldn't shake the feeling in the pit of his stomach that something was terribly wrong.

When the phone rang, it woke Kit from the dream. She opened her eyes slowly, still caught in that other world, and reached for the phone. "Hello?"

"Is Luke there?" Belinda asked in a hurry.

"No. Why?" Kit sat up and tried to shake off the warm memory of the dream, then remembered that it hadn't been a dream at all. She and Luke *had* made love. Her body still felt alive with the feel of him—and sick with missing him, worrying about him.

"Good," Belinda said, confidentially. "I just talked to Sanders. He said there's something about this guy, this Luke St. John, that he needs to warn you about. Maybe you ought to give him a call."

"Something about Luke?" she asked. "He didn't say what?"

"No, but I've got to tell you, I've never heard Sanders sound so...desperate."

"Luke thinks Sanders is involved with Jason's murder," Kit said. "He doesn't trust Sanders any more than he does Derrick."

"Yeah? What about you?"

"I'm not sure anymore," Kit said.

"Well, we both know Sanders has always jumped when Derrick said 'jump,' but I'd check it out if I were you. Sanders is too upset and there's something about Luke St. John that just seems too good to be true, you know? I think if anyone can trust Sanders, it would be you. He's always had a major crush on you."

Kit hung up and sat for a long while staring into the darkness, thinking of Luke. She knew how he made her feel. She knew she loved him. But what did she really know about him? Nothing. Was there something she *should* know?

Worry niggled at the back of her brain. Why had Luke refused to tell her about his past? Even when she'd asked about the scar on his thigh, he'd put her off. What didn't he want her to learn?

Kit hugged herself, thinking about the man she'd come to know intimately. Did it matter how he'd gotten the scar? Why he limped? What had happened to him in the past? Wasn't it enough seeing how he was with Andy, feeling how he was with her, remembering the tenderness of his kisses, his touches, his lovemaking? She trusted Luke with her life. With Andy's. There was nothing Sanders could say that would change how she felt about Luke. Nothing.

Then what did she have to fear? She picked up the phone and dialed Sanders's number.

Sanders answered on the first ring.

"Oh, Kit, I'm so glad you called. I've been so worried," he said quickly. "Are you all right?"

"Yes." She said nothing else for a moment, remembering Luke's claim that Sanders had set her up. "Derrick would have been waiting for me in Huntsville, wouldn't he?"

"Yes." Sanders sounded both guilty and sorry. "I thought it was the best thing at the time, Kit. Please, believe me."

"And now?" she asked.

"Now I'm not so sure. I just know I'm afraid for you, Kit. Are you still with Luke St. John?"

"Why?"

"Kit, I think you might be in danger," Sanders said. "Did he tell you what happened four years ago?"

She didn't answer.

"That's what I thought," he continued. "Four years ago, Luke was one of the leading structural engineers in the country. He had jobs all over the world. He was at the top of his field."

That surprised her. Luke didn't seem like someone who'd want that kind of success, or need it. That didn't jibe with the man who made furniture in his cabin back in the woods at Big Sky. Maybe she didn't know him as well as she thought.

"He was engaged to be married," Sanders said. "He had everything—success, fame and a woman he idolized."

Kit felt her heart drop. He'd said there hadn't been anyone in his past. No one who mattered. She'd known even then that he hadn't spoken the truth. Why hadn't he?

"Then something horrible happened."

Kit found herself holding her breath.

"The wedding was called off just days before the ceremony. No one knows exactly why. There was a rumor that his fiancée, a woman named Ashley Westford, dumped him. Some said she'd fallen in love with a friend of his, Paul Carlton."

No wonder Luke was so afraid of her saying she loved him.

"That isn't all, Kit," she heard Sanders say.

"The day after Ashley broke the engagement and canceled the wedding, there was an accident at one of St. John's buildings."

Kit gripped the phone tighter, afraid of what Sanders was going to tell her.

"St. John was hurt when part of the building fell."

The scar on his thigh. She felt a chill.

"Ashley and St. John's friend Paul were both killed."

Kit let out a gasp.

"No one knows what the three of them were even doing in the building that late at night. The cops couldn't prove Luke was responsible, but they still think it was a double murder," Sanders said. "St. John dropped out, pretty much disappeared. He left his high-powered, successful career to become a small-time furniture maker in Big Sky."

Her heart ached. That explained why Luke hadn't wanted to talk about it. "He didn't purposely hurt those two people. I know this man."

"Do you? What if you're wrong, Kit? What if you're wrong about Derrick?"

"I'm not wrong about Derrick. Nor am I wrong about Luke. Be careful, Sanders. Please. Derrick isn't who you think he is." She hung up.

Sanders stared at the phone for a few moments after the line went dead, amazed at himself for staying so calm, for not giving away his feelings. Then he looked over at his brother.

"You did good," Derrick said, and took the phone. He dialed his friend at the sheriff's office. "Was it long enough to get a trace?" He smiled. "And where exactly is that? The Pinecone Motel. Number nine. Thanks. I owe you." He hung up and looked at his brother. "I'm going to go get my son."

"Are you sure you don't want me to come with you?" Sanders asked, worried.

"Don't worry. I know what I'm doing. But I have something I need you to do for me, Sand."

Luke worked the metal detector slowly back and forth across the concrete floor. It reminded him of water-witching when he was a kid. There was an old man who used to find water with only a forked stick. He'd called it a divining rod, and he found water when no one else could. He was never wrong.

Luke just hoped this metal detector worked as well. He only wished he were looking for water instead of his brother's body.

He glanced up. Afraid Derrick or one of his goons would sneak up on him while he had the earphones in, listening to the steady beep of the machine, he'd gone with the digital readout. The room had remained empty and quiet. He figured Derrick was held up in his home, thinking it a fortress Luke St. John could not scale. How wrong he was. But he would find that out soon enough.

Luke had covered a quarter of the floor when a second light began to flash, then a third, just like the man who sold the metal detector to him had said it would. Luke watched, his heart pounding so loudly that he wouldn't have been able to hear Derrick even if he were right behind him.

Luke stared at the lights, seeing everything too clearly, seeing Jason's motorcycle under the concrete, seeing his brother's body in his mind's eye.

He moved the metal detector around the spot on the floor, slower now, and felt defeat in the sag of his shoulders with the realization of what he'd found.

He turned off the metal detector and stood for a long time just sucking in the cold night air that had settled like cement in the empty building.

When he turned the metal detector back on, he'd pointed it at one of the outside walls of the condo complex. For a long moment he didn't move; he just stared at the dial. It wasn't picking up any metal at all. That wasn't possible. He ran the detector along another wall. Nothing.

Then he heard a sound. Footfalls on concrete. He swung around quickly, expecting an attack. Belinda stood in the doorway behind him.

"You found it?" Her expression said she already knew.

"Yes. What are you doing here?"

"Looking for you." She stepped into the room and stopped as if she didn't want to walk on whatever he'd found under the floor. "There *was* another folder and I think I know what Derrick is so afraid of. The invoices just don't add up. I hid the folder. Under a flower pot behind my condo. For insurance purposes."

He waited for her to tell him what "the invoices just don't

add up" meant, although he had a pretty good idea that he already knew. She seemed more nervous than he'd ever seen her, and it made him nervous too. "What's wrong?"

She looked sick. "It's Kit."

"What?" he demanded, closing the distance between them.

"I told Kit that Sanders wanted to talk to her." She grimaced. "About you. He sounded so afraid for her. I thought— But then the more I thought about it—"

Luke swore and dropped the metal detector. "How long ago?"

"Maybe ten minutes."

Luke ran, fear driving him. For an instant, he considered taking Belinda's Suburban, but decided he could get there faster on his snowmobile.

He raced through the darkness, headed for the Pinecone Motel. Kit. Oh, God. He should never have left her alone.

Chapter 18

Luke roared down the mountain, through shadows deep under the dark pines, the sky above him ablaze with stars. Kit. His heart felt close to bursting. She'd talked to Sanders. Luke didn't doubt for an instant that Sanders told her about Ashley and Paul. Luke didn't even want to imagine what Kit must think of him now. Worse yet, what if she trusted Sanders enough to meet him somewhere? Kit could already be in Derrick's clutches.

The thought drove him down the mountain, all control gone. He had to get to Kit. If Derrick touched one hair on her head—

He could see the Pinecone Motel sign as he came up over the ridge and picked up the road. In the distance, a pair of headlights raced toward him. Derrick? Luke slowed, afraid it would be Derrick's pickup and that Kit would be inside.

The pickup drew nearer and he felt himself tense. As it passed, Luke saw that it wasn't Derrick's. It was his own truck, and Kit was driving. She threw on the brakes and jumped out, running back toward him. He stepped off the snowmobile and stood watching her, afraid.

She ran into his arms. "Luke. Oh, God, Luke," she cried. "I had to come to you. Sanders told me. I know what happened four years ago. I know it was an accident. I know you wouldn't hurt anyone."

"Kit," Luke breathed into her hair as he hugged her to him. "I thought I'd lost you. I should have told you myself—"

"It doesn't matter. None of that matters now."

He hugged her tightly, promising himself he would never let this woman go.

They stood in the middle of the gravel road, the lights of the pickup and the snowmobile pointing across the expanse of snowy white, the night clear and cold, the stars looking on.

After a few moments, she pulled back to look up into his face. Her expression saddened. "You found Jason, didn't you?"

He nodded.

"Oh, Luke, I'm so sorry. I wish there was something I could do or say."

He hugged her to him, wishing he could tell her that he no longer needed to avenge his brother's death. He felt such relief that Kit was safe, that she didn't think he could have hurt his ex fiancée and his friend. But there was still so much hatred in his heart for Derrick. He glanced up and saw the Big Dipper hanging over the dark purple rim of the mountains etched against the sky, and felt as if his heart were being pulled apart.

"With the motorcycle and the body, we have proof," Kit said gently.

He pulled back and nodded. "We might even know why Jason and Derrick argued. Belinda found some papers."

"What did she find?" Kit asked.

"A possible motive for Jason's murder. She says she's discovered another file folder, this one with invoices in it that don't add up. I told her we'd meet her at her house at Mountain Village. I have a pretty good idea what those papers will prove." Then they'd have enough evidence to at least get Derrick thrown behind bars. But for how long?

"I just want this to be over."

"Me too." But when he released her, Luke saw something that turned his blood to ice. Below them, the light from the Pinecone Motel flashed in neon, and Luke saw that Derrick's pickup was parked by the end unit.

"Thank you," he said, relief in his voice.

"What for?"

"For believing in me." He pointed down the mountainside at the motel. If Kit had hesitated just a few moments after her call with Sanders, she would be in Derrick's hands right now. Luke couldn't believe how lucky she'd been... how lucky *he* was.

"Sanders. He betrayed me again," she said, her voice soft with hurt.

"I'm sorry, Kit. I know you hoped you could trust him."

"You were right about him," she said, shaking her head. "I wonder when I'll quit being so naive?"

"Never, I hope," he said, lifting her chin to gaze into her eyes. "I like you just the way you are." Then he released her, wishing like hell that this was over, worrying how it would end. "Let's load up and see what Belinda's got."

Luke backed the pickup up to the snowbank, and Kit drove the snowmobile into the bed. When she climbed in the passenger side of the truck, Luke pulled her over close to him, wrapped his arm around her.

He wanted to tell her everything was going to be fine. He wanted to believe it. But he couldn't get the words past his lips. He couldn't lie to her. He loved her too much.

He drove toward Mountain Village, watching the road behind him in his rearview mirror. He spotted another set of headlights, but they pulled off just before the road to Belinda's.

As Luke turned onto the lane that led up to Belinda's house, Kit noticed there were no lights on. The house sat on a small rise overlooking the ski resort. "Are you sure she said she'd wait for you here?"

Luke nodded and slowed the pickup. Snow now fell, silent and thick. "Her Suburban's in the garage." He pointed to the tracks in the fresh snow that had drifted in front of the door. One set of tire tracks showed her vehicle had entered the garage not long ago. It hadn't come back out.

Luke parked, and they climbed out of the pickup. Kit walked up the rock steps, glancing back over her shoulder. The lights of Huntley Lodge glowed golden against Lone Peak.

Luke rang the doorbell. It rang inside the house, but Kit heard no sound of footsteps coming to answer it. He rang the bell again. Then he tried the knob. The door fell open.

Kit glanced over at Luke. He gave her a concerned look, then stepped inside and turned on the lights.

A soft moan came from within. Kit moved toward it, Luke at her side. As she turned the corner into the kitchen, she caught sight of something on the floor. Belinda lay sprawled on the floor.

"Quick, call 911," Luke cried as he hurried to Belinda.

He knelt beside her, and Kit grabbed the wall phone and started to dial.

"The line's dead," she said.

Belinda moaned again.

"Belinda, can you hear me?" Luke asked.

Her eyes flickered open. "Substandard." Her eyes closed. The next words came out like a curse. "Derrick." Her head fell over to one side and she didn't move.

"What did she say?" Kit asked, not sure she'd heard correctly.

"She said, 'Derrick,'" a voice announced behind them. Kit spun around to find a man silhouetted in the doorway, but she'd already recognized the voice.

"Get to your feet slowly. Both of you. And no fast moves, St. John, or Kit pays the price," Derrick said as he stepped into the light and Kit saw the pistol in his hand. It was pointed at her heart.

"Do as he says," Luke whispered.

Derrick smiled. "Oh, dear Kit, if only you *had* done as I said. We wouldn't be in this predicament, now would we?"

Luke tensed, but he didn't move. And Kit knew he didn't retaliate only because he was afraid of risking her life.

Derrick grabbed Kit and pulled her in front of him, holding the pistol to her head. Then he motioned Luke back and dragged her over to Belinda, kneeling down to check for a pulse. He smiled and straightened, and Kit felt sick inside. "Come on. Try anything, St. John, and I kill Kit."

Luke led the way out the back door to where Derrick's pickup was parked. Derrick motioned Luke in the passenger side, then he dragged Kit around to the driver's side.

"You drive," he told her. "One wrong move and I shoot you, then your boyfriend."

She didn't doubt him for a moment. He slipped behind

her into one of the king cab seats and pressed the barrel of the pistol to her temple.

"We're going to the complex," he said. "Take the back way, I'll show you a shortcut."

Kit started the truck and put it in gear. The truck lurched forward, and she felt Derrick's arm come around her throat, the barrel of the pistol press hard against her temple.

"I wouldn't do that again, if I were you, sweetheart," Derrick said through gritted teeth.

Luke let out a low growl. "Let her go, Killhorn."

"Don't push me," Derrick snapped at Luke, but slowly let up the pressure of his arm around her throat. She took a couple of breaths and, this time, got the pickup going.

Kit could see Luke's face out of the corner of her eye. He looked like he could kill and she feared that if he got the chance, he would.

"I found my brother's body where you'd buried him in concrete," Luke said quietly. "I think I know why you killed him. He found out about the substandard construction in Killhorn Condos. Just like Belinda did. What were you doing, trying to cut costs? Leaving out a little steel here, a little concrete there?"

"Aren't you clever," Derrick said. "Not that it's done you any good."

"I wondered how you got the crowbar out of that wall so easily," Luke continued as if he hadn't heard Derrick. "When I ran a metal detector along the walls, I realized you hadn't been reinforcing them according to building codes. Jason would have been worried about the people you planned to sell the condos to."

"Your brother shouldn't have butted into my business," Derrick snapped. "And you shouldn't have either. Turn here."

Kit turned and started up the hill. "The building isn't safe?"

Luke let out a snort. "Not even close. This whole area of Montana is rated four, the same earthquake danger as San Francisco, California. One good quake and Killhorn Condos will crumble like sand castles."

"By the time there's an earthquake, I will have made my money and won't be around here to worry about it," Derrick snapped. "Neither will you."

As Kit topped a hill, the condo complex appeared on the horizon. It loomed dark and sinister: a death trap.

"Stop here," Derrick demanded. He reached up to open the door and slid out to pull Kit with him, the gun to her head. "Now you, St. John." Luke got out, and Derrick ordered him to the lead the way.

Kit stumbled along with Derrick toward the complex. He kept a tight grip on her.

The moon had crested the mountains and now cast a brilliant golden sheen over the snow, making the night bright.

As they neared the structure, she heard an odd sound that she'd heard before but couldn't place. A motor was running on the other side of the building. But it was the odd rhythmic swooshing sound that pulled at her memory. She had a bad feeling that she needed to remember where she'd heard it before, because Derrick seemed to be dragging her toward the sound.

When they reached the plastic-walled building, Derrick pushed Luke back as he maneuvered himself and Kit up to the opening. He released Kit for a moment to take a flashlight from his coat and hand it to her.

"Light the way for your boyfriend," he instructed as he latched on to her again, the pistol pointed at her temple.

Kit took the flashlight, her gaze darting to Luke. In the

moonlight she saw him nod almost imperceptibly. For a moment, she pretended to have trouble, because of her mittens, pushing the switch.

Derrick cursed and started to reach for the flashlight to help her, releasing his grip on her.

She snapped on the light with the beam aimed directly into his eyes. At the same time she brought her elbow up into his stomach as hard as she could and dropped away from the cold barrel of the pistol into the cold darkness of the building.

"Run, Kit," Luke cried as he flew through the air and caught Derrick in the chest, driving him back. They fell, hitting the concrete hard. The gun skittered across the floor and away into the darkness of the massive empty structure.

Kit hesitated only a moment, then ran deeper into the building, the flashlight beam bobbing on the concrete floors in front of her. She had to get to the trailer and the phone. She had to help Luke.

Chapter 19

Luke got to his feet. He could see nothing. He stared at the pitch blackness, trying to pick up Derrick's shape, expecting the man to come barreling into him at any moment.

But nothing hit him. He listened. Off in the distance he could hear footfalls on the concrete. Kit's? Or Derrick's? His heart raced for a moment, then he realized he could hear only one set of feet. It had to be Kit. *Run, Kit.*

The plastic behind him flapped in the breeze, and he spun around, anticipating Derrick's attack. Derrick hit him hard and low, sending them both tumbling deeper into the darkness of the complex until they rolled into a block wall and stopped, Luke on top.

Luke had planned for the day when he would come face-to-face with Derrick Killhorn. He'd looked forward to the moment when he would avenge his brother's death.

Then Kit had come into his life and everything had

changed. Or had it? This man had murdered his brother. This man had hurt Kit.

"Killhorn," Luke said, amazed at how calm his voice sounded as he pulled Derrick to his feet.

Derrick stood stone still, but Luke felt him look toward the darkness where the gun had gone as if considering his chances of finding it in time. Nil. Luke tightened his grip on Derrick's collar and slammed him back against the block wall. He could smell fear coming off Derrick in waves.

"Why did you have to kill Jason?" he demanded. "Don't you realize it was for nothing?"

"Nothing?" Derrick repeated. "Everything I own is tied up in this building. Everything. And your brother threatened to destroy me."

Luke shook his head, remembering a time when his whole life had been tied up in huge buildings. When material things had mattered more than people.

"You killed my brother for money?" he demanded in disgust.

"I killed him because he dared to tell me how to run my own business," Derrick snapped. "I offered him money to shut him up, but the damned fool refused it. He would have gone to the authorities. He would have destroyed me if I hadn't stopped him first."

Luke felt a surge of anger so powerful that his body seemed made of steel. He lifted Derrick and flung him across the room. Derrick hit the floor. Luke heard him scamper toward the sliver of light in the thick plastic.

Kit ran, weaving her way through the empty building, knowing she was hopelessly lost. All the rooms suddenly looked the same. She stopped, fighting to catch her breath.

Her pulse thundered in her ears but she could still hear that odd sound coming from the far end of the building.

She picked up a foot-long piece of board and tried to bust her way out of the plastic, but the material was too thick, the fibers in it too strong. She gave up, threw down the board and began to run again, this time away from the strange sound—as if she knew instinctively that the noise meant her harm.

Behind her, she thought she heard someone calling. She stopped to listen, thinking it was Luke looking for her. She heard it again, only this time she recognized the voice. Sanders's. He was calling for Derrick.

What was Sanders doing here? Where were Derrick and Luke? She fought back the horrible feeling that Luke was in trouble. She had to get to the trailer and a phone, even if it meant backtracking.

That's when she heard it. A flapping sound. Plastic snapping in the breeze. She followed the flapping and spotted the gaping hole in the thick plastic. Just wide enough for her to force her way through and out into the winter night.

Luke caught Derrick before he could slither through the plastic doorway. They rolled out of the building and into the snowfield. Luke felt the hatred drive him, the way it had driven him for seven months, as he fought Derrick in the snow.

"I'm going to kill you, Killhorn," Luke spat when he got the upper hand and had Derrick pinned to the ground. "Just the way you killed my brother."

To his surprise, Derrick quit fighting. He lay back in the snow, breathing hard. With the moonlight reflecting off the snow, Luke could just make out Derrick's expression: a smile.

It took Luke a moment to register the smile and realize what it meant. It was a moment too long.

All he heard before he felt the blow to the back of his head was Derrick saying, "About time, Sanders." Then everything went black.

"Are you all right?" Sanders cried, helping his brother to his feet.

"He tried to kill me again." Derrick looked around. "We have to find Kit. God only knows what he did with her." His gaze fell on Luke lying in the snow, facedown. "We'd better take care of him first."

"You don't think he's dead, do you?" Sanders asked.

"No, he's not dead," Derrick snapped impatiently. "Let's lock him in the tool shed though, where he can't kill one of us when he wakes up, all right? Hurry, we have to find Kit."

There were a dozen questions Sanders wanted to ask but he realized this wasn't the time. Kit was missing, and Derrick seemed to think she was in trouble—that Luke might have done something to her. That didn't make a lot of sense to him, but Sanders concentrated on finding Kit first and asking questions later. He forgot about her betrayal, forgot everything but how much he cared for her. Derrick, too, seemed to have put his differences with Kit aside.

Derrick grabbed Luke by the ankles. Sanders went around to pick him up under the arms. They hauled him around the back of the building to the shed and they lowered him to the floor. Derrick grabbed a couple of flares and slammed the door, snapping the padlock, locking Luke inside.

"We'll find Kit, then call the police and let them handle Luke St. John," Derrick said as he handed Sanders a flare.

"Let's split up and meet at the trailer. If you find her, set off one of these flares. I'll do the same."

Sanders wondered why they didn't call the police first, but Derrick's fear seemed to be catching. He took the flare and started back through the building, calling for Kit.

Kit glanced around as she burst through the plastic, trying to see where she was. The trailer. She could see Derrick's pickup parked in front of it on the far side of the complex. She ran along the front edge of the building where the snow wasn't quite so deep. The wind whipped the falling snow around her, blinding her. But ahead was the trailer and a phone and help. She prayed Luke was all right and that help would arrive in time.

But when she reached the trailer, she saw that the door stood open. She slowed her steps, fear clamping down on the back of her neck like a hand.

"Hello?" she asked in a hoarse whisper as she peered inside. What did she expect—Derrick to answer if he was waiting in there for her?

She took a tentative step and tried to see into the darkness. She didn't want to turn on the light, but saw no other option. It was much too dark to find the phone and she had to know whether she was alone—or not.

She turned on the light and blinked into the bright blindness, her heart in her throat at the thought of Derrick sitting behind his desk smiling that horrible knowing smile of his, that gee-you're-a-stupid-woman smile.

To her utter relief he wasn't there, although she could feel his presence like a nasty headache. She picked up the phone and quickly beat out 911.

When the dispatcher answered, Kit frantically told her there'd been a murder at Big Sky in the Killhorn Condos complex under construction across from Mountain Village, and that the murderer was still in the building.

"There's another man in there too," she cried. "The victim's brother, and I'm afraid—"

"Calm down. A deputy is on his way. Where are you? Are you safe where you are? Can you stay on the line with me?"

"No, I'm in the job site trailer, but I can't stay here. He'll be looking for me."

"Hide somewhere until the deputy—"

The line went dead.

"Hello?" Kit felt him behind her, and swung around to find Derrick framed in the trailer doorway, the telephone cord he'd just jerked out of the wall in his hand.

She screamed and dropped the phone.

"Well if it isn't my sweet wife," he said, advancing menacingly toward her. "I ought to—" He held up the phone cord as if he planned to strangle her with it.

Kit stumbled back against the desk, momentarily intimidated by him. But the fear left her at the thought of Luke. "What have you done with Luke?" she demanded.

One eyebrow shot up. "He's under lock and key."

"If you hurt him—"

"Who do you think you're talking to?" Derrick demanded.

"A murderer."

"No wife of mine talks to me like that." He grabbed her arm.

"I'm not your wife, I never was," she said, wanting to spit in his eye. She jerked free of his hold and, reaching behind her, picked up the lamp and swung it hard.

It struck him on the side of the head and he stumbled back, but he didn't go down and he didn't offer her any escape. He wagged his head and looked at her sadly. "Killing you is going to be a pleasure." He grabbed her again, this time with both hands, and hauled her out of the trailer and into the night.

"The police are on their way," she said as he dragged her toward the back of the building.

"By the time they get here, you and Luke will have disappeared just like Jason."

She glanced back. "Where is Sanders?" He had betrayed her, but still she couldn't believe he'd let Derrick kill her. Could she be so wrong about him?

"Sanders will do whatever I tell him to. He always has. Who do you think took care of Luke for me?"

"I don't believe that."

"You always were a fool, Kit. Do you really think I carried Luke's body all the way from the building to the shed by myself?" He pulled her around the corner of the building, his flashlight beam slicing through the snowfall. She could see the shed in the moonlight.

"Come on, I have something special planned for you and your boyfriend," Derrick said.

He dragged her toward the odd noise she'd heard earlier and feared. It seemed to take shape as they neared it, growing in both form and volume. She finally recognized the sound. A truck was parked at the back of the complex, its engine running, the drum full of concrete on the back turning, the concrete inside making a rhythmic swooshing sound as the blades stirred it.

Derrick drew her closer and she saw that the truck sat at the edge of a deep pit. He pulled her to the rim and she knew what he intended to do. The hole looked to be four or five feet wide and at least eight feet deep. The chute from the mixer had been placed to empty its contents into the pit. He planned to bury her under the concrete just like he had Jason.

She glanced toward the shed. In the moonlight she could see the double set of footprints in the snow. Sanders *had* helped Derrick put Luke in there.

"Luke!" she cried, struggling to free herself. But Derrick held her in an iron grip. No answer. "My God, tell me you didn't kill him."

Derrick laughed. "And ruin my plans to bury you both alive in concrete? Not likely." He tightened his hold on her, his face twisted in a hideous smile of satisfaction.

"Luke!" she screamed, only this time instead of pulling *away* from Derrick, she shifted her weight toward the pit—and pushed. It was enough to throw Derrick off balance. He loosened his grip. In that instant Kit brought her knee up into his groin. He let out a groan and stumbled backward, toppling into the hole he'd dug for her and Luke.

Kit scrambled away from the pit and Derrick, almost falling in herself. She rushed to the shed, only to find it padlocked.

Hurriedly she glanced around in the moonlight for something to break the lock. What wasn't hidden by shadow was covered with snow and Derrick had taken the flashlight with him when he fell into the pit.

She dropped to her knees and dug in the snow with her mittened hand until she felt something round and hard. She brought the rock up and was about to slam it down on the padlock when the sky lit like the Fourth of July around her.

She spun around. Fire blazed from the pit. Derrick held a flare in his hand, the light blinding.

Kit knew he was signaling for Sanders, and Sanders couldn't have missed the flare. She lifted the rock and brought it down hard on the lock. Once. Twice. Three times.

The fourth time, the wood around the padlock splintered, but the lock held. She raised the rock to strike again. Sanders grabbed her from behind and twisted the rock from her hand.

"Sanders!" Derrick cried. "Get the ladder and get me out of here."

Sanders held Kit to him, his arm around her waist, as he pulled her over to where the ladder rested against the building.

"Sanders, listen to me," Kit pleaded. "If you let him out, he'll kill us."

"You're in love with this St. John guy," Sanders said, sounding hurt. "That's why you're trying to frame Derrick for murder."

"Is that what he said?" Kit couldn't believe the lies Derrick had told. "I'd never seen Luke until he picked me up in Galveston. Luke brought me here because I knew the exact room where Jason was killed. Luke found the motorcycle under the concrete—proof that Derrick killed Jason." She felt a little hope as Sanders's steps slowed.

Kit hurriedly told Sanders about the fake marriage and the fact that Andy wasn't Derrick's baby.

"Derrick said you would lie and say the baby was St. John's," Sanders said, grabbing the ladder with one hand and keeping his hold on Kit as he dragged her toward the hole.

She struggled, fighting him, knowing that once Derrick got out, she and Luke were as good as dead. "Sanders, Derrick plans to bury me and Luke in the concrete the same way he did Jason. You have to believe me."

Sanders dropped the ladder into the pit, his hold on her tightening.

Derrick climbed out of the hole and pulled the ladder up after him. He stepped to where Sanders held Kit and shone the flashlight on the ground, a hot circle of light at her feet.

"I can handle this now, Sanders. Go up to the trailer and wait for the police."

He grabbed hold of Kit, his face so full of rage and vengeance that she recoiled, stumbling back against Sanders.

Sanders let go of Kit and took a couple of steps away, then stopped, turning to look back at his brother, who now had an arm around Kit's neck. "What are you planning to do with her and St. John?"

"Look, we don't have time for this now," Derrick snapped. "You're my little brother. You've always helped me. Help me *now*. Go stall the police."

Sanders shook his head. "*This* is why you wanted the truck here tonight? Not to pour a slab. You planned this all along."

In the distance, Kit could hear sirens coming up the mountain.

"Sanders, listen to me," Derrick pleaded.

"No, I can't let you do this," he said, and reached to pull Kit from his brother's grasp.

Derrick moved quickly. He grabbed his brother's arm and swung around to shove both Kit and Sanders toward the black opening of the pit. At the last moment, Sanders turned his body so he was the one who hit first, breaking Kit's fall as they both tumbled into the hole.

Kit heard a loud crack beneath her. She rolled off Sanders as Derrick shone a light down into the hole. She could see the rock beneath Sanders's head and she could see the blood.

He didn't move as she stumbled to her feet.

"Your own brother," she spat at Derrick. "You'd kill your own brother!"

"Shut up," he yelled down at her. "This is all your fault. Yours and that—"

Derrick disappeared from view and she thought for one heart-stopping moment that he'd gone to the shed. An instant later, concrete began to flow down the chute and drop into the pit. She tried to pull Sanders up to keep the concrete from covering him, but finally gave up, realizing she was trying to save a dead man.

She moved as far from the chute as she could to avoid the concrete that splattered thick and heavy into the hole and began to grow deeper, rising first to her ankles, then to her calves. She looked up into the falling snow to see that Derrick had returned. Where was Luke? Still locked in the shed? Had he managed to escape or was he lying in there injured? Or dead? She couldn't bear to think that.

Derrick smiled down at her. "I will find *my* son. I'll raise him to be a Killhorn. I'll raise him to hate his mother."

"You're sick, Derrick. You need help," she said, praying that Luke was still alive and that somehow he'd gotten out of the shed. "The police will be here soon. Don't do this."

He laughed. "My uncle will be here eventually. But by then all trace of you and Luke St. John will be gone."

"What about my 911 call?" she asked incredulously.

"A prank call. I caught some kids in my office."

"And Sanders? How will you explain that?" she demanded, watching the concrete rise. All she could think about was Luke and Andy and the possibility that she might not see either of them again.

"Sanders will be off searching for you and my son," he said confidently. "No one will miss him. No one has missed him this last seven months."

She would, Kit thought, heartsick. She looked down. She couldn't see him anymore. The cement was up to her knees and steadily climbing. She told herself Derrick would never get away with it, but knew she was only kidding herself. Look what he'd gotten away with so far. If anyone could convince his uncle that he was innocent, it was Derrick.

The concrete seemed to come faster. It rose past her thighs. She couldn't move. The weight of the concrete pushed against her and she knew it would crush the life out of her before it drowned her.

"About time to get St. John," Derrick said. "You're so fond of him? Spend eternity together."

Luke came out of the darkness, moving fast and furiously. He hit Derrick with a force that sent the man slamming into the side of the concrete truck. Then Luke was on him with only one thing in mind.

Destruction.

Again Luke smashed Derrick against the truck, holding him there by his throat. All the hatred and vengeance he'd felt for the man seemed to explode inside his head. Derrick's flashlight lay on the ground, the beam like an arrow pointing at the two of them through the snow and darkness. But for Luke, the night had turned red with his anger. He could see nothing but Derrick's face in that red haze, and he knew he was going to kill him.

Over the thunder of his pulse in his ears, Luke was vaguely aware of the sound of the concrete sliding down the chute, the steady *slap, slap, swoosh, swoosh* of the mixture inside the drum as it turned, and the truck motor running, running. But those sounds were far away, just like the sound of someone calling his name.

"Listen to me," Derrick rasped, gasping for breath as he

fought to free himself from Luke's hold. "You don't want to kill me."

"That's *all* I want to do," Luke said between clenched teeth. He thought of his brother Jason and his heart swelled with such rage that he thought it would burst from the pain. "No one deserves to die as much as you do."

Luke looked into Derrick's face and squeezed his fingers. He watched the dark eyes widen in fear, then horror. Derrick fought frantically to pull Luke's fingers from his neck. Nothing could save him. And Derrick Killhorn and Luke St. John both knew it.

"Luke!"

From a great distance, Kit's voice seemed to come out of the red haze. Luke heard the frantic tone of her cry, heard his name. He looked down at his hands around Derrick Killhorn's throat as if he didn't recognize them as his own.

"Luke!"

He shook his head and let go. Derrick slumped to the ground in a heap and Luke stumbled back, disoriented.

"Luke!" Kit cried as the concrete reached her waist, growing rapidly deeper. "Luke!"

Just when she thought there was no hope, Luke's face appeared at the rim of the pit. He disappeared again. Concrete slowed to a trickle down the chute; the engine died on the truck. And there was Luke with the ladder. He threw it across the hole, then crawled out on it and lay down. He reached a hand toward her.

"Grab hold," he said and with a great effort, he pulled her up and out. The next thing she knew she was in his arms beside the pit.

The sound of sirens filled the air. Sirens and snow. Beside her, Killhorn Condos stood etched into the skyline, dark as sin.

"It's over," Luke whispered against her hair as he held her. "It's over."

She clung to him, wanting desperately to feel relief instead of fear, happiness instead of horror.

Then the truck engine started up again, the drum began to turn and concrete began to slide down the chute.

She and Luke both turned, but too late. "Luke!" Kit got out only that one word as a figure burst out of the darkness.

Derrick made a running dive at them, no doubt hoping to drive them both back into the pit and the concrete. But Kit and Luke, still in each other's arms, moved too quickly. Together, like people who had danced with each other all their lives, they swung away from him and fell back from the pit.

Derrick sailed through the air, a human projectile on a deadly mission. Kit felt the air stir as he brushed past, barely missing them. He made one final desperate attempt to save himself, arms flailing. Luke grabbed for him, but Derrick was beyond his reach.

Derrick toppled backward, falling under the full power of the chute and the concrete, and disappeared.

Luke crawled over to Kit and pulled her into his arms, holding her as if he never planned to let her go again.

Chapter 20

In a room at Huntley Lodge, Luke stripped Kit's clothing from her chilled wet body and pulled her into the shower, not taking the time to remove his own clothing.

She stood shaking, her teeth chattering. Her skin where the concrete had touched it was pink and burned. He soaped her, rubbing the skin where he could to warm it and washing the cement away quickly and gently so as not to hurt her.

Then he stripped off his own clothing and they stood under the hot water, just holding each other.

"I almost killed him," Luke said against her wet hair.

"But you didn't."

He shook his head, still amazed. "I came so close. I thought it was the only way I could live with Jason's murder. But then I heard your voice calling to me and I knew I couldn't do it."

He'd fought his demons, he thought, looking down at Kit. And he'd won. But it wasn't over yet.

They made love, and later Kit lay in his arms, warm and safe. She wished Andy were sleeping beside their bed, but Luke had promised he'd get them a flight out the next day so she would be with her baby again.

"I want to tell you about Ashley," Luke said. "I need to before I can move on."

Kit snuggled closer and waited, afraid Ashley had been Luke's true love, only love. And that Luke would never let himself love again.

"I met her at college. At the time, I thought she was everything I ever wanted. Smart. Wealthy. From a blue-blooded family. My dreams became her dreams, and she had big dreams for me.

"She talked me into going back east to live after graduation although she'd professed to love Montana—that's why she'd been going to college here. Later I realized Montana had just been a passing fancy, as most everything was with her."

He took a breath and pulled Kit closer. She snuggled against him, listening to the steady beat of his heart, the deep softness of his voice as he continued.

"I drove myself to find a high level of success so I felt I deserved Ashley. I felt I had to be 'somebody' for her.

"The truth is, I'd been having some doubts about my career. I missed Montana, I yearned for something, although I wasn't sure what it was. Ashley and I hardly spent any time together alone. She loved parties and knew a lot of people. I knew I would have preferred a quieter, simpler life, but I never said anything, I was so busy trying to please her.

"Then, out of the blue, just days before the wedding,

she said she couldn't marry me because I had turned out not to be what she wanted. I was devastated. I had tried so hard, and failed."

Kit closed her eyes, hurting for him.

"The night of the accident, I went to the building I'd designed and climbed up onto one of the steel beams."

Kit held her breath.

"I guess Paul thought I might be suicidal. I just needed to be by myself, and that was the only place I could think of that I could be totally alone."

She leaned her cheek against his chest, his skin warm and soft and scented with the smell of him. She thought she would burst with love for this man.

"Paul brought Ashley with him. I guess he thought between the two of them, they could talk me out of doing something stupid. He knew I'd go to my building. He knew me too well."

Luke took a breath, and Kit waited, wanting to stop him but knowing he had to do this.

"Paul started to climb up to where I was. It was my fault. I tried to stop them but…"

Kit could feel the tension running through him, the anguish.

"It happened so fast. There was a stack of beams on the second floor. I tried to get to them before—" he closed his eyes for a moment "—the beams fell and took me and Paul with them. Ashley was standing below us."

Kit wrapped her arms around Luke. "I know they were killed, Luke, and I know the police thought it was murder and you were a suspect," she told him quickly. "It was an accident, Luke. A horrible accident."

He raised his head to look at her, his handsome face twisted in agony and grief. "Then you really do believe me?"

"Oh, yes, Luke." She cradled him in her arms, hoping her love could heal his hurt, his grief, his guilt.

The next morning, Luke let the deputy sheriff into their room so they could answer his questions. When they'd finished making their statements, the deputy closed his notebook. "I thought you'd like to know that Belinda is in the hospital, doing fine."

Luke could see the relief on Kit's face. Too many people had died at Derrick's hands. He was glad Belinda was going to be all right. Now she could also be free of Derrick, although he wondered if she wouldn't be one of the few people to mourn his loss. What would she do with all her time without him to torment?

The deputy hesitated. "We found your brother's body. It was with his motorcycle, just as you thought. I'm sorry."

Luke felt Kit squeeze his hand.

The deputy got to his feet. "I suppose you've heard about Judge Killhorn."

"No," Luke said, but could have guessed.

"He took his life early this morning after he'd heard about his sons," the deputy said. "I guess he blamed himself."

Luke nodded. He understood guilt better than almost anything. Guilt and loss, sorrow and regret.

The deputy turned his hat in his hand and said nothing for a moment, as if searching for the right words. "If your brother hadn't found out about the problems with the construction up there, a lot more people could have died. You know that, don't you?"

Luke nodded. "Thank you," he said and shook the man's hand. Then Luke let the deputy out and closed the door behind him.

"It's over," Luke said and looked up at Kit. It was time to tell her how he felt, as much as that frightened him. But if he didn't, he would most surely lose her. "Kit, I came so close to losing you too many times," he said as he crossed the room to her. "For a while, I lost track of what was important." He cupped her face in his hands and looked down into the clear blue of her eyes. He felt tears fill his eyes and realized that he hadn't cried in years. "You're all that matters, Kit. You and Andy. I love you. I want us to be a family. I want us to make babies. I want to marry you."

She smiled up at him, tears flooding her eyes, then spilling down her cheeks.

"But I have to warn you. I like living up here, making furniture. I'm never going to be rich or famous, but I will take care of you and the kids. Can you live with the kind of man I am?"

"Oh, Luke," she cried, throwing her arms around his neck. "I love the man you are. The man who makes beautiful furniture. And beautiful love."

He hugged her for a long moment, unable to believe his luck. "Let's go home."

Luke took Kit to his cabin—the cabin she'd loved when she hadn't even known it was his. And he made love to her in the big bed he'd built. He made love to her slowly, lovingly, cherishing her for the woman she was and giving thanks that he hadn't lost her.

Afterward, Kit lay in his arms and he told her his plans for adding on to the cabin.

"I think it's fine the way it is," she said.

He laughed. "We're going to need a studio for you to paint in. And a nursery. And more bedrooms. I want us to start a family right after the wedding—or maybe before the wedding."

Kit laughed. "What makes you think we haven't already started one?"

He smiled over at her, amazed that so much good could come out of so much sadness. "I'll always love you, Kit Bannack. Always and forever."

"And I, you."

And Luke knew right then and there what he had to do.

Chapter 21

Kit woke to what she thought were sleigh bells. She opened her eyes to find Luke beside her in the cabin, lying naked in the wonderful bed he'd built. She hoped they'd conceived a child in this bed, but she knew even if they hadn't yet, they would.

"Do you hear that?" she asked.

He smiled over at her. "I think you just hear my heart beating."

She grinned. "Oh, yeah? Sounds like bells to me."

"Bells?" He frowned. "What day is today?"

She couldn't be sure, too much had happened. All she knew was that they would be flying out this afternoon, and by this evening she would be once again holding her son in her arms. Luke had made all the arrangements, having to pull a lot of strings to get them tickets at this time of year.

"Kit, it's Christmas Eve," he said when she didn't answer. "And unless I miss my guess, that would be Santa

Claus." He hopped out of bed, pulling on his jeans as he rushed to the window. "Quick, come here!"

"What?" she asked suspiciously as she got up, wrapped herself in his robe and joined him at the window.

"You aren't too old for Santa, are you?" he asked and pulled her closer.

She giggled. "Depends on what Santa has in mind."

It was snowing, huge flakes that floated down from the heavens making everything white and clean and new and beautiful. Like a new beginning, she thought. A rebirth. She could hear the bells, closer now, but could see only snow.

"Come on," Luke said, taking her hand. "We don't want to disappoint Santa." He stopped at the door to slip on his boots, and waited while she pulled on hers. Then he opened the front door and pulled her out onto the porch.

She took a deep breath of the mountain air and snuggled against his bare chest. "Aren't you freezing?" she asked.

He laughed and hugged her. "I'm never freezing when you're around."

Bells jingled and she looked up to see the sleigh. It was bright red and led by two beautiful white horses wearing red bows. Santa sat on the front seat, the reins in his hands, and behind him...

Kit blinked, tears rushing to her eyes, blinding her. She caught her breath as she saw what Santa had brought in his sleigh. The best present she could ever have hoped for.

"Oh, Luke," Kit said, crying and throwing her arms around him.

"I guess that means you like my present?"

"Oh, yes," she said as she rushed through the snow to meet the sleigh.

"Merry Christmas!" Aunt Lucille said as she handed Kit a brightly wrapped baby boy in a Santa-red snowsuit.

Kit hugged her son to her. Andy laughed as she covered his face with kisses. Luke joined her, wrapping them both in his arms.

"Merry Christmas, sweetheart," he said, gazing down at her and Andy, his eyes so filled with love that she thought she would burst.

"This is the best Christmas I've ever had," she cried, and saw Luke wink at his aunt.

"It's only the first of many," he promised.

* * * * *

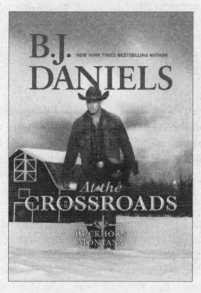

At the Crossroads

Bobby Braden wiped the blood off his fingers, noticing that he'd smeared some on the steering wheel. He pulled his shirtsleeve down and cleaned the streak of red away, the van swerving as he did.

"Hey, watch it!" In the passenger seat, Gene Donaldson checked his side mirror. "All we need is for a cop to pull us over," he said in his deep, gravelly voice. It reminded Bobby of the grind of a chain saw. "If one of them sees you driving crazy—"

"I got it," he grumbled. "Go back to sleep," he said under his breath as he checked the rearview mirror. The black line of highway behind them was as empty as the highway in front of them. There was no one out here in the middle of Montana on a Sunday this early in the morning—especially this time of year, with Christmas only weeks away. He really doubted there would be a cop or highway patrol. But he wasn't about to argue. He knew that would be his last mistake.

He stared ahead at the narrow strip of blacktop, wondering why Gene had been so insistent on them coming this way. Shouldn't they try to cross into Canada? If Gene had a plan, he hadn't shared it. Same with the bank job that Gene said would be a piece of cake. Unless an off-duty cop just happened to be in there cashing his check—and armed.

Concentrating on staying between the lines, Bobby took a breath and let it out slowly. He could smell the blood and the sweat and the fresh clean scent that rose from his shirt, which he and the others had stolen off a clothesline somewhere near the border. The shirt was too big, but he'd liked the color. Blue like his eyes. It bothered him that he'd gotten blood on the sleeve. The smear kept catching his eye, distracting him.

At a sound behind him, he glanced in the rearview mirror and saw Eric's anxious face. Bobby regretted letting Eric talk him into this, but he'd needed to get out of the state for a while. Now here he was back in Montana.

"How's Gus?" he asked, keeping his voice down. He could hear Gene snoring but not his usual foghorn sound. Which meant he wasn't completely out yet. Or he could be faking it.

Eric moved closer, pulling himself up with a hand on Bobby's seat as he leaned forward and dropped his voice. "He's not going to make it."

Bobby met his gaze in the rearview for a moment, a silent understanding between them. They both knew what would happen if Gene's younger brother died.

"We aren't leaving Gus behind," Gene said without opening his eyes. "He'll pull through. He's strong." He opened his eyes and looked around. "Where the hell are we?"

"According to the last sign I saw, just outside Buckhorn, Montana," Bobby said.

"Good. There's a café in town. Go there," Gene said, making Bobby realize that had been the man's plan all along. "We'll get food and medical supplies for Gus and dump this van for a different ride." He pulled the pistol from beneath his belt and checked to make sure the clip was full before tucking it under the cotton jacket he'd gotten off the line.

Bobby met Eric's gaze again in the mirror. Things were about to get a whole lot worse.